CHINA GIRL

INTEL 1, BOOK 6

EREC STEBBINS

TWICE PI PRESS

Only one thing is impossible for God: to find any sense in any copyright law on the planet.
—Mark Twain

China Girl. Copyright © 2019 Erec Stebbins

Published 2019 by Twice Pi Press, erecstebbinsbooks.com

Cover and internal design by Erec Stebbins © 2019. Antibody image, Martin Brändli, Creative Commons Attribution Share alike license, Wikipedia. Other image elements royalty free licenses from DepositPhotos.com, Shutterstock.com, and iStockphoto.com.

Developmental, line, and copy editing by Loni Crittenden, critandpen.com. Proof reading by Edee Lemonier, bossladyproofreading.com.

ePub ISBN-13: 9781942360599

Kindle ISBN-13: 9781942360582

Paperback ISBN-13: 9781942360605

Hardcover ISBN-13: 9781942360629

Content Guide

This novel contains depictions and references to events and ideas that some will find disturbing, possibly including, but not limited to, battery, assault, murder, imprisonment, captivity, severe illness, pain, fear, medical procedures, torture, and war. There is also profanity and strong language, the challenging of some accepted norms, and the questioning of different kinds of authority, religious and secular. The book also contains religion, partisan politics, Oxford commas, and, despite the heroic efforts of my editors, an unnecessary number of tpyos and, grammer misteaks from my endless and unwise meddling with the text.

Readers are asked to prepare accordingly.

To the Mother of Exiles

A mighty woman with a torch, whose flame
Is the imprisoned lightning.

— The New Colossus, Emma Lazarus

ATTACKS SURGE IN SOUTHWEST

by Mary Hernandez and Lorrie Miller, *New York Times*

Fueling President Suite's call to Congress for expanding domestic counterterrorism programs, the spate of terrorist violence in the nation continues to accelerate. Major attacks on United States federal officers and national infrastructure in the last month have seized headlines and overtaken the administration's scandals and debates over executive authority.

The epicenter of the violence again centered in the Southwest. The May 5th bombing and destruction of the Memorial Bridge spanning the Colorado River near the Hoover Dam significantly escalated the terrorist target profile. A convoy of thirty immigrant transport container trucks was halted by the devastating explosion. In the ensuing chaos, guerrilla fighters emerged from the sands, attacking the convoy and abducting hundreds of detainees. Two subsequent attacks, one on another convoy in Arizona, the second on an immigrant detainment camp in Nevada, have led to substantial disruptions in federal efforts to establish a national highway pipeline to deport illegal immigrants.

"President Suite wants eleven million people shipped out of the country," noted Arizona governor Fred Johnson. "That's not going to happen anytime soon if these terrorists keep blowing up the roads and bridges along the way."

To date, no organization has claimed responsibility, although rumors in immigrant communities persist of a mysterious figure called *El Marcado*. Local, state, and federal law enforcement have been stymied to discover anything about this domestic Che Guevara, while President Suite has been highly critical of ICE division leaders and Homeland Security's leadership.

"Former president York was a terrible leader," Suite declared at a rally in Phoenix, Arizona over the weekend. "Just terrible. Now we have to clean up her mess. She picked weak people. Too many currently in Homeland are because of her. They're soft on terror. Her appointments. They're soft on crime and terrorists invading from the border. We're not safe until things change."

Democratic leaders have accused the president of using the attacks as an excuse to purge law enforcement agencies of career agents and to staff the departments with political operatives.

"We've seen what's he's done with the FBI his first term to quash the investigations into his alleged criminal activity," said representative Damon Rolf, Democrat of Massachusetts. "Now he'll use these attacks as excuses to do the same with the rest of Homeland. We're approaching a frightening place in America, one-party rule and executive overreach like we've never seen before. The government is unrecognizable."

The terror attacks have tracked ICE deployments and removal missions to secure and detain undocumented immigrants. These large-scale governmental raids have increased in number, performed in accordance with last summer's Presidential Security Decree. The new laws, drafted by the Republican-controlled Congress over staunch Democratic opposition, provided forty billion dollars for border wall construction and ten billion in additional discretionary funds, much of which has gone toward what some have called a "militarization" of ICE and related border security forces.

"President Suite is declaring war on legal and illegal immigrants," said recently elected Senator Anastasia Ortega-Cruz of New York. "Are we surprised that someone is returning fire?"

Calling her comments anti-American, Florida Rep. Mark Graf fired back. "The young Senator is crossing a line, giving aid and comfort to the enemies of the United States. More than ever, we see the need to curtail the reckless rhetoric of the radical Left that endangers our soldiers and law enforcement officers. That is why I will be voting to introduce the Patriot Speech Act to criminalize seditious and otherwise anti-American rhetoric. Enough is enough. We're under siege. Under attack. In times of war we have to line up behind our leaders and the flag or be revealed as traitors to the United States."

Director of Homeland Security Kiltss Neerijnen escalated tensions with Mexico by blaming the recent violence on foreign meddling.

"These terrorists are well trained and equipped. They demonstrate high level, professional, state-sponsored skills beyond anything we have seen before. You can rest assured that we are doing everything in our power to determine if they have received help from outside the United States. As the president has warned, any such meddling by our neighbors will be considered an act of war, hostile to the United States, and will be dealt with accordingly."

Mexican president Miguel Ángel Garcia Gonzalez sought to defuse tensions in an international statement following Neerijnen's press briefing.

"Mexico remains a staunch ally of the United States," his letter began. "We condemn these acts of violence and terrorism. We assure the United States president and the world that our nation has had no hand in such deplorable actions in any manner whatsoever. We hope that our long history of cooperation and peace will reassure the American public of our continued friendship and support."

He reiterated his country's recent hardline stance on returnees, however, vowing to keep the border closed to alleged undocumented migrants.

"While the United States builds a wall between our two countries to protect its sovereignty, Mexico cannot accept millions of planned returnees who are verified only by the government of the United States. Until such a time as a mutually agreed upon treaty can be established, one in which we are allowed to determine who is and is not a Mexican citizen, the border to human traffic will remain closed."

The recent closing of the border to everything but commercial traffic has enraged Washington and, particularly, President Suite. Opinion polls in the United States show a majority of US citizens oppose Mexico's actions.

PART I

DOMESTIC TERRORISTS

There comes a point where a man must refuse to answer to his leader if he is also to answer to his conscience.

— SIR HARTLEY SHAWCROSS

1

EL CAZADOR

Sara Houston returned to the convoy. She clipped the handheld transceiver to her belt beside her holstered Browning 1911. Blond hair danced over her shoulders, whipped by the parched wind from the nearby desert. Adjusting a black Stetson hat, she packed the strands underneath to clear her vision.

She scanned up and down the road. Disabled vehicles lined the shoulder, maneuvered to the side to clear a path. Drills and clanging metal signaled the installation of armor plates and machine gun mounts. Trucks pulled into the gaps of the convoy. Not federal, but they'd made them to appear so, professional paint jobs and exterior modifications achieving the façade.

For what was to come, they would need to look the part.

Their teams were elite. Ex-military, recruited with paranoia. They chose those with skills and passion, men and women resisting the growing authoritarian power of Daniel Suite. Latinos, both citizens and permanent residents, filled their ranks. Many felt called to resist the Deportation Act. But they were not alone. Ex-soldiers of every race, culture, and creed joined them. In the face of an endless flood of dispiriting news, the melting pot of their forces strengthened her resolve.

"Sara!" came the boom of Francisco Lopez, his broad frame silhouetted in the bright beams of an SUV. "Let's move!"

She signaled with a high thumbs-up and strode to the truck.

Let's hope this crazy idea works without one or both of us getting killed.

Since she'd met Lopez, every day began with danger, and each night ended under threat. Their only respite was a short stay in the defensive bunker underneath Manhattan with Intel 1. That turned sour after the election of Suite and his white nationalist minions.

The election had transformed Lopez. The assassin-priest who once struggled with the carnage of his black ops assignments had vanished. Hesitation with hard deeds became a relic of the past. He'd discovered a burning purpose that clarified his actions.

She opened the driver's side door and slid into the seat. Grit stained her teeth. Once, they hid as fugitives, framed for murder and terrorism. Now, they embraced the lies. They'd blown up roads and bridges, rescued abducted immigrants from federal detention, attacked and killed the blackshirts conscripted by Suite. Federal officers, every one of them.

We're the terrorists now.

It didn't matter to Houston what anyone called her. The nation was upside-down. Orwellian language spilled from the airwaves. Monstrous characterizations of the vulnerable mutated into monstrous actions against them. Evil normalized. Legalized. Glamorized in marriages of state and media. Increasingly, traditional media either buckled or turned the other way.

A nightmare America.

In that reality, the true patriot was the traitor.

She slammed shut the door, a cloud of dust fogging the air. The heat and mass of the huddled forms in the bed of the truck struck her like a blow. They murmured in fear and anticipation. She caught pieces of Spanish dialogue. Again and again, *El Marcado* floated through the air. Always, the name rang with hope.

And the lives of a convoy of migrants are in our hands.

Their guerrilla fighters had ambushed the ICE convoy, slaughtered federal agents and some local law enforcement officers. As they had done repeatedly since the migrant roundups had begun, they'd interrupted the flow of detainees toward the camps. They'd thrown a wrench into the administration's mad plan to deport millions.

But tonight was different. Tonight, they did not disperse with their charges into the night, leaving dramatic headlines in the next day's papers. Tonight, they remained and dangled their charges to lure a most dangerous of sharks.

Her transceiver buzzed. She mashed the button on its side with one hand while starting the engine with the other.

"Maria here, over," she said, using her codename. She released the button, adjusting the clip on her belt.

Static burst. The engine coughed as she turned the key.

"Unfriendlies on approach, boys and girls," came a woman's voice. "ICE forces in two."

Shit.

"Roger that, Seraph. Maria out."

A male voice grumbled over the device. "Copy. Batten and exit. This is it."

She removed the key and turned to the crowd behind her. At the sounds of her transceiver, all speech had ceased. Fifty sets of eyes stared wide in her direction. She swallowed. Death approached, and she had to convey that reality without panicking her passengers. And all of it in her broken Spanish.

"El cazador viene," she said, her accent painful even to her own ears.

They gasped. A woman began to cry.

Houston raised her voice, hoping to God she was going to get through.

"¡Todos bajen! No te muevas. Ignoren los sonidos." Voices chattered with tones of growing panic. "¡No hagan sonidos! Hay un *plan!*"

Funny how the plan is always to step in front of some damn rifle.

"Pronto estarán a salvo."

She placed her finger to her lips, the terrified group lapsing into silence. She motioned downward with her hand. They lowered to the bed of the truck. Mothers coaxed frightened children with gentle whispers. The young aided the younger and elderly.

Houston turned, set the brake, and leapt out of the truck. Her hand moved instinctively to her sidearm. She scanned the hard hills around them. The terrain outside of Vegas glowed, a moonscape reflecting the wan radiance from above.

Lopez approached her. After so many years, she still winced seeing the inflamed tissue on his forehead, a mark a madman had branded him with during the chaos when they had fallen in love. When America had betrayed them. When corrupt fanatics in the CIA had terminated their old lives and the lives of those they loved.

El Marcado.

The precise diameter of a gun barrel, a circle with a cross at the apex, the scar was now shrouded in dangling black hair that gave him the look of some crazed Sandinista. She smiled and reached her hand to his cheek, running her fingers through the curls of his long beard as he spoke.

"He's going to fire on anything moving. He's an ex-trophy hunter, remember?" He glanced at her Browning. "Especially anyone armed."

"I know!" she frowned, running her other hand from her firearm to his hip. "Can't a girl feel up her weapon in peace?"

Lopez brushed his gloved fingers through her hair. "Peace isn't what's coming."

They kissed. Warmth radiated through her even in the Nevada heat. She savored the touch. Each kiss was precious. Each could be their last.

Especially tonight.

Their forces dashed about, propping the dead from the skirmish earlier. ICE uniforms were stripped, replaced with camouflage. The macabre mannequins lounged around the vehicles. Finishing, their teams darted underneath, hiding from the coming storm.

She took a deep breath as they pulled apart. "No backing out now," she said, swallowing. "This had better work."

"Only if our divine intervention can haul ass. We're lucky the bastards are hitting us at the ambush site." He touched his forehead to hers and removed his hand. "Time we go to ground."

They ducked under the back of the truck, dragging themselves over the rough road and under the axel. She grabbed his hand. "I didn't realize how desperate you thought things were until this plan."

Lopez grunted. "Because we're making ourselves sitting ducks? Risking our lives?"

"No. Because you're risking theirs. The detainees."

Risking their own lives was always on the table, but Lopez had devoted himself to saving as many of the detained as he could. Risking their lives had shocked her.

He sighed. "Yes. We're that desperate."

"One of these nights, Francisco," she said, closing her eyes. "You've always been right. One night will be the last."

"But not tonight, O Lord," he said, squeezing her hand back. He recited a prayer as the roar of tires and approaching engines grew louder.

Contend, O Lord, with those who contend with me;
Fight against those who fight me.
Take hold of a buckler and shield
And rise up for my help.
Draw also the spear and the battle-axe to meet those who
pursue me;
Let them be like chaff before the wind,
May God's angels scatter them.
Let destruction come upon him unawares,
And let the net which he hid catch himself;
Into that very destruction let him fall.

Dust kicked into the air from a sudden thunder. A searing spotlight erupted above, burning down and raking across the convoy. The fake soldiers they'd arrayed cast shadows in its beams.

The beat of helicopter blades drummed.

2

TRAMPA INVERSA

A rumble of heavy vehicles joined the thunderous helicopter. The trucks stopped with a hiss of hydraulic brakes. Soldiers spilled out the doors, their boots tramping along the convoy. They didn't wait to discuss anything with the dummies, or they might have discovered the ruse. Instead, they immediately discharged their weapons.

Lopez gritted his teeth as gunfire burst truck tires and shattered windows, raining glass inches from his face. His thick muscles tensed at the dull thuds of rounds embedding in the plating around the human cargo.

Lord Jesus Christ, let the shielding hold.

Around the vehicles, the dead props exploded. Their debris joined the growing dust storm created by the circling helicopter overhead. He doubted the feds could still see what they were shooting.

And that's what they've come to. Under Suite, we're nothing better than mercenaries.

The gunfire ceased. His strike team coughed in the choking grit. Muffled cries of pain clawed their way through the sounds of heavy boots and the shouts of men. He glimpsed the stilled forms of some of his fighters under nearby vehicles, his dangerous gambit extracting a price in blood.

"They're under the vehicles!" cried a voice.

"We surrender!" yelled Lopez, the phrase taken up in turn by each of the groups cowering under the automatic weapons fire. Weapons discharged near the truck beside them elicited muffed screams from inside.

Will it go like this? Pure execution?

"Hold your goddam fire!" came a commanding voice.

The silence returned. Footfalls tromped around them.

"Throw out your weapons! I swear to God, we see one thing out of place and we mow your asses down!"

Lopez stared at her hip. She shook her head.

"Sara—"

She placed a finger to her lips. The other hand removed a holster and looped it over the grimed axel, fastening the buckle. The 1911 hung and brushed against her chest.

"We're coming out!" Lopez called. "No weapons! Hands in front of us from the rear of the truck!"

The feds dashed, gun barrels pointed underneath from outside. "Do it slow! We'll shred you!"

Like boot camp recruits, Houston and Lopez forearmed their way over the rocky road. The dirt caked his beard, and Houston lost her hat to the low clearance. They emerged from underneath the transport. Two officers slammed them to the ground and mashed their wrists together with restraints.

"Him!" shouted another voice. "Yes, goddammit! That one! Get Childs. Holy hell, boys we got him. We got the bastard!"

Houston grunted as a black boot slammed into her ribs and turned her over. Lopez had no time to process the violence against his lover; another kick struck his side. Failing to move his massive frame, he received two more for good measure. Frustrated agents stooped and struggled to flip him onto his back.

He stared up into the cold eyes of The Hunter.

Darren Childs's face rested in a perpetual smirk. A gold-capped tooth glinted from the red taillights of the truck beside them. An epic brown mustache reminded Lopez of bad '70s reruns. His eyes twinkled as he rested a pump action shotgun over his shoulder.

"Well, ain't today my lucky day."

He turned and spat a stream of tobacco into the dirt besides Lopez. Tannic droplets sprayed over their faces.

"And to think, I told the missus I was gettin' a little discouraged. Felt El Marcado was gettin' the upper hand in too much territory. Hell, son, you were about givin' me a goddam midlife crisis."

He grinned, teeth sharp like a cat's.

"But we finally bagged you, bad hombre numero uno. *El fucking Marcado.*" He bent down and glared at Lopez's forehead, scoffing. "Good name, even if that mark don't live up to the *mojados* boogieman."

He stepped over Lopez and planted both feet on either side of Houston. "And what have we got here?"

Her sweat-stained hair was dirt caked, her face tanned several shades by grime. Blue eyes blazed from the stained exterior.

He leaned the shotgun on the large tire of the truck. After removing a cigar from a front pouch, he chewed the top off, tonguing the rod in his mouth.

"This one yours, scary man?" Childs grunted. "So the big bad brown savior of migrant filth kept a little pale tail to squeeze at night. Looks like pure white trash to me. Bet that cooch got a hundred things crawling out of it."

Houston's glare didn't waver.

"Yeah, well," grinned Childs, "maybe we'll find out."

Lopez ground his molars but stilled his body. He wasn't going to give the monster the satisfaction.

Childs stepped away from the pair, a match's flame flaring in the darkness near the tip of a cigar. A pungent aroma of pepper creosote and eucalyptus mixed with the fog of dust. "Hard to track you down. But that's why they call me the Hunter."

A tack-sized circle of red light appeared on Childs's gun arm.

Lopez rumbled. "Pride goeth before destruction, and a haughty spirit before a fall."

"What did you say?" The Hunter turned toward Lopez, dropping his match. He grabbed the gun. "You're worth much more alive than dead, spic, but there's all kind of in-between."

A calm smile spread across Lopez's features. Childs furrowed his brow. His eyes widened, and he spun around.

"Ambush! *Ambush!*"

Too late, amigo.

The Hunter's right shoulder ruptured in a puff of red. His flesh and bone spray painted the dark side of an SUV. He pivoted, stumbled, and toppled over the body of a slain man.

Automatic weapons fire burst from all directions. The federal agents spun in confusion, bullets spraying into the hills. Their bodies dropped in a maelstrom launched from Lopez's guerrilla forces in the surrounding hills.

Light flashed from the top of one of the rocky hills. A sizzling rush accompanied an orange streak that sped into the sky. The helicopter exploded as it banked around the road. Lopez squinted at the fireball. A thunderous roar tore at his eardrums. Heat assailed his skin, and fragments of metal and glass rained over the convoy.

The bulk of the firefight was over in half a minute. A handful of holdouts delayed the inevitable surrender, but soon the shooting stopped. Camouflaged forms rose like ghosts from the hillsides.

A lithe figure strode toward them, her wiry arms bare and painted in camouflage. A shock of white hair erupted over a pair of piercing green eyes. Smoke trailed from the barrel of an M27 machine gun in her hands. Halting, she ejected a magazine and slammed in a new one, scanning the road as her soldiers sprinted about.

Angel Lightfoote grinned at the pair of roped killers on the ground.

"We've really got to stop meeting like this."

3

MINISTRA DE LA LLAMA

"You do manage to crash all our parties," said Lopez, a grin on his face.

"Parties?" Lightfoote smirked back. "So that's what you call getting your ass kicked. I thought Tehran was bad, but this is next level."

Fires flickered around the stalled convoy. The remains of the helicopter flared like a bonfire as a group of men and women sought to dampen the flames. Disoriented and frightened civilians spilled from the vehicles, demanding answers, shepherded to return to the trucks by dust-caked combat veterans.

Lightfoote stood above Lopez and Houston. Orange light danced over her face, smoke and dust framing her in a dystopian portrait. She jerked her head toward several men. "Get them out of those restraints."

Boots thudded as broad shapes jumped to her command and sprinted over. Brown shadows transformed into men as they passed her. Soldiers helped Lopez and Houston sit up, scrounged downed federal agents for keys, then released the bonds.

Lightfoote bent to one knee and brought her gaze to theirs, leaning against her weapon as she planted it on the road. Her glance flicked to Houston. Both women tensed, eyes locked.

Girl's alive.

She breathed out. "Looks like some kind of military role-play. If I didn't know better, I'd say you were into some kinky shit."

She saw immediately she'd overstepped boundaries. Again. Houston grimaced and turned away.

Focus, Angel. Stay on mission.

"We're sending up smoke signals here and need to move out soon," she said. "But it looks like we're getting paid today."

Lopez laughed. "I see you've modernized the troops." He gestured to her weapon.

"Nothing like hitting some military storage depots while performing tangential terrorism." She padded the large magazine. "Hell of a man dropper. Portable. Great for urban war with the magazines, but lugging a bunch of them around to reload is a bit of a pain." She turned toward the others, yelling. "Patch the transports! Medics and mechanics to each, like we planned!"

The camouflaged soldiers raced to her commands. Some set to work on any damaged vehicles patching tires and engines, cleaning shattered glass. Others crouched around the wounded with medkits. One group dealt with the handful of unharmed federal agents, restraining them and marching them off to a specific transport.

"Last time I swooped in like this, Tehran, that was on the fly," she said. "This job had some good prep, and it was still a damn close call. If they'd hit you down the road, not sure we'd have made it in time." Her voice dropped. "Hate to lose you two."

Houston's gaze passed over her and away again. Things were so damn awkward now.

Probably shouldn't have kissed her.

Lopez broke the tension between the women. "You sterilized the perimeter?"

"Nothing for miles," Lightfoote answered him, looking away. "Childs put all his forces into the reverse-trap. Too damn eager. Too sure of himself." She smiled. "So, what do you call a reverse-reverse-trap?"

"Winning," said Lopez, standing with a grunt. "Now maybe we

can get to the bottom of where this butcher has been disappearing people."

Houston pulled her arms from behind her back and rubbed her wrists. She marched to the truck and retrieved a hat, gun, and harness from underneath. After placing the Stetson on her head, she strapped the harness over her shoulder. Her 1911 glinted in the moonlight. She spoke over her shoulder as she adjusted the holster. "Speaking of the devil, where's that piece of shit, Childs?"

Lightfoote stood and rested the machine gun over her chest. "Thought you might want to have a word with him."

* * *

The Hunter wasn't far. His attempted crawl had failed near the open door of a jeep. He'd collapsed five feet away, two men planting a boot on his back. Bullet wounds stained his right leg. It looked as if a bomb had gone off in his shoulder.

Lightfoote called up more soldiers and instructed them to guard and tend the wounded ICE agent. They pointed rifles toward him. A medic dressed his wounds.

Lopez stood over the semi-conscious man. He growled at the medic. "Prognosis?"

"Serious," he said, his hands bloodied and tugging on gauze. "Especially the shoulder. He needs surgery soon."

"How soon?"

"Hours. The sooner, the better."

"A few hours will do," said Houston, "for what we need."

The medic glanced up with a grimace but returned to his work.

A ragged whisper croaked from Childs. "Got lucky tonight, *spic*. Matter of time." The muscles in his jaw bulged. He struggled to move, but winced, pain distorting his features. Lightfoot felt his anger radiating outward. Lopez cut through it with a laugh.

"Lucky?" Lopez scoffed. "No, no. Not luck. *Love.*"

Childs scowled.

Lopez stretched his arms out to his sides. "Can't you see how much we love you? I know it seems strange after all the innocent people, families, and children you have thrown in concentration camps or murdered because of our Beautiful Leader's plan of ethnic cleansing.

But seeing all this—the work, the patience, the blood—can you deny it?"

"What?" Childs's eyes widened.

"Luck? That you could set your trap, follow us, that we'd never be the wiser. Really?" Lopez shook his head. "You should have been afraid it was so easy. We played you from the beginning."

Childs's eyes narrowed. Anger mixed with lines of pain on his face.

Lightfoote lifted a smoldering cigar from the ground. She gestured around them with it. "El Cazador struck fear in the helpless," she said. "He's the boogieman in the campfire stories, the monster that steals children in the night and puts them in cages." Lightfoote dropped the cigar on the ground beside Childs, her boot crushing its smoking tip. "*I hate cages.*"

Lopez recited, "Woe to the world for the causes of sin. These stumbling blocks must come, but woe to the man through whom they come."

Lightfoote sneered at him, her bleached hair dingy and yellow in the night. "Now, the hunter is hunted. Welcome to *our* world, asshole. We have a lot of work ahead of us."

4

GONE, NOT FORGOTTEN

"**A**nd let's welcome our newest member to the group, Tyrell!"

Tyrell Sacker smiled from one side of his mouth, his eyes daggers.

Shitburgers. Here we go.

On cue, the whispers began in the sterile therapy room. *The Eunuch Maker. Grace Gone.* He thought he caught *nigger* and *chink,* but it could be the lingering effects of alcohol withdrawal. His brain stumbled like a Tesla on diesel.

He glanced from the circle of chairs to his trembling hand. *Delirium tremens.* He was already wet with sweat. His heart drummed in his head. Damned neural system all hyped up, compensating for years of heavy drinking, turning him into a ball of quivering anxiety.

Thanks, Gracie. Thanks a whole hell of a lot.

Grace Gone insisted. Made it part of the employment deal she knew he desperately needed. Because being fired and blacklisted by the NYPD didn't exactly do wonders for one's cop cred.

Of course, his association with Gone and the ballsy serial killer case helped him score some gigs. Security. Bodyguard. A long list of other humiliating temp jobs. All opened for a former detective who helped break open the crime of the decade.

I should've written a goddamned book.

Why not? Hire a ghostwriter for the torture-porn of the case. Land a series of two-bit TV appearances. Might've seen him through three or four years.

And how long for your liver, Tyrell?

After Ladner and the NYPD sent him packing, she'd practically begged him to stay. Offered him a chance to start over. And proud old Tyrell Sacker said no.

Face it, brother. More fear than pride.

Four years and a lake of bourbon later, he'd turned up on her office doorstep in Queens, tail between his legs.

"You're killing yourself, Tyrell," she'd said. Dwarfed behind her desk, this tiny Chinese chick had punched way above her weight. "It hurts to see you this way."

And she'd seen him, all right, good and hammered during that crazy time four years ago. Bigoted president elected. Serial killer making a mockery of the NYPD. Her big brown eyes, a master key opening him up. He'd let *her* see him at rock bottom.

Unless this damn group therapy was it.

The therapist held up his hands. What was his name again? Josh something? He was a hippie type. Gray hair to his shoulders, glasses and blue eyes behind them. Sacker noticed scars on his forearms. Ex-heroin junkie.

"Now, now. That's enough," Josh said to the buzzed muttering. "*Remember*—whoever we are on the outside doesn't matter in *here*. We're all here because we share *a problem*. One that has wrecked our lives enough that we have *stepped out of that other world* to this place. To *stop*. To *detox*. To learn ways to *cope*. So that when we go back out there, we find a way to live our lives *without* the poison that brought us here."

You're killing me, Hallmark man.

"So, *Tyrell*, please know that you are *welcome* here. Like with each of us, you will *not* be judged for your past. Good *or* bad. You could be a street wino. You could be a celebrity. You could have committed crimes," he paused just a second too long, "*or helped solve them.* Doesn't matter."

Sacker nodded but had nothing to say.

"So, then. Would you like to *introduce* yourself?"

"Not particularly."

"I *know* it's not easy, but it helps in managing your addiction if you can stop isolating yourself. Not just in here, but *outside*. There are people who will care for you out there *if you let them*. And those people can be the difference between life and death." He smiled. "So, why don't we start *practicing* with the group?"

Oh, good God.

Sacker checked his watch. Ten more minutes. He could do this. He had to do this. He'd signed a damn form allowing Gone to track his progress in therapy. She was ruthless. So, time to pretend and play along.

"Yeah, sure."

He sat up and cleared his throat. The room spun. His stomach lurched. He kept it down, the faint taste of bile a familiar by-product of his withdrawal.

"Like you said, name's Tyrell. I'm a cop."

Again, the whispers.

"Everyone, *please*," snapped the gray-haired guru.

"Well, I *was* a cop. I don't have to go over the whole sorry story. Seems like everyone here's been reading the papers." He smirked. "A friend of mine got me in here. Was worried I was harming myself. Maybe she was right."

"And *how* were you harming yourself, Tyrell?" asked Josh.

"Booze. Hell of a lot of booze. Maybe the cigarettes, too, but those ain't gonna kill me for another thirty years. Booze wasn't gonna wait that long."

"So you were a *heavy drinker*. How long?"

"Since the war. Iraq. I used to party a lot before that. Maybe a little too much." He laughed. "Definitely a little too much. But I didn't go pro until after Fallujah."

"Fallujah? That's what exactly?"

What was Fallujah?

How the hell was he supposed to explain that? The peace freak didn't even know the name.

"City in Iraq. Hour from Baghdad in Al Anbar."

"And *something bad* happened there?"

"Everything that happened there was bad."

Sacker glared at him. Josh squirmed a little in his lotus position.

"We all have difficult *experiences*," said Josh, bringing it to something relatable. "What's important is that we *find* coping methods that allow us to live productive *lives*."

The ringtone on Sacker's smartwatch erupted into Drake's "God's Plan." Heads jerked toward him and away from the discussion leader. He indulged himself with a broad grin.

"Hour's up, doc," he said, standing. He slid the Ice Topper over his low-tapered afro. Banished from the NYPD, he'd moved toward scruffy. His curls pushed against the sides of the hat. "I got work. Got to go."

He walked to the exit, the group silent and attentive to his every movement. Grabbing the handle, he pushed without looking back. The door clicked shut behind him.

Grace Gone stood in the middle of the hallway. She sported a bright outfit, pants and a flowing blouse. Colorful but controlled, flattering but not revealing. Cooling in the summer heat. Her long black hair was ponytailed. She leaned to one side, supporting some of her weight on a cane.

Her lips were pinched in a pensive pout.

His squinted. "Gracie, don't even start."

"War stories are only half the real story. You need to work on the other half. The half you *really* don't want to talk about."

"Jesus. You sound like New Age Guy in there."

Gone cocked her head to one side. "Yeah, he was a bit affective."

"You were listening?"

Sacker reached into his pocket and pulled out a box of cigarettes. Gone limped forward and placed a hand on his, covering the box.

She's so warm. A velvet compress.

"Yes, I was listening. You signed off on that, remember?"

"Yeah. Stupid, but I needed the money." He tugged on his cigarettes. She didn't let go. "You gonna take my smokes, too?"

"Absolutely," she said, holding up a blue-tinted box with the words

NicoPatch. "Transdermal delivery of your drug. A thousand times less damaging to you than breathing in a forest fire every day."

Sacker rolled his eyes. "I'm not sure this job's worth it."

"You're worth it, Tyrell," she said, her lips in a thin line. She gazed up to his far greater height, boring into his eyes. "As long as I'm around, I'm going to see that you treat yourself in a way that reflects that worth."

Sacker handed her the cigarettes and turned away. *Punching way above her weight.* "Let's get out of here," he rasped.

"Indeed," she said, smiling. Her arm slid around his broad bicep. She leaned into him. "We have a boatload of cases to look over and decide on."

He slowed his stride, matching her gait as she limped. Their footfalls jibed, echoing down the corridor.

5

GONE PUBLIC

Gone pushed the steaming tea toward Sacker and smiled. He gave it the side eye.

Come on, Tyrell. Work with me here.

"What's this?" he asked. "Green tea from Shaolin monasteries?"

"No yellow-baiting here," she snipped. Her eyes darted to the china saucer. "I made it myself. Brewed it."

Sacker squinted at the cup. "Yeah, I've seen you huddled over the tea before. You're worse about that than your damn lab experiments downstairs."

She followed his gaze across the dim first floor of her private detective business. It landed on the doorway to the cellar. A new set of locks ran up and down the side.

His eyes widened. "Keeping the masses from the mad scientist's lab?" he smirked. The sarcasm belied his slumping shoulders.

He knows he's missed a lot.

No doubt he'd noticed the fancy, backlit *Gone Investigating* sign outside. The spruced-up exterior made the building stand out in the dilapidated Queens neighborhood. After the Eunuch Maker case, queues of deep-pocketed clientele swelled her coffers. The flow surged after successions of high-profile cases kept her name in the news. Even her third-hand lab equipment in the basement looked shinier.

Gone chewed her lower lip. Her success, her skyrocketing fame over the last four years would never have happened without him. He'd sabotaged his career in making it possible. *To solve the case,* of course. He'd be sure to emphasize that. But she knew he'd done it for her as well. Sacker had believed in her, respected her skills from their first unorthodox meeting where she'd picked apart his life. At rock bottom on the verge of eviction and failure, he'd seen something in her.

That's what made it so hard. When he'd turned his back on her offer, the sting was as personal as it was professional. She'd missed him.

"It's a brew for the sick," she said, bringing her mind back to the present. "My grandmother used to make it when we still lived in China."

"I'm not sick."

Her eyes narrowed.

"Al*right*," he sighed. "Fine."

He fit his finger into the handle of the cup. Lifting it to his mouth, Sacker wrinkled his nose at the bitter, earthy aroma.

"Don't be a baby, Tyrell."

He gave her a thin smile. "Bottoms up."

"Whiskey it isn't."

He forced it down, his face tightening. "It's great."

She rolled her eyes and placed her hand on a stack of folders. "We get a lot of traffic now. The challenge is intelligent selection. We need to decide. I hope you did your homework assignment."

"The Labriola case," he said, sipping the tea, "that's clearly mob. Big money. Bad men."

"Agreed."

"We don't need the heat with that one. Common *interfamily* dispute. Bunch of thugs. Risk-reward is too low unless you got Getting Whacked insurance. We pass?"

She nodded, flipping pages to one side of the table. She pointed to another stack of papers. "What about Greenwald?"

Sacker leaned back in his chair. He winced, but she was glad to see the symptoms lessening. He'd crossed some hump. She hoped it was going to be easier surfing for a while.

"That's easy green," he said." White collar financial crime. I bet it's a bit convoluted. Bit of a puzzle, so you'll like that. If they get a little pushy, I'm there. My business sense says take that baby."

She smiled, wanting to reach and touch his hand. "We're sounding so corporate, now, Tyrell."

"Got to pay the bills. Especially if we're going to take on some impossible cases."

"Indeed!" The grin grew. "Which brings me to our supposed Deep State security contractor!"

Sacker held the cup near his face, the steam obscuring his features. "You're serious?"

Gone stared forward, her eyes focused in the distance. She had to convince him, but conveying the mental labyrinth of an unfinished puzzle was her great weakness. She could see the overall pattern, know it wasn't random, but without the connecting pieces, describing the puzzle usually ended up making her sound like some internet conspiracy theorist. But this one was too important. Too big. And she'd likely need a man with his skills to have any hope of penetrating the bureaucratic enigma.

"I did some IP tracking," she said. "Our whistle-blower was trying to use proxies, but they got sloppy. The cord plugged into some generic dot gov servers. After that, the firewalls worked."

"Yeah, so? Plenty of nutcases working meaningless jobs for the US government."

"But the illegalities he's claiming! They're not some common skim-ming-off-the-top or gold-plated Pentagon toilets." She tapped the folder without consulting it. "These are major capital entities. *Equipment.* The records he teased are intriguing, but clearly tampered with. Someone has gone to a lot of trouble to mess with military, Home-land, and ICE records. Construction companies. *Mining.* There's even the Department of Transportation."

"The contracts with the vaccine company did catch my eye, I'll give you that. Especially after the Eunuch Maker's doomsday virus hell trip."

She beamed. "See? What an enigma!"

He set the cup down, shaking his head. "If they're real, Gracie. People can fake a lot of things these days. Maybe someone's using you in a setup to bring someone else down. Maybe it's some ticked off incel who wants to humiliate the female Sherlock Holmes." Sacker grinned. "Isn't that what the Post called you?"

"Yes."

"That was damn patronizing."

"That was great advertising."

He gestured over the table. "Look. Isn't this all just a little, well, *big*, wouldn't you say? Unbelievable?"

"Yes." Her intensity flared. "But the pattern is too startling. Somebody risked their job, possibly their *freedom*, to bring these to us. Either we're dealing with a psychotic possessed of a novelist's mind, or we have the pieces of a giant scandal."

"Well, you've had a good run with those."

"Much more interesting than another lucrative, but ultimately repetitive, case of financial malfeasance."

Sacker waved his hand over the file. "But isn't this big tinfoil hat, government money cover up the same thing? Just on the federal level? It's always about money."

"No. White collar crimes always have the same motivation. Simple greed. But this thing," she said, flipping through the folder, "this is too wild for such a simple motivation. I'm sure opportunists will leech off the mountains of cash. But what set this giant fraud in motion? What's driving it? Disparate governmental organizations, private sector contractors, completely unrelated areas? All brought together under a secret and unified umbrella?"

"Maybe it's just bureaucratic incompetence, nothing more."

"It's too broad and integrated to be random stupidity." She slapped the folder. "No. There's something here. Something big and *weird*. All my meters are in the red."

Sacker stared at the empty cup in front of him and back at Gone. "One thing you won't catch me doing is second guessing you, Gracie." He yawned and checked his watch. "I've devil advocated enough for tonight. You say we do it, then we do it."

"Great," she said, grinning like a schoolgirl before a fair. "The Greenwald case goes to Jennifer."

"The new hire?"

"Tyrell, *you're* the new hire. Jennifer's good. She's handled white collar cases with her previous firm. This mysterious Uncle Sam scandal is for you and me. We'll work on it together."

His teeth shone, the smile devoid of his common dose of snark. "Like old times," he said.

He's happy to be back. The truth of it warmed her. "A lot like old times."

She wanted to return his expression, but her mind couldn't shake the data. The pout returned, her lower lip plump.

"Like before, there's something very rotten here." The pout finally stretched to a smile. "I can't wait to find out what it is!"

SUITE SIGNS "TRUE AMERICANS ACT" PROTESTS SEIZE CAPITAL

by Renat Kegel, *Washington Post*

With a smile for the cameras, President Suite posed over the recently passed True Americans Act with pen in hand, then signed it to the applause of the conservative Congressmen surrounding him, putting controversial legislation in motion that represents the most sweeping reform of American citizenship in a century. His actions all but ensured a court challenge to the constitutionality of the new statutes.

"Elections have consequences," he said, continuing to remind the public months after the overwhelming GOP midterm victory.

The bill remakes three long-standing pillars of American citizenship. Its first article broadens the set of executive actions by Suite that revoke naturalization. Among his first set of executive orders, Suite dictated that any naturalized citizen could have their citizenship revoked, and be subject for deportation, for a growing list of infractions, including previous felony or misdemeanor arrest, evidence of fraud in identity, finances, or residence, as well as membership in organizations now listed by Homeland Security as Unlawful Combatant groups.

"Of course, many of those organizations are activist groups or associations of marginalized communities slandered with claims of ties to terrorists," said Ahmed Andoni, spokesperson for BDS Now!, a pro-Palestinian non-profit. "And the other so-called violations are often trumped-up charges with little evidence, but they allow for the arrest and deportation of individuals while their case supposedly awaits review. It's a violation of constitutional rights. It's a green light to disappear undesirables."

The new law goes further than the previous orders, broadening the revocation to natural-born citizenship for the same infractions. Civil libertarians and conservative constitutionalists have voiced their opposition.

"This is in clear violation of the 14th Amendment," said ACLU spokesperson Miranda Hogoth. "We will fight this in the courts and have already filed for an injunction. And we will win."

Challenges to Suite's hardline orders and his GOP-backed agenda have found consistent success in the lower courts. But now, with Suite having confirmed four ultra-conservative justices to the Supreme Court, there is an increased likelihood that the challenges will fail at the highest level.

"The court is now a 6-3 institution heavily biased toward an extreme right-wing agenda," argued William Francis, professor emeritus at the Columbia University Law School. "They have shown an unwillingness to respect precedent in many of the recent decisions on executive power and the rights of minorities. I'm not too sanguine about their respect for traditional interpretations of the 14th Amendment."

The second article of the new law extends the controversy on citizenship, requiring an ancestry record of citizenship for natural born citizens for the first time in American history. All US citizens will be required to produce evidence of parental citizenship by the next census or risk immigration review to re-evaluate their own citizenship status.

Activist groups have filled the streets over these two aspects of the law, claiming that the Suite administration is seeking to delegitimize Americans based on color, arguing that the new statutes disproportionately affect immigrants from Central and Latin America as well as Africa and Muslim nations.

"That is simply not the case," responded Press Secretary Vokol Stammers. "This new law helps preserve American exceptionalism, ensuring all citizens share the culture and values of freedom. It will be applied to all recent migrants to the country, whatever their race, religion, or country of origin."

Human rights activists have challenged that assertion, noting that the wording of the new statutes is vague, allowing the potential for tremendous leeway in how the rules are interpreted and enforced.

"Suite is stacking the immigration offices with white nationalists," noted former Obama administration official Dirk Lendry. "How do you think these guys are going to be applying this new ethnic cleansing act?"

The final provision of the new law uses the rules in the first two articles to immediately strip voting rights from anyone whose citizenship status is questioned or under evaluation.

"We can't have potential non-citizens casting votes on American issues," said Stammers. "That would be foreign meddling in US matters."

As these controversial laws are moved to the judicial branch, activists are taking to the streets. Massive rallies swarmed several major cities this week, including Washington, New York, Chicago, Los Angeles, and Philadelphia. In Washington, over one million people filled the streets, only to be disbursed after violence flared in one of the largest deployments of the National Guard in recent history. Accounts differ about what started the violence. Protestors claim far-right groups affiliated with the Proud Boys were responsible, whereas city and federal law enforcement echo White House statements that Antifa members threw Molotov cocktails at assembled riot police.

The crowds thinned quickly, ending the protests before they reached the White House. However, five protesters were killed by guardsmen, in events recalling political riots not seen in America since the 1960s.

"Of course they framed the protestors," said Vermont Senator Benny Sonners. "Suite wasn't going to allow a protest of this size to reach the White House. He doesn't want those kinds of images on national television. It might remind a lot of the nation that his policies are deeply unpopular with millions. Instead, the protest was quashed with violence, giving a week of talking points demonizing Americans exercising their First Amendment rights on Canid and other conservative media. It's shameful. It's threatening our democracy."

For his part, President Suite made it clear that he viewed the strikes and protests as unacceptable, seeming to threaten again to impose martial law on targeted urban centers.

"It's dangerous and un-American activity. That's why Congress has to pass the Protect America Act. Radical Antifa leftists are thugs, threatening our economy, trying to destabilize the nation. Their socialist masters will stop at nothing to harm us. Good, patriotic citizens are in danger for simply going to work, their children threatened for going to school. Deadly gangs are joining the protests, fueling violence across the nation. Murderous illegals are invading our country, attacking federal agents, blowing up buildings. It has to stop. It's time we make our law enforcement strong again. With the military. National Guard, Special Forces. We are going to make America safe again."

6

SNARA

"John, you're not going to like this."

The words came from a short brunette with back-length hair. She marched from an adjoining room into John Savas's office. His office for the time being, at least. He still ran Intel 1, the clandestine agency buried deep beneath the streets of Manhattan. He continued their pursuit of problems that others could not. But Savas heard the approaching feet of doom.

Any day now, and Suite is going to throw our asses on the street.

He removed his glasses, scraping his hands over cropped gray hair. The white offset a deep tan, acquired from a recent vacation to his grandfather's homeland of Greece. A vacation that did little to lighten the load of a grandson's country gone mad.

"Who'd we lose today?" he sighed.

Rebecca Cohen sat across from him, a stack of papers in her hand. She tossed them on his desk. Her brown eyes smoldered. "These cowards don't even have the ovaries to do anything in person. I don't know the full extent, but it looks like every one of our senior management staff has a great big bullseye on their backs. We're losing Reddy, Pérez, and Chandra just from the first pages."

"Reddy? The new one?"

Cohen nodded. "I'd already promoted her. She's a phenom. Or *was*. I wish I had her skills and cool at twenty-nine."

She's the wrong color.

He didn't have to say it. Cohen knew. The pattern was painfully obvious. Suite was bleaching the DoJ, the Cabinet, the DoD. Any government agency that he wasn't starving or shutting down.

Minus the politically chosen tokens to throw before the cameras.

Wonder Bread lackeys replaced solid agents across the DoJ. These yahoos jumped to their master's bidding. They suppressed the investigations into the President's purported illegalities. American apparatchiks leaking the right pieces of the right documents at the right times, all for the maximal political advantage. They swung the ax, ending the careers of devoted agents and career public servants. Anyone who didn't fall in line or who dared pursue the spiraling legal case against the sitting president.

"So why are you and I still here, Rebecca?"

She bit her lower lip. "That's the mystery that's keeping me up at night."

"Yeah, something sure is," he said, smiling at his wife.

Their relationship had been a problem when the pair worked together at the FBI, but those days were long past. Incredible events had scrambled protocol; a genius hacker plunged the US into chaos, and a civil war led to the undoing of a global conspiracy. In that chaos, they'd found themselves reincarnated as the former president's private black ops agency, planted deep in a remodeled Cold War bunker packed under the streets of New York. But Savas knew that their privileged status had been cemented before this.

Even before he ran Intel 1, he and Cohen worked side by side for it as parts of a team. In those early years, an American terrorist group called Mjolnir slaughtered half that division in their mad plan to start a world war. The bloodbath restructured the experimental FBI branch. When Intel 1 finally brought down the group, everything had changed.

But a new president had seized power on a platform of bigotry and xenophobia. Now this dangerous man controlled Intel 1. The rulebook had gone out the window.

"They *are* tearing us apart," she said, grabbing the papers and waving them around. "But why keep *us*? It's clear we aren't on board with his agenda. We won't run his game for gold or power, either. He's gutting and re-staffing everything, consolidating his stronghold on the Executive. We should be gone."

"Maybe we should be grateful. We can limit damage, maybe even help with the assignments we do get."

"Something doesn't add up. I've got the feeling that we're missing some trapdoor they're setting for us to fall into."

"Setting us up? So we make a mistake, discredit all the agencies and people we've been working with?"

"Maybe." She shook her head. "And don't forget, we're working in violation of federal law. Unaccountable."

He squinted at her. "But you don't think they're setting us up for a scandal."

"It's the other things going along with it." She leaned back in the chair, folding her fingers together in front of her face. "We could be asking ourselves why we haven't quit, instead."

He barked a laugh. "I do. Every day."

"Exactly. The motivation to stay is obvious. We're working to limit the damage, do some good. But good people are being fired or are quitting left and right. And why wouldn't they?" Her hands danced in the air, highlighting imaginary text on non-existent slides, as she entered what he called her *graduate seminar mode*. "Extremist hate crimes are spiking. Mosques and synagogues, defaced. Muslim and Jewish academics, harassed. Kids in cages, attacks on migrant families at the border. A militarized wall."

He rubbed his temples. "At least the damn deportation program's failing. Suite didn't factor in Mexico resisting as they have."

"Failure has consequences on the ground. Those mushrooming camps are overflowing. The press is gathering like flies to ratings honey. I can't watch the footage anymore."

"Well, it's a bad look for the new administration. I think it's even dawning on his cultist base that this will take a decade, cost in the trillions. Total fiasco."

Cohen leaned toward him.

"But that's what I'm getting at. We're part of the problem for him. He's a vindictive bastard. He's pink-slipped people for much less. He loves firing people. Our passive-aggressive resistance is excuse plenty." Her eyes burned into his. "So why the hell are we still here?"

Savas tensed. He didn't have the answer, but he also trusted Cohen's intuition as much as her deductions. When there were missing pieces to any puzzle, she was always the one to notice them. Her anxiety and surety spooked the hell out of him.

"I don't know," he said. "But something tells me we're going to find out."

Her expression softened. She rested back into the chair. "When they were sworn into power, those wonderful introductory meetings. Remember those?"

"Like a colonoscopy."

"*That* at least made sense. They were all over our assess about domestic terror from El Marcado. They knew who was likely behind it all as well as we did."

"Suspected," he said. "We still don't know. There's not a shred of proof, no contact with Angel or the pair since. They could just have gone underground, trying to ride this period out."

She held his gaze. "You just don't want face the truth. Even the possibility is too much for you. You work down here in this unconstitutional secret police force, but you just can't stomach the idea of their vigilante war."

Stop being right, Rebecca. Just this once.

He turned away. Was the trio behind the attacks? The deaths of law enforcement officers? The theft of government property? The destruction of national infrastructure?

It was too close to sedition. These were *his* people. Lightfoote, a former agent with Intel 1. Lopez and Houston, adoptees he'd taken responsibility for. Their lives, destroyed by criminals in the Deep State. The three had put everything on the line to save the nation. Again and again.

"We break some rules down here in the service of the nation," he said. "We *saved* the country doing that. These terrorists, whoever they are, are *attacking* the nation."

Cohen set her jaw. "Half the nation's gone rogue. Suite's regime is pushing through autocrat straight to tyrant."

"Messy as hell, I'll give you that. But until there's some modicum of actual evidence, I'm not going to engage in that kind of thinking about them." His face fell. "I just can't."

"They aren't terrorists. Not in the sense you know."

"They *weren't*, no. But if that's them out there, if they're responsible for all that murder and wreckage, I'm not so sure about what they've become."

The lights flickered, and a tremor ran through the underground building. Dust misted from the ceiling, and a stack of papers spilled over his desk. He didn't move, but he stared at Cohen. The only sound was the soft scratching of grit settling.

"What the hell was that? Earthquake?"

"In Manhattan?" Cohen rasped, the dust inducing coughs. "That would be new."

The lights stabilized. A buzzing commotion rose from the neighboring rooms.

"Maybe a construction charge?" He blew over his keyboard, a puff of dust trailing into the air.

"It'd have to be a dangerously strong one. We're several layers down."

A woman burst into his office. Her face was pale, coffee spilled over a white blouse. "I'm so sorry to interrupt."

Savas straightened his back. "Jenny, you okay? You want a tissue?"

"No. Thanks."

"I guess you experienced our little earthquake."

"Not an earthquake," she gasped. "A bombing." Her voice rose in pitch. "In New York."

Savas blinked. *Right above our heads.* "Where? How bad?"

"Harlem. Data's just coming in from multiple cameras and sensors. A building was destroyed. Surveillance AI predicts that it's the Harlem Mosque."

His stomach tightened. An old ghost placed a cold hand on his shoulder. He shuddered and blocked it out. "All right. Let's get to the Operations Room and into crisis mode."

She gave him a curt nod and ran from the office. Savas angled his head up, squinting at the ceiling.

"Bombing of a mosque in New York," he whispered. "Now that's something I never wanted to hear again."

Cohen reached across the desk and cupped his hand. "That was a decade ago. Focus on the now. You don't need to revisit old wounds. Mjolnir is gone."

He continued to stare upward.

"Yeah. Let's hope so."

7

COME AND GONE

"Mr. Sacker, how may I help you today?"

And so it begins.

Sacker parked his briefcase on the ground. Gone had decided to pursue the mysterious government fraud case with her usual enthusiasm. Over the last few days, she'd made him dizzy with a mental map of corporations and federal departments, zeroing in on some entry points to begin the investigation. They were to start with some of the smaller irregularities, governmental contractors holding unusual arrangements with Uncle Sam. The goal was to gather real world information from something beyond a shadowy whistle-blower, verify that there was something legitimate in the documents. That, and to stir things up and see what moved.

The mid-grade sales manager for Reliant Construction frowned behind a mammoth desk. The wooden behemoth was adorned with woodland scenes by some poor OCD artist during a manic episode or chiseled out by a CNC machine gone mad. A giant, ornate plaque with the name TURNER in gold-plated letters faced the door. Sacker nearly pulled out a set of shades.

Compensating for something, this one.

Stout, balding, and red-faced, Turner radiated impatience like heat from a bonfire. But Sacker was prepared. Gone Investigating sprang for a corporate suit and the gold-plated briefcase at his feet. If this was going to have a prayer of working, he had to look and act the part.

Time to turn things around.

"I appreciate the meeting," began Sacker in his best Ivy League. "Especially as I could only be vague on the phone about my purpose. I represent a client group interested in your low-security detainment facilities. This is a delicate matter. A private-sector investment. These types of prisons carry such an unfortunate stigma in society. My clients would rather remain anonymous at this stage, at least until we ascertain how serious we might be about adding Reliant to our portfolio."

The man's demeanor upshifted. He leaned forward. "My apologies, Mr. Sacker, but your record—NYPD and some security jobs—well, I wasn't expecting…."

An articulate negro?

"No problem," said Sacker donning a moneyed grin. "I'm a security consultant now for some exclusive interest groups. As you've likely realized, with the way things are going in the country, more and more people are interested in the ability to break into the prison-industrial complex."

The man coughed. "Well, sir, we don't like that name. Other terms, such as *security industry*, much better reflect our products."

"My apologies. It's not very important what we call it. Only that there's money to be made."

"Indeed, indeed." He coughed again. "Let's put this on the right foot and begin again. My name is Harold Turner. You can't do better than Reliant. We are well positioned to compete with the GEO Group and CCA in the coming decades. It's good you came to me today, because I'm authorized—"

"Before we get into any details," he interrupted, "I've been asked by my clients to perform due diligence. Part of that involves trying to obtain some answers to questions I can't ask through any means except by direct contact with Reliant."

Turner furrowed his brow. "I'm not sure I follow you."

Time for the deep state goods. *Let's see how you like these, money man.*

Sacker popped open his leather case. He pulled out a dark folder and flipped on a pair of fake reading glasses. He pretended to scan the contents of the folder, making eye contact with Turner from over the edge of the lenses.

"Performing my research," Sacker said, frowning, "I came across some anomalies that troubled my clients."

Turner sat upright. "Anomalies?"

"You are part of a number of highly lucrative governmental contracts." Sacker smiled. "This is, of course, a very good thing. However," he said, glancing back down to the papers, "there are several recent contracts my investors flagged as suspicious."

"What do you mean, 'suspicious'? What contracts? How do you know so much about our government deals?"

Sacker removed his glasses and placed them on the folder. "Mr. Turner, as I said, we perform our due diligence. And we have considerable resources to do so. When my clients invest their considerable resources, it is only when we are satisfied with the fundamentals." Again, the glasses went on. "These are the contacts to which I refer."

He held out a slip of paper. Short lines of text and numbers ran across the top of it, all from the document cache their enigmatic contact had supplied them. Now the rubber was going to meet the road.

Sacker surprised himself with a wish that it would all dissolve in the wind. That Gone would be wrong just this once and they could turn their attention to safer, more lucrative cases. That there really wasn't some giant conspiracy in the US government that would take them into the bowels of…what exactly? He'd paid enough dues in his life.

But that wasn't to be. Turner blanched, the red in the face melting away as his eyes widened. So their whistle-blower wasn't crazy.

Ah, hell.

His back stiffened. He kept his face neutral. "There were some irregularities in protocols between government agencies and financial transfers that we would like clarified."

"Where did you get these? These are top…these are only…these are not available to the general public." Turner stood, the paper partially wrinkled in his grasp. "I'll be right back."

He fled the room.

Damn. Maybe pressed too hard.

But the ground had shifted. Once again, Gone was right. These contracts, these bizarre government financial and capital transfers, were TNT. *Radioactive.* She was on to something.

Footsteps bustled behind him. Turner had returned, but not alone. A bulky man with a security badge and handgun strapped to his side had joined the party.

"Mr. Sacker, I must apologize," said Turner, "but your thirty minutes are up. Mr. Pucci here will escort you outside. Our facility can be a bit of a maze for newcomers."

He did not offer his hand.

Sacker stood and placed his mock glasses back in a case. He smiled. "And the paper I gave you? You know, the one with the contract names and codes?"

Turner swallowed. "I apologize. I seem to have misplaced that."

Mmmm-hmmm. Sure you did.

Sacker grinned and closed the briefcase, gesturing with his hand to the armed guard. "After you, Mr. Pucci."

The guard led Sacker away from the sweating form of Turner, a slammed door the final exclamation point on the illuminating interview. The muscular man stayed glued to him, his breath hot on Sacker's neck, stirring memories of department stores that weren't so friendly with young black boys sneaking peaks at the latest nerf guns. Dozens of turned heads and the electric swish of glass doors later, he was outside.

The cruel summer painted the northern New Jersey landscape a shade of parched tan. Plants drooped and flowers wilted around the offices of Reliant Construction. Workers dashed between several buildings to huddle within the air-conditioned spaces.

Sacker loosened his tie. At least today's sweat was respectable. The shakes were gone. The nausea now spoiled his meals only if he overate, marking the slow return of an appetite. He gazed down at his narrow waist, the pounds having melted off him the last few months.

He wiped sweat from his eyebrows and pulled out a smartphone. Face recognition unlocked the device, and he tapped Gone's face to start a call.

"Tyrell?" she chirped. His face filled the screen. "Please hurry. My appointment's in five minutes."

"They didn't say a thing."

"Really? Nothing? I'm surprised. I thought this would shake them up."

He laughed. "Oh, it did. It was *how* they didn't say a thing that said everything."

A short pause. "I see. Low-level staff now in high-stress mode."

"Exactly." He adjusted the nicotine patch. The thing irritated his skin. "The second I showed him the contracts, I think his life flashed before his eyes. Two minutes later, the meeting was over and I was being shown out by a dude with a Glock."

"I'll score this as very positive. We'll have to find other routes to the information, but now we know there's something here. We aren't on a wild goose chase."

Sacker removed his Armani jacket and slung it over his shoulder. His taxi was approaching the circular drive in front of the Reliant buildings.

"You didn't ask if the massive detention center orders were related to the deportation program?"

He shook his head, moving to the vehicle. "No. Things ended pretty quickly. But it's the best hypothesis. I think you're right."

"We'll see," came Gone's clipped voice. Her face softened, and she smiled. "I think the esquire look is a good one for you."

Sacker winked at the screen. "Now that you mention it, I could get used to this new dress code. I make these suits look *good*."

"Well, we'll talk about that. Gotta go. My appointment's in five. Let's see what HFP Corrections has got for us."

8

GONE ON THE OFFENSIVE

"Ms. Gone? Mr. Fairchild will see you now." The blond beauty plastered a fake smile on her face. "Last door at the end of the hallway."

Grace Gone smiled back at the receptionist and stood. She straightened her blue pastel blouse and matching pants. Patting her hair bun, she returned the phone to her satchel.

Now that Tyrell has made this real, let's see what we can get here.

Sacker had landed at Reliant in stealth mode. His fifteen minutes of fame four years ago had been forgotten, his history since then buried in low level security work. That's what happened when you avoided the press and disappeared.

But she could hardly conceal her purposes. The Asian Holmes. Charlie Chan in drag. The Girl who Cracked the Case of the Missing Junk. There were frequent appearances on CNN and *The Today Show*, even an odd reboot of the *Mr. Wong* mysteries with some Japanese actress. She might have taken it as a compliment but for the bounding anime breasts and faux-Confucian proverbs.

At least it wasn't a white chick in yellow face.

Gone took the opposite path to Sacker. She leveraged her fame and sent them a message they couldn't ignore.

It is unfortunate that I am unable to secure an appointment with anyone on the staff of your brand-new company. Currently, I'm preparing my list of possible cases and need to ascertain whether an investigation into HFP Corrections is worth my time.

I don't think this mystery will make the cut, but I can't cross it off the list until we talk. I would appreciate the chance to do so.

Yours sincerely,
   Grace Gone

PS: Did you know that I blog? It's mostly updates on finished cases and some detective "how-to," but it does get a lot of traffic. Especially after the Eunuch Maker case.

She'd received a return email from some management VP within an hour.

In front of his office door, Gone removed a pair of thick glasses and slid them on. Her hand pressed the right side of the plastic frame. She blinked and stared forward for several seconds, letting the special lenses adjust. She knocked.

The door opened immediately. Another robotic blond assistant held the handle. Perfect teeth beamed back at her. The woman stepped to the side, her form-fitting dress more like body paint than clothing.

"Ms. Gone," came a baritone behind a glass desk. "Please come in. Meghan, please wait outside."

Gone scanned the room as the woman's heels clicked behind her and the door closed. *Glass.* She arced her head in a slow, awkward, and controlled curve. The desk, the chairs, and the sofa in the room were all made of glass or some kind of acrylic. The lamp on the desk, transparent. The picture frames of wife and kids, clear. The walls were similar, but opaque, tinted for privacy.

Might as well be an aquarium.

"I guess I shouldn't be throwing any stones in here." Gone approached a see-through chair in front of his desk.

Mark Fairchild was the inverse of his surroundings. Heavy-set, bronzed, and sporting a black suit, he frowned through his teeth. His eyes were cold as he barked a false laugh. "Funny, I've never heard that one before, Ms. Gone. Please have a seat."

With deliberate precision, she moved her head back and forth across his desk, making sure the glasses took in every inch. She sat, adjusting to the stiffness of the plastic chair.

"So, let's get to the point, Ms. Gone." He dropped into a translucent executive chair. The acrylic squeaked. "Your email stirred up a lot of people. Someone of your *profile* considering some kind of investigation into this startup." He shook his head. "Beginnings are sensitive times for companies. That last thing we need is any bad press. If the great Grace Gone is looking into us, it will be all over the papers."

"You are a very new company," she opened. "Remarkable capitalization in such a short time. You've never built a building. And yet, suddenly you've netted a series of government contracts."

Fairchild squirmed. "Thank you. We are proud of our fund-raising and the faith the American people have put in our product."

"It's especially eyebrow-raising considering the makeup of your founders. Paul Wistern, for example. Your CEO. He has no experience in the prison industry."

"Well, neither do I, Ms. Gone. But we're businessmen. Running a business from the top is more about good management than specific knowledge of given products."

"Perhaps. But Mr. Wistern hardly had any of that, did he? He's a former marine biologist, started a company a year ago designing and building pressurized submersible habitats. Suddenly, that company disappears. Then he's a co-founder of a new corporation that advertises as a prison construction company."

"I'm sorry, I don't really follow you. Why is any of this troubling you?"

Gone smiled. "I'm good at identifying patterns, Mr. Fairchild. That's why I'm successful at what I do. That, and pushing through deductions based on data. Right now, I don't have much data on HFP Corrections. Mostly because there isn't any to be had."

"That will change, I assure you," he said, beads of sweat growing on his forehead.

"So all I have are patterns. Or rather, holes where normal patterns should be. Help me understand." She crossed her legs and leaned forward. "How does a brand-new company, devoid of any names with significant experience in construction, architectural design, or the prison industry, suddenly appear, grab three or four lucrative contracts from Uncle Sam, all without ever having produced so much as a portable potty?"

His mouth hung open a second. "We have kept our proprietary work a closely guarded secret, Ms. Gone. Industrial espionage is very real. Our plans were only revealed to the government under confidentially agreements, and only when we competed for the contracts."

"A strange competition. One where no other competing firms are listed."

"Since that is also confidential, Ms. Gone, you're only speculating."

"Am I?"

She held his gaze as his fingers drummed on the clear armrests. *How much to lead, and how much to let the silence push him?* Without knowing his access to information, it was a dice roll. But the right pressure could mean a break. She studied his eyes. His gaze didn't waver. If she pushed too much, she could tip her own hand.

Keep it causal, Gracie. You're a PI checking out her potential new cases. No emotional commitment.

"Perhaps I am," she said. "But I must say that I've never heard of so much secrecy for simple prison design. What miraculous inventions in housing criminals might your R&D wing have come up with to require such complete secrecy?"

Fairchild ground his teeth. "Of course, being proprietary, I'm not at liberty to—"

"And your collaborations! *The DoD.* Very impressive. Are these innovations for military prisons? And then there's Homeland Security. You know, when I see contracts with Homeland, detention facilities, and the military, I can't help but think of the exploding need for space to hold the flood of detainees in the expanding deportation program. Could any of these have to do with that?"

"Again, all speculation on your part, ah, Ms. Gone." He licked his lips. "I just can't comment."

She pouted. "You're really just not giving me much to go on, here."

Her hand ran over the top of her thick rims as she aimed her stare at his desk. Her eye twinkled, and she raised her gaze to a reflective portrait on the shelf behind him. She continued to rub the top of the frames, praying that the miniature lens motors could not be heard across the desk.

"But I can't help but think that your secrets are related to hiring Wistern," she continued. "Why him? Makes no sense to make him a founder. Unless something about underwater habitats is important to your work?"

She snapped her attention to Fairchild. He flinched.

"You're not going to put those poor children and families at the border underwater? Exile them to the sea if Mexico won't open its doors?"

Fairchild's eyes went wide, and he barked a laugh. "Ha! Ms. Gone, you have a very active imagination. But I can assure you on that question, we are building no underwater structures. Our CEO is here because he has a keen business mind and is leading our new company to great heights."

She worried the smile he held might break his face.

"Okay, Mr. Fairchild," she said, standing up. "I swear—this is all very odd, but uninteresting. The man who referred you to me clearly saw something worthwhile that I don't. I'll move on to other cases."

The cramped muscles on his face slackened, and for the first time she glimpsed an honest smile.

"Well, that's good to hear, good to hear." He stood and offered his hand. "Great to hear, Ms. Gone. Is there anything else?"

She shook her head, touching the heavy glasses again. If they had captured what she thought, he'd given her perhaps quite a bit.

"No, thank you. I can see myself out."

9

FACHADA

ngel Lightfoote crouched in the dim interior of the command-and-control van. A panel of flat screens cast a pale glow over her alabaster skin, her bushel of hair a white fire lit above her head. The vehicle lurched to a stop. Tense voices outside mixed with a man's repeated phrases. They spilled from computer speakers in front of her again and again.

"The terrorist El Marcado escaped. But we saved the convoy. And we've got wounded. Some of my people are bleeding out."

Almost there.

They'd never tried something so audacious, infiltrating a major detainment camp without a shot fired, using only their wits and a good dash of modern digital trickery. Lightfoote set her jaw. Tonight's break-in would succeed or fail because of her. She continued tweaking the videos.

The face of the Hunter, Darren Childs, filled a boxed-off portion of half the screen. In the other half, Francisco Lopez spoke the same words. Lines caged the lips, eyes, and cheeks, differential vectors connecting the two faces. The algorithms had nearly mapped Lopez's words to the video elements of Childs, blending the movements so that their digital puppet of the Hunter said exactly what they needed it to say.

The other monitors were paneled nine-by-nine. They ran footage of Childs from TV appearances and internet videos. The majority came from *Canid News*, the near state-run media outlet that was little more than an arm of the billionaire president. The same diagram lines boxing in Childs's facial features played over each video, annotating the reference footage with high-mimicking visemes, phonemes, reflectance, and three-dimensional face pose and geometry. Numbers flowed down the sides indicating the fit of the neural nets between the two subjects.

The van door slid open, headlights from nearby vehicles reflecting off the displays.

"Close the door!" cried Lightfoote, her hands darting over the keyboard. "Glare!"

Houston slammed it shut and peered over the monitors. Her Stetson and holstered gun gave her the vibe of a tech cowgirl bending over the screens. "The compound's just over the hill," she gasped. "How close are you?"

"It's good. Just tweaking."

"It's got to be good enough now."

Lightfoote spun in the chair, her head just below Houston's midsection. Her eyes flicked up her form, her mouth drying out. "Deep fakes are still cutting edge. The more processing time, the more realistic. Childs is a media whore. We got all the background images and dialogue we need. Francisco's a decent match. Not ideal, but good enough without imposing too much of a computational burden."

"English, please," said Houston, her breathing slowing, deepening.

"I've got most of the dialogue we need. Video too. But every minute processing makes it more realistic. Video conferencing in will be very effective if we've got it polished."

Houston stepped back, creating a distance between the two. Her head pressed against the van ceiling. "Angel, we've got to move, or we'll become far more suspicious than a glitchy deep fake video. Add some static. Hell, video chat freezes and distorts so much, your deep fakes look better than my bad reception calls."

"Ahead of you. Incorporated." Lightfoote pivoted to the screens, then to Houston again, her gaze intense. Houston was right. It was now or never. "Okay. Let's do it, cowgirl. Good to go."

"Yeah." Houston licked her lips. "Okay, I'll tell Francisco." She turned to open the door.

Lightfoote touched her arm. "Sara…"

"Not now, Angel." Houston didn't turn, her face lost to the brim of the hat. "I know. *I know.* But not now. There's too much. Too important. Everything else waits."

She slid the door open and bounded out, her thick boots crunching the gravel beneath.

Lightfoot followed her swaying hips as Houston's form faded into the night. Wiry and strong, energized by a spit-fire attitude and a sailor's vocabulary, Houston's spirit always hit her with a burning rush. *Like the whiskey she loves so much.* It was a struggle to stay still, to refrain from dashing into that tornado of personality. That's what did it years ago. That's why she'd violated the trust among the three of them. One day, when her own demons threatened to climb out of the dungeon again, when the Eunuch Maker brought back memories of a personal hell, she'd taken that tornado into her arms for a brief moment.

Now Houston was a taut bow around her. She just wanted her to loose the arrow. Lightfoote felt her chest rising, her heart beating in her head. Their crazed life of guerrilla warfare had given them plenty of distractions. Always, there were more important things. It was never the right time for Houston.

"Some things always wait," she whispered to herself. "Until they never are."

Lopez's broad frame pivoted around the front of the van. "We ready?" he asked.

Lightfoote nodded. She hated being a wedge between them, even if she was sure Houston had said nothing. Lopez wasn't sensitive to nuance in relationships, but he wasn't stupid. More and more, his face betrayed something she could only identify as suspicion.

"So where's Sara headed?"

That look. Right there. A suspicion related to them, not the mission.

"Out looking for you. She basically ordered me to stop playing and get this going."

He held her gaze a moment, the look fading. "She's right. We need to move now. I'll grab her."

He dashed off, the pair returning in minutes. Side by side, shoulders occasionally touching. Lightfoote envied Lopez in moments like this. Would she ever walk openly side by side with Houston?

The mission took precedence over any other concerns. They huddled together in the armored SUV as the convoy approached barbed fencing of a new and secretive detention camp. Two makeshift concrete towers flanked a metal gate. Armed guards aimed weapons both inside and outside the compound.

"You called it in?" asked Lopez, glancing at Lightfoote.

"Two contacts. Used Childs's transceiver. Added some static to mask the synthetic dialogue. No sign of suspicion."

Houston frowned, scanning the entrance. "Security's gone up a lot. This tent city is what, three months old?"

"The fifth in this area in a year," noted Lopez. "And more a fort than a tent. Doesn't make sense. The growth of camps at the border fits. Gonna export millions, gotta pile them up at the bottlenecks. But here?"

"No doubt. What the hell do they need five camps in Nevada for?"

"*Loads* more security," smirked Lightfoote. "They're scared they're going to be our next target. But they'll drop their pants for Big Boy Childs here." She glanced at the other two. "I'll initiate the video call."

She tapped the keyboard. A classic landline ringtone filled the van. There was a click and a male voice.

"Detention Center N5. That you, El Cazador?"

An older man's face with short trimmed gray hair and sharp-rimmed glasses appeared on the screen and stared from the computer monitor. His image was flanked by the visage of Darren Childs, artifacts of poor reception and all. On computers beside the conference call, images of Childs tiled several monitors. Text descriptors lay underneath each.

Lightfoote's hand darted to the mouse, and she clicked on one of the Childs panels. The deep fake spoke.

"Childs here. Reception's all to hell. You getting this?"

"You're freezing and skipping, but loud and clear." The old man smiled. "Been too long, Darren."

"Wait," said Houston, "isn't that—"

"General Stephen Miller," finished Lopez. "One of the early architects of Suite's deportation plan."

"What the hell's he doing here?"

"Something bad." Lightfoote inhaled. "Okay, we need to cut off pleasantries, or this high-roller is going to out us." She clicked on other panels.

"No time for a chat," barked the image of Childs. "This convoy was hit earlier by El Marcado."

"So your earlier communication noted. You didn't get him?"

Lightfoote clicked on another panel of Childs further down on the screen. The video froze and skipped as the panel engaged.

"El Marcado escaped, but we saved the convoy. And we've got wounded. Some of my people are bleeding out."

Miller grimaced. "That son of a bitch. Understood, Childs. I'll have medical routed to you immediately."

Another click, and the video skipped again.

"Thanks. And I'd man as many guards on the gate as you can. For all I know, that bastard followed us back and is waiting to spring."

"Good advice." The man's face hardened. "We'll get him, Darren. I don't doubt that for a minute. And it'll be you who does it."

Lightfoote cut the video call. Several seconds passed in silence.

Lopez bared his teeth. "Did they buy it?"

Metal clanked. The double doors of the gate vibrated, the steel shimmying under the headlights. Dust clouded the air as the metal dragged across the ground.

Lightfoot whispered. "And Cassandra spoke to the Trojans as they toiled with the giant horse, *'Unhappy people, who carry doom into our city! Already mine eyes witness these very streets flooded with fire and murder and blood.'*"

"Remember your roles," said Lopez. "Act it out until we get inside the main structure. Take up your positions until the signal."

10

MJOLNIR

A stream of black SUVs sped through the cleared streets of Manhattan's Upper East Side. Police cruisers lined critical intersections, blocking traffic. They created a path for emergency vehicles and other official personnel.

And unofficial, thought Savas.

They sat in the back, shielded from the outside world by metal and bulletproof glass. But there was only so much they could screen out from the world around them. Smoke dimmed the sun as he and Cohen approached the bombing site. The tinted glass failed to stop the particulates as a foul stench, acrid and burning, irritated his throat. At least the bombastic re-election posters featuring Daniel Suite's smirking face were defaced by angry New Yorkers with all manner of inappropriate graffiti. A very small win as they seemed to lose a bigger war.

Cohen, ever in command of the data, rifled off facts and figures as they sped into Harlem. "Massive explosion. The entire mosque is gone."

She pivoted the laptop toward him. His eyes flicked to the screen and away. He'd seen the preliminary images. High resolution, on the ground, enhanced, whatever—it wasn't going to change the assessment.

"High skill set for terrorists," he said, memories of the same words like an echo as he spoke. "Like nothing we've ever seen."

Cohen whipped her head toward him, her eyes narrow.

"John, you're not—"

"I still remember when you first gave that assessment on the UN bombing. A decade ago now. In a different world. When we were different people."

She exhaled. "And terrorism has changed a lot in that time. Many groups have upped their game. Let's not see ghosts."

The vehicle lurched over potholes and bulges in the road. The chemical reek of a burning building intensified.

"That's just it. I'm always seeing ghosts." Savas closed his eyes. "It's just, now they're starting to talk to me."

He reached to the floorboard. A sharp purr hummed as he unzipped a black duffle bag between his feet.

"I was going to ask you what that was all about," she said.

Savas removed an instrument the size of a breadbox. A dark LCD screen framed by small buttons protruded from one side. Circular openings with porous grids lined the top. Two handles protruded from each of the short sides.

"Is that what I think it is?"

"Sure is. Our FBI requisitioned portable mass spec. Never used. First field test was right after Gunn and those bastards murdered our teams."

"It still works? Did it *ever* work?"

He laughed. "Kind of like me, now, huh?" He pressed a button and the LCD blinked to life, coded letters and numbers flashing across the screen. "The labs certified it way back when. And I've kept it serviced."

Her eyes widened. "All these years?"

The corners of his mouth twitched up. "Every year. Didn't want you to think I had too many issues, so I kept it on the down low." He turned away from the concern in her eyes. "Some upgrades and specifications were added. Basically, it's an S-47 detector now, optimized for the compound. Key units inside are modernized. Looks prehistoric, but it's cutting edge."

"Jesus." Her face tightened. "Mjolnir is gone. Gunn is dead. There's been nothing from any remnants of that group for years."

"Well, a mosque in Manhattan just blew up."

"Okay, but how many arsonists hit mosques after Suite was elected?"

"This wasn't arson. It was a precision bombing. Even in today's gamed-up terrorists, how many hits like this have you seen?"

She put her hand on his arm. "Let's get some evidence before we go off the cliff here."

Savas turned back to her, smiling. He patted the device.

"That's what this is for."

* * *

Savas and Cohen stepped out of the dark truck and into the failing summer light. Buildings aligned to the city's grid-carved horizontal canyons. An orange glow from Jersey poured through them.

Flashing firetrucks and armored police vehicles walled them from the inhabitants of Harlem. He glanced around at the towering housing projects nearby. The faces of tenants pressed against windows, cameras likely streaming everything to various online sites.

Talk about a surveillance state.

"Uh, Mr. Savas, Agent Savas?"

A mustached hulk of a man approached them. Savas turned to him as Cohen aligned herself to greet the official.

"That's me," he answered.

"Special Agent in Charge Fred Collins."

The giant grasped Savas's hand in a vice and crushed it.

Goddamned Hercules.

"Nice to meet you, Agent Collins. With me is Rebecca Cohen." He removed the remains of his hand and gestured toward her.

"I didn't get which agency you're with." Collins peered at them, his face tensing.

Even his face is on 'roids.

"You've been instructed to work with us from your superiors, correct?" Savas locked eyes with him.

"Uh, yes, but—"

"Good. Then we know where we stand." He motioned with his head toward the still smoldering crater. "Take us to the scene."

Collins frowned but relented. "This way."

As if we'd miss it.

Approaching the barrier of tape, Savas angled his face away from the heat. The fire department performed to their usual professionalism. Small flames burned deep within the structure, unextinguished. The city had shut down the gas lines to the surrounding area.

Cohen spoke. "The damage around appears minimal."

"Sure is," said Collins. "I served in Afghanistan. I've seen a lot of bombing sites. I ain't seen nothing this *clean.*"

Savas glanced at several sheets covering bodies and body parts in the road. Flashes popped around them as detectives and federal agents documented the crime scene.

Collins followed his gaze. "Well, you're not going to blow up half a block in the middle of the day and not leave some remains. But normally, this kind of thing—"

"We know," interrupted Savas. "This is precision. Surgical. Artistry." He gazed under his eyebrows at Cohen. Her mouth tightened.

A short spurt of beeps sounded from beside Savas. Collins turned and gazed at the source of the sound, a black box gripped in Savas's left hand. "What the hell is that?"

Savas brought the box to his face and flipped on a pair of reading glasses. The LCD light glowed in the growing darkness and painted his face green.

"It's part air sampler, part mass spectrometer."

Collins scoffed. "We've got investigative teams with much better gear."

"I'm sure you do," said Savas, holding the device toward Cohen. Her eyes widened. "But none that are designed specifically for one compound."

"What compound?" Collins appeared on the edge of his patience.

"Variant of Semtex called S-47. Cutting-edge about ten years ago. A favorite of a terrorist group called Mjolnir."

Collins stiffened. "Mjolnir? You mean, Thor's Hammer? The one that…"

"Targeted Muslims," finished Cohen, glancing at the flickering hole before them.

"That's the one," confirmed Savas. "S-47 was their go-to. They had some highly trained demolitions people. Like Michelangelo with that stuff."

He turned away from the bombing site and gestured into the air. "And according to this thing, we're breathing in high concentrations of it right now. Raining down on us with the ash."

Cohen grimaced, staring into his eyes. He shut off the device. His blood was already cold, a dark certainty weighing on him the entire drive. Now ice ran through his limbs.

"They're back."

His mobile phone buzzed in his pocket, a quick glance confirming his worst fears. He glanced at Cohen.

"White House calling."

REPUBLICANS PUSH PRESIDENT'S CHARGED AGENDA

by Fred Usher, *The Guardian*

Today, House Republicans moved swiftly to bring the US President's so-called Sovereignty Act to vote. Cast as a response to a national emergency at the border, the appropriations bill would authorize the transfer of monies from safety-net programs such as Medicare, food stamps, and various welfare statutes to the Department of Homeland Security.

These funds, the amount still under debate on the House floor but suspected to range in the tens of billions, would be earmarked for increased militarization of the US-Mexico border, the continued construction of a border wall, and the expansion of existing "alien centers" along the border for undocumented detainees. Labeled concentration camps by political opponents and colloquially known as "tent cities," existing structures are reportedly filled to dangerous levels by the forced displacement of undocumented persons rounded up across the nation.

"It's a hellscape, a nightmare," said Amnesty International's Gordon Hill. "The family separation policy continues and is now applied to those families in the US, many living in the nation for years or even decades. There's no trial. No *writ of habeas corpus*. It's unlawful abduction and indefinite detention in what are unsafe and deteriorating conditions."

British and European leaders have expressed concern over what some have termed the growing xenophobic climate in the United States, but few have been directly critical of Suite or specific policies for fear of how the mercurial and unpredictable US president would respond. Russia and China have remained neutral, calling the problems internal affairs that should remain within the purview of the United States.

Only Germany, through its UN representatives, has consistently voiced opposition, openly attacking the new policies.

"I never thought we'd see sights like this again," said UN representative Helmut Kern. "Not in the Western World. And never in my wildest dreams could I have believed that it would occur on the soil of the United States of America. In Germany, we remember. Remember what we once became. But the world forgets. History repeats. Vulnerable minorities are scapegoated, fears stoked and used to gain and consolidate power. People are dehumanized. Latinos and Muslims attacked, their businesses ransacked, their houses of worship defaced. Now they are disappearing. Communities suddenly emptied. I see videos of children ripped from their parents, and the world will not act. I see emaciated figures that were once hardworking members of a society that is being consumed by darkness. I fear for the soul of the western world."

The controversies over the border and undocumented immigrants are only part of the agenda for the president and GOP after their resounding victories in the midterm elections. With the House and Senate firmly in hand, the Republicans have moved aggressively to implement small government, business-friendly legislation. Several bills loosening environmental regulations, opening up oil drilling along the Atlantic seaside, and privatizing national parks are in the works. Legislation to extend and expand the corporate tax cuts of Suite's first term has been rumored, but this time centering on oil and gas companies. The President is also working with Congressional allies to end governmental support for alternative energy research and subsidies, looking to transfer the funds to other areas.

The Democrat party leaders appeared stunned and defeated after November's elections and the announcement of policies and executive orders dismantling former President York's agenda.

"Decades of work to clean up the environment is

disappearing before our eyes," said Minority Whip Thomas Kline. "While Suite distracts with the legitimately terrifying Sovereignty Act, which itself is going to harm millions of people as it steals funds from vital programs for the vulnerable, what isn't in the headlines are a host of changes that will make America worst for our children and grandchildren. This presidency will damage generations of Americans."

11

GONE SOUTH

Sacker scowled, scanning the compartment as the train pulled out of DC. A lifetime as a black man had honed a supersense for detecting potential racial animosity and danger. The proliferation of black Suite hats announcing allegiance to the bigoted president, even in this northeastern corridor, had his hate-dar on alert. He was glad Gone remained absorbed with her laptop, spared the adolescent guffaws and loud-on-purpose off-color jokes.

It didn't help that some of the young bozos were cheering the flat-screen stream of *Canid News*. Even in Blue States, Canid had become the default station for public locations. Hospitals, public transport, it didn't matter. After last year's Accuracy in Media Act and the subsequent crack down on "libelous content," too many local and even national newscasts had found themselves shut down by government action. Most had challenged and won in court, at least so far, but the disruptions meant that only Canid, the media arm of Daniel Suite, was sure to be available. The telecast today set Sacker further on edge.

"Good morning. It's a bright six a.m. here in New York City, and you're watching *Canid & Colleagues*! The number one show on *Canid News* and favorite of our Commander in Chief, President Daniel Suite."

Three telegenic hosts sat on a couch, a woman between two men. A coffee table rested in front of them. Bright, perfect teeth gleamed in the camera lights.

Barbie and Ken dolls for the damned KKK.

They introduced a guest linking in by phone.

"Joining us is author and columnist Granne Voulture," chirped one of the men.

Sacker shook his head. *That blond witch hatching ratings gold with every racist vomit out of her mouth.*

"She'll talk about her new book, *Suite Sound of Victory: How a Real Man Defeated the Limp Left.* Granne? Can you hear us?"

"I sure can, Ryan." The voice was devoid of bass and full of nasal. Intermittent static popped. "How are you?"

"We're great, Granne. Great. This new book of yours," he continued, "I gotta say, it's something. You hit hard."

"We're at a crisis point," said Voulture. "The Left nearly destroyed this nation. First under Barack Hussein Obama and then Elaine York. A black man and a woman president. So you can see what their affirmative action plan has done for us."

Jesus. In some warped way, he actually had to admire the genius of her hate riffs. The black-hatted boys hooted.

"That's funny," laughed one of the hosts along with them.

Voulture's tone remained harsh.

"It's not funny. Because I love this country, and I didn't know whether it could be saved. Not until Daniel Suite won. But the Left will do anything to stop his plan to make the country great again. They'll burn everything to the ground before letting our president's programs get off the ground. That's what my book is about."

One of the male hosts wagged his head. "Yeah, we're seeing that with the protests, the activist judges, the ACLU. Suite is trying to get these criminals, illegals, and killers out. Now Mexico is closing the border."

"It's the Deep State. The remaining Leftist traitors are loyal to disgraced president York. It's no coincidence that John Reynolds was speaking to the Mexican president. He's a hold-over at State from the

York Administration. All right before they took this hostile action toward America."

"You don't think he was negotiating," said the host. "That's what the *New York Times* is running with."

"Please," scoffed Voulture. "More fake news. And why do you think this terrorist organization, this *El Marcado* and his killers haven't been caught? In this age, with drone surveillance, cameras, inside America itself? The FBI can't find a well-financed, large and deadly group of terrorists? Leftists constantly take the side of primitives against civilization."

"You think the Deep State is involved?"

"Of course it is!" shouted Voulture. "It's a slow coup. They can't catch this Mjolnir either. But at least those guys are blowing up secret terror cells. These Muslim sleeper cells in the US masquerading as legitimate organizations, hiding behind mosques. They're doing us a favor."

The female host furrowed her brow. "But it's still terrorism, right Granne? I mean, you can't just blow up buildings and gun people down. That's for the police."

"If they'd do their jobs and protect us. But a decade under liberals has left us soft. I'm more a real man than any leftist out there. Now these terrorists out west are killing our officers. They're sabotaging Suite's deportation program to clean America of these vermin. The FBI would look incompetent if they weren't so obviously in on it. No liberal ever passed on a chance to betray the United States."

"This book is going to be controversial!"

The voice on the speaker continued. "The President is going to have to take extreme measures. What we're seeing is sedition. Let's call it what it is—treason against the President, an act of war as he tries to protect our national sovereignty and the American people. Maybe the liberals don't want protection, but we do!"

"But what about those on the Left crying about civil liberties and rights and all that?"

Static burst on the speaker, and the woman barked a laugh. "Oh, the liberals love to defend so-called civil liberties. Sure. But only when they're talking about Muslims, perverts, and criminals! One day they're defending communists, the next, crying for Islamic terrorists. They're always against America. *Always.* They are either traitors or complete morons. There may be some bad conservatives, but there's not one good liberal. None. Ever."

The male host laughed. "Then they can all move south of the border wall. We won't miss them."

Voulture concurred. "Clean out the country. Like Suite is doing with these criminal vermin aliens. But that's a good point, Ryan. Maybe the president should be more thorough. Clean out the country of the Left as well. Like I said: this is treason. In normal times, the nonsense liberals vomit is cute in a sad kind of way. But in wartime, it's life-threatening. The Republican Congress is rewriting the citizenship laws as we speak. Why clutter our jails with Leftist and Antifa riffraff? Strip these traitors of citizenship and deport them with their gangbanger buddies."

"Powerful words from a woman President Suite is known to respect and take advice from. We'll be back to continue this interesting conversation after this break."

Sweet Son of God.

Sacker tipped his hat down around his face. As a police officer, he'd faced down hardened criminals. He'd stared into the face of death in Iraq. But what scared him more was the direction of his fellow citizens. Some kind of mind virus was eating brains faster than a zombie outbreak.

The clacking of a keyboard beside him drew his attention. Sacker turned to face Gone in the adjacent train seat. He needed to occupy his mind with something else. She had said the train ride would give them a chance to go over their efforts of the last few days. He was ready to have a conversation.

"You sure this is a good place to talk?" he opened, his eyes darting to the boisterous Suite supporters in front of them.

She stared ahead into her open laptop and leaned in. He caught his breath. Her scent, some fleshly version of mixing chocolate and nutmeg, hit him like a fifth of bourbon. Black strands of hair brushed his face as she whispered.

"Keep our voices low," she said. "It's a train. Half the people are plugged in with headphones. Those other idiots have the confidence of privilege to ignore their surroundings. We're the only two in this row. We need to go through all this. We need to talk."

She angled her head towards him. Catching her eyes was diving into a deep and warm pool. He tipped his hat forward more, obscuring his vision.

I'll drown in there.

"So then," he coughed, "Department of Transportation checked off the list. We were lucky to hit a useful idiot. All hail the bureaucracy."

She pointed to a digital flow chart. "Right. So, our whistle-blower handed us these contracts with the DoT. But now the big numbers begin to make sense. Entire recommissioned rail lines. New train cars for livestock and chemicals. Everything in the Southwest. Everything centered in Nevada. Not bad for a week's work."

Nevada. What's in Nevada? "So, what the hell is going on there?"

"Something big, Tyrell. The big picture is starting to give me pause."

She closed the device and turned to him. He needed to look away, take in the data, process the implications.

Stay sane. Stay sober.

"Lady Holmes is stumped," he smirked, reaching for a distraction.

The pout protruded. "We need to get our hands on insider details. Our contact has gone dark. It's up to us."

"Not sure how we can dig any deeper here. We don't have access." He tapped his finger on his knee. "Can we go back to the smart glasses? You said you had something to show me."

"Yes. It's finished. You need to see this."

Gone flipped the computer back open and scrolled through several windows.

Sacker grunted. "I have to say, that took some guts, walking in there and spy-graphing the entire thing. So what didn't you show me before?"

"His computer screen."

She opened some software that showed several graphs and a series of pixelated frames. Sacker struggled to process the disparate images.

Trucks. Mining equipment. Company logos and spreadsheets. It was information overload.

He cocked his head. "Wait. This is from his screen?"

"He didn't close his PC or put it on screen saver. Guess he thought I was on the wrong side of it."

"Well, weren't you? Those X-ray lenses, too?"

"Mr. Glass, remember? Well, with all those reflective surfaces, after some hunting, I found one behind him. A photo of the family, with the right polarization and angle. It was a functional mirror. Aimed right at his display."

"Damned Ms. MacGyver."

"I didn't want to say anything until I was sure. The image quality was terrible. I've had it processing with enhancement software for the last two days. Background work during our little trip to DC. But it's done."

She clicked on the last series of pictures. On the right was a dark shoulder. In the middle and left portion of the picture was an LCD display. Photographs and text. The letters were jagged and blurry, but legible.

He squinted at the display, tapping several dark rectangles with black circles blurred underneath. "Those are eighteen-wheelers." He leaned in further. "And this photo, what the heck are those sacks?"

"Impossible to tell. Look down here." She pointed to the lower right of the monitor. Photos of large machinery peeked around Fairchild's shoulder. Bright letters branded each.

"ADS. What's that?"

"The first strand of a web," she said. Several windows opened with bank records.

"How'd you get those?" He held up a hand, cutting her off. "Nevermind. Plausible deniability is useful when the Feds come after you for cybercrimes."

"There's a cluster of shell companies, all traced down to a principal subcontractor of the Yucca Mountain project."

"The what?"

"The deep mine where they were going to bury the country's radioactive waste."

"Right." Sacker had fogged flashbacks to news reports. "Some controversy or something? That still going?"

"No. Killed by the Obama administration in 2011. Well, sort of. Lots of legal wrangling. But essentially killed after ten years of funding, digging, and construction. The politics were as radiative as the mess they wanted to entomb there."

"Well, nobody wants that shit buried next to them."

"Exactly. So, why are contracts suddenly converging on it?" She flipped back to the reconstructed image of the laptop. "American Depository Services, or ADS. That's our acronym. Want some more alphabet soup and shell games? It's a wholly owned subsidiary of SRU Corporation. That's now part of something called AORC. AORC has supporting principal subcontractors Wash Corporation. Wash is part of McDonney International Inc., held by Avera Government Services, LLC. Which is, of course," she said smiling, "now Orlando Contracting."

"I'm totally lost."

"You're supposed to be. These businesses are nothing more than transfer points. They obfuscate the money trail. It'd take a very dedicated reporter or governmental audit to get through this."

He stared at her. "Guess we're lucky you're on the case."

"The best part for last." She touched to the top of the screen. "The letters are a bit cut off. What do you make of the title for this slide he stupidly forgot to hide while I was there?"

He squinted. The words stumbled out of his mouth.

"China Girl?" He gave her a side glance. "You're kidding, right?"

She shook her head.

He stuttered. "This can't be...I mean, there's no way..."

"No. It's not me. Of course not. They didn't know I was involved with this until recently. This is a code name for the big program. They've always got some cute name for stupid things they're doing."

The adrenaline receded, his pounding heart slowing, the chill rushing through him lessening. For a moment, he'd imagined a crosshair on Gone.

"All right, so what's China Girl?"

She shrugged. "I don't know. Internet searches drown in the David

Bowie song. Push beyond that and there are some novels, a restaurant or five, and, of course, street slang for fentanyl."

"Fentanyl? The drug?"

"Powerful opioid. One hundred times more powerful than heroin."

"Yeah, I wasn't on vice, but I've heard of it."

"Cheaper to make than heroin, too. So of course, lots of labs in China crank it out." Her mouth formed a thin line. "Lots of Chinese labs in other places, too."

He shook his head. "Chinese labs in other places? What do you mean?"

"Not important." She waved it away with her hand. "It's a problem because dealers cut heroin with fentanyl. If they do it right, addicts get the same high for far less cost to the dealer, but it's one hundred times the potency. If the dealer gets it a little wrong, the addict's dead of an OD. Most of the overdoses in the ER now are from fentanyl adulterants or even straight."

"China Girl. Okay. So what could that have to do with this government thing? You think someone's using government as camouflage for drug running?"

"Not sure it has *anything* to do with it. A lot of code names are distractions from the real scheme. Maybe whoever's behind this had a thing for Bowie. Right now, I'm much more interested in what ADS and Yucca mountain have to do with this."

"Gracie, this is starting to feel like *Beautiful Mind* material. Your flow chart's a conspiracy theorist's pinup."

"Complex doesn't mean crazy," she said. "We just need to ferret out the connections."

He frowned. "Okay, how? Where do we start?"

She whispered, her eyes darting like arrows around the cramped space, hands dancing. "We have a new but upcoming member of the US prison-industrial complex bankrolled on suspect deals with its origins and purpose covered up. Another's on the same list, whose CEO used to design and build underwater habitats. What's marine biologist Wistern doing with Homeland Security and the DoD? Meanwhile, folded into this project *China Girl,* there are other massive arrangements with outside business. Pharma. Biotech. *Mining.* Layer over it the DoT reserving rail lines, trucking capacity, all for trips to the Nevada desert. What *is* this thing?"

He stroked his chin. "It's too big. There's no place to insert. The low-level stooges we probed were a good start, but we've reached our limit. And it's a big gap between them and the heavy hitters you're talking about. Access. That's the problem. We don't got it."

She clacked on the laptop. He fought a smile. The girl was not going to give up that easy.

"We need to go one by one," she said, setting her jaw. "The DoT and prison companies are tapped out. We need to look at the chemical synthesis plant on the list. That vaccine biotech, Vaxagen. Also," she said, pulling up the image of a bearded man, "the mining connection."

"Who's that?"

"Ex-CEO of ADS. Board fired him for internal disputes, according to the press. He left right in the middle of all this."

His brows leapt toward his hairline. "You think he balked? Didn't want part of something he saw?"

"There's a chance. Timing's right. All we need is one person to crack. One to talk. Could break it open."

"Talk." He smiled. "I think I know where you're going with this."

"I've got an address." She said, beaming at him. "And a plan."

12

CABALLO DE TROYA

Houston adjusted the black flak vest and stepped out of the truck. A rush of camp personnel and medics greeted her. A team of their clandestine forces waited close by, playing their roles.

Looking the part, they sported standard-issue ICE uniforms and tactical gear stolen by raiding other camps and sites. With an eye to the future, she always stocked up.

Let's hope Angel's satellite hacking got us the right camp images.

So far, it appeared so. Buildings rose where they were supposed to. On her right, metal siding loomed. *The armory.* Always a good place to visit once they'd secured a location.

The warehouse should be behind the trailers she approached. If so, it was one of the largest she'd seen to date. It could hold tens of thousands of detained immigrants. If it matched the previous camps they'd hit, most would be Central American. All brown. In Suite's world, ICE passed by the Nordics with expired visas.

That's how you put the ethnic before the cleansing.

Medics and soldiers sprinted past her. She tightened, knowing that Lopez was taking great risks. They applied a latex covering to his stigmata. He'd broken out his old priestly robes and assumed the form of a cleric. Huddled with the others in the transport trucks, the camp guards would usher him into the warehouse as a prisoner.

The plan was simple. Fan out. Assess security and vulnerabilities. Assume strategic positions. Then coordinate an assault from within.

But first there was the General to deal with. She picked out his tall gray head approaching with a group of guards. She prayed Angel had done her job.

Time for a redirect.

"General Miller, sir?" she called over the din.

"Yes, who are you?" he said, sizing her up, staring into her eyes.

"Special Agent Sara Houston, sir. Lead on the recent raid."

"Where's Childs?"

"Evac'ed to medical."

"What?" His eyes widened. "He's wounded? He looked fine!"

"It's serious, sir. He doesn't let on more than he has to."

"God damn."

"A hero, sir."

He nodded. "You knew where to take him?"

"Yes, sir," said Houston, pointing in the direction of where the medical complex should be. "Behind the armory. He needs blood and was rushed out the second we entered the gate. It's touch and go."

"Thank you. Get those damn illegals in storage." He turned to a stout soldier beside him. "Grant, work with Agent Houston and clear the entrance. Childs warned El Marcado might be looking for a throwdown. We need this area emptied of all civilian personnel."

"Yes, sir," said Grant, stepping toward Houston.

"You've got the helm, Grant. I'm heading to medical. Richards and Johnson, with me."

Houston suppressed a grin as the older man jogged across the compound, bodyguards in tow.

Grant spoke. "Take me to the convoys and we'll unload these vermin. It's getting damned packed. We're gonna need another camp here soon."

Another camp? What the hell was going on in Nevada?

"Roger that."

She gazed to the towers and fencing. A growing contingent of armed men took positions around the perimeter.

Now to mark the fence sentries they're posting.

She locked eyes with key members of her disguised team, her eyes darting to the fences. As she led Grant to the transports, they assumed positions around the perimeter, behind the camp forces.

* * *

The guards shoved Lopez and the others through the warehouse doorway. He feigned a stumble, exaggerating his age and clumsiness. His hands gripped a bulky cross around his neck.

"¡Demonios! ¡Es un sacerdote!" came a woman's voice.

One of the guards struck the woman who protested, knocking her to the ground. No one else spoke. Terrified, the groups from the convoy marched into the giant building.

Lopez stared in horror. It was beyond anything he had anticipated, even from the other camps he had liberated. Tens of thousands were crammed together in a space designed for one-tenth the size, so packed that the cots and privacy screens had been shoved to the side or stacked. People slept on floors in tight bundles. It stank. Human body odor and sewage assaulted his sinuses. Children wailed. A persistent coughing signaled spreading infections.

He made the sign of the cross over the masses. He'd hardly finished when a baton slapped across his back. A prod shoved him forward.

The guards treated them like hardened terrorists. Even the old and infirm. They hadn't searched anyone. They were unfocused. The least professional agents he'd ever seen.

Recent hires. Untrained. They're desperate.

Lopez thought back on their guerrilla attacks over the last year. A pattern was emerging, strengthened all the more by what he saw here. All the new camp constructions, the sloppiness of ICE raids and transfers, had made their strikes easy and devastating. Staff grabbed to handle the exploding detainee numbers, hires made with poor vetting and minimal training. A perfect recipe for disaster and abuse.

And for getting their heads handed to them tonight.

The camps enforcers led him to a group of several families at the edge of the crowd. A guard shoved him down and marched the others along the periphery.

A mother with a young son stared at him.

"Ruega por nosotros, padre," she said. Her eyes were dead. Her son appeared malnourished, sickly thin and unresponsive.

Lopez responded in Spanish. "What is happening here?"

She misunderstood his question. "You have to sit. They will come by. Later. Maybe with food. Usually not. They will scan you then."

"Scan me?" he asked.

"Yes." She squinted. "They did not scan where they took you?"

"No. What do you mean, 'scanning'?" Nothing was making sense.

"They process you. Give you the shot. But they check. A machine with a light, like this." She mimed holding something in her hand and passing it over his arm. "Some don't have it. They give them the shot. That's all I know. They don't tell us why."

A chill ran through him. The inhuman care. Injections and scans, whatever those were. Camps popping like kernels in the desert heat. Something had gone completely off the rails.

Another woman spoke. She nursed an infant swaddled and hidden within folds of fabric. Two toddlers huddled behind her, staring wide-eyed at the priest.

"Father, please. My children are hungry. They took their father. We don't know where. When can we leave?"

"Soon, my child," said Lopez, the weight of their suffering a mountain. "Tonight brings danger. and you must pray."

His priestly robes buzzed. He silenced the phone.

It's time.

He scanned the enormous room. Figures around the interior stood. He followed suit, concerned stares adhering to him like glue.

"Father, sit! They will punish you if you stand."

Lopez smiled, stepping away from the crowd to the edges. Two guards noticed and shouted, moving toward him. They waved weapons toward his face.

"Sit down, asshole!" one shouted, only feet away.

Lopez brandished a hefty cross, the men's faces constricting in confusion. The cross clicked. A glinting blade extended from the apex of the crucifix.

The pair froze at the absurd sight. Lopez pivoted, his leg whipping like a propeller blade into the jaw of the man on his left. The kick crunched the guard's face, teeth scattering as his limp body dropped to the ground. The movement left Lopez facing the other guard, who fumbled in panic with his weapon. A thick blade entered the front of his windpipe and exited the back of his neck. Lopez twisted and yanked the cross back, side-stepping a spray of blood. Stooping, he grabbed the machine gun off the fallen man.

Gunshots exploded as the federal agents were set upon by members of his team. He touched his forehead and ripped the glued latex away, revealing his stigmata. He shouted over the din, sweeping the heavy firearm toward the warehouse entrance.

"No one move! This will be over soon!"

Cries of *El Marcado* rocked the building.

13

LA MARCA

The gunfire stopped. Isolated cries and moans sounded from the shadowed fog of smoke in the prevailing wind. The battle had been intense, but short-lived, the element of surprise providing their team an insurmountable advantage. Once the violence flared, their opponents' poorly trained staff and weak organization in the camp had fallen into complete disarray. She wasn't sure who Odysseus was in this Trojan Horse of theirs, but the ruse and subsequent execution was devastating.

Houston cut through the pungent fog and entered the medical building. It was filled to capacity with wounded. Federal agents. Members of her teams. Isolated non-combatants caught in the cross fire.

Always, the vulnerable pay the price.

She adjusted her hat, having retrieved it after the skirmish. Her mouth set in a hard line. She spoke to one of her medics. "Where's Angel?"

Had that mad FBI girl made it? Had Lopez? In the chaos of battle, leading their separate teams with different strike points, there was no way to know. But it was Lightfoote that preyed on her thoughts.

Losing Lopez was a threat she repeatedly immunized herself against. The pair had faced death so many times that their relationship was one of living intensely in the moment. Lightfoote was a recent wildcard, bursting into her emotional space without warning. She didn't have a handle on any of it.

Maybe that's why I can't shake her.

The two women had denied what was brewing between them. And it was Houston's doing. She wasn't going to change that. She couldn't betray Lopez or their life together. But the fear of losing an unborn love set her to a near panic.

The medic glanced up, her uniform coated in blood. "She left as soon as the shooting started."

The man under her knife trembled, his anesthetic insufficient. Only severe blood loss kept him from screaming.

"Well," said the medic, "as soon as they'd tied this one up." She pointed her needle to the far corner, then returned to her suturing.

Houston glanced to the back. General Miller was hog-tied and gagged, his eyes a combination of fury and fear. Beside him lay an unconscious Darren Childs, his shoulder wrapped in bandages. "Angel gets all the fun."

She spun on a heel and stormed out. Bodies decorated the rocky soil, but they clustered around the fences. Miller had positioned the bulk of his forces facing out, blind to the enemy inside the camp.

All for fear of the Mexican boogeyman.

But combat was never clean. Their invading teams had taken fire. They'd lost good soldiers, even if the cost was heavily one-sided. Now, the camp was theirs.

A broad figure exited the warehouse, a small bundle dwarfed in his massive arms.

"Francisco?" Her eyes locked on what he carried.

"Get Angel! She'll be in records. We need to find out what the hell is going on around here. Something is off. I'm getting this one to medical."

He sprinted off. Houston blinked to remove the image of the wounded child from her mind. She failed.

Records.

Angel's mission. As usual, they'd turned the digital sorceress loose on the computer systems. She closed her eyes and recalled the images of the compound they'd obtained from the satellite data. A smaller building came into focus, antenna and communication dishes on its surface. The command center of the camp.

This way.

She dashed through the chaos, dodging bodies and debris, converging on the location. The front door hung at an angle from the hinges, bullet holes studding the surface.

They held out until the last here.

Browning in hand, she slid along the door and peered into the small room.

Computer monitors lined a long desk. Several were sparking, an acrid, plastic smoke burning her lungs. Wires dangled from the ceiling. Thick bundles of ethernet lines and power cables snaked between the racks of metal chassis. A body lay slumped over a keyboard near the door. The man's head was dissected from the side, blood coating adjoining equipment. A group of her soldiers stood guard over several restrained federal agents at the far end of the room.

Before an unblemished monitor, a white mane glowed in the dim LCD light. Lightfoote's fingers danced on the keys, her face etched in lines of concentration. As Houston was about to speak, she held up a finger.

"Moment." The figure returned to the keyboard and the clacking intensified. "Angel is digging."

Houston stared, unmoving, Lightefoote's cold focus clashing harshly with her own relief to see her unharmed. But if Lightefoote was speaking in the third person, progress was being made. Houston holstered her firearm and pulled up a chair.

"The numbers of detainees are skyrocketing," said Lightfoote, shaking her head. "Not just at the border. Recently, not at *all* at the border. They're bringing them all here."

"Here? Nevada? Why? Is this why they're building all the new camps?"

"Gotta be. Look at these manifests." She whacked a finger on the keyboard and pointed to the screen. "They're roping in the trucking companies, packing migrants and anyone on a list into eighteen-wheelers."

"There were rumors."

"Rumors no more. They must be carrot-and-sticking the companies. The trucks have huge capacity, except, what to do when they get here? The numbers don't make sense."

Houston squinted. "What do you mean?"

Lightfoote puffed snowy strands from her forehead. "Five camps. A few tens of thousands, right? This one the biggest."

"It's shoddy. Security lax. They're rushing this."

"They have to," she said, the typing uninterrupted. "They're trucking in more than they can put here. Already have."

"Already have? What does that mean?"

"The manifests, the number of people they've brought here, it's too much. These five camps can't hold them."

"Are there camps we don't know of?"

"Have to be. A *lot* of them. Ten times what we know about, or more."

Houston blinked. "Ten times? How can—"

"What?!" Lightfoote's halo of white hair shook as she shouted at the monitor.

Houston paused, the tone of the exclamation stunning her, the former FBI agent pounding the keyboard like a drum. Her finger traced a line across the screen. She sat back in the chair and closed her eyes.

"All right, Angel," said Houston with a hesitant pause. "What is it?"

She didn't move, her face pointed to the ceiling, eyes remaining closed. She spoke with a whisper. "They're chipping them."

Houston shook her head. "Chipping? What's that? Who?"

Lightfoote opened her eyes and turned to Houston, a green light burning in each iris. "These motherfuckers have contracted with some company called PowerID." She scanned web searches on the name.

"Some startup in Boston. Subdermal implants, each with a unique ID number."

"What?" They were injecting devices into the detainees? Violating their flesh, their personal autonomy? This was from some dystopian science fiction film.

"Each links to external databases. Names. Documentation. Medical histories. Jesus, some have DNA data." Windows popped open across the monitor. "Vitals monitoring, even. And, of course, GPS tracking."

"Wait, like pet microchips? That kind of chipping?"

"Exactly. But ten times more sophisticated. More current and cutting edge."

"How is this remotely legal?"

Lightfoote scoffed. "How is anything these bastards do legal except under a shower of emergency degrees Suite keeps unrolling?" Her eyes narrowed over lists of names in a window. "There are hundreds of thousands in this database."

Houston shivered. "You mean they've chipped a hundred thousand people?"

"Nearly four hundred thousand."

The chill spread through her body. "But, how can the program be that big?"

"It means we, the press, the damn world, have missed a mass roundup bigger than anything suspected. Sure, Suite is talking millions, but it was supposed to be logistically impossible. Not without massive infrastructure use, huge numbers of law enforcement."

"There aren't those kinds of numbers in law enforcement," said Houston.

"Which means they're getting people to work in this program from other places."

"Four hundred thousand missing people. Microchipped."

"And they're trucking them in daily. Huge numbers to the deserts of Nevada," said Lightfoote. She stared without blinking. "Sara, something's very wrong."

An explosion rocked the camp command center.

Dust showered the pair. Lightfoot glowered from the computer screen and coughed. Houston's black Stetson shielded her face from the debris. The display went black as power cut from the building. The electronic hum inside ceased.

Lopez stormed into the shack.

"Ground and air assault!" he called, an automatic weapon in his hands.

Lightfoote rose from the chair. "Holy FUBAR, Batman."

14

DRAUGAR & JÖTNAR

The storm battered the cliff's edge, a blinding flash of lighting searing her eyes. Rebecca Cohen screamed, her arms burning from the strain, the ropes tearing the top layers of skin off her hands.

"Rebecca!" screamed Savas. "Now! Pull me up!"

The thin grass tore, and her feet slid on the mud towards the overhang. She wept. Her tears melded with the howling rain. A weight crushed her, the final sense that she was overmatched, ultimately powerless. The rope slipped through her bloodied hands. Savas cried from below, and the sound struck her chest like an arrow.

"Rebecca?"

The background hum of the plane's engines mixed with a soft light as she cracked her eyes open. Her neck was stiff, her head lodged against the window. Rain and flashes of lightning speckled the dark morning sky.

"Wake up. We're descending. Pilot says the storm's going to make it bumpy."

John.

Relief flooded her, an existential salvation from the fading reality of the dream. She opened her eyes wide and rolled her head away from the window. Her free hand grabbed his wrist.

Savas's eyes narrowed. "What is it? You look like you've seen a ghost."

"Haven't we both?" she deflected, wanted to erase the memory of the dream. She pushed her disheveled hair out of her face.

He nodded, turning away. "The worst kind."

She exhaled.

Is my subconscious trying to tell me something?

The discovery at the bombing site in New York burst a dam. The past could reach forward and possess the future. A poltergeist materialized, and a dark spirit sat on her husband's soul.

The cabin lurched and rumbled, turbulence rocking the small twin-engine plane. Intel 1 had its perks, a small collection of secure and secretive airplanes among them. But she preferred a larger bodied aircraft in torrid weather.

Savas noted her tension and grasped her hand. "You didn't need to come, stubborn girl. One humiliation is enough. Suite loves staff firings. At least according to the flood of tell-all books coming out of that sewer. Gets off on the adolescent power games." He smiled. "I could have delivered your pink slip and saved you the trip."

Cohen huffed. "Are you kidding? I wasn't sitting pretty for this. I'm not getting fired by remote control. They can look me in the eye when they do it. See how Reality TV President likes that."

He laughed. "You do have an unnerving stare."

The plane rattled side to side. She leaned back and closed her eyes.

"Was the all-nighter worth it?" asked Savas, squeezing her hand.

"Master distractor."

"I try."

She sat up and gazed forward, her tongue at the tip of her teeth.

"I poured back over all the data from Tampico. Security cameras. Eyewitness testimony. Everything. Slogged through the shelved effort to identify Patrick Rout. Passports. Credit cards. Face-recognition data for the last ten years. *Nothing.* Maybe it *is* a ghost because we haven't found any evidence of a corpse or living body."

"It has to be him. He was Gunn's right-hand man. Maybe more

the heart of Mjolnir than Gunn, even. No one else was so committed, so capable. Or so ruthless."

"He was shot up pretty bad. He could have died."

"You did him some serious damage, that's for sure." He glanced into her eyes. "He had me dead to rites. I thought that was it. I *knew* that was it. I'll never forget you walking out of that cloud of smoke like some damn commando in a war film."

"Don't remind me."

Savas ground his teeth. "I saw him fall against the car. Blood smeared on the hood. I heard that soft and wet smack when a body hits the pavement hard. I thought he was dead."

She squeezed his arm. His muscles were taut, the lines in his face pronounced. "We all did. You killed Gunn. Husaam detonated that warhead. Total chaos." She sighed. "We took our eyes off Rout. Our minds were fried for weeks. We dropped the ball." She shuddered, staring out the window. "I don't know how he walked out of there. It was inhuman."

"Pure hate. A powerful venom driving him. That, and the constitution of a rhino."

Cohen shivered. The monster *should* have died after that. Bled out quickly from the ammo she'd fired into him.

"That S-47 in the air of New York says he survived."

Lightning strobed the window. She shifted her weight in the seat, no position comfortable. "I'm inclined to agree. But all this does is put us on red alert with very little data."

"What about any of the Western extremist groups?" he asked. "US and EU. We never got anything close to complete records on Mjolnir as an organization, who worked for them and where. But we know where they recruited from."

"Yeah, disaffected and militarized white dudes. Problem is, now they all work for Suite."

"Funny."

"I'm serious, John. More generally, they're all empowered. They aren't hiding anymore. Rout would likely be with groups far more careful. More under the radar."

"They've already gone public. Announced themselves. Ten years ago, they were in stealth mode even after many attacks."

"There's something political with that. On the operations front, I still think they'd choose more carefully."

"Army? Those he served with or commanded? Family?"

"What else do we have? They obviously preserved their stock of S-47—it's been out of circulation since that time. No one will touch it, so we can't use that as a trace like before."

"But it doesn't matter, does it? Now, it's over. Right when those devils return, another devil is going to throw us on the street. Timing's so perfect that I might need to order me a tinfoil hat."

She grimaced, the corner of her mouth twitching. Savas continued, his expression hard, sending a chill through her.

"We've been so focused on our Iranian mastermind, Mirnateghi, we forgot about the other monsters out there. We knew Rout escaped. We should have done better. We failed."

"Let's keep some perspective here," she countered. "I'm not going to say Rout or whoever running some resurrected Mjolnir isn't a problem. They just blew up another mosque after a decade of silence, but that doesn't mean they're the threat they were before."

"Rebecca, don't. You—"

"Listen! They don't have Gunn's resources anymore. They don't have his money. They lost the logistical connections of his shipping networks. Their global reach has to be impacted. They can only be a shell of what they were."

"We can't take that chance."

"Mirnateghi, however," she continued, soldiering forward, "we know what she's capable of. We know she still has major resources in Iran. With Bilderberg, she pulled the strings across the world, then loosed the strings on her own. She nearly destroyed it. We can't lose sight of that great of a threat. And we know there's a connection between her and this presidency. Whatever the GOP-controlled Special Counsel has to say, the evidence is there."

"For however long they last. But it doesn't look good. Suite's going to burn the DoJ to the ground."

Stay on target.

"Rout escaped our best efforts, and a larger monster took our attention. Rightfully so. Don't blame yourself. You need to let go of this. Don't let it eat you up like before."

He refused to look at her. "Tell that to those who lost loved ones or friends in Harlem yesterday. Ask them if our failure to catch and end these terrorists isn't a failure. Let's see if they think we did just fine."

The speakers over their seats crackled.

"This is the cockpit. We've been cleared to land in Dulles. Make sure you're tucked in and comfy."

Cohen stared back out the window, the storm still raging.

She shuddered again.

Official vehicles met them on the tarmac and whisked them to DC and the White House. Within the government-provided SUVs, they kept conversation minimal, unsure of who might be listening and how. Once at 1600, aides escorted them through the executive departments toward the Oval Office and the smirking face of the president's National Security Advisor.

"Agents Savas and Cohen," said George Darton, the mustachioed former U.N. Ambassador. "He's been waiting for this day for a long time."

Savas half expected the old war hawk to twirl his gray facial hair like some cartoon villain. Cohen stood on his right, her posture austere, the tension in the room a thick fog. The veneer of professionalism poorly disguised the murderous undercurrents around them.

He smiled, extending his hand. "Mr. Darton, a pleasure to meet you. That almost sounded like a compliment."

The older man's smile wavered a half second, and he turned to Cohen. "I'm surprised to see you, Agent Cohen. I thought that the president was explicit. He required a private meeting with your boss, the head of Intel 1."

"Did he?" She feigned confusion and cocked her head toward him. "Obviously there were some errors in communication, but perhaps for the best. John and I work as a team. Whatever is going to happen to Intel 1, we are always there together for it."

Darton smirked. "What is going to happen to Intel 1? Do you believe you are here concerning such an important topic?"

Savas fought off a scowl, weary of the man's slithering. The bastard held all the power and he knew it, teasing the very real possibility of ending Intel 1.

"We did assume a request to speak at the White House signified something significant. Unless it's going to be a golf invitation, in which case, Rebecca really should have come alone, as she at least routinely makes par."

The smile vanished.

Eat static, asshole.

Darton turned to a door leading to the Oval Office. "He'll see you now."

Inside, Daniel Suite beamed at them, jovial like the clown in *It* sheathed in a business suite. His unnerving smile swam in a sea of spray-on tan. His smirking eyes were two pink holes in an orange face. Thinned hair was dyed a deep black, like the widows in Greek churches who refused to surrender their youth.

Don't be fooled, John. He's a clown suit filled with adders.

Savas took note of the attendees. Secret service guards, the White House staff, and a tall man in a form-fitting blue suit. Savas sensed Cohen stiffen as she stared at the same man.

They stopped before the large Resolute desk. Nobody moved. Suite continued to grin like a child about to open his Christmas presents. Savas willed himself to stillness, masking his face from any expression.

I'm not going to give you one penny.

"Well, don't just stand there," waved Suite, his smile mutating to a frown. He motioned to the chairs in front of the desk. "I don't have all day."

They sat. The rest of the men in the room stood silent as sentries, glaring down at them. Ten years ago, Savas would have been intimidated, but he'd seen too much since then. Lived through fire and murder, civil war and the death of close friends. These presidential lackeys meant nothing to him.

Except for the Iranian-American.

He glanced at the thin man on the right who stood at attention behind Suite, an expensive watch framed by his tailored clothes. Rectangular eyeglasses matched the hard lines of his face. He was thin, his posture erect, a goatee giving his youthful face a sinister slant.

"And this will be our new ambassador to Iran," bragged Suite, his humor returning. "Reza Kazemi, these are the great agents from that secret division I was telling you about. The best people. Super job they've been doing."

Reza Kazemi. The billionaire hedge fund manager. Savas clenched his jaw. The proof was thin, but a lot of circumstantial evidence placed him in Mirnateghi's orbit of influence. That the young investor had landed beside Suite in the Oval Office on the day they visited solidified those links in his mind. *The new Ambassador to Iran.* The bastard was not only going to fire them. He was gloating that he'd turned over Intel 1 to Mirnateghi. Conspiracy in plain sight.

"They said it couldn't be done. Tanks and airplanes shot up. Ships seized. Almost a war after those unfortunate rebel attacks on Saudi Arabia. They said no way anyone can fix Iran and America. Broken relationship." That beaming grin again. "But I'm a deal maker. Only I could do it. Now we're partners again. So much oil. So much security. We needed an ambassador. Reza's the best. Wall Street. He made billions. And an immigrant! They say I don't like immigrants. So much fake news. But I have the best immigrants. Like Reza."

"Pleased to meet you, Mr. Kazemi," said Cohen.

Savas glowered. "So much interest in Iran."

The new ambassador's eyes flashed, telegraphing the reality. "And between these two great nations," he said. "I look forward to helping change that relationship. Hopefully, that process will not be held up by people or organizations trapped in the past. In old ways of doing things. They won't survive the new reality."

Not only was there a reanimated Mjolnir in America, but now POTUS was conspiring with one of the deadliest criminals in the world. A vile conspiracy wrapped up in the guise of a great diplomatic breakthrough.

Our worst fears materializing.

Suite laughed. "That's so true. So true. Big things happening in Iran. So much happening. This president has made more things happen, I'd say, than any other president. I've heard people saying that. I think it's true. That's why we won so big. The biggest victory ever." He reached to the side of his desk and removed a framed illustration of the United States. "Have you looked at the Electoral College map? They said I couldn't do it twice."

An aide whispered into his ear.

"Right," he said, putting the photo down on the desk. "So, today, this business with mosque bombings and stuff. Horrible. Very sad."

Savas stared at the smiling man. *Smiling.* America's leader radiated everything except concern over the incident.

"Thor's Hammer?" He gazed at the aid who confirmed. "Good name. Strong name. Those people know how to promote, let me tell you. But terrible. Yes. And we need you, Intel 1, to put everything aside. Stop everything else. Work on this case only."

Cohen inhaled, leaning forward. "Excuse me, sir?"

"With this other terrorist stuff happening out west, we've got big problems. We've got to delegate. I'm a businessman. I know how to delegate. You were part of the FBI team that stopped them the first time?"

"Yes, sir."

"Didn't finish the job too well, did you?" He beamed, his blue eyes sharp. "But you didn't completely fail. It's been a while, right? I'll give you a B-minus. But now, so many dead. Just terrible. A shame really." He paused for emphasis. "Sad. Our dear Muslim brothers and sisters".

The hypocrisy took all Savas's willpower to ignore. This man threatened to shutter mosques on national security grounds, calling them terrorist breeding sites. His actions generated a flood of First Amendment court filings. He recounted historical accounts of westerners killing Muslims. He was a shambling Mjolnir recruitment ad.

What the hell is going on?

"Intel 1, you and this lovely lady here." Suite leered at her. "You're the right people for the job. The best. And I always hire the best."

The Commander in Chief had landed a hard right. Savas was dazed and flat-footed. He resisted the urge to glance at Cohen.

Cohen spoke, her voice clear and cold. "And what of our other work, especially with El Marcado?"

That's not what she's really asking. Cohen wanted to know their general leeway to pursue the Iranian angle and continuing their hunt for Mirnateghi, but Suite made things crystal clear.

"It all stops," he barked. "Everything. That's for other agencies now. Intel 1 is one hundred percent on Thor's Hammer. I don't want to hear of one of your agents touching anything else." His eyes were lasers.

And so it was laid bare. Cohen had avoided centering on the biggest case in their docket with Mirnateghi. That would tip their hand too obviously. Instead she'd brought up a situation that the president and his people should have begged them to solve. El Marcado had reached the level of folk hero. Robin Hood for oppressed communities. A constant in the news cycle. Those terrorists were interfering with the administration's deportation program, repeatedly embarrassing them. But the president was forbidding them to touch it. Solving the Iranian problem, the *real one*, was clearly off the table as well.

"The Mjolnir case has been cold for some time," said Savas, "but we've—"

"I have complete faith in you," said Suite. "But to help in this most important case, we will be making some structural changes to your agency."

"You mean beyond those already made?" said Cohen.

His eyes darted to her, the flash of anger poorly concealed. "Yes. Sadly, some more people will need to be let go or reassigned. But we have great agents coming to replace them. The best. You'll get so much help you'll be sick of winning by the time they're done." The president stood, his right hand indicating the door. "Some of them are waiting outside and will start today. They'll make my agenda clear. I want this case solved soon. I know that you don't want any more deaths on your hands with these terrorists."

Adders in a clown suit. The man knew his way around emotional poison. Rage and guilt burned through Savas. He fought it, balled his right fist, and ground his teeth.

"Of course not, Mr. President. We'll get these bastards." He glared at the new ambassador. "All of them."

15

GONE DIGGING

I *still can't believe he went for this.*

Gone stared out the window of the taxi as it sped northward in Manhattan. They'd left her office in Queens and cabbed over the 59th Street Bridge, the driver cutting to the middle of the island and taking Park Avenue toward the more posh residences.

She'd told Sacker that she had a plan, which was only partially true —confront the former CEO of ADS with the very government malfeasance that likely drove him out of the company. By his reaction they could assess the veracity of the documents and her theory of why he left. But she was hoping for much more. *An ally.* Could the man who had refused to play along with the corruption also be tempted to join efforts to get to the bottom of it all? With his access to the raw information, the details of the business he had abandoned, it could blow the lid off the case.

Well, we're going to find out today.

Sacker grunted as the bouncing taxi slung his head against the ceiling. He winced and rubbed his scalp.

"Small has its perks," she smiled, unscathed by the bumps. "I need to get you tall ones a helmet for the city."

"I had a hat before you promoted me to PhD," he said frowning.

After pulling out the fake glasses, he slipped them on and looked down his nose at her. "And is that any way to speak to your mentor?"

His eyes sparkled, the half smile from one side of his mouth inviting.

Always the charmer.

"Passable. But you'll be more convincing in the moment. You're a pressure player."

He sighed. "I hope so. This plan's on the edge."

Canyons of concrete lined their way north through New York's grid. The cabbie blared his horn as cars bottlenecked around a parked UPS truck.

She grasped his hand and squeezed. His body tensed alongside her and then relaxed.

"Stop fretting," she said. "It's a solid game plan. Everyone has their mortal sin. It's useful to be able to identify them. Stephen Burleson, bowtie-sporting ex-CEO of a very profitable mining company. Loves to give lectures on digging. Gave a TED talk on energy diversity. Pundit on Canid News about how great the industry is to America. Limelight moth." She stared out the window. "His sin is pride. We're academics seeking out his expert opinion for a thesis. This will work."

"You should be the professor, not me."

"It doesn't work that way, Tyrell. We need as few red flags as possible to make this fly. We overcome a huge activation energy barrier if we have the gender power structure right. Man on top. Woman on bottom."

He shifted in the seat but remained silent. *He's not going to touch that one.* She tried to make herself feel a little guilty for her choice of words, but it didn't work.

"Second," she said, "is the expected age differential. Caucasians underestimate my age with high frequency."

"And overestimate my threat level," he grumbled.

She glanced over his tall form. There were minorities and then there were *minorities. Stupid Oppression Olympics.* All of them suffered real toxicity in the culture, but the truth was that dealing with the slights and discrimination varied group to group. She couldn't imagine the stress, the very real risk to life and limb that Sacker had dealt with regularly, systematic obstacles that made his every achievement all the more impressive. Threats that could have killed him outright at any time.

"Your false title covers that a little." She patted him on the shoulder, suppressing the urge to wrap her arms around him. "We'll have to make do."

"I can't believe he hasn't done any checking up on us."

"I doubt *he* has. I'm sure some of his people have. So I concocted some fictitious personas."

He raised his eyebrows.

Gone distressed her shirt, wrinkling it. She disheveled her hair. She donned her bulky smart glasses. Glancing in the rearview mirror, she decided it was an excellent picture of an overworked grad student.

"Hacked web pages at the University of Rochester will likely not be noticed for a few days," she said. "We look real with our university presence, fake LinkedIn accounts, and CVs."

His eyes widened.

"I planted some minor malware that will erase it all in a few hours. No one will be able to finger us. I even used generic photos. Asian babe and black dude with glasses. We all look the same to them, anyway."

The corner of his mouth twitched. "I'm not sure if you're a crazy genius or just genius crazy."

"We're about to find out."

The driver pulled up to an East Side brownstone in the mid-80s near Central Park. Gone ignored her usual taxi app and paid in cash. Sacker hastened around the cab and swung her door wide, helping her navigate the exit. She clung to the window frame to stabilize herself and stepped out into the late morning sun.

Humidity synergized with the heat, the atmosphere hazed and suffocating. They were about to approach the gate when a short man shuffled toward them.

"Spare some change, pal?"

Gone flinched instinctively, unsure of the man's intentions. She scanned his person. Late sixties, Caucasian, worn and stained clothing utterly inappropriate for the heat of the day. His body odor assaulted her nose. His leathered skin, tanned from years in the sun, was wrecked with wrinkles, his beard caked with filth. But his sunken eyes pled. Defeated. Not a threat. Another broken citizen in the richest nation on earth.

"Hey, friend," said Sacker, positioning himself between the beggar and Gone. "You lost? Hitting this neighborhood's gonna put you in lockup real fast."

The man's slumped shoulders twitched. "Desperate, man. They took everything, now. They took my food stamps. Stamps are gone. I'm hungry."

"Who took your food stamps? You get robbed?"

"No, man. The gov'ment. That damn Suite guy. Took all ours. All the money's for that wall."

"Shelters are still open."

"Money's drying up there, too. I always ate better with the stamps. Come on, man. I'm a vet." He held up a set of dog tags.

Sacker stared at the dingy metal. "Franklin, huh?" he said, handing them back.

"They called me Li'l Frankie after the Vinh Moc Tunnels. I'm small. Could fit in places only the Viet Cong could go. Killed a lot of gooks." His eyes flashed toward Gone. "No offense, ma'am. It was bad times."

Sacker flashed a ten-dollar bill. The old beggar took it without hesitation.

"Get out of this area," said Sacker. "You've been around. Don't push it."

The man stared at Sacker, his eyes slits. "You serve?"

Sacker nodded, putting his hand on the man's shoulder and pushing him gently forward. "Yeah. Now get the hell out of here before you run into one of those Patriot Corps. Don't come back."

The man stuffed the money into his jacket pocket, shuffling away and down the street, mumbling to himself.

A tingling rushed through her. Sacker watched the beggar leave, but Gone only had eyes for the former detective, his form surrounded by the concrete monoliths. A very human essence in the midst of so much inhumanity. She'd seen it the first day he walked into her office, some strange combination of rough and tender. A soldier. A detective. But with decency.

She touched his hand. "You have a good heart, Tyrell."

"Caused me all kind of trouble." He glanced back to the brownstone and straightened, patting the slight bulge under his jacket.

Gone arched her eyebrows toward his chest. "Professors rarely come packing for interviews. I hope they don't have a detector or pat you down."

"I'm not a professor. And I'm not taking any chances." He frowned. "Let's get in character."

The pair stood before a black metal fence surrounding the property. A sphere-shaped camera was perched over a set of buttons. Gone gestured toward it. He drew a deep breath.

"Showtime, Tyrell," she said.

He pressed the larger button and waited. A woman's voice came over the speaker. "Professor Marshall?"

Sacker shifted into a polished Ivy League dialect. "Hello. We're here to see Mr. Burleson. Eleven o'clock appointment."

"Yes, he's expecting you."

There was a buzz, and the lock clicked on the metal gate embedded in the fence. He pushed on the bars and the doors swung inward. Before them rose a steep and long set of stone steps.

Gone gazed at the slope with grim determination. She planted her feet and grasped the cane like a warrior. Sacker glanced at a recent addition to Gone's wardrobe: a brace kept her foot aligned forward, reducing the tendency for it to drag. She concealed it as best she could with flowing pants. But he'd seen. It was getting harder to maintain a semblance of normalcy. "May I have your arm, Dear Professor?"

He was already offering. She grabbed hold, and together, they ascended.

"You know why the stairs are so high on these classic brownstones?" she asked, her breath increasingly ragged.

"I hadn't thought of it. Just a New York City staple. Like Yankees game traffic and dog shit."

Sweat trickled down her back. "Related to the last. Pre-dates motorized vehicles. The city used to have horse gridlock."

He laughed. "I see. Different kind of pollution. And the well heeled wanted to get to higher ground."

She didn't speak further, the effort leaving her breathless. She worried she might need to be carried toward the end, but her determination brought her to the top.

A door to the house opened. A stern woman with cropped gray hair waited with a tablet in hand. Her eyes danced from Gone to Sacker, her brow furrowed.

"Good morning, ah, Dr. Sacker," she said. "I am Mr. Burleson's personal assistant." She didn't offer a name. "He is waiting for you in his home office. Please follow me."

She clicked down the hallway in short but high-end heels that matched her pink pantsuit. The front door led to a hall lined with closed doors. An unwelcoming lobby for such a fancy home.

A business location as well.

She brought them to a stop in front of a wooden door. A keypad was embedded in the wall beside it. "He rarely entertains guests," she noted. "As stipulated, you have an hour of his time. At most. Please use it wisely."

She didn't smile to lighten the words. Pressing a button, she announced their presence. The door clicked and swung open a few inches. She motioned for them to enter.

Continuing the roleplay, Sacker took the lead and pressed the heavy portal inward.

16

EINHERJAR

The Oval Office door closed behind them. The VIPs and higher-level staff had vanished. A nameless aide waited in the drab hallway, the beige walls and black and white photographs offset with color only from the pair of American flags on short stands. The aide's expression was as naive as her dress-to-impress attire. She led them without a word to exit the West Wing, not pausing at the reception desk. Cohen frowned.

Don't let the door hit you on the way out.

A hot breeze stirred the shrubbery as she and Savas waited at the entry portico. The double wooden doors clicked behind them. There was no car waiting by the curb. She fumed.

Intentional disrespect. They didn't call for it in advance.

They stood unaccompanied except for a lone Marine sentry posted by the entrance and a groundskeeper tending the landscape. A gaggle of school children of various ages sang as they marched to the White House. She smiled, but something was off with their words. She reappraised. Chanting, not singing.

Cohen's smile faded as their black uniforms came into focus. The elementary students shuffled cluelessly in their dark trousers, but the middle school kids adopted a more self-aware and aggressive march.

Instructors lined the sides of the group like drill sergeants, keeping them in line and encouraging a military cadence.

Patriot Academies. They were springing up like weeds in every city. A cohort of funding groups with deep pockets and rich donors were supplying the resources for the president's new educational mission. Her stomach tightened when she saw the tower symbol on their patches, the stitched "DS" of Daniel Suite on each side. Most of the children were white. Browner hues were sparsely peppered within a sea of beige, a decidedly unreal demographic slice for DC.

She shivered in the hot sun. This wasn't America. It couldn't be. It was a scene out of some 1930s documentary where half her ancestors had disappeared in ovens. Her usually analytic mind failed her. She could only speak trivialities to Savas. "Must be so hot in those in the summer."

Savas stared without a word, his jaw clenched tightly. She could imagine his back teeth grinding.

The school troop passed to their left, heading to the doorway they had just passed through. An older boy hurled insults at the groundskeeper.

"Go back to where you came from!"

More kids joined in. Cohen winced, seeing the hesitant slurs from the mouths of black and Asian kids. She couldn't imagine the mad calculus of assimilation churning within their minds. The dark-hued man paused from his work but did not acknowledge the slur. He turned back to his tools, ignoring the growing shouts spreading through the group. The instructors did nothing to stop it.

"Hey! That's enough!"

Savas stepped toward the kids. His eyes blazed, the children and even the instructors loath to hold his stare. The grumbling subsided as he glared up and down the line approaching the entrance. Breaking the tension, the doors opened and several White House representatives escorted the Patriot Academy students into the building for their tour.

"Well, that was interesting," sighed Savas. He stared across the circular drive and White House grounds toward Pennsylvania Avenue.

"Interesting like that bass music they play in a horror film right before things go terribly wrong." She peered up at him. His silence and continued gaze unnerved her. She snapped her fingers several times. "Earth to Agent Savas."

He blinked and turned. She continued.

"Suite sure is pushing every one of your buttons. And what happened in there today wasn't a coincidence."

His face hardened. "I don't understand exactly what happened in there, but I agree. Something was off. Wrong. *Bizarre.* Maybe it's some kind of political cover for all their Islamophobic policies. But whatever they're up to, the truth is that Mjolnir is real." He pointed out over the city in front of them. "They're out there. I can't tie myself in knots about how Suite and his gang are going to use this, use us, for political gain."

"What if it's more than that?" she asked, hoping he could let go of his obsession with Mjolnir "What the hell was Kazemi doing there?"

It didn't take Einstein to puzzle that one out. Between Kazemi's connections to Mirnateghi and Suite trotting him out as they forbade any work on cases beyond the Mjolnir bombings, the signal was clear. He had to know that. But he waved it off.

"We can't chase everything right now." He exhaled. "Look. I thought we were done. That Intel 1 was *done.* Especially because of Mjolnir returning. No way Suite and Brennem would let us take this on. But if this administration's supporting our hunt for these bastards, I'm taking it."

She shook her head, grasping his arm. "But that's just it! They're giving us tons of time. Too much time. We're to drop everything else, including our hunt for Mirnateghi! We dealt her a blow in Tehran, but she's regrouping. Our assets confirm it. It's only a matter of time before she makes another move. The last one nearly released a doomsday plague on the planet!"

"We can't do it all."

"And there was Kazemi, today. Do you think this is a coincidence? They're boxing you in, ordering you to go after what they know you have to, all the while closing the door on Iran and Mirnateghi. It's so obvious, it's genius!"

He stared at the ground. "You're probably right," he said, his lips forming a thin line. "But what else can we do? We disobey, and they'll shut us down for sure. Then we can't do any good. No hunting terrorists in New York or out West, or taking out the ghost of the damn Bilderberg group living through Mirnateghi. They gave us an out, a way to continue, even if it's to ensure we don't pursue Iran. How can we turn away from something so monstrous as Mjolnir?"

She put her hands on her hips, exhaling. "We need to slow down and think. They're running their chaos offense on us. They've perfected spinning the press and the rest of the country. We need to parse what just happened, look at the chess board and see what they're trying to do. There's something nefarious here, John. I smell it."

He stared at her, blinking. "Okay. We'll think it through. We've got the flight back and the weekend. Let's—"

The double doors behind them burst open, and the Marine guard jolted. National Security Advisor Darton hustled out with a pair of comely aids behind him. One of the women held a tablet computer to her chest.

Darton approached Savas as they turned. A black SUV pulled into the circle drive, slowing as it neared the portico.

"I hope you took the president's words seriously," he said, ignoring Cohen.

"Deeply," said Savas.

"Then you'd better get back to work. Mary?"

The young woman with the tablet approached. She and Darton flanked Savas as she pressed a button on the side. An image lit the glass surface. Cohen forced her way between them and Savas so that she could see.

"Images just came out online," said Darton, his tone bemused. "Those dead guys are members of the Islamic Center of Washington."

She stared at the screen in horror. Bodies lay scattered around a red-tiled walkway. Stairs behind them led through a set of decorated arches. Green Arabic script swirled across the stone overhead.

"Guess they don't plan on bombing everything," said Darton.

Cohen turned to Savas, her face pale. "This just happened?"

The car came to a stop. The sounds of doors opening and footsteps jogging toward them pulled her attention. She saw several men in dark suits approaching.

"Yes. And as part of your new directive, you're on the case." He gestured to the approaching men. "DC FBI agents were called here on my command. They'll bring you to the scene of the crime."

Cohen glowered. Her eyes were bright, her face tight.

Chaos offense.

She shook her head to clear it, resisting paranoia. Mjolnir wasn't Suite, no matter how much their hearts aligned on Islam. But all the same, this was fuel on the fire for Savas, feeding his obsession. All objectivity would be lost.

Darton motioned with his hand to the cars.

"And I wouldn't delay anymore, Agent Savas," he smirked. "Maybe you can finish the job this time."

17

FUERZAS ESPECIALES

Shouts filled the detainee camp as the rumble of the explosion faded. Lightfoote had just briefed Houston on the insanity she had hacked from the site's data center. Microchipping of detainees. Transports of tens of thousands from the Mexican border to Nevada. Then the madness spread as an assault hit the camp and Lopez had dashed into the tent. She spat the dust from her mouth and rose from the chair.

"ICE?" said Houston, leaping up as well, her eyes squinting.

Lopez loaded a new magazine. "Not ICE." Sweat dripped from his face. "Too professional. I got two repelling down the fencing. Barely. They're good. Special forces."

Lightfoote shook her head. "What now? Domestic deployments?"

"A new era," he said. "We have minutes before they've locked this place down. We can't beat them." He wiped his face with his sleeve. "I've given the order to our teams. Scatter and ground, contact through secure channels when safe."

Another explosion rocked the compound.

Lightfoote frowned. The sound zeroed in her mind to the gate, a combination of experience and the odd sixth sense she'd developed years ago that unnerved those around her.

"Front gate." She yanked a thumb drive from the dead computer and shoved it in the pocket of her flak jacket. "We need an exit. *Now.*"

Automatic weapons erupted, shattering the air around them. Houston grabbed a backpack and slung it over her shoulders.

"The side tower," she said. "Saw it earlier scouting the fence. Very fortified. Opens to Red Rock. They won't expect retreat there. Should buy us some time."

Lopez scowled. "You have a plan for that?"

Houston tapped her backpack. "C4. Enough to tear a hole in the fence."

Lightfoote strapped a shotgun to her back and picked up an automatic rifle. She smirked at Houston. "Remember Tehran? Demolition Woman will take down the entire camp."

"Let's move!" shouted Lopez, turning to the doorway.

They raced outside. Chaos churned. Civilian detainees scrambled in all directions. Gunfire cut many of them down. Dust from blasts and tramping feet turned the clear day into a dry soup of sand. Screams and weapon fire blended in cacophony.

"Follow me!" screamed Houston, sprinting forward.

Lightfoote fell in step behind her, the pounding feet of Lopez a racing rhino to her rear. A burst of bullets tore through the air. A round whizzed past, pinching her hair, making her ears ring.

The trio dropped to the ground.

"Left!" roared Lopez. "Two shooters!"

Houston crouched behind a jutting boulder, her gun barrel stabbing forward. She tipped her hat back to clear her view. At least she had a stable position. The former CIA agent was their best gun.

Wild West shootout.

The ground erupted around her. The stink of gunpowder filled her throat. She dragged the weapon into position. The targets were moving, one limping from a wound. She sighted the unhurt soldier, tracked his motion, and fired.

Her shots synched with a second burst of gunfire from her partners. The man below staggered, tripped, and fell forward.

"Move!" she cried.

They jumped to their feet. Again, they sprinted. She glimpsed the tower approaching over the cloud of dust. Cheap scaffolding with a bare platform, the tower's fencing might as well have been duct-taped to the supports. In the haze, she couldn't see what lay behind.

Hope you're right about this, CIA girl. Or this is going to be a very short trip.

Houston waved her arms. "Flank the approaches. Getting shot's not on my todo list." Her bag hit the dirt with a thud. A sharp zippering followed. "Phones, please."

They tossed her their burner cells. She taped them to the C4 bricks.

"Planting charges!"

The ground sloped up toward the fence. Smoke billowed and visibility was poor, but at least they'd have a height advantage.

Lightfoote sighted with the scope on her rifle. Gunfire flashed in the vapors below. A helicopter's blades sounded in the distance. "Suite's not playing around."

"Guess we're getting to them," said Houston, slapping gray bricks to the metal feet of the tower. "Glad the detonators are here."

"It won't be long," growled Lopez. "*Hurry.*"

"Hurrying me?" Her voice rose in pitch. "You remember my last demolition? I need some real training."

A figure broke through the smoke below some fifty yards away. Desert camo, automatic weapon, helmet, glasses, and face covering.

"Jesus," Lightfoote huffed. It was full clandestine assault gear. *Black ops.* Not only was Special Forces replacing the domestic troops of ICE, but these were full-on clandestine commandos. America had turned its world-beating military back on itself.

The soldier scanned in their direction.

"Hold fire!" she hissed. "Unless he spots us. We don't need to give our position away."

She relaxed her trigger hand, slowing her breathing. The man headed down the slope and disappeared from her scope.

"Move away!"

Houston charged from the structure, her right hand securing her hat.

The three slid down the slope, taking refuge behind an overhang of red stones. Small compared to the looming structures outside the fence, but enough for shelter.

"Charges set," she panted. "Ready?"

Lopez grunted, Lightfoote giving a thumbs up.

"When that blows, we make like cheetahs. If that *is* Red Rock Canyon on the other side, it's wide open space. A football field until we hit any cover."

"Let's hope they have their hands full down there," said Lopez.

Another explosion rocked the compound below. A fireball climbed toward the sky.

"Perfect cover!" yelled Lightfoote. "Now!"

Houston raised a controller and pressed a button.

The ground shook, and debris slammed around them. Sand rained. The three sprang forward, coughing in the smog, and dashed toward the mangled steel. A gaping hole greeted them in the tall fencing.

Lightfoote braced her back beside the smoking metal, waving the pair through. She spat grit from her mouth, her eyes watering, surveying the compound a last time. Satisfied, she turned toward the breach, scurrying down the rocky slope outside.

18

GONE DOWN

The door to the office of mining mogul Stephen Burleson swung open. It revealed a space as muscular as the man himself.

Photographs of safari kills decorated the wall. A bloodied elephant. A leopard and lion. A massive horned Cape buffalo. A heavy rifle was racked on the wall. Sacker fought the urge to whistle.

Rich enough, I guess you get to hunt endangered animals.

The furniture was broad, leather, and studded with brass. Straight ahead, a thick oak desk glared back at him. A window behind it opened to an internal garden, offset to the right by an expansive couch and spacious armchairs around a coffee table. On the left, a fireplace sprawled across a wood-paneled wall underneath the gun.

Burleson rose from behind the desk. His black shirt rippled with the musculature of an action movie hero. He sported an ample beard, thick like his frame, black like his shirt. It was punctuated with sharp lines of gray.

He strode over and grasped Sacker's hand in a vice. His bulk loomed beneath the more elegant and taller frame of the former detective.

"Professor Marshall," he boomed in a deep tone. He turned to Gone. "And this is your student, Miss Wu?"

"Good to meet you, Mr. Burleson," said Sacker. "Yes, Ms. Wu is a fourth-year graduate student in our department. I am her primary mentor."

Burleson frowned. "Fourth year? You won't catch me on my deathbed crying that I didn't get more education," he scoffed. "But I'm a libertarian. To each his, or her, own. Have a seat, let's get this done. I have a very full schedule today. That includes an interview on Canid News about the new rare earth mines opening up in California."

They followed his lead to the coffee table. The broad man took a lounge chair for himself. The professor and student sat on the giant couch.

"Rare earths are in the news a lot," Gone opened. She assumed a high-pitched, nasal voice Sacker startled to hear. "But they're not all that rare. So much hyperbole about them and the electronic market."

It was Asperger's stereotypes broadcasting at a hundred decibels. Sacker fought the urge to stare at her.

Always a surprise, Gracie.

The former CEO angled toward her. "Indeed, my young lady. Indeed, yes." He nodded toward Sacker, his shoulders joining in. "Your student knows her material, professor."

Sacker smiled. "She's my best. And she's the one who wanted to talk specifically with *you.*"

The flattery struck its target. Burleson smiled and turned to Gone. "Well, then, what can I do for you, *Ms. Wu?*"

"Let me just say it's such an *honor* to meet you, Mr. Burleson," she lilted, eyelashes fluttering. "Gosh, you're even more impressive in person." Her gaze ran over his ample body.

Oh, good God. I never knew you, Gracie.

"Yes, thank you," he purred.

"I've been following your work on fracking. That's my thesis topic. *Reassessing Materialism: The Dialectic Discourse of Fossil Fuel Extraction in Modern American Media.*"

"You don't say," he hummed, eyes glazing over.

"You're a luminary, defending fracking and, generally, all mineral extraction," she said. "Your TED talk has over eleven million views alone!"

Her praise perked him up. "Yes, I know."

She frowned, her shoulders slumping. The energy drained from her body. "I couldn't believe what happened at ADS."

Burleson blinked. Sacker saw the wheels downshift in his mind. The ex-CEO sat straight in the chair. "Well, um, yes. But really, there's nothing to say on that..."

"For a man of your accomplishment, it seemed so *sudden*. Disrespectful, sir, if you were to ask my opinion."

The muscles in his jaw spasmed.

Gone reached into her burlap satchel and removed several papers. "In my research, I came across some startling findings."

She held out several sheets to him. Sacker tensed.

Here it comes.

"These contracts, they're in the billions," she whispered. "And look. These appropriations are not legal. They're taking money for many programs and routing them to the construction and mining companies you headed." She swallowed. "Before you were let go."

Burleson glared at her. "Where the hell did you get these?"

"Financial crimes," she said, her sharp eyes belying her naive tones. "Is *that* why you left? You're a good man, Mr. Burleson. I know you couldn't be involved with this. Did they try to make you go along?"

He stood, hands shaking in rage. "I don't know what you think you're up to. How you got this confidential information. *Top secret* information. But we're done today. You're out of my office." He stormed to the door and yanked it open. "Harriet!"

Sacker exchanged glances with Gone as they stood. A hurried trot of heels echoed and the flushed face of his assistant appeared in the doorway. "Yes, Mr. Burleson? Is something wrong?"

"Escort these two out. Immediately. I don't want to hear from them again."

Sacker turned to the ex-CEO. "Mr. Burleson, if we could just—"

"I have nothing more to say," he snarled. "Get. Out."

Gone tugged on Sacker's jacket sleeve. Bracing herself on the edges of the couch, she limped with her cane toward the exit. He held her arm and helped steer her forward.

The door slammed shut behind them.

Gone stood still a moment, panting and catching her breath. She smoothed her blouse and ran her fingers through her disheveled hair, wrapping it into a bun.

"So," she exhaled. "That went well."

"Another boot to the ass," said Sacker. "This is getting a little repetitive."

They paused at the top of the steps, the doors to the brownstone shut and locked behind them.

Gone stared down to the street and sighed. "Down is not my favorite."

He placed his hand on her arm and gave her his warmest smile. "One step at a time. I'm right here."

She glanced up at him and closed her eyes. "Ok, *professor*. Down we go."

His smile faltered. A flash of light glinted from glass on the roof across the road. His eyes telescoped and focused, spotting a crouched shadow. A dark extension protruded from the form. His mind folded to Iraq.

"Grace!"

He shoved her. Air split, ripped apart by hurled metal.

Her chest ruptured in a burst of red.

"Oh…God," she gasped, collapsing.

Sounds ceased. Manhattan vanished. Fallujah shimmered around him.

Sniper.

There was no thought. His gun was in hand, the weapon zeroed on the crouched shadow. A thousand survival instincts activated.

The shooter moved on the rooftop. Sacker locked on the flash of the scope, subconsciously calculated angles, distances, compensations.

He fired. The handgun was a terrible instrument for this battle, but all he had. He fired and sighted, again and again. The shadow buckled, but did not fall. Still he fired. Fifty yards from the steps to the roof. Control recoil. Shave lock time.

Hold under. Hold over. Hold off. Hold on!

The target vanished from the roof's edge. Sacker's magazine was empty. His ears buzzed with adrenaline. The dust-choked wreckage of war-wrecked Fallujah dissolved. Screams and car horns faded into his awareness.

"Gracie."

Her body lay at the bottom of the stairway, wedged against the black steel fence. Blood splattered the lower steps around her.

His lanky frame leapt down, his work shoes slapping on each landing. A crowd had gathered. Bystanders yelled, whispered, and gawked. Some held up phones toward the crumpled woman. He glared at them.

"Call 911! Call now!"

His voice, but it raged from somewhere distant. All he knew was Grace. Her face was pale, flesh lacerated from the fall.

But most of the blood came from her chest.

"Gracie, *please*. Come on, girl. Don't do this. *Don't do this!*"

She didn't respond.

PART II

THE DEVOURERS

When Fascism came into power, most people were unprepared, both theoretically and practically. They were unable to believe that men could exhibit such propensities for evil, such lust for power, such disregard for the rights of the weak, or such yearning for submission. Only a few had been aware of the rumbling of the volcano preceding the outbreak.

— ERICH FROMM, *ESCAPE FROM FREEDOM*

19

LIFE SUPPORT

"I'm going with you, dammit!"

The EMT placed a firm hand on Sacker's chest. "Sir, I have requested that you stand back. Let us get to the hospital. Time is critical."

He'd lost his mind, but he was also losing Gracie. *God help me.* A part of him fought to stay sane, but a rattling earthquake inside him drowned everything out.

Inside the ambulance, a paramedic darted around Gone. He cut her clothes open. He hooked her up to a red bag. Her blood soaked his gloves.

The EMT's eyes flashed behind Sacker. Red and blue flashing lights told the story.

Great. Arrested by my old boss.

"What going on here?"

A woman's voice from behind him. Familiar. *It can't be...*

Sacker turned to see two uniformed officers on each side of a plainclothes detective. Detective Kathy Hill. He couldn't dwell on the randomness of encountering his former pupil. At that moment, he didn't even care about the ugly end of his tenure at NYPD and the support Hill had given him, one of the few in the division to do so. Right now, all that mattered was Grace.

The EMT barked past him. "We have a gunshot wound. Critical. This man insists on accompanying us. It's against protocol."

A cry came from the inside of the truck. "Now, Higgins! We move!"

The EMT turned with a final glare to the police. Sacker's shoulders slumped. A modicum of his sanity returned. He let them go, facing Hill. "Hey, Kathy. How you doing?" Nothing was real.

"Jesus Christ, Tyrell? What's going on?"

The sirens blared, and the emergency vehicle roared down the side street. The world spun. He put a hand on Hill's shoulder, trying to anchor his reeling mind in something tangible and supportive.

She steadied him. "You okay?"

"Not sure. Depends on what happens next."

She stared at the disappearing ambulance lights. "Let's sit down."

"Not here!" he shouted. His eyes avoided the sight of Gone's blood pooled and coagulating over the brownstone steps.

"Yeah, sure." Her glance darted to the other cops. "Get this roped off. He's an eyewitness. I'll take his statement."

She walked him away from the crime scene, stopping beside a parked van.

"That was Gone?"

An odd stupor ebbed over him. He floundered, trapped, gasping on the rocks with the low tide. Next plunged back into bracing arctic seas.

"Yeah. Professional hit. Sniper shot. I tried to get her out of the way." He shuddered. "Too slow."

"Okay. I'm going to need you to come down to NYPD and give a full statement. We have an attempted murder in broad daylight in the streets of New York. And the target is going to make the presses."

"Wait, a statement?" The fog receded a moment. "No! I can't. I have to find out where they took her." He grabbed her by the shoulders. "I've got to get to the hospital!"

"You're in no shape to be going off on your own." Hill squared up to him, her lips in a thin line. She held his gaze. "I'm assigned to this shooting. It's my call how we do this." She placed a hand on his shoulder. "We'll go together. To the hospital. She's the victim and also a possible witness. I'll get your statement there and deal with Ladner later."

"Let's hurry then," he said, dropping his hands and scanning the street. He stopped and glanced back at her. "Thanks, Kathy. I can't thank you enough."

He didn't remember much about the drive to the hospital. Somehow, he'd gotten into Hill's town car. He'd sensed her presence beside him, driving. The buildings had flashed past, horns blaring. He'd been dissociated from his body, his awareness floating nearby, flashes to the horror of the attack buffeting him like seismic waves.

Years seemed to pass by the time they arrived. Hill led him from the car and looked him in the face.

"Tyrell. You're nearly in shock."

Her voice tugged his awareness back to his body. He was at the hospital. Gone was inside.

I have to focus.

"I'm okay, Kathy." He swallowed, trying to see through the mental fog. "Let's get in there, find out what's happening."

"Let me handle this."

The words were curt, but she was right. Her clout with NYPD was sure to get answers. He was certain to get security on his ass.

With a final glance to ensure compliance, Hill spun around. Bypassing a line of people who glared at her, she marched up to the reception desk.

"NYPD." Hill showed her ID. "I need some information on a patient who just came in. She's the victim of, and potential witness to, an attempted murder."

The receptionist behind the counter frowned at her. "NYPD, huh?" The woman's eyes darted behind them. "Oh, look, the vultures."

Reporters streamed in, cameras flashing, lights on. Staff intervened, pushing them out of the ER.

"So, she's a name," the lady chirped.

"Female. Asian. Short. Gunshot wound to the chest."

The woman checked the screen. "Yep. Just brought in. Straight to surgery."

"What's her status?"

"Critical. Not much more information. They've got a trauma team and the ER docs on her, so it's serious."

Sacker tried to appear nonchalant. He rested against a marble pillar within earshot. His hands trembled.

Another man behind the counter approached and whispered into the receptionist's ear. She glanced from the screen to Hill. "If you would like to learn more, please follow Mr. Hansen here. He'll take you to an office where you can talk."

With a final glare at Sacker, Hill followed the man through a door and disappeared.

Sacker paced. He walked outside and jogged back in. No Hill. He hiked around the large lobby space, dodging the reporters at the hospital entrance. Still no Hill. He watched forlorn patients rolled in wheelchairs. Sick children on crutches. Another gunshot victim fired in on a stretcher, howling, the room in stunned silence until the thrashing patient was out of sight.

No Hill.

The scene at the bottom of the brownstone steps assailed him. The wound was near Gone's vitals. Exactly where, only the trauma team knew. Depending, she was either in for a rough time, or…. He wasn't going to think about "or." Right now was the most crucial time. Her fate would be decided in the next few hours.

His limit came and went. He told himself to stop, but his legs rebelled. He marched toward the receptionist.

How long until they toss me out of here?

The door opened, and Hill stepped out. Spotting him and frowning, she sped in his direction. "Calm down, Tyrell."

"She's okay?"

Hill shook her head. "It's serious. But you need to calm down. Let's sit over here."

She led him to a bench along one of the far walls. The area was deserted.

"I spoke to a doctor in the trauma center," she said. "This is not going to be easy to hear, but the reality is that she might not make it."

His stomach dropped. The muscles in his legs spasmed.

I'm dissolving.

"Only one bullet," she said. "And it missed all her vital organs. By inches. But there's significant blood loss and shock. It's a matter of finding the leaks, plugging them, getting blood into her."

"Before she dies."

He had to square up to the truth, like he had done many times before when lives were lost around him. In the deserts during war, it was handle the trauma or die. Back in the comfort of peace, separated from the action with nothing to do, he felt even more helpless and vulnerable. But the truth still needed to be reckoned with, even if this loss would be far more devastating than any he'd known.

"Before she dies." She held his hand.

Tough love.

"Thanks, Kathy. I owe you."

"I already owed you." She shook her head. "I'm forever grateful for what you taught me. Before NYPD screwed you. A lot of us owe you a hell of a lot more than we can give."

He couldn't process her words. His mind drowned in visions of the operating room, the sound of the sniper's gunshot. Gone dropping to the ground.

Hill coughed. "All right. I'm going to see if we can find a better place to hole up here. I *do* need to ask you some questions, pretend to do that job you taught me how to do. But not here. I'll call this in, get Lander's rant, ignore him, and get us some privacy."

Come back, Tyrell. Thank her. Something!

He tried to smile. He couldn't. He stared toward the entrance of the trauma center.

Hang in there, Gracie.

GONE A GONER?
Daylight Hit on PI Makes President's Case for More Security

by Dan Williams, *NY Daily News*

In a shocking turn of events, Grace Gone, dubbed the Chinese Sherlock Holmes for her unraveling of the Eunuch Maker murders, was shot in Manhattan today. Eyewitnesses told the *Daily News* that they came across the young Asian detective sprawled in a pool of her own blood in a wealthy Upper East Side enclave. Brought by ambulance to the New York Presbyterian Medical Center, she remains in stable but critical condition after what some hospital staff called an hours-long emergency trauma surgery.

Gone burst from obscurity to stardom four years ago when she almost single-handedly discovered the identity of one of the City's most notorious serial killers. While the killer erected pornographic displays of his castrated victims in highly public locations, law enforcement came across as impotent to stop him.

Enter the perky Peking PI, her whiz-bang brain, and her photogenic smile. Since the killer was caught, Gone has been a media favorite, appearing on talk shows and featured in numerous magazines, solving many cases and putting bad guys behind bars.

It looks as though someone might have held a grudge. Details are still emerging, but sources claim that the killer used a high-powered rifle to shoot the young detective in broad daylight.

Hospital staff have refused to comment on the record, but they indicate that Gone is in serious condition with life-threatening injuries.

Little is known about Gone's personal life. She has been seen in the company of disgraced homicide detective Tyrell Sacker. Gone partnered with Sacker on the Eunuch Maker case before he mysteriously left the NYPD. Reports place Sacker at the scene of the crime and in the lobby of the hospital when Gone was brought in, but it is unclear whether he played any role in the shooting.

A spokesman for Homeland Security released a sharply worded statement. "It's this sort of lawlessness that only makes it clear how necessary President Suites's criminal quarantine plan is," said Howard Dorson, referring to a highly controversial document leaked from the White House. The plan as described proposed dividing highly populated urban areas into "safety districts" based on crime statistics and other measures. As written, it would station national guard forces and erect fencing and gate systems around high-crime zones. Suite subsequently called it a "border wall for crime." But not all reacted positively.

"This insane plan would be a true ghettoization of America," said Gail Nelson of the ACLU. "There is no hiding from the fact that it would isolate populations based on race and ethnicity. It's a terrifying proposition."

Rather than refute the leaks, the White House doubled down on their content. Dorson justified the idea of districting.

"Here we are, in broad daylight, and an upstanding citizen like Ms. Gone is gunned down. The law-abiding members of our nation are living in fear for their lives. Crime is up. Those living in high-crime districts are not our best people. They're criminals. They're druggies and dealers. They're murderers and rapists. Some are good people, I'm sure, but the real America has to be protected from the rest of these vermin. And that's the president's job. One that he takes quite seriously."

20

DIVISION

Cohen fumed beside Savas on the ride to the Islamic Center of Washington. Their driver had followed Savas's instructions; the black SUV made like a bat out of hell. They plunged through the crowded streets of DC like some wailing banshee with sirens flashing. Nausea churned in her gut, but it cowered before the raging storm inside.

Suite was manipulating Savas. To what end, she shuddered to think. But Mirnateghi was involved, that much she would stake her life on. The administration was so deep in *quid quo pro* that Suite might as well be a foreign asset. And Savas *knew*. How could he not? He'd said as much. But with Mjolnir back, it was a perfect storm. One that welled up around him like a tempest.

So I might as well come out swinging.

"We should've told Darton *no*," she stated.

"What?" Savas's eyebrows jumped.

"Let the DC FBI and police handle this. We can get the briefings, handle it from New York. We don't personally need to rush off like junior agents into another jurisdiction."

"Rebecca, this—"

"You're not *that* hands-on. They're shooting you full of adrenaline and angst to keep you high on this. Addict you. Push you to go all in. This is crack for you."

"We *are* all in!" he shouted, turning away at his outburst. He exhaled. "We have *orders* from the president. We *work* for him, remember? And this is a case worthy of our full attention."

"Normally, under other conditions, I might go with that. But this is *not* normal! You know what's going on! Don't let the past swallow everything we've worked for!"

Savas shook his head. "There's no choice."

"There's always a choice!"

"Do you really think these guys are going to play dumb or nice? If we're not one hundred percent engaged, focused on these attacks, if I'm out there hunting for our Iranian princess or whatever, if they don't see that we've committed, they'll pull the plug on Intel 1. Certainly on us, anyway. We just went over this!"

The vehicle navigated police barricades as they approached the site of the attack. Onlookers gathered. Flocks of smartphones rose in the air, snapping pictures. News trucks crowded together. Reporters stormed the pavement like troops hitting Normandy.

"I'm more worried about you than the cases," Cohen said. She fought for eye contact. He dodged and scanned through the tinted windows.

"Okay," he muttered, hesitant. "You're right. I can't let go of Mjolnir. But the other work is too important." He sighed, finally turning toward her. "Since I can't let this damn thing go, it has to be you."

"Me?" *What's he saying?*

"You've practically run Intel 1 several times. Suite keeps jerking me around and up to the DC sessions. You've been the steadying force at home for the last few years. And you made some great calls during the Eunuch Maker crisis." He put a hand to his chin. "I'm going to lead a team to investigate these attacks. Find Mjolnir. Stop them. You're going to head back to New York and continue our work there. You have full control, full discretion on how and what."

Cohen swallowed. The weight and opportunity pressed down on

her. The familiar foundations of very dangerous work were shifting under her feet. "That's a big step."

He smiled. "Maybe a good one. At the very least you can start cleaning house, round up the Suite lackeys they keep assigning us. They're clearly spies. You're much better at identifying and handling them than anyone. If we don't get Intel 1 back under our complete control, the hunt for Mirnateghi will be sabotaged from inside."

He's right. Damn!

He needed her with him on this case. But Intel 1 was under siege. *And...* She flushed, ashamed of her thoughts. Part of her also saw the promotion as a career opportunity. One she had always desired but suppressed.

"I think it's a mistake," she said. "I think you should let this go and come back with me. But if you're determined, and I see you are, I'll go. Intel 1 is in trouble. If it goes down, no one is left who can go after Mirnateghi."

The truck stopped. Only the growing churn outside broke the silence within.

"Plan made," said Savas. He turned and pulled the handle. "You're with me for one more crime scene. Then get your pretty little self on a shuttle back to the Big Apple."

She grabbed his arm and yanked him toward her, planting a hard kiss on his lips.

"Be careful, John," she said when she'd pulled back.

"I don't underestimate them," he said, stepping out of the SUV.

Cohen sat still a moment, watching him walk toward a group of police. Several competing emotions roiled through her. Excitement to head the search at Intel 1. Terror at the same prospect. Anger at the manipulative corruption in the Suite administration.

And lastly, fear for Savas.

He took the killers of Mjolnir seriously, the ruthlessness of those fanatics not forgotten. Both she and Savas had watched their friends die at the hands of monsters. No, she wasn't worried he'd underestimate them.

It was the psychological assault she feared. His son's death. An FBI division's massacre. The death of Muslim CIA agent Hussam Jordan. Mjolnir mixed 9/11 and a near nuclear war on the Arab countries with her husband's internal struggles.

Nitroglycerin. Just one shake…

She grimaced and slid out of the truck.

21

MESSAGE

Local police enforced an eerie calm over the remains of chaos. Radio chatter spilled across the courtyard as vans disgorged helmeted officers in black body armor. Savas turned from the huddle of senior police officers. Cohen approached from behind.

"Captain Lemont," said Savas, "this is Rebecca Cohen. She's my right hand in everything we do. But she'll be heading back to New York this evening to run things from our home office."

Right, Rebecca?

"Glad to meet you, Captain," she said, tipping her head, her eyes flashing to Savas.

He exhaled. Events were accelerating. He'd just made a huge decision on the future of Intel 1. If he was wrong, it could be the end of their covert division.

Could be the end, even if I'm right.

He knew the survival odds under Suite were low. But he trusted Cohen. There was no one better to steer the ship.

"Agent Cohen," returned Lemont, shaking her hand. He indicated a thin and bespectacled man in a suit beside the police captain. "This is Tim Cox, Assistant Director in Charge from the local branch."

"Heard about your work on the Anonymous Signal," said Cohen.

"Likewise," replied Cox, grasping her hand. "As well as what happened with William Gunn. Mayhem seems to follow you two."

"Perhaps it's the other way around," smiled Cohen.

"Of course." Cox tipped his head to Cohen. "Poor phrasing on my part. Seems like we can't cut the heads off this dragon."

Savas scowled. "Show us what you have."

The police captain led them to the site. Yellow police tape fluttered in the hot breeze, the smell of copper thick in the air. Bodies sprawled without pattern, the doomed efforts of victims to flee heartrending. Forensic teams dispersed, documenting the crime scene.

"The building is a mosque and cultural center," said Lemont. "But most of the deaths were inside the mosque."

They weaved around the bodies. Old and young. Even the very young. Savas made a fist, staring at the crumpled form of a small child. Mjolnir reveled in indiscriminate slaughter.

His stomach turned. The intricate geometrical decorations of the mosque clashed with the grotesque, crimson-soaked corpses. A helicopter roared around the site, forcing them to shout to each other.

"No explosives?" yelled Cohen.

"No!" cried the captain. "Multiple attackers. We don't know how many. Military level precision. Automatic weapons. Surgical. No one stood a chance."

Savas bent his head beside the captain's ear. "Casualty count?"

"Fifty! At least. Double that number wounded."

"Anyone apprehended?" The aircraft pulled away and his voice boomed in the returning quiet.

"Not peacefully," said Cox with a frown. "But we got one. Wounded seriously, currently getting patched up with tax-payer dollars. He killed two of our agents."

Savas spun in his direction. "Still alive? Prognosis?"

"Far too early to tell. This is still in real time."

He dipped his head to the FBI man. "I'm sorry about your people. I know what it's like to lose good agents to these bastards."

He felt for the man, but his heart rate surged. Taking a soldier of Mjolnir alive was a breakthrough he had not expected.

"I assume he has three special forces teams assigned to him for protection?"

Cox's eyebrows angled downward. "Security is heavy. We're not going to lose this guy. Assuming the docs can pull him through."

"Mjolnir doesn't play by any rules. If he's in a hospital, the entire building's in danger. They won't let him talk."

"Ahead of you. We played this like my old days in the Secret Service, scrambled dummy teams like this killer was POTUS. We'll move him to a safe house as soon as he's medically fit to travel."

Captain Lemont indicated the entrance to the mosque. "Agent Savas, there's something you should see inside."

The body count increased as they approached, forcing them to the edges of a short set of steps. They rose to the arched entrance of the mosque. Giant Arabic letters flowed in blue script over the stone above as they ducked into the interior.

Dear God in heaven.

Bodies tiled the prayer hall. An enormous carpet was buried beneath them, pools of crimson leaking from the sides. Ornate columns plunged from the ceiling, resembling swords hurled by God to earth.

The shapes of men dominated the middle of the prayer hall. In a back corner of the room, set off by a seven-foot wooden barrier, the female victims massed. Despite the shock, Savas couldn't stop his mind from analyzing the setting. His words spilled out as he gazed around the room.

"A complete surprise. So many killed before they realized what happened."

"Seems so," said Cox. "Only a few had time to start running, and the bodies begin to scatter."

He glanced at Cohen. She'd seen as bad before. Her focus was sharp, and she held her gaze toward a central pillar in the room. She was a professional. But he would never lose an older-style upbringing that made him protective of her.

"Who's that?" she asked, tipping her head forward toward the body in question.

Cox breathed out his nose. "That's what Captain Lemont wanted you two to see. Especially you, Agent Savas."

They navigated the massacre at their feet as best they could. The forensics teams glared at them but let their superiors through. A dead man rested at the base of the pillar. Blood stained his white robe and long beard.

"Sons of bitches," Savas whispered.

A note was taped to his chest, the edges soaked red. The scrawl of a black marker weaved across the paper, reading "*Remember Thanos.*"

Cox coughed. "So, the name of your son, if I recall?"

Jaw clenched, Savas glared at the ghoulish script. *The bastards dared.* They dared to plaster his name over this scene of horror. As if other extremists hadn't desecrated his son enough on 9/11. As if the slaughtered worshippers in this mosque had as much value to them as cheap poster board.

He removed nitrile gloves from the bag of a busy forensic technician. He stepped back to the murdered Imam as he popped the gloves over his hands. Reaching down, he grasped a glinting chain of metal dangling from the note.

Savas raised it and opened his palm. Inside was a pendant linked to a chain. Drops of blood smeared the polished metal. The pendant took the shape of an anchor with the harsh face of a bird carved in its side.

Cox shook his head, turning around and stepping back through the bodies.

"What is that?" asked Lemont, his brow creased.

Savas stared at the golden artifact in his hand without turning.

"Thor's Hammer."

22

ON THE RUN

The Nevada sun had set, its blinding rays blasting across the landscape of colored stone in Red Rock Canyon National Conservation Area. The air temperature dropped immediately, the little humidity in the air allowing sweat to cool any fools still outside in the wasteland. Artificial lights burned a day's hike away, centered on a smoking detainment camp.

Lopez welcomed the evening with a growl. His hands ached, fingers dug into the red clay. He dangled over a ledge on the latest climb. The two women were already up, their smaller masses an advantage in this terrain.

Heavyweight is a bad division for free climbing.

The pair grasped his shoulders and helped hoist him over.

"Five minutes," he gasped, opening a canteen and emptying it. "And we're in trouble with water."

"Bugging out leads to shit planning," puffed Houston, dropping beside him. She plopped her wide hat on the ground. "Rather we had some fucking whiskey, anyway."

"I'm sure you would."

He smiled at his lover. She glowed from the exertion even in the dim light. Sweat covered her and dripped from her matted hair.

Salty skin and salty tongue.

Wild scenes of them together exploded through his mind. Fires and bombs. A tortured lunatic branding his forehead with the barrel of a smoking gun. Decoding another madman's equations of doom. Accelerating a vehicle out of an airplane and blasting their way to freedom. Too many trips through hell.

Is there some kind of redemption in it?

But this time was different. Especially for her. They'd continued to cross lines after Suite announced his deportation plan. The risks, the deaths, turning against a country she had worked her life to defend. All from his burning passion to protect the immigrants now treated as vermin.

She'd signed on without hesitation because she wanted to stop a monster, end the injustice, but also because she loved him. Because this mission, this seditious quest, consumed him like nothing ever had.

He glanced at Lightfoote.

And what about you, wild FBI girl?

He met her during the near collapse of the nation. A time when the digital world had disintegrated under the cyberattack of a crazed genius. The hacker-agent from Intel 1 had joined them in the chaos. She'd cast her lots with the pair of ciphers. Fought with them. Risked her life with them. The trio had ended a global conspiracy together.

But this wasn't her fight. *Or was it?* He shifted his gaze back and forth between her and Houston.

Maybe it became so.

Lightfoote scanned the star-filled sky. The distant pin lights and thwack of a helicopter drifted through the air. "They know we got out," she said, her voice in a trance. "But they've lost our trail."

"For now," he grunted, wiping the orange chalk from his hands.

The trio resembled painted acrobats in a circus show. Multi-colored clay stained every inch of their clothes.

He coughed up colored phlegm. "At least we're getting our iron supplements."

"Aztec Sandstone," noted Lightfoote, sitting cross-legged beside them. She spread her hands over the landscape like some meditating goddess. Her tone turned mystical. "Therapod tracks. Petroglyphs. Mineral strata. *Geologic* time." She grinned like a kid. "Nice park."

"Not how I'd hoped to visit."

"It was a special forces strike team at the camp," said Houston. She dumped sand from her boots and picked at the blisters on her feet. "They have to hold it. They don't have the numbers for a wide search. Not yet, anyway."

He scowled. "They're definitely going to bring in search teams soon. We'd better keep moving. No sleep tonight. Stay out of sight. Then it's a game of square miles and luck."

"And time," she said, placing a hand on his arm. "Without a lucky water strike, we've got a day before we drop."

He reached over and grasped her palm in his broad fingers. "But that town's close. Right?"

"Mount Charleston," she exhaled. "Half a day, I think, if I remember the map right."

"But it's a climb?"

"About fifteen miles and seven thousand feet. The elevation will cost us the most time." She reached back down to her battered feet. "But it will mean a cooler climate. Still, we have to get through this painted desert first." She grimaced as blood spat from a lanced boil. "It's a vacation area. Tiny town. They'll have communications we can monitor and a place for a rendezvous."

"You're the eagle scout, Francisco," said Lightefoote. "You're in charge of navigation to the mountain."

"Easier if we had the GPS," he laughed. "But Semtex Sara had to blow the phones up."

"No damn choice." Houston replaced her boot with a moan. "They'd have triangulated our position with the cellular signal. We can check Twitter later. I'm sure Suite will still have nothing but good to say about you."

Love you baby.

"All right," he smiled. "But what's the plan when we get there? Who are we calling in? Our core team just got fried. Those who got out have all gone to ground. We've got to give an 'all's clear.' If we don't make it, there's no one who can lead them. Our plans are frozen until we're safe and back in contact."

"I think we'll need to change our plans," said Lightfoote, palming a thumb drive.

"Every mission Angel's got to get herself a radioactive storage stick." He stared at the device. "We haven't had a debrief. What the hell's got you two so spooked? What's on that?"

She coughed, drinking from her own canteen. "I haven't had a chance to look it over. I copied a massive pile of personnel files. Data on all the camps. It's much bigger than we imagined. Certainly far larger than the public numbers. They really are making a go on rounding up ten million people."

He shrugged. "We suspected. What else?"

Houston grimaced. "They're chipping all the detainees. Men, women, kids. Every one of them has an ID code, GPS coordinates."

His eyes widened. Flashes of the woman in the camp fell like puzzle pieces into place. "Now I see."

She turned to him. "Francisco?"

"An old woman in the last camp. She said something about injections and scans. She was surprised I hadn't been injected. She meant the chipping. Lord God have mercy."

"It's worse," whispered Lightfoote, her eyes to the stars. "Much worse."

He sat up, his broad arms over his knees. "How?"

"It's not just the numbers, ten times what we've known about. It's the gathering."

"Gathering?"

"Shipping manifests. Trucks. Buses. Repurposed train lines. They aren't taking them to the border."

He angled his head down, his eyes fixed on her face. In the dark, her green irises were black with glints of starlight. "Where are they taking them?"

She gestured around them. "Here. Somewhere. These camps sprouting like shrooms around Vegas are feeder camps."

His muscles tightened. The air cooled after the sun dropped. The land's stillness was otherworldly. "Feeding what?"

She waved the stick in the air. "I hope the answer's on here. I'm afraid we might not have much time."

He held his hand out toward the device. She held his gaze and handed it over. It floated like a canoe in the lake of his large palm.

"You know how this sounds," he said, staring at the flash drive.

"We know how it sounds."

He made a fist around the stick and stood, looking away from the distant lights of Vegas. He examined the stars, pinpointing due north, examining the shadows of the terrain.

"Then we'd better get to Mount Charleston. Soon. But Uncle Sam has a hell of a price on our heads. I still don't know who has the resources to get us out of there safely."

"Intel 1 does," said Lightfoote, her eyes flickering a dim green.

Lopez laughed. "Something tells me that they might have an issue or two with what we're doing. They might come pick us up, all right. It's the destination after I'm worried about."

Houston concurred. "No way that's a good route."

"Rebecca would help us. And John's fighting his demon right now." Lightfoote's eyes teared up. "I'm afraid it's going to win."

And our Cassandra returns.

He never knew what to think of Lightfoote's strange declarations and intuitions. Except that one ignored them at great peril.

He stood, pebbles rattling from his soiled clothes. "Chickens before hatching. We still need to get somewhere to make a call. Any kind of call."

The sounds of the helicopter were a little louder. Lopez glanced over his shoulder at the blinking lights in the sky over the silent desert.

"And I'm not sure we're going to make it."

"ACCURACY IN MEDIA ACT" NOW LAW

Washington Post and Jeff Bezos indicted

by Odette Johnson and Herman Hempelmann, *New York Times*

Amid protests from the Left and the Right, President Suite signed the recently passed AMA bill, transforming American historical approaches to the Fourth Estate. The law severely curtails what is permitted for the press to publish about political leaders, limiting the use of anonymous sourcing and broadening the definition and prosecutorial authority to go after libel.

In signing the bill into law, Suite met another of his campaign promises to "expand laws on libel" and sue the press from his position as president:

"When I won, right at the top of things to do was expand and broaden our laws on libel. When these leftist liars print lies, negative and terrible, Americans need to be able to sue them for lots and lots of money. That's only fair. So, we're planning to take a hard look at libel laws with the Congress. So when the *Amazon Washington Post* writes some kind of hit piece on me or someone in Congress, all of it totally disgracing, the victims can seek justice to their damaged reputations from these degenerates. Make them pay right out the nose. Right now, these awful people are totally protected. We'll change that."

The law was immediately challenged as unconstitutional and is expected to go to the Supreme Court. However, with a six to three majority filled with several highly conservative justices appointed by President Suite, and with Clarance Thomas on record as favoring much stronger libel laws, many legal scholars believe that the new law will be upheld.

The legislation also creates the new Department of Media Accuracy. Today, Suite appointed Kluckor Snarlson, former media pundit on Candid News, to head this organization.

"Mr. Snarlson has been taking on the Fake News Media since they waged their dishonest and criminal campaign to slander me and my administration. No one is better to judge media content than he is."

While details of the new department's structure are vague, it is expected to be imbued with the power to examine, review, block, and refer any content deemed "malicious libel" to the DoJ for prosecution. The resulting judgments issued by the DMA could range from fines and loss of broadcasting licenses to trial. One provision of the new law specifically focuses on penalties for any defamatory content against the president, members of Congress, and the Judiciary.

"This is the next step toward tyranny," said former advisor to Elain York and Navy intelligence officer Jason Rite. "The press is the only private institution granted specific rights in the constitution. That was for a reason. Its job, its duty to society, is to challenge authority, to make the lives of those in power that much harder. They are the watchdog of our democracy and we're shooting that dog in the leg today."

The first enforcement of the AMA was carried out before the ink was dry from Suite's pen when the new Department of Media Accuracy issued an injunction against the *Washington Post* and indicted its owner, Jeff Bezos, the billionaire founder of Amazon.com Inc. Although court challenges reopened the presses that same day, the incidents sent a chill through the American press.

Speaking for the Post's competing newspaper, Arthur Sulzberger Jr., publisher of this paper, released a statement following the DMA actions:

"When the President of the United States labels the free press 'the enemy of the people' for doing its constitutionally protected duty of holding those in power to account, the government has discarded democratic principles for those embraced by tyrants," Mr. Sulzberger said. "A free press is a notion previous presidents have strongly defended on a non-partisan level, even in the face of staunch criticism from the Fourth Estate."

The publisher added, "I have often warned President Suite that his inciteful rhetoric is encouraging the rising spate of intimidation and violence against journalists, both domestically and across the world."

President Suite has faced recurrent criticism for his attacks on the press. His first year in office, he praised the violent assault of a reporter by Wisconsin Rep. Joe Colombo. He has called several major media outlets like this paper the "enemy of the people" in language similar to that of dictators such as Stalin, Mao, and Nazi propagandists. And he worked with conservative members of Congress, many who are expressed "Constitutional Conservatives" to draft the AMA legislation.

Suite has expressed a desire to regulate free expression and First Amendment rights beyond the press and to the internet, noting in a recent USA Today interview:

"Americans lose so many because of the web and the internet. We have to respond. We have to go see Mark Zuckerberg, somebody, and a lot of other computer people who can tell us what's going on. I have to sit down and talk to these people. Because I know how to fix things. So, we might have to look at shutting down the internet in some places, some ways. The internet is where the terrorists meet. It's killing us, folks. Common sense to control it. Radical leftists will protest all day, 'freedom of speech, freedom of speech.' These are crazy people. Really bad people who put us in danger. We have a lot of crazy people. We have a lot of very, very crazy people."

Anonymous sources, now outlawed by the AMA, have claimed in several papers that the DMA authority will extend not only to the press, but also to Internet Service Providers. Time Warner and other ISPs have been given instructions for future content filtering, according to these sources, with the claim that they will be monitored for compliance.

Public responses to Suite's attacks on the press have been divided sharply along partisan lines. A recent poll from the Pew Research Center asked whether Americans would support "allowing courts to silence news outlets for printing or televising content that is biased or factually inaccurate." A plurality of Republicans respondents— 43 percent — were in favor of allowing news groups to be shut down, whereas only 18 percent disagreed with the idea. The remaining Republican respondents were undecided. This is in contrast to Democrats and independents, who largely oppose such actions (with a margin of 25-points with Democrats).

However the law is enforced and interpreted, whether or not it survives a constitutional check at the Supreme Court, Daniel Suite and his administration are celebrating the victory. The president ended his signing ceremony with another broadside at the Fourth Estate.

"The Fake News Media is more dirty and more wrong than ever before. Incorrect articles, wrong on purpose, what we used to call lies, and phony fake anonymous sources fuel their program. This is honestly disgusting, how the press can write anything they want and not care about the truth. That ends today."

23

STABLE

S acker motioned to his team. They sprinted across the glass-strewn road, dust swirling around them. The sounds of automatic fire reverberated through the shattered urban landscape.

They rounded the rubble of a flattened house. Bombing runs the night before had reduced this neighborhood of Fallujah to wreckage. In the back were the remains of a garden. Olive trees smoldered. A children's playset survived unharmed, colorful poles and slide tarnished with soot. A long series of steps led from the flattened home to a demolished courtyard below.

Shots came from a gutted, but standing, structure across the block. Two of his team fell, one toppling forward into the pit. He sighted the sniper from a series of controlled shots exploding on a high balcony.

A figure darted to the side. Sacker pulled the trigger. The shape stumbled, cried out, and fell off the balcony to the rubble below.

"Secure that!" he yelled. "Medic!"

He scampered down the stairs, the moans of a soldier mixing with the gunfire and the sound of his boots. The body lay on its side in a lake of blood. A hole the size of his fist opened in the back.

Sacker moved toward the front, kneeling down toward the soldier's face.

Black hair. Brown eyes. A woman?

"Grace?"

"Tyrell. Wake up."

Light stabbed his eyes. He shielded them with his hand, turning away from the window in the musty hospital office. He sat up, resting his back against the couch.

Hill's voice rang like a PA system in his ears. "They're going to need this room soon. We were lucky to get it last night."

"Grace. What happened?" His voice rasped an octave lower than normal.

"I didn't think you'd last through the second surgery. Looks like you tried."

The smell of coffee swirled through the room. Sacker opened his eyes. Hill sat across from him in an office chair.

"Good news is they found the last bleeder. They had to open her up again, but she's stabilized."

Sacker leaned over his knees.

Thank God.

"She's still critical. I'll let you talk to the doctor for details. God knows I'm no med student."

"When can I see him?"

"Her. Dr. Lena Patterson. That's the one they kept sending to me. Besides the medical, I had some things to talk to her about."

"You got her the extra security?"

"I pulled some strings. Pissed Ladner off because, well, it's you two. You're not a popular man at NYPD. But she's not the first, let's call it, *special case* where imminent threat was involved. They have measures. She's isolated, and I've posted two guards."

"Glad they didn't give you problems."

"Sniper rounds. This wasn't an ordinary hit. This is something really big and bad."

"Yeah. I know."

"What the hell are you two poking around in?"

"I'd tell you, but, as you see, it might get you killed."

She glowered. "I'm serious!"

"So am I!"

He rubbed his eyes and stood, fixating on her coffee. She rolled her eyes and shrugged. He took it as a yes and downed half the scalding liquid. The pain helped him wake.

"Look Kathy," he said, "if telling you would help, I'd tell you. I owe you that. But right now, I don't see how it does anything except put your ass on the line. I don't want to see another friend bleeding out anytime soon."

"So Gone is your friend." She tilted her head, gazing at him.

"We're friendly. A close, professional relationship," he stuttered. "Look, she hired me recently. We get along."

"Yeah. Right." She held his gaze, but Sacker looked away. "Go home, Tyrell. Get some real sleep. You look like shit."

"Thanks."

"I mean it. You've done beyond the call of duty for your *boss*. There's nothing more you can do right now. She's in the ICU. No one will be seeing her for at least a few days. Go home. Sleep. Hell, take a shower. You smell like a compost pile."

Sacker glanced down at his rumpled clothes. He should get sleep. Get his shit together. Someone put a professional hit on Gone. It nearly killed her. Walking around like a fetid zombie wasn't going to get to the bottom of it. Or help protect her.

But Kathy doesn't understand.

He was terrified to leave her alone. His heart raced, and cold rivers ran through his limbs at the thought of walking away.

"Yeah. For sure. Gonna crash for a few hours and come back this afternoon."

He tried to smile. He failed again.

Ten minutes later, he stood outside the hospital. Hill was gone. A line of yellow cabs glared against the asphalt in the bright sun. One by one, they pulled into the circular drive in front of the hospital. Doors opened. Patients or family climbed in. Doors shut. Patients or family drove off. He watched in a stupor, detached from the process.

He reached into his pocket and pulled out a box of smokes. He was also detached when he bought them last night. Only a distant onlooker watching a lanky black man drop fifteen bucks at a corner kiosk.

He stared at the pack. A high-pitched voice sang in his mind.

"As long as I'm around, I'm going to see that you treat yourself in a way that reflects that worth."

His shoulders shook. He threw the box to the ground and wept.

24

GROTTO

Houston squeezed her right calf muscle as it threatened to spasm from dehydration. Her swollen tongue stuck to the roof of her mouth, the skin rough and tasting of dust. Grit coated her eyes, gluing the lids, but rubbing them would just throw more dirt into the mix.

This desert harasses everything in it.

The sharp rocks of Bridge Mountain obscured the sunrise. Shadows darkened around Houston in the strengthening light. She kept to the brush beside Rocky Gap Road with the other two. The path hugged the rougher terrain next to the mountain, hidden from traffic.

Their pace was brisk, danger always behind them at an unknown distance. Several times they were forced to conceal themselves in the sparse brush along the rocky walls when a search helicopter flew overhead. The crafts were reminders that they were hunted prey.

They'd followed water flowing from the higher elevations, Lopez guiding their course. Trails converged on the jagged valleys carved into the stone.

Lightfoote pointed toward one ahead of them. Her fair skin

glowed a bright pink in the sweltering light, pulsing and alive to Houston's eyes. Muscles striated along her arm. "That what you meant?"

Lopez nodded, sweat coating his face and dripping from his beard even in the early morning cool. The black hairs were stained yellow from the grit of the Mojave.

"If there's water around here," he panted, "it'll be in there. All the hiking paths lead inside. Perfect geologically, but it's the middle of summer, so it may be all dried up." He swallowed, grimacing in pain, his throat raw. "Even if we find water, we're going to need those high-tech canteens with the filters."

She exhaled, her shoulders slumped. "We can't afford to be slowed by any infection. Might as well shoot ourselves."

"Wait!" whispered Lightfoote. "There!"

They followed her finger to the base of the mountain. Gray-brown shapes shuffled around a small oasis of vegetation. The horse-like creatures brayed, necks craned toward the encroaching bipeds, then the herd dispersed.

"Wild burros," she chirped, beaming.

Houston shook her head. "A herd of donkeys?"

Lopez laughed. "They don't look happy to be disturbed. That's a water hole they gathered around. For sure."

The three picked up their pace. As they neared the site, the animals had distanced themselves. Trail paths ran from several directions to a small pond. A thin trickle of water fell from between cracks in the rocky walls surrounding the site.

"A waterfall," said Lopez.

"Pretty sad one," murmured Houston, coming to a stop in front of the water.

He knelt to the water and inhaled through his nose. "Not bad for a desert. Don't like the smell. It's fresh water coming in over the rocks, but this pool's got issues. Get the water into the canteens and get out of here. This is a tourist magnet."

The three emptied the contents of their packs. Each had two large green canteens in carrying cases. They lined them up on the rock by the water.

Houston turned to the former priest, removing her hat and wiping her brow. "What's the protocol?"

"Fill them all. Try to minimize particulates. Stay on the surface. Keep the mouthpiece clean. Get some spores or bacteria there, and the filter's useless. Don't worry if you taste some iodine. Part of the filter composition."

They moved to the water. He demonstrated by dipping his canteen into the water, halfway submerging it lengthwise.

"These hold about fifty ounces. They're heavy. But at our pace out here, we're going to need close to two canteens a day."

Lightfoote bent to the water, filling her first canteen. "Meaning we need to find a water source once a day." Her hair blew back in a warm breeze, the piercings on the side of her face revealed and glinting.

"About right. We might can get away with less for a short period, but we need to be careful. Dehydrated, we'll tire faster, be prone to cramps and dizziness. Don't want to cramp up if we need to run. Or faint and fall off a cliff."

"How many more water sources you think are in these mountains?" asked Houston.

"I don't know." He scanned the area. "But we're heading into higher altitudes. Water flows downward. And these areas do have caves and other grottos like this one, I'm sure."

Lightfoote finished and strapped the canteens to her belt. Lopez squinted toward the mountains.

"If we stick to the trails like we planned," he said, "we'll find more. These trails are old. Hikers likely settled on routes with water."

"Let's hope so," said Houston. "Special forces crashing our party shot to hell any planning."

He stood, sealing his second canteen, moving it to his left hand. With his right, he made the sign of the cross over the water. "Lord, grant us seasonable weather and an abundance of the fruits of the earth. Especially water."

"Amen, *Padre*," chanted Lightfoote turning from the grotto.

He grunted and put his arm out for Houston. She grasped it and pulled herself up, dropping the hat back on. She gazed toward the brightening sky.

Going to be another hot one.

The three moved out of the grotto and back to the desert. The herd of wild donkeys had vanished. Lopez pointed to a valley between the mountain beside them and one across the roadway.

"We make for that passage, careful to avoid being seen. I don't think they've got enough people to set wide sentry points, but that's an obvious location. Right now, I'd rather not climb anything until we have to."

"Seconded," added Houston. She again pressed into her calf to halt spasms. The packs gained weight every minute. Exhaustion was setting in.

Lightfoote stared toward the sheer walls forming the passage. "Petroglyphs," she hummed.

Houston frowned. "Sorry?"

"Thousand-year-old wall drawings from ancient tribes. Myths and magic. We'll pass right by them."

"Well, Angel, we might not have the time to explore."

Lopez gestured before them. "When we get past the valley between the two hills, we're going to hit a series of peaks toward Charleston. It's uphill from there on. And we're going to need food. Water's critical, but food will give us a boost to our step."

"Any drive-throughs on the way?" asked Houston.

Lopez flicked a quick glance at her. "No. But there's wild game."

"Like those burros?" smirked Lightfoote.

"We might can do better. But we'll have to know where to look and how to track. Sara and I have done some in the years since we hit the FBI's most-wanted. Up in the mountains. Isolated. I don't know this area, but we might get lucky."

"I'm all for non-donkey rations," said Houston. "Otherwise, it's their asses for dinner. I'm starting to feel pretty damn hungry."

Lopez put an arm around her shoulders. "It's no joke. We bought some time with the water, but we need food. We're burning calories like hell. We've got to have the strength to get to the town. It's our only chance to reach someone, get out of this dragnet."

Houston tilted her head into the nook of his neck, the tight muscles a brawny nest. A false sense of safety, but she needed to feel it. She arced her gaze toward the sky as the faint sound of helicopter blades grew.

"Assuming they don't catch us first."

25

NETTED

Rebecca Cohen stepped out of the dark SUV, an assistant holding a black umbrella over her. The rolling thunderstorms of East Coast summers raged and boomed. The downpour sizzled like bacon around them. A dedicated, government-issue jet awaited her at a secure gate at Reagan National Airport in DC. The aid lowered the umbrella as they entered. TSA ushered them through a private and quick security check.

It had taken her two days to leave Washington. The plan for her to return to New York hit delays. There was too much going on after the attack. That included the capture of one of the wounded killers.

The visit to the mosque still played in her mind, an equal combination of horror show and chess match. She tried to map out a strategy. Except in chess, you could see all the pieces. You knew their abilities and limitations.

And they weren't waiting to kill you if you slipped up.

Patrick Rout opened with a hell of a gambit. If indeed Mjolnir's prime killer had survived to resurrect the terrorist group. Using S-47 amounted to raising a flag of the hateful organization. Planting a note on their recent victims naming Savas's son was declaring war.

Savas had killed their leader, William Gunn. Even as the madman tried to convert Intel 1 to his cause: destroying Islam. Like Savas, he'd lost a loved one on 9/11. Like Savas, he held deep anger and biases because of it. But Gunn had not struggled with those emotions. He'd fanned their flames into a genocidal plan. The billionaire had nearly sparked a global war.

As Gunn's right-hand man, Rout knew every detail. Mjolnir did their research. Savas struggled with the death of his son, a rookie officer crushed in the Twin Tower collapse. The note was a dagger in the heart, twisted with hate in the midst of a massacre for maximum impact.

She'd tried to steer him to sanity, begged him to step back from this vortex. But the vortex had a dark will of its own and reached out to grasp him.

Now there's no turning back.

She shook her head, trying to clear it. The TSA handlers waved them through with no delay. She slowed her pace, realizing that she'd left her young aid scrambling behind to keep up.

Breathe, Rebecca. Breathe.

She gave a curt nod to the pilot and crew waiting beside the door to the jet bridge. Thunder rattled the windows, the air outside a soup flecked with lightning. The small governmental plane was going to get the crap kicked out of it.

Two storms in a row. Is this a sign?

But she couldn't lose focus. Not for some storm turbulence. Not for the turbulence of her life and work. Savas had charged her with guiding Intel 1 and its critical cases, ensuring that it could survive this critical period in American history. Hate crimes were surging. Terrorists out west were approaching the level of a guerrilla insurgency. Meanwhile, their long quest to end the conspiracy of the Bilderberg Group floundered.

Mirnateghi is pulling so many strings.

More and more, her mind linked the strands. An election that evidence argued was won because of the meddling of foreign powers. *Iranian* powers, amongst others. An administration that undermined US institutions, particularly law enforcement. Organizations warped into a private cudgel of the Executive to quash Suite's enemies. A nationwide crackdown on scape-goated minorities like Latinos and Muslims. And now, the return of Mjolnir. All coupled to the president's personal involvement in handcuffing Intel 1 to that single case.

With a personal note of venom to John at the scene of an attack.

Cohen ignored the advertisements in the jet bridge. She did not acknowledge the waiting members of Intel 1 on the plane. She sat before computer monitors and satellite hookups. There was much to do. Information to gather. Chess pieces to put in motion to counter a wild gambit.

Time to enter the fray.

Savas wiped the rain from his brows and dabbed his face with a towel. He gestured to his armed escorts. The pack trekked through an isolated hospital wing in the trauma center at George Washington University Hospital. A tense group of armed soldiers patrolled the hallway. IDs were inspected, superiors consulted, and Tim Cox intervened to grant Savas access to the patient cipher inside the secured room.

"So he's back from the dead?" he asked.

"Yes," said Cox. "Even conscious an hour ago. He's being held as an unlawful combatant. Bastard knows his rights, screaming about getting a lawyer."

"A lawyer?" He sneered. "Quick recovery."

"Kept shouting about the Posse Comitatus Act and telling us the military had to go."

"Unexpected."

Savas stared at the door and the pair of military police on either side of it. Mjolnir soldiers fought to the death, took their own lives rather than betray the cause. They didn't come crying about their legal rights and quoting Civil War legislation.

Maybe the sequel doesn't live up to the original. Maybe Rout can't recruit like he once did.

"Most of the killers from Mjolnir were ex-soldiers," he noted. "Top shelf. Handpicked. They made mistakes sometimes, but this guy doesn't sound like he fits the profile."

"He was a shooter," said Cox. "Video footage tracks him from the scene, even to the subway where he engaged some of my best."

Savas rubbed the side of his face and chin, staring down. "I'm sure you're running his prints and DNA."

"Of course. It's still our jurisdiction, unless your phantom agency has the clout to take over." He smiled without showing his teeth. "I'll let you know what we find."

"Meanwhile," said Savas, a glint in his eye, "if he's well enough to sing for his Constitutional protections…"

"My thoughts exactly. He's sedated, and we're going to move him to a safe house," said Cox. "And you're invited, of course."

A pale blue light spilled over Reza Kazemi in a dark room. He faced a flat screen, a python of cables wrapped together running from the monitor through several blinking boxes on the floor. A radiant woman's brown eyes bored through the pixels, her face surrounded by thick black hair. She spoke in Farsi. Her tone was imperial.

"I don't care about Suite's obsessions," said Mirnateghi. "That is a tool to harness his apparatus, and eventually to sow discord and destabilize the nation. All this is part of a longer strategy. But Intel 1 must be stopped. They have revealed themselves to be our greatest threat. Your focus must be on turning the American system toward Mjolnir. Our plan must succeed."

Kazemi nodded. "My dear Sonbol, that is my only priority. I only wish to return to the problem of the private investigator. Her efforts threaten to expose both Suite's project as well as our ties to him."

The Iranian woman waved it away with her hand. "Our connections to him are nebulous. They're no threat to us and only a danger to him in his position. The woman could be a tool to publicly disclose Suite's efforts and inject chaos into the American political system."

"And yet," said Kazemi, "her track record is anomalously successful. I worry she will ferret out connections even we have not antici-pated, some potentially threatening our efforts."

Mirnateghi paused. "Your concern is valid. Should it come to that, we will revisit the effort to shut her down. In anticipation of such a contingency, gather the needed assets."

Kazemi smiled. "It is already underway."

26

FLOWERS

"**M**r. Sacker?"

He spun toward the sound, adrenaline spiking. "Yes?"

A young nurse stopped beside him, her focus upward. "Nice hat," she smiled.

She had a pleasant demeanor. Short, full-figured, chirpy little thing with blue-streaked hair. Normally, she would've tempted him to a few choice looks. Discrete. Non-threatening. But today he couldn't care less.

A series of blurred days had passed since the shooting. Gone had seen multiple surgeries. Sacker had seen little sleep. He was sharp with everyone even by his standards. He needed rest. He needed to eat a decent meal. Most of all, he needed to see Gracie.

"Can I visit the patient now?"

Her smile faded. "Right this way, Mr. Sacker."

She led him across the length of the hospital building. Sacker's patience ebbed. Every unfortunate relative or visiting friend who crossed his path offended him.

He passed a series of large flat panel monitors, CNN blaring in front of blank-faced groups. Four years under Suite had defanged the media. While Candid was still the mouthpiece for the administration, the other news organizations had changed their tune. Criticism was muted. Missteps or outright atrocities by the newly re-elected president were ignored or skimmed over. Increasingly, any praiseworthy action by the government was given headline treatment.

Sacker scowled. They were a bunch of cowards terrified for their bottom line or getting thrown in jail for violating the growing list of libel statutes. It was the same with the tech industry and nearly every corporate sector.

Fascism and business. Match made in hell.

The density of people thinned as they reached a little-used end of the large building. The nurse led him through a more abandoned wing one floor down from the normal ICU patients. NYPD Blue flanked a doorway on the left where she stopped. They stepped to the side, allowing them to enter.

Before they could do so, a woman stepped out. She was tall, Sacker's height, trim and forty-something. Dyed blond hair, glasses, and intelligent eyes behind them. She closed the door.

"Mr. Sacker?"

"Yes, ma'am."

A soft smile touched her lips as she offered her hand. "I'm Lena Patterson. I led the trauma team that worked on Ms. Gone. I'll be your contact here at the hospital."

"Good to meet you, doc," he said, shaking her hand.

With a motion of her eyes, she dismissed the nurse, who scampered back down the hallway.

"Let's take a short walk, shall we?"

It wasn't a question.

"Sure."

Patterson took him out of earshot of the guards. She stopped at a corner and removed her glasses. They hung from a string to her chest.

"Look, as far as I can tell, there's no family here for her. Is this correct?"

"No one I know. She's got a mysterious past." He managed a weak smile. The doctor's expression didn't change.

"She asked for you. Now, I've got twenty-five years trauma experience. And I've seen a lot of gunshot wounds. A lot of deaths. Two mass shootings." She paused to let the words sink in. "Having family, *anyone* who can serve as family, makes a positive difference in recovery."

"I believe that. I'm here."

She held his gaze, assessing him. "You need to understand. This wasn't a handgun wound. This was a military-grade bullet. What we call high-velocity rounds."

"I'm a combat vet, doc. I'm familiar."

She returned a sharp smile. "Humor me. I don't know you from Adam, except she asked for you. Weapons like this impart tremendous amounts of kinetic energy into tissue. She was lucky in several ways. First and foremost is location. Had this been a few inches over, it would have exploded her heart."

His mind flashed to the brownstone steps. The glinting light. His scream, him shoving her away.

"The round didn't pass through very much tissue. It blew right through the upper area between her shoulder and neck, here." She tapped her collar bone. "The exit wound was golfball-sized. If it had gone through the chest, it would have been an orange by the time it exited."

He grimaced. "The bad news? What'd it hit?"

"Stay positive a moment. No major organs. The round exited her body just as it was beginning to blow up tissue. Again, had this happened in a thicker part of her body, it would have been worse." Her mouth tightened. "But the bullet did make a mess. Basically, several bones in the shoulder area were shattered. Not just broken, but highly fragmented. The soft tissue damage was also critical."

He tried to stay focused. He'd seen worse. Much worse. He knew the drill. He'd held dying men.

But this is Gracie.

All he could see was the flash of her smile. The soft glow of her skin. Those piercing eyes puzzling out the whole goddam world. That just didn't mix with blood and metallic violations strewing flesh.

"There was a puncture wound to the lung. The organ escaped, for the most part, but she nearly bled out because the subclavian artery ruptured."

He cocked his head before he could control it.

"That's a major artery running from your chest down your arm." She traced the path of the vessel on her body. "A lot of blood moves through it. Fortunately, help was called quickly. The response team was prepared for a gunshot wound, but it was touch and go with the blood loss before we had that under control." She frowned. "Alongside that artery is the brachial plexus, a large nerve bundle controlling the arm. It was shredded."

"How much arm function will she lose?"

"Function? She almost lost the left arm. I'm afraid her prospects for much use of that limb are very, very poor."

"I see." His stomach spasmed.

"I know this is distressing. I'm not telling you this to upset you. She has *months* of recovery coming. Very likely a second surgery to help repair the blood vessels, bone, and other tissue damage. We saved her life, but the hard work for her is just starting. She's going to need someone. Especially with her chronic condition."

"Condition?"

The footsteps of some ignored doom beat in his head. The limp. The cane. The falls. Of course he'd seen. He was a detective, which was as much about studying people as crime scenes. He just hadn't wanted to know. In the chaos of how they first met, in the nearly blackout drunk years after, he'd buried the thoughts. But the time for self-delusion had passed.

The doctor studied him a moment. "Well, if she hasn't told you, I've said too much. It won't be the primary factor physically. Not in the immediate future. But there are going to be a host of emotional weights for her in this."

Gracie, what are you hiding?

Sacker stared at the ground, smiling. "You don't know our Gracie, Doc," he said, glancing back to her. "If she's conscious, it's the rest of us who'll need help by the time it's all over."

Patterson gave him her first warm smile. "I don't doubt you. She's already exasperated the nurse with detailed medical questions. For now, though, her stamina's low. Good for the nurse, but bad for too many visitors. I'll give you ten minutes."

"I'm very grateful."

They walked back to the guarded ICU room. She turned the handle and pushed open the door. Sacker swallowed, held his breath, and entered.

Aw, hell.

He'd stepped inside a scene from some sci-fi horror film. An alien womb throbbed with tubes and wires plugged into a helpless shape. Machines beeped, pumped, and gurgled, extracting fluids and squirting them in. A raw smell of flesh raked his nostrils. In the center, cocooned in it all with blankets and pillows, a small form huddled. She lay on her back, her side facing him.

"Was worried about you," Gone rasped, her head still.

He approached the bed, grasping the metal handrails on the sides. Her skin was deathly pale, eyes sunken, the sockets black. Like she'd been in a twelve-round fight. Her left shoulder was twice the size of the other with tubes and bandages.

"Worried about *me?*" He shook his head, knuckles white on the rails. "You're something."

She tried to speak, but her throat caught. She tried again. "The killers could have gone after you."

"Maybe, but you're the Steve Jobs of this operation. I think I'm pretty safe. That's why we've got the guards outside."

"You smell of flowers."

He slumped. In all the chaos, he'd forgotten to get her anything.

A simple damned gesture of flowers, you moron! How hard?

"Stop," she coughed, swallowing several times. "I don't want flowers." She cleared her throat. "I smell the Hyacinths on you."

Never lie to this woman.

He'd intercepted the hyacinths sent to her. No note with them. No address. Plain, unremarkable box. He'd turned them over to the police, but he was sure they'd find nothing. But there was no hiding from the meaning of that delivery. He figured she didn't need any more stress right now. "Bullet didn't hurt your nose, I see."

"Mirnateghi," she whispered.

Gone would not have forgotten the calling card of the deadly Iranian. Known to many in her home country as *Sonbol*, which meant hyacinth, she left the flowers with the bodies of her kills. She also used them as an intimidation tactic. Intel 1 had opened their eyes to that underworld. Hyacinths from Mirnateghi were a serious threat.

"Yeah," he growled. "Beautiful and poisonous flower. That monster sent a message. I was going to save that until later. I think everyone in the know has nightmares with hyacinths now."

Gone closed her eyes. She lay there, silent and unmoving, for several minutes. Sacker didn't dare bother her. He was about to leave when she spoke again, eyes still closed.

"They said there were reporters outside."

"You heard that? They ought to keep it the hell down and let you heal. We're keeping them at bay. But you're all over the papers."

"Let them in."

"Sorry?"

A flame lit in her eyes. "Let them in. Make sure they have photographers."

"Gracie, what…"

"But first, go buy me purple hyacinths. Bring them up." She leaned back into the bed, the efforts draining her. But her voice didn't waver. "I'm going to let my NYC fans know I'm okay. Smile real big and hold the flowers for the papers."

The left side his mouth twitched upward.

"You're one sassy bitch, little girl."

GRACE NOT GONE:
DOCS PATCH GENIUS PI

by Alexander Manning, *New York Post*

There's no keeping down the Big Apple's female Charlie Chan. Only a week after she was the victim of an assassination attempt in Manhattan, Grace Gone posed for photographers in her hospital bed, a smile, bandages, flowers, and all.

"You make enemies in my line of work," the diminutive detective said at the makeshift press conference. "It's a risk you take. The bigger the case, the bigger the risk. But I'm here to tell all my enemies: I'm not going anywhere."

And if a sniper's bullet can't stop her, what will?

Reporters were hustled in and out of the room quickly by the hospital staff. NYPD officers were stationed along the hallways and in the room.

The press had a host of questions. When asked if she saw the shooter, the answer was no.

"My colleague, detective Tyrell Sacker, saved my life. If he hadn't pushed me out of the way, the bullet would have hit my heart."

Inquiries into the seriousness of her injury were met with suggestions that many months of recovery awaited the PI.

"There's a lot of damage to the shoulder. It's too early to tell how much function will return. Luckily, I earn my living with my mind."

When pressed about rumors that there were tensions between her and the NYPD, Gone strongly denied them.

"Of course not!" she said loudly. "It's just gossip that I have any problem with our officers in blue. Only the highest professional respect. We worked together on the Eunuch Maker case, and we continue to do so often. I've never felt safer now that they're here to protect me."

Mike Lander of the 12th precinct was also present and echoed Gone's words.

"NYPD is forever grateful to Ms. Gone for her help in many an important case. The police serve the people, and when citizens aid our efforts, as Ms. Gone has done so well, it makes our job that much easier."

Speculation has run rampant about who could have targeted Gone. Despite her praise for former NYPD detective Sacker, rumors persist that he could be involved. As for Gone herself, she played coy.

"Let's just say that I always have ideas. I've got nothing better to do in this bed than think. Sift through evidence. Connect the dots. As you can imagine, I'm very motivated to solve this crime. And I will."

27

VISITOR

Detective Rick Snyder flipped through a notepad, peering over the pages toward Gone. Sacker stood in the opposite corner of the room with his arms folded. His face muscles twisted, his eyes glaring at the young man.

Gone leaned back into the hulking pillow.

Going to have to get rid of this guy before Tyrell smacks him.

It was more than a week since the shooting, and after Gone's public press appearance, the NYPD concluded she was fit to be questioned. And of course Sacker's former chief had sent Snyder, the one man who had taken it upon himself to turn coat on his mentor years before. She tried to center the room on her, get Sacker's eyes off the arrogant detective.

"Is there anything on the shooter?" she asked.

"We have his blood type."

"Tyrell shot him?"

Snyder scoffed. "Seems like. Just wounding him, though. Dragged himself to the stairwell and bled all the way down, but he got out. No prints. He got away."

He smirked at Sacker, who gave him a death stare.

"I wondered," said Sacker. "I thought I might have hit him. But he pulled back from the roof. I had more important things to do with Grace bleeding out than chase the bastard."

All right, intervention required.

"So many questions, Detective Snyder," said Gone, feigning fatigue. "Is there much more?"

Gone placed the blanket over her hand by the bed keypad. She pressed a button. Snyder was dim, smug, and overconfident, all accentuated by an unpleasant leer. One of the men to avoid in social settings. She understood why Sacker hated him.

Betraying Tyrell at NYPD likely had a little to do with it, too, Grace.

Snyder huffed. "We still have many unanswered questions, Ms. Gone." He wagged a finger at Sacker. "You still haven't clearly explained why former detective Sacker was with you."

"Like I said," she yawned, "he's an employee now. We were investigating leads on a confidential case."

"About that, now—"

A nurse opened the door and stepped in. "Everything okay, Ms. Gone?"

"Thank you, Mr. Snyder, but my recovery has drained me. Let's arrange for a time after the weekend to talk more, yes?"

She beamed at him. Snyder's mouth hung open. His eyes narrowed.

The nurse frowned in his direction. "My patient needs some rest, sir. Please arrange for a visit another day."

Snyder fabricated a smile, the grin from a slasher villain. "Of course. We will definitely get back to this soon."

"Have a nice night," yawned Gone again, closing her eyes.

Snyder's lip curled, and he stormed out of the room.

"Now that's a type," mumbled the nurse, checking the vital signs monitors.

The shooter flared in her mind. Snyder's data triggered a rush of energy, the implications critical. If the shooter was still alive, he provided a direct connection to Mirnateghi. Gone opened her eyes and sat up in the bed. Her heart rate jumped, flustering the nurse.

"Carefully, honey. Let's not burst anything."

Need to get rid of her and talk to Tyrell.

Gone leaned back in the bed, trying to relax. The woman frowned.

"Dinner's in an hour. Let me know if you need anything. Or need to get rid of anyone else." She threw Sacker a glance and then closed the door behind her.

"So, the shooter may still be out there," said Gone, her eyes bright.

"Mmm-hmmm," hummed Sacker, pacing the room.

"That's our most direct connection to the core of this. You've got to talk to Hill. Make sure we're in the loop if NYPD finds anything."

"Hill's out. Ladner reassigned her as fast as he could. No accident Snyder's here. He's a spy, not a detective."

"She can still help. Meanwhile, you can talk to others in the force. Call in favors." Gone pouted, her lower lip cracked and dry. "Maybe we need to call in bigger guns."

His eyebrows rose. "Intel 1?"

"Maybe. They have resources we could use."

"Makes sense with the Mirnateghi angle. They'd want to know about the hit."

"But it's not just Mirnateghi."

"What do you mean? You even got the flowers. She's not exactly being subtle."

"No," she said. "Of course she's behind it. I mean she's part of something bigger." She was out of breath. "We triggered something. We're poking around where we shouldn't."

He shook his head. "After everything that's happened with that Iranian devil, I understand. I get conspiracy theory. But not everything is on. Mirnateghi's been murderous toward Intel 1 for years. We're just on her radar now because we helped foil her doomsday man-virus. We don't need to try and weave government malfeasance into her web."

"No, we don't. She could be an independent confounding variable." Sacker shrugged. She set her jaw. "But she's *not*. The timing is suspicious. So is the scope of what we're uncovering. And what's the Special Counsel investigating president Suite for?"

"Conspiracy with the Iranians to influence the election, campaign finance violations, and violations of the emoluments clause." He exhaled. "But Gracie—"

"Let's just pretend for a minute that this giant scandal we've stumbled across goes high. It *has* to go pretty high to be this big. Multiple large government departments, including Homeland? The odds are good that someone as corrupt as Suite is overseeing it."

"We don't have evidence for that."

"Not yet," she said, leaning back into her pillows, groaning. She touched the bandages over her wounded shoulder. "The paper trail is clear. Crimes have been committed. But prosecutable evidence, who's running what, that's usually hard to get in cases like this. Unless they're really stupid and careless. But the separate pieces would synergize if they interacted: government malfeasance, Suite, Iran, Mirnateghi, assassination."

"If she *is* involved with Suite and this Nevada thing, it's got to be really bad. Like brand new apocalypse bad."

The door swung open and two burly men stormed inside.

Sacker's arm dropped and rose with a handgun in his hand. "Stop right there," he shouted.

The men did not attack or display a weapon in response. They said nothing. Gone stared at the pair. Chinese. Tall and muscular. Suits. Black earpieces.

Oh, no. Please don't let it be.

"Excuse me," repeated Sacker in a louder voice. "Who the hell gave you permission to come in here?"

An older Chinese man stepped through the doorway. He was short like Gone, slender, with thick white hair trimmed short on his scalp. His bottom lip protruded in a pout.

"I gave permission," said the man in accented English. "She knows me."

Sacker's weapon remained trained on them. His eyes darted from them to Gone and back. "You know these people, Gracie?"

Gone grimaced and sat up again in bed, staring at the older man.

I can't believe this.

"It's okay, Tyrell. Put the gun down. We're safe."

He lowered his weapon and holstered it, his face scrunched.

Gone closed her eyes and shook her head. When the lids fluttered open, she wore a sad smile.

"Hi, Dad."

28

DAD

"Dad?" Sacker gawked.

He grabbed a chair and placed a foot on the seat. *Dad?* His head had spun enough the last week for a lifetime. He'd barely downshifted from Snyder to talk shop about the case with Gone when his gun was out, adrenaline flowing, spying two hulking bodyguards escorting a man Gone called her father. He glanced back at the thin figure flanked by two hulking guards. She'd never mentioned him. He'd never seen a single family photo. It figured their introduction would occur at the barrel of a gun.

Gracie, we're going to have a talk.

The older man spoke in a language he couldn't decipher. Probably Mandarin, but he wasn't a linguist.

Gone interrupted him, her expression pained.

"English only. It's rude. Have you forgotten all the things you pretended to teach me?"

The man was silent, his face set, an irritated glance at Sacker his only response.

"And Tyrell is the one person in the world that I trust. So he hears everything."

Sacker inhaled, his jaw slack. In the middle of all this madness, she upped and reached her hand through all his armor to touch his heart. He couldn't take his eyes off her face.

"The former police detective," said her father, a flat smile on his lips. "Man of many faces. He saved your life, as I understand it."

Sacker held the man's gaze. "I was returning the favor."

"Of course, I've known of both your whereabouts, and exploits, for years."

Gone sighed. "You have your ways."

"Indeed. But you had made your will known. I suffered to see a Gon struggle so, impoverished, helpless. And yet, look what you have done! Stopped a madman. Saved millions of lives. More famous than even your father."

"Dad, you're infamous, not famous." She gestured with her functional arm. "Tyrell, meet Fan Gon. International, shall we say, *businessman*."

"My idealistic daughter. You ran away to avoid conflict. But conflict has found you."

"There are different kinds of conflict."

Mr. Gon turned to Sacker. "And it is *Gone* without the 'e'. My daughter's spelling is a product of her artistic streak."

"An expression of my desires as a child."

The old man exhaled, fixing his gaze on his daughter. "I don't want to fight the past yet again. I know you will not come home. I know you will never accept me. But that is not why I am here."

She scowled, her lip curled like a rebellious adolescent. "Why *are* you here?"

"Whatever our differences, *Qiānjīn*, you are my child."

"Don't call me that."

"When you were small, it pleased you, our game. The name—"

"Don't call me that."

"You are of the Gon family." His back stiffened. "And I will be buried in my tomb before some Iranian whore attacks my own blood, brings such dishonor to my family."

Sacker's eyes widened. "How do you know—"

Fan Gon spoke over him. "I have resources that bitch knows nothing about." He turned to Gone. "I will help you."

"I don't want your kind of help. I want nothing to do with you!"

Sacker marveled. The conversation changed directions like a carnival ride.

What's going on here?

The prospect of learning about her life exhilarated him. The deep mystery surrounding her past only intrigued him more. Perhaps over time, she would trust him enough to open up. She'd just said she trusted him more than anyone. Enough to truly share herself?

But the angry, hurt, and child-like woman before him was a shock. He'd never seen her so flustered.

"You need my help!" her father shouted. He frowned and smoothened his black tie. "But I do not expect you to allow me to help. You are too much like me, *little daughter*. So I've always told your mother. The only one smart enough to carry on the family name is Grace. Your brothers, ha! When I am gone, they will be fighting each other and the other families within months. They understand only strength, not strategy."

She shook her head. "I don't want any part in your *business*. Or your *strategy*."

"Of course. And that is your mother in you. But I have anticipated this. Rest now, daughter. Know that I am watching, and when needed, will descend with fury on your enemies."

Gon turned to leave, pivoting back toward his daughter.

"Two last things."

"Finally. Spit it out and go."

He stared at Sacker, his expression cold. "This *man*. He, or whatever it is. Unworthy of you. Unworthy of a Gon."

Why you son of a bitch.

He took a step toward her father. The two guards faced him. Sacker balled his fists.

Control yourself, Tyrell. Not like this. Not with Gracie here.

Gone growled, her voice unrecognizable. "How dare you? I never expected you to respect the lives of others, let alone their privacy." She teared up. "But this is low. Get out of my room or I'm calling the police."

"The police are well paid," smiled Gon. "I do not fear them."

Her lower lip quivered.

"Still a child, I see. Emotions still your master." He pouted. "The second item is your medical reports. How long have you known?"

Tears dropped down her face. "How did you get my records?"

"I have my ways."

She lowered her head. Her shoulders shook.

"Okay, *Dad*," growled Sacker. "I didn't want to make a scene with Gracie here. But I will if you don't leave. Now."

He took another step toward the guards. They did not move.

"I hope you can see that she's hurt," he tried. "Bullet in the shoulder, now Dad in the heart. Let her be."

Gon spat curt commands in Mandarin to the hulks at this side. They bowed toward him and left the room. He scowled at Sacker and turned a look of pity to his weeping daughter.

"Some enemies always win, no matter how great the warrior. And death is the only final champion. But at least, while we all wait for that last stroke, we may yet bring death to the doorstep of our enemies."

He spun on a heel and marched out of the room.

29

ON THE TRAIL

Houston startled as Lightfoote sprinted around the curve in the rocky wall. She stopped beside the remains of their campsite. Grime covered her from head to foot and stained her bleached hair to a filthy cream, but it accentuated her musculature. The tawny striations in her bare arms and exposed back were a walking anatomy chart.

Needs a bath, but she looks good.

Lightfoote had returned from a scouting run of some likely hostiles they'd spied yesterday evening. The idiots had lit a fire at night and flashed lights in the darkness, giving away their existence and position. It wasn't the first they'd seen over the last week. Search parties and the occasional helicopter forced them to zig-zag up the mountain. Even hikers presented a risk of discovery. All that extra distance meant more time. Fortunately, they became adept at locating sources of water. They had even found decent game. Unfortunately, it meant the additional week in the wild had given their pursuers that much more time to plan and mobilize. They had to reach the town of Mount Charleston soon. Once there, they had to concoct a true getaway.

Houston shook her head to clear her mind and returned to the task in front of her. She angled her Stetson to block the sun and grabbed a hunting knife.

"ICE agents, for sure," said Lightfoote. Rivulets of sweat carved darker streaks down her face and arms. "Three of them."

Houston kneeled in front of a bloodied carcass. Massive horns wrapped around themselves at the head. The animal was opened up, the broad knife bloody in her hands as she eviscerated the beast. "How close did you get?"

Lightfoote stared. "Bighorn sheep. Didn't hear a shot. Nice job."

"Thanks," she muttered. "Used a suppressor. One shot kill. Francisco had to lug it up here."

Lightfoote nodded, staring past Houston. "Thanks. Getting pretty hungry. That the cave water?"

The deep bass of Lopez boomed as he stepped from behind several boulders. "Filled and ready to go." He gestured to a row of canteens near his feet. "Should have enough for another day out here."

"Hopefully we'll be gone by then," said Houston, the animal's outer layer of skin and fur pulled back. "So, your scouting?"

"Right," said Lightfoot, crossing her legs and sitting next to her. "They're definitely hitting the trails. And I got real close." She gestured to her filthy body. "Dug in like a tick on the trail side. They came right past with a group of hikers, doing the expected. Closing off the trails. Rounding people up. If we want to stick to the trails and not free climb again, we've got to either double-time it or take them out."

Houston sighed. "I'm tired of killing people."

Lightfoote's green eyes pierced her.

She feels what I feel.

She turned away. *Angel, I can't. It's not that simple.*

Lopez approached the pair. "And we're *tired*. Not sure we can keep up that pace. Maybe we can neutralize them without taking them out, incapacitate them for a time."

"They'll die out here," said Houston, the parched landscape shimmering around her. "We can't haul them back to the grotto. We've got to move forward."

"We passed a small cave. They'd fit inside. *Restrained*. If they don't report back, someone will come looking, trace the last coordinates of their phones. That will take a day. If we're not gone by then, we're dead anyway."

She looked away. Lopez struggled the most with the life they lived. When a former do-gooder priest turns assassin, there's a price to pay.

At least there was before.

Now he was changed. How much, she didn't know. He quoted scripture less. His insomnia was gone, his conscience seemingly pacified despite their deeds. Did he want to minimize death today, or was this a show for her?

"Three, huh?" Her eyes flicked toward Lightfoote. "Three of us. If they're standard ICE agents, should be able to take them alive."

"Besides," he said, "I'd like to get a shot at questioning them. Get some raw intel. Might save our lives."

In agreement, they doubled back and set a trap near the cave. The trail cut between two house-sized slabs of rock, the entrance to the cave some six feet up on one side. The passageway was tight, three people wide, and the stone around them was terraced by erosion.

They concealed themselves on several broad ledges over the trail. Houston gazed across the path toward Lightfoote. The lithe former FBI agent hung from the rock like a spider. Lopez squatted within a shallow hollow near the opening to the path. Their height over the trail and the sheltering rocks shielded them from sight.

Her muscles tensed as voices rang through the stone. She locked eyes with Lightfoote, who grinned across her.

Crazy girl. Let's hope they aren't paying close attention. And hope we don't end up with some innocent climbers ICE rounded up dead in the crossfire.

A group of five hikers entered the crevice. Three ICE agents followed behind, their black uniforms oppressing them in the sun. All heads were bowed, the incline toward the mountain steep, the heat of the day intense.

"Keep moving" rasped one agent, wiping his neck with a rag, sweat glistening on his skin. "We've got some climbing to do to get to Mount Charleston."

A pair in the hiker group mumbled. Their vacation was ruined, a day of exploration ended before it began. The agents passed Lopez, who drew his arm back and lofted a stone into the pack. The trio of agents was centered in the middle of the narrow tunnel, the hikers exiting past Houston.

"Hey, what the hell?"

A hiker's voice echoed as the stone landed. They stared down at the object, startling at the sounds of boots slamming into the rock around them.

The terrorists sprung like snakes. Houston lunged toward one of the agents with her right arm, her blow absurdly telegraphed. He over-reacted, unbalancing his weight in a wild effort to dodge. She pivoted, her left leg a carving knife, the boot striking the man in the midsection. He collapsed, a blast of air hurled out of his lungs. He gasped on the ground, cradling his side.

Behind him, an unconscious body lay crumbled in the dust, the bright, white ICE letters facing the sky. Lopez stood over him, fists clenched and wrapped in climbing gloves. She turned to her left.

A man groaned in agony. Lightfoote held the agent's arm behind his back, the wrist twisted sharply. He dropped to his knees, blood dripping from a shattered nose.

"Please, God! Stop it! It hurts!"

The hikers simply gaped, frozen in place. Lopez pushed past the two women, his eyes focused behind them.

"Over here, now!" he yelled at the hikers.

"Oh, God, it's them!" came a high-pitched shriek.

"El Marcado," one whispered, his eyes wide and staring at the scar on Lopez's forehead.

A firearm appeared in Lopez's gloved hand. He aimed it at the trembling group.

"Quiet. There's one way you walk out of here alive, and that's if you do exactly what we say, when we say it."

Five heads bobbed in panicked unison.

DOJ ANNOUNCES NEW LIMITS FOR PRESIDENTIAL INVESTIGATIONS

by Sophia Hatzivasiliou, *The Atlantic*

"The witch hunt era is over. The new McCarthyism is finished."

These were the words from Attorney General Liam Newton today as the Department of Justice announced sweeping new policies, revamping procedures and limiting the authority of federal investigations into the Executive Branch.

Foremost among the new rules is a bulwark against the investigation and indictment of a sitting president. It is no secret that Daniel Suite had long chafed at the appointment of a special counsel to investigate purported links between his campaign and presidency and foreign influence peddling, particularly from Russia, Iran, and Saudi Arabia. Many speculated that his appointment of Mr. Newton, an attorney with a public history of opposing presidential inquiries, to the Attorney General position was to ensure that DoJ policy would be altered to "relieve some pressure" from investigations, as he famously put it in a televised interview with CNN.

Conservative lawmakers and legal experts expressed enthusiasm for the change, voicing long-standing concerns that the growing set of probes into the president were impairing his ability to govern the nation.

In a rare public statement, recently confirmed Supreme Court Justice Rett Dravan sided with the DoJ. "The president must be freed from the more onerous burdens of normal citizenship during his tenure in office," Dravan wrote. "In the 1980s and 1990s, I might have disagreed. I held positions similar to many Americans at that time, convinced that the president ought to be required to shoulder the same requirements we all carry. But I have come to rethink this position, that it was a lapse in judgment."

When reporters challenged the Justice to address the claim that such policies put the president above the law, he replied, "Our Constitution prescribes that it is through the Congress, and not elements of the Executive Branch like the DoJ, that investigations of the president occur. Criminal investigations must wait until the accused departs from the Office of the Presidency."

He continued by suggesting that legislation should be enacted to protect the Executive from such inquiries. "Given the current climate, the Congress could consider legislation that exempts a sitting president from any investigation or criminal prosecution, including the demands of questioning by prosecutors or defense attorneys. Any such inquiries into a sitting president become politicized by critics as well as supporters, damaging both the function of government and the rendering of justice."

How this will affect the results of the recently concluded investigation of Special Counsel Ronald Tiller is unclear. When asked about this, the Attorney General replied in a guarded manner.

"We are looking into that. Some of this investigation has certainly violated the new protocols. Whether or not any information obtained in such violation will be considered admissible will need to be reviewed. The Special Counsel report is not a public report. It is confidential, subject to my review. This office will determine what is relevant, admissible, and share what we believe is pertinent to the Congress as stipulated by law."

Such words raised the specter that the report submitted by the Special Counsel would remain heavily redacted or buried from the public.

"This is third world dictator stuff," said Harry Karplus, former Deputy Attorney General under President York. "We have before us a situation that is unique and requires pushing past simplistic statements about governmental function. This is the president. This is about the election. This is about the sovereignty of the United States of America and whether it is compromised by foreign influence. There is nothing more relevant to the public than the full disclosure of a comprehensive, unexpurgated, and unadulterated report by the Special Counsel. We as a nation need to know the full truth."

30

SQUEEZED

S avas studied the killer in the hospital bed. Medical equipment surrounded the patient. Hanging bags of plasma dripped into tubes. A repeating tone from a monitor raked the nerves.

The clinical elements clashed with the residential furnishings of the house. Inside and out, the building was an unremarkable suburban family home. Two stories and a basement and a manicured lawn. The owners were Home Owners Association regulars, a graying couple without children. The wife was known for her pumpkin pie at the local fairs. Her husband hailed from California. He'd made some money back in the day at the dawn of the tech era.

But the house was anything but normal. High-tech security systems blanketed the plot. Video cameras, motion detectors, and microphones inside and out all linked to a central command desk in the basement manned 24/7. The charming elderly couple were retired assets long-experienced in witness protection.

You might need protection today, asshole. From me.

Maybe this bastard hadn't written the note. Maybe he had. But he was part of the mission. Savas wouldn't forget the killings or the message they sent

The patient was shackled in restraints, arms and legs. His wounds were serious. By luck of the Irish, there were no life-threatening complications. The pain medication was minimal, and the subject's mind would be clear. His eyes certainly appeared focused.

"No lawyers, my friend," Savas began. "Unlawful combatant against the United States. You signed away your rights the second you decided terrorism on US soil was a good life choice."

Drawn shades cast the room in darkness but for one bright light. The lamp focused on the patient's face. He squinted, eyes darting around the room. They settled on the shrouded shadows of armed guards posted at the door to the room.

"It doesn't matter," he rasped. "We're trained to take any torture you can dish out."

Savas smiled. He lifted a manilla folder and leafed through the pages, pulling one out and brandishing it at the man. "You're not very photogenic."

Savas hovered a passport photo with the patient's personal data over the bed. The picture was of a blond man, crew cut with a chiseled jaw. The face was years younger than the patient strapped to the metal railings.

"Bruce Maynor, thirty-three years old. Born and raised in Dayton, Ohio."

Maynor set his jaw and looked away.

"Honorably discharged from the Army, which does beat many of the rag-tag scum Mjolnir was scraping the barrel-bottom near the end."

"It's not the end!" Maynor hissed.

"Some infections take a dose of curative, that's for sure." He continued flipping through the pages. "The Army concluded the honorable part of your career, it seems. Some time with mercenaries— sorry, private military contractors. Blackwater. Not bad. If you're going to break the Geneva Conventions, they're the best."

Savas sat down in a chair pulled close to the bed. He folded his glasses and stuffed them in a shirt pocket under his gray suit jacket. He paused and stared into the shadows. The folder in his hands was a weapon. A dirty one. One he was about to use because he was sure it was going to work. He didn't like it. He probably should have talked himself into trying something else. But something had to be done, and done fast. Penance would come later.

"Fingerprints. DNA evidence you provided from one of those popular sequencing companies. US law enforcement has special deals with them all. We know who you are."

"So, what?" The man barked a laugh. "Lots of people know who I am."

"And perhaps your family, as well. Your wife. Sophia, isn't it? And what's the cute little girl's name…"

Maynor turned and glared at Savas.

Bingo. Take the bait, asshole.

"Oh, yes." Savas dragged out the syllables with a smile. "Isabella."

"Law and order, huh? You threatening my family?"

Savas smirked. "That's some Olympic level chutzpah coming from a man who just slaughtered children in DC."

Maynor's face constricted, and the veins in his neck bulged.

Make sure the hook takes. Reel him in carefully.

Savas continued.

"But it's not really me who's interested. Just the man I work for. President Suite has taken a hard line on illegal immigration. A very hard line."

"My wife is Christian! Not some towel-headed savage!"

"I'm afraid that the president and his policies are not so forgiving as you might be. As he's noted, some immigrants are very good people. But it's so hard to know them from the thieves, child traffickers, rapists, and killers. They all must go. And, if you read the news reports, they're all going. Willingly or not."

He removed another folder from a satchel on the floor and waved it toward the man.

"We have everything about your wife and child. Address. Schools. Shoe size. ICE would love to deport her and her anchor baby south of the border. Of course, chances are they won't be together. You know how alien families tend to get split up these days. Sometimes they're never reunited, I'm sad to say."

"You son-of-a-bitch! I'll kill you!" Maynor thrashed against the restraints.

The guards moved closer but Savas held up his hand, aiming a stern glance in their direction.

"I wouldn't worry. I hear sometimes the little ones get adopted by some of the hyper-religious groups in the states. It's a growing child-seizure-to-Christian-adoption-agency racket. 'Saving the children' and all that. Most are nice homes."

The man yanked wildly and moaned, arching his bank and collapsing.

"Now, you don't want to tear those staples the good docs put in you. And you don't want to die without giving me what I want." He again waved the folder back and forth. "Their deportation is a done deal."

The man on the bed squeezed his eyes shut, his mouth drawing up in a distorting grimace. With a long release of breath, his body relaxed.

Reel. Slowly, but firmly.

"I can't give you much," said the patient.

Savas kept his voice flat. "That may not be good news for your family."

Maynor's eyes flashed open and he turned his head toward Savas. "Dammit! We're all *blinds*. Mission cells are separated! From each other and central command. Nothing's traceable. We get two missions, then we reprogram."

Two missions? I see.

"I hope you're telling me that you haven't completed your second mission."

The man rolled his head back and focused on the ceiling. "That's exactly what I'm telling you."

Easy, John, don't blow it now.

The fish was nearly in the boat. The balance was tight. The man's devotion to Mjolnir weighed against the threat to his family.

"So then, the question is how much is your daughter worth to you? Is she equal at least to a single Mjolnir mission? Or less?"

The Mjolnir soldier closed his eyes. "I get a lawyer. And some guarantee about my family."

"How about naturalization for your wife? Fake papers to prove ancestral citizenship as well to get around the new laws."

Maynor stared Savas, his eyes intense. "You can do that?"

"That's the easy part. The hard part is whether any piece of paper is going to matter for them in a few years. But you'll have that, at least."

The man held his gaze for several seconds, turning back to the bed and slumping. "Okay."

"The next attack, Maynor," he demanded. "Location, time, and nature. In exchange, once we see that you delivered, Uncle Sam doesn't throw little Isabella into a cage in the desert. He even wraps up some top-flight witness protection documents. Call it an early quinceañera."

Maynor's eyes remained closed. "Deal," he whispered.

"We need you to focus on the more serious threat, Mr. President."

Reza Kazemi rested unmoving in an antique chair in the Oval Office. The lights were low, a desk lamp on the Resolute desk the only source of illumination. Across from him fumed a disheveled Daniel Suite. The pair were alone in the room.

Suite slammed the old wood underneath him. "They're still out there! This Mexican-funded spic is still alive." He pointed an index finger at Kazemi. "They hit the new camps. They might have information. They could blow it all up!"

"Your projects out west do not directly concern me. My superior in Iran is far more focused on the Gone woman and her actions."

Suite smirked. "Then maybe you should've finished the job. Some killer you brought in."

"Bringing in a foreign asset to do a job your infrastructure would be much better positioned to complete is wasting resources. Isn't there some immigration violation you are working on? Just send a wagon to pick her up."

Suite sighed, looking away. "It's not that simple."

"Perhaps not yet. But you have taken the system a long way toward giving you such control."

"The records are complicated. And she's famous. They love her on TV. They're making shows and films about her. If we use ICE, try to deport her, she'll just scream to the press and reveal everything!"

"Surely you have ways of disappearing people?"

"Why not just kill her? You tried once."

"Perhaps it will not come to that. As you note, suddenly the bright spotlight of the media is focused on her for that failed effort. The initial attempt has left her seriously wounded, however outspoken she is. With luck, her injuries will curtail any further efforts for the coming months and give us enough time to complete our little project." He straightened his tie, gazing around the dark room. "We will monitor the situation and see how well able she is to continue her investigation. Your help and the help of US law enforcement powers in this would be much appreciated."

Suite's mouth morphed to a snarl. "Then I want help out west. This situation is fucked up. I've even brought the goddamned military in now and they still can't find those sons of bitches."

Kazemi leveled a gaze at Suite. "This is not our fight."

"Well, you'd better make it your fight. Don't forget I know who you are. Who *she* is. You don't want your secret society revealed to the world, do you?" He smiled, victory in his grasp.

Kazemi sighed. "Threats without teeth are such pitiable creatures. Unlike you, Mr. President, we have left no paper trail. No witnesses besides yourself and your co-conspirators. Should you stupidly make public some half-baked conspiracy theory, you will only look the desperate fool when we dump the very real proof of your malfeasance for all to see. But we need not go that route. Let's be reasonable. We have had a productive collaboration from your campaign through our work on Intel 1."

Suite's face reddened and his hand crumbled papers on his desk, but he swallowed, saying nothing. Kazemi continued.

"So we are in agreement. The terrorists out west are your problem to solve. We will monitor the detective using the full force of your intelligence apparatus. Should she resume her problematic inquiry, we will strike again. And this time, some disgraced policeman will not be able to save her."

31

GONE HOME

Gone watched Sacker thank the driver with some palmed bills and turn away from the van. Sweat from the sweltering heat stained the edges of his Bailey Ice Topper. He grasped the handles on the back of the wheelchair just as the engine coughed. The wheels of the hospital shuttle synced to the turn of those at her sides.

This is the last week in this chair.

But the truth was harder. She knew getting back on her feet would take time. Already she'd lost weeks in the hospital, under constant surveillance by the staff and hardly able to work. The physical burden of her injuries also took its toll on her ability to concentrate. She hoped that as she gained strength and returned to the comfort of her own space, she could get back to the case that now had taken on life and death significance for her.

I wasn't doing so well before the assassin.

She had to face that reality as well. One compensation at a time, the loss of function in her body continued to mount. And now with her father in the know, spilling the truth before Sacker without regard for the consequences, she would also have to deal with that.

She needed to eat. Anything with iron. Her hematocrit was still quite low from the blood loss. Weak and anemic, Gone was dizzy even when sitting.

Bloody steaks, a giant side order of clams and mussels, spinach and tofu. I'll mix it up with beans, liver, and rusted scaffolding if I had to.

The wheelchair bounced as Sacker pushed, the jarring sending bolts of pain down her arm. "You sure they have this thing set up correctly?"

He frowned. She immediately regretted the tone. Sacker was the one person she could count on.

"You're not ready to be out of bed yet," he said. "Look, there's only one reason you're not still in the hospital. That's because you had the green for homecare and rehab."

"Perks of skimming eight-figure hostile divorce cases."

"At least something good came out of them. Although by 'going home,' I think the hospital staff assumed *home*, not the damn office."

He accelerated with increasing annoyance, which made the bumping worse. But she was irritated herself. "I'm not going to sit at home and do nothing."

"I think going back to work with half a shoulder missing is the definition of a workaholic."

She tried to peek over her shoulder to see him, but the pain snapped her head back. "You seem in a great mood," she said, wincing.

"I'm happy you're out. Don't get me wrong. I've got some kind of PTSD about you in that hospital. Out here, back to the office, whatever — resets things a bit."

They reached the doorway and Sacker fumbled with the keys. He opened the door, squeezing the wheelchair through the frame. It gouged the wood lining.

"Sorry."

"Forget it. We'll fix it. I can't wait to get out of this thing."

She glanced around the interior of Gone Investigating. Not a soul present. Magazines in the lobby tossed in haphazard places. Empty chairs and couches. The only movement were the particles of dust glinting in the sun's rays from the window. The stillness unnerved her.

"It's so strange to see the place empty now," she said. "I suppose that's good. When I started, I could never imagine it full."

"We'll get it back up and running. You can't be taking on new clients right now. Shutting things down for a bit was the right move."

And watch my client base hemorrhage as much as I did.

Sacker dropped a stack of mail and a duffle bag on a chair. The bag landed with a thwack as well as the rattle of pills in bottles. In his hand, he held up an envelope.

"You got your ancestry form from ICE and Uncle Suite," he smirked. "Now in my case, I got all kinds of evidence for ancestors in America. Back to the damn slave ships." He eyed her. "But what's your story, China Girl? This going to be a problem?"

"Maybe," she sighed. *Time to change the subject.* "Is that bag a delivery for the pharmacy? I heard enough pills to stock the shelves."

"Can't a man bring his goods without an inquisition?" He winked at her. "This heroic body needs some nectar of the gods. Or something like that. But I'm not telling you nothing you don't know, am I?"

She'd called him out on his physical realities years ago in an interview for the Eunuch Maker case. She'd done her homework. She knew the typical maintenance of hormones. She wondered what it was like for him to keep his body in a form far from its default biochemical equilibrium. After he'd demanded the subject never come up again, she avoided broaching it. His bittersweet reaction today showed her something had changed within him about the subject. *Changed about how he feels about me.*

"I know it can't be easy."

"You got that right, sister. But it's easier for me than you right now."

She pointed to a couch in the lobby, once the living room of the repurposed home. "Dump me there. We need to map things out. I've got to get my head back in this case."

"Now? Today?" His eyebrows scraped the top of his head. "How about we put you in that ten-G hospital bed you're leasing and you take it easy? You've moved more today than since the incident."

"The *incident*?" she laughed, wincing again from the pain. "When I was shot down near dead on the streets of New York, you mean."

He stared at her, his face slack. She sighed.

"I have all night to cocoon in another hospital bed. Couch please."

He shook his head. "Okay. Let's try to do it better this time."

Getting from the van to the chair had been an awkward dance, but Sacker was a fast learner. This time, he bent much lower and spread his feet like a sumo wrestler. He wrapped one arm around her waist on her good side. His other stabilized her wrecked shoulder and arm. Her legs buckled again as he lifted her out of the chair. Wobbling, she managed to plant her feet and not topple. Groaning with the effort and pain, her face wrinkled.

Three feet, Grace. Three feet. One foot…in front of the other. There!

She slipped across the slick leather, a long purr escaping as she sank into its back.

Praise be endorphins. This is going to take a while.

He sat across from her in a chair, gaze forward and brows creased.

"So, Gracie," he began, the hesitancy putting her back on alert.

"Tyrell, let's not."

He ignored her.

"Something the doctor said bothered me. And your dad's words about your medical records."

"It's nothing."

"Nothing. I'm sorry but phrases like 'how long have you known' kind of get my attention."

She ground her teeth, focusing her thoughts. "Not now, Tyrell."

Please let it go. Please.

Different expressions played across his face, an internal battle waging. He changed the topic of the conversation.

"And what about dear old dad? I was getting the feeling that we were talking to a mafia boss."

"This is hard."

She wanted to jump across and hug him. Hold him tight and cry. One hundred emotions spun her, pummeling, stabbing, pulling. Gone put her fingers to her forehead and pressed. She had to clear her mind and focus.

"You have no idea how much your presence has meant to me," she said. "Beyond saving my life. Being here. Everyday. I know having a bleeding, bed-ridden invalid hasn't been pretty or fun. Thank you."

His face contorted into conflicting expressions. Concern. Affection. Frustration.

"But...." he began.

"But Dad," she said, shaking her head. "I just...can't. It's not about you. It's about me. Me and him. I've run from some things in my past. Run to escape them and do something with my life. I can't face that. Not now. Please understand."

She held his gaze.

"Well, when? I'm cool with secrets. I've got my own, remember? Even if you're too damn smart for me to hide anything from you. But maybe I need to know some things." His long arm extended toward the door. "In case you haven't noticed, it's getting a little crazy out there."

"Not because of dad. He's not part of the crazy that tried to get me killed. We need to focus on that." Her shoulder throbbed.

He threw up his hands. "What's the mystery? There's a killer after us. Left us flowers. Maybe Mirnateghi has a beef with us because of the Eunuch Maker."

"But wouldn't she be more focused on the ones chasing her for years at Intel 1? Why *me*?"

"Less fortified target. But we're going to change that."

Gone's lip moved outward, and her eyes narrowed. "I hope so, because it's clear to me that we were shining light where they couldn't let us, threatening to uncover things they need buried." She raised her good arm, her hand toward Sacker as he began to argue. "If we're going to prevent this from happening again, we need to get to the bottom of why someone hired a professional to gun me down. It *has* to be related to the investigation."

He pursed his lips, studying her. "So you said in the hospital. Too much coincidence for Mirnateghi to have hit at this time."

"Yes! Things just happened to come to a head? Right after asking questions about a top secret government project called China Girl?"

Sacker scowled. "That title is starting to worry me."

"We find a guy who left the project. Left a lot of money on the table, because he couldn't stomach something? Burleson's the kind of man who gets kicks from shooting animals in Africa. What turned a guy like that away?"

He chuckled. "Yeah, I wasn't seeing a soft side to him."

"The day we go see him, *bang*." She put a hand to her bandages. "Someone tries to take me out. Mirnateghi could have done it more quietly, had me disappear or die mysteriously with flowers in my hand. But some sniper on a rooftop in NYC at midday? That makes a *public* spectacle of me. Now what does that sound like to you?"

Sacker squinted. "Desperation."

"Exactly. We *scared* someone. We hardly have a handle on this criminality and we scared them enough to move so flagrantly. It's all tied together. I *know* it."

He opened his palms to the ceiling. "So, now what? You're in no shape for sleuthing. No pounding the pavement."

Gone scowled, glancing toward the wheelchair. "I hate those things," she whispered, a shudder running through her. "But maybe I'll need to bite my tongue and ride it a little longer."

"You're not thinking to—"

"There's that vaccine company. I want to visit. That's the craziest connection in all this. But at least there, I'm on home turf. If we can get some time with the scientists, maybe I can ferret out a connection."

"Vaxagen? You think there'll be leads there?"

"A giant scandal in the tens of billions likely involving a compromised president and his Iranian connections, prison conglomerates, weird construction companies, transportation department, and...a *vaccine* company?" She shook her head. "Always look for the outliers in the data. That's one of my rules."

He shrugged. "But everything in this crazy case is an outlier. Nothing's normal."

"But vaccines? That's the neon-light flag in a pile of red flags."

"So, we're planning a trip upstate." He rubbed his forehead. "Against doctor's explicit orders."

Gone smiled. "As soon as we can arrange it. Time to see what these guys are vaccinating against."

32

FIRST STRIKE

The sun arched down toward the entrance of the narrow crevice. Eight shadows stretched along its path. Light set the surrounding orange stone on fire.

Lopez finished searching the fifth hiker. Their group stood facing the sun, eyes slits, faces wrinkled in discomfort. He picked each clean. The burning radiance bathed his back, the setting sun reminding him that their time might be running out as well. They had to move faster.

We don't even know when the buzzer rings.

Six phones. He didn't ask why one of them had two. It didn't matter. They wouldn't be calling anyone. He tossed the last device to Lightfoote. She caught it mid-flight and dropped it in a bag.

Stealing from nature enthusiasts. It wasn't a high point, but phones were replaceable. Lives were not. And he'd taken many of those in this growing underground war. If the hikers had those phones, one of them would call his group in. It could very well mean capture. And he didn't fool himself: without the trio, the movement would falter. Ego had nothing to do with it. It was a critical reality he had to factor into his calculations.

"We might need to use the phones for help," one whispered, terrified to speak.

Lopez stepped in front of him. His shadow fell over the hiker's face, blocking the sun. The man's eyes opened. Their gazes met.

"You need to be alive for that. That only happens if you shut up. If you do as you're told." Lopez darted to the side, the glare assaulting the man's eyes again. Lopez pointed toward the light. "You head back to Vegas. You do not pass Go. You do not collect two hundred dollars. You do not come back in this direction. Or you die."

The man swallowed, his face scrunched and lower lip trembling. Houston slapped him on the back. He jumped.

"You're experienced," she chirped. "You'll find the way. We did, and this terrain is virgin to us." She sauntered off.

The hikers' eyes remained on Lopez.

"Don't tell anyone you saw us," he commanded. "Go. And don't look back." No one moved. "Go!"

The five dashed off down the slope, soon lost to sight. Now that they were out of the way, the information gleaned from the ICE agents could be put to use.

"They're gonna tell," sang Lightfoote. She stared down the path, one leg propped up on a fallen boulder, the other holding the sack of phones.

"Of course," he rumbled. "But the more threat, the more they'll keep to themselves until they're around others. It's a day's hike back to Vegas if you're not hiding from the law. Downhill. That's the easy route. No way they're coming back this way."

"Loose end. A lot of loose ends."

"Hopefully not enough to hang us with."

He turned toward Houston, who had scaled the ledge beside the cave. Her feet jutted from the hole and over the ledge.

"What if he falls out?" He frowned. "Cave's not as deep as I thought."

Houston hopped back down. "ICE gets pretty good standard-issue restraints. It's going to be hard for them to move much. Other than that," she winked, "I hope they get hazard pay." She turned to Light-foote. "The phones?"

"We can't risk getting tracked. Any cellular signal is going to be detected. These brought ICE straight to those hikers. They could to us."

"Nothing we can get from them?"

"Dick pics to unsuspecting girls, maybe. We don't need the GPS. I say we just leave the bag here with the blackshirts. Better chance they're found."

Houston exhaled. "We've lost an hour, but gained a lifetime of information."

"It does make sense the search is focused around Vegas," said Lightfoote. "Or we'd be swimming in blackshirts. Path ahead should be relatively clear until the town."

"The *conscious* pair were useful," said Houston, eyes darting toward Lopez.

He shrugged. "There were three. We got what we needed."

She glared at him. "What we *needed*? We're getting fucked. Special forces are going to set up a center of operations at Mount Charleston. I saw the agent's eyes. He wasn't lying. Weren't we headed there?"

"That was the plan."

"So what now? Where else can we go in this dead zone?"

"We don't have the supplies to take our time out here." Lopez glanced toward the mountains. "We don't have a choice."

"Necessity is good," said Lightfoote, "But invention is its mother. You two aren't thinking straight. Best news we had in a while was that they're headed to Mount Charleston. They'll bring some kind of command-and-control vehicle. Unchecked, that's bad news for us. They'll coordinate a much more effective search with those troops and tech. But, if we can take that unit, we neuter their search grid in this region. We'll have access to their intel and communications. That just might be enough to get us the hell out of Dodge."

"Bold move," said Houston.

"It's not a big town," said Lopez, shaking his head. "If we get there first, we should be able to set an ambush."

"Assuming they don't have a damn platoon," Houston gestured. Her matted hair stuck to the sides of her face.

He approached and brushed the strands back. "You said it yourself,

Sara. They don't have the numbers for that. Not yet. It will be a small team."

"Or we're screwed. Even so, it'll be Seal Team Six or the like," she sighed. "Not like those bozos up there. We'll need to be ready."

He glanced to the ground beside them. Laid out was the full collection of arms they took from the camp. Three of the newer-issue M4 assault rifles and three standard Sig P320 handguns. A limited set of magazines for the weapons. Two boxes of shells for a lone shotgun.

"On our best game," said Lopez. "If we don't strike hard and end it fast, we won't last."

Lightfoote walked between the pair, placing a hand on the shoulder of each. "Get me in that thing. I can use their digital links to hack into their system."

The corner of Houston's mouth twitched upward. "That's usually very bad for our enemies."

Lopez stooped to collect his weapons of choice. "Then we get up there fast. Middle of the night, I predict. Scout the town. If they're not there already, we figure out the likely locations they'll stop."

Lightfoote smiled and grabbed the shotgun from the ground.

"We'll be ready."

Suite Presidency, Term 2, 1st Year

"PATRIOT EDUCATION ACT" UNVEILED

by Marsha Kaye, *the Washington Free Beacon*

Surrounded by some of America's most promising students, spanning from elementary school to college age, Suite spokeswoman Kim Young announced the creation of a wide-ranging program revamping federal education standards. The Patriot Education Act will create a series of capitalistic incentives, both financial and regulatory, for local, state, and private institutions relying on federal grants to enact curriculum reform.

A long-sought creation of Suite's master campaign manager Stan Brennem, the Act is set to revitalize and correct every level of the struggling American educational system.

Under the new regulations of the PEA, teachers at all levels must adhere to English as the sole, official language of the nation. All classroom activities will be conducted in English, as the Founders intended, and alien language speakers will be sent to remedial programs created by the local and state governments until they can assimilate into the US culture. "American exceptionalism," a long-standing patriotic term objected to by many leftist groups, is declared as a cultural value to be instilled in schoolchildren from an early age, correcting years of liberal influence.

All schools will employ textbooks produced by a federally approved organization as yet undetermined. In the running is the textbook giant O'Connor-Mountain of Texas, a company that has suffered mob justice from the Left from controversy over its boldness to teach that the Civil War was economic based, labeling slaves as workers in the plantations of the Old South.

Higher education advocacy groups continue to seek the

status quo, complaining that these facts are partisan political motives coloring the content of the textbooks produced under the PEA. In a familiar case of overreaction, they predicted doom, extending their hysteria to the discredited science of evolution, fetal development, and global warming, as well as historical depictions of controversial ideas and persons.

The coastal elites have been particularly vocal. "They're already teaching revisionist history," moaned Ria Evans, once-jailed activist of state education in Seattle. She and other so-called intellectuals raised the discredited claims of a Native American genocide, the absence of communistic socialism in the New Deal, and other favorite propaganda talking points of anti-American influence groups. Their words remind many of the Soviet Union in the 1960s with the Orwellian lies brainwashing entire generations.

Provisions in the PEA provide government agencies with both positive and negative incentives to adopt the new policies. Universities, secondary and primary schools, as well as researchers and professional academic elites, can be stripped of their tax status and federal funding for failure to adequately adopt the national guidelines. Seditious or anti-American acts by faculty or students can also lead to financial consequences. Examples of these seditious acts given by lawmakers include dangerous protests, flag burnings, and other subversive actions.

"It's blatantly unconstitutional," complained Susan Romero, head of the discredited American Civil Liberties Union. "We will fight this until our last breath."

Conservatives have long fought to protect America from the corrosive teachings in the liberal bias of higher education. Many in the Republican education reform movement have argued that steeping young children in traditional viewpoints on social and scientific issues would be as important as addressing the known bias at higher levels. The PEA attempts to right these wrongs in a single effort, although the president was focused on colleges and universities in his recent remarks.

In a well-received speech before the Heritage Foundation,

Suite highlighted the suppression of speakers advocating for traditional values at many universities due to radical student protests.

"Today this sends a strong message to the teachers and institutions working to suppress conservative dissent, to those seeking to keep young Americans — and every American, not only the young — from challenging biased, crazy, far-left ideology. If the university blocks free speech, they will lose funding. It's that simple."

The president also turned to other aspects of the bill in an interview with the Chronicle of Higher Education, asserting that the changes would be sweeping.

"This is just the beginning. The first in a series of steps we will take to defend students' rights. Our children are under siege from degenerate, leftist teachings that seek to brainwash them from an early age. Lies. So much of it. Lies that hurt our children and our country. Anti-American lies that have to be stopped to protect our children and our future as a sovereign nation. Our culture is at stake. Our history. Our people. The leftists want to exterminate it all, replace us all with lies and immigrants and traitors. We won't have it."

The new PEA act was outrageously labeled as "redundant and unnecessary" by the head of a group of public universities. Ignoring the brainwashing and intimidation tactics of liberal elites, he claimed that "Under the Constitution, all Americans, public and private universities included, must support freedom of speech and the press. Conservative viewpoints are free to be expressed. They are often expressed. Universities pay conservative speakers millions of dollars every year for the privilege to speak from elevated podiums in our schools. Rescinding such paid privileges is not in violation of the first amendment. They are not owed our podiums. Teaching the broad consensus of scientists and historians is not violating free speech or is anti-American. It's teaching the truth. When the government starts telling us what we can teach, we aren't free, we stop being a place of learning and inquiry. We become propaganda mouthpieces for those in power."

Such outrageous claims were not making much of an impact on our administration or their patriotic supporters in Congress.

"The politically correct thought police were just fine imposing their lies and traitorous ideas," said Senator Patrick Oldman of Nevada. "Well, real Americans have had enough. Real patriots are in power now, and these radical socialists are not going to brainwash our children anymore. A new American generation will rise in the place of the decadent old."

33

QUEENS

A fogged moon hung in the sky in Queens, silhouetting the skyscrapers across the East River. Ghostly behind the thin clouds, the orb took on an orange hue from the reflected street lights. For John Savas, the air was pregnant and ominous.

Everything is charged before a mission.

He returned his gaze to the warehouse across the street, leaning against the edge of the roof. His hand rested on a set of binoculars. He adjusted the micro-earpiece compulsively.

He was working on several days of little sleep, but the adrenaline tonight promised to keep him sharp. After flipping the terrorist in Washington, he'd flown back to New York to lay a trap. He maintained the forced division of Intel 1, remaining separated from Cohen and the bulk of the agency. He wasn't going to give Suite or his minions any excuse to shut anything down.

He deployed a special set of operatives for this job, resources allocated from Intel 1 at a distance. Either they hit pay dirt tonight, or they began again from square one.

With the advanced intel, his teams had prepared well. Portable cameras with night vision and several motion detectors covered all the warehouse's possible angles. They'd swept the surrounding buildings. A team in a nearby van monitored the surveillance. Snipers waited atop buildings around the entrance, two flanking him. A crack strike force from Intel 1 lay hidden on the ground, awaiting instructions.

The trap was set.

The Mjolnir soldier had spilled the details. His precision convinced Savas the man was broken, that he'd handed them real information. And it was every bit as horrific as he had expected.

The terrorist group planned a morning strike on the Masjid Al-Mamoor mosque in Queens. Called the Jamaica Muslim Center, it housed a mosque, community resources, and a cafeteria. It was also attached to a school. Pre-K through twelve. It would be a bloodbath.

The plans were for another bombing. That meant those gathered tonight would be their demolitions experts. His team did not fool themselves. Every Mjolnir soldier was an experienced combat veteran. There was no escaping the likelihood of casualties in his team. But the monsters summoned to the abandoned warehouse tonight had to be stopped.

His cell vibrated. He pulled it out of his pocket and glared at the screen.

Rebecca? She knows what's happening tonight!

He unlocked the device. "Targets are assembling. It's game time."

"I'm sorry. Some news. I would have messaged, but I wanted to tell you."

"Quickly." He strained below as another vehicle approached the entrance. Headlights bounced at each pothole.

"It's Grace Gone. The detective who helped us catch the Eunuch Maker."

"I'm not likely to forget her."

"She was shot last week in Manhattan. Assassination style. Rifle. Heavy rounds. She's recuperating."

"Jesus." Savas glanced to the side. "That's not random violence. That's a hit. That's Mirnateghi."

"My thoughts," came Cohen's voice over the speaker. "There are, of course, other possibilities. She's angered powerful people. Mobsters."

"A hit like that's beyond mob. This is resource heavy. Deeply professional intention. That's one vindictive woman."

"Be careful, John. You're sure about this soldier?"

"As I can be. We broke him. It's not the old Mjolnir. This recruit had a family. He was vulnerable."

"What did you do?"

"Bent the law. I needed a shower afterwards. But I think hundreds of lives, lives of children, that's worth a little bending."

"Sometimes you keep bending until you don't know what's straight anymore."

"We can talk morality later. Right now, we have to stop them. I need to get my head back in the game."

"Of course. You message me the second this thing is over."

"Will do. Later."

He hung up and exhaled.

Grace Gone shot?

That pushed the envelope. The PI certainly wrecked one of Mirnateghi's plans, but that was a one-off, a fluke that Intel 1 happened to overlap with her case. It was unlikely to happen again. So why spend the resources to take her out? Was the Iranian really that vindictive?

If so, it meant clouded judgment. It meant mistakes that Intel 1 could exploit if they were ready. More and more he was confident putting Cohen in charge of operations was the right move.

"Eagle 1, this is Sentry."

The voice crackled in his earpiece. "Eagle 1, go ahead."

"Van pulled up. Armed escort for a VIP. Over."

Savas pulled out a pair of binoculars and scanned below. The terrorists were entering the building.

"Copy that. Sighted. Got to be the mission leader. They'll just be setting up. We don't wait for them to get comfortable. Greenlit. Signal the strike team. Do you copy?"

"Affirmative. Sentry out."

And so it plays.

A door rolled up from a rusted delivery truck parked across the road from the warehouse entrance. Out poured twelve Intel 1 agents. They were met with the same number sprinting from the sides.

Spits cut through the city soundscape. The snipers around him fired. Several of his men below dropped from corresponding sniper fire from the terrorists.

They had their outlooks placed well.

He traced several weapons flashes to windows scattered across the building. Glass shattered as the Intel 1 forces unloaded a heavy barrage at street level and above. A shadow plummeted to the ground from the opposing building. The strike force rushed in, disappearing from sight.

And then the gunfire erupted in earnest.

34

AMBUSH

Lopez ignored the moonshadows dancing from the ponderosa pines. He welcomed the cool breeze after the desert heat, but his focus was elsewhere. Fatigue threatened to dull their responses and minds. They couldn't afford to fail now.

The trio had reached the resort town of Mount Charleston. A gray radiance glowed off the surrounding peaks that dwarfed the small village. The height of Mount Charleston itself shimmered in the distance.

They approached off the main road. It afforded the easiest path while providing them advanced notice for incoming traffic. They expected an important arrival, if it wasn't already waiting for them in the town.

Our escape window is closing.

Rustic holiday lodging greeted them as they exited the pines. Upscale Levittown log cabins from mass producers sprouted like mushrooms. They sat in the middle of older, less picturesque homes.

Houston held up her hand and halted the march. They squatted under the needles in the rocky landscape. She indicated two sets of thicker power lines above.

"The military's going to want a center of functionality. Power.

Water. Internet. Space. We follow the lines into the town, size up the possibilities."

"They could choose a bunch of sites," said Lopez. "The town's small, but we'll still have to cover some ground to check them all."

She sighed. "We don't want to give them time to dig in. We have the element of surprise. That won't last much longer."

"Tourists," said Lightfoote.

Houston cocked her head to the side. "Tourists?"

"Tourists are change. Modernization. Money. Lodging for the well heeled and spoiled. They like their amenities. They pay for them." Her head bobbed back and forth. "Find a nice ski lodge. Views. Power. Internet. Parking space for the damn military trucks."

"Good idea," he agreed. "Still, Sara's right. The power lines should get us in the right direction."

Lightfoote rolled her eyes. "Well, duh."

They returned their attention to their surroundings. The electrical trail was simple to follow. Within minutes the three entered a more expansive area with broader roads. A collection of taller buildings of several stories rose before them. To their left a series of log cabins on stilts exploded like flowers in a field beside a steep drop off.

"This is it," said Lightfoote. "They're coming here. Angel says so."

Lopez and Houston glanced at the former FBI hacker and then locked eyes with each other. He smiled. "Promising, I agree. And we never disagree with an angel."

Houston pointed toward the larger lodge. "They'll commandeer that. Good space in front. Vehicle space. Generator in the back. The logistics are good."

He smirked. "And what soldier doesn't want to invade a mountain resort."

"Lot of civilians," muttered Houston, her eyes dancing over the elevated cabins.

"A lot more disappearing into Suite's internment camps," growled Lopez. "We need a way out, or we lose the bigger fight."

Collateral damage. A term that once nauseated him. *What have we become?* Lopez stared at the ground. Maybe they were becoming what was required to stop even greater atrocities. But who was to decide?

Where were the lines? What risk was too much? And why was God so silent?

"And we need a way in," said Lightfoote. "Into their network. I'm counting on them bringing the best high-tech mobile assault vehicles Uncle Sam could buy."

An engine roared in the distance. Lopez squinted at a glow of artificial lights spilling over an incline in the road.

"Diesel. Heavy motor," said Houston, yanking on the straps of her Stetson. "We've got sixty seconds."

He indicated the cabins. "They'll pull to the front door of the lodge. Sara and Angel position on either end of the building. Cover behind the sign in front. The back's out of sight. Short sprint to the middle."

They nodded.

"I'll take that utility building in the center of the lot. We wait until they check with the locals inside. Then I'll hit the truck from behind, Sara from the front, Angel from inside."

"If civilians show?"

"Neutralize them," said Lopez, his jaw set. "Quietly."

They sprinted across the road and into the parking lot. Both women assumed their positions along the wooden walls of the building. At one end, Lightfoot checked the chamber in her shotgun. At the other, Houston placed her hat on the ground and readied her Browning.

Lopez reached the utility building. To maintain the rustic theme, it was designed to match the lodge. Aged wood and pioneer windows glinted back at him.

Praise be to God it's not a metal structure with real locks.

He smashed the door in, wood fragments splintering. Luckily, it faced the resort. He entered, propping the wrecked structure against the frame. He peered through the window and down the road.

Gravel crunched as headlights blasted through the soft moonlight. An engine churned like a tornado. A lumbering six-wheeled vehicle rumbled past the shed.

Holy hell.

Suite's administration had been militarizing domestic law enforcement, but this was something else. It matched the raid on the camp where they'd deployed US military forces within the country. But the sheer bulk and hostility of the vehicle struck him.

If that thing's filled with soldiers, we're dead.

A large machine gun protruded from the roof, and beside it, thick antennae rose skyward. The truck resembled a motorized box cutter, only sharp windows in the front replaced the cutting blade. The rest of the vehicle was plated with thick armor.

He racked his brain to recall any similar military vehicles but came up empty. He'd be charging that thing ignorant of what might lay within.

The assault vehicle rocked to an angry stop before the entrance. Lopez chanted under his breath.

> *Arise, O LORD. Stand against them,*
> *and bring them to their knees.*
> *Rescue me from the wicked with your sword.*
> *By the power of your hand, O LORD, destroy those who*
>   *look to this world for their reward.*

The front side doors swung open. Soldiers in desert combat gear leapt out and slammed the doors. They moved toward the lodge entrance.

He strained to listen. A hinge squeaked, and a door clattered shut. The men were inside the lodge.

Now.

He shoved the broken door to the side and raced out of the shed toward the armored beast.

35

CBRN

The door to the lodge swung shut, the soldiers out of sight.

Go!

Houston sprinted toward the metal monster. In the corner of her eye, she saw the blur of Lightfoote racing toward her and the entrance. But her focus was on the truck and the parking lot.

Lopez was charging across the asphalt toward the back of the truck. She didn't know how many they had inside that tank, but he was going to need help. He disappeared behind the thing. There was a metal clank. She held the automatic rifle against her chest and spun around the side of the vehicle.

She jumped away from the truck as Lopez fired into the interior. The soldiers' screams were cut short.

He held up his hand toward her. "Two inside. Dead. Keep the peace."

He darted inside. She spun in an arc, surveying the lot and road. A few lights popped in the adjacent cabins.

We've got to move fast.

Two muffled shotgun blasts came from the lodge.

Angel.

A wet slap hit the pavement behind her followed by another. She didn't need to guess.

"See to Angel!" he yelled. "I'll hold the truck!"

She dashed around the monster wheels and to the lodge entrance. Her back slammed against the wall as she prepared to pivot and enter the structure. At that moment the door swung open. She aimed.

"Angel arriving." Lightfoote leapt out of the lodge. Trails of smoke issued from the barrel of her pump-action shotgun. She sprinted to the back of the vehicle. "Come on, Sara!"

Houston followed her around to the back of the van. Lopez waved them inside.

"Holy bloodbath, Batman," gawked Lightfoote. Red goo spattered a foldout panel with keyboard and monitor. She sat in one of the benches arrayed on either side of the interior. "I'm gonna need a long shower after this."

Houston surveyed the lodges around them. More windows lit up across the street. She turned back to the vehicle. "What happened inside the main lodge?"

Lightfoote fiddled with thick panels on the sides of the vehicles. She popped several open to reveal its hardware. "Two soldiers checking in. They won't check out. Manager was agreeable to lock himself in the closet. I took his mobile."

"Why only two soldiers inside?" barked Lopez over his shoulder, scanning the surroundings with Houston.

Her fingers clacked over the extendable keyboard attached to the wall panels. "It's a Fuchs 4. Newest German CBRN export to NATO."

"CBRN? English!" he growled.

"Chemical, biological, radiological, and nuclear. It's a reconnaissance vehicle. Next-gen satellite-linked, mobile warfare armored doohicky-majig. Two reconnaissance personnel in back, standard." She flicked her head toward the bodies outside. "Appears they're neutralized."

Houston frowned. "What the hell is a chem-bio-nuke truck doing up here?"

"No idea," said Lightfoote, adjusting knobs on the panels and staring at the screen in front of her. "But let's see what we can find out."

Static popped, and there was a whistling tone. Distorted voices chattered on the com.

"We have confirmation," came a voice. "Bunch of hikers came across armed suspects, one with a scar. Repeat, positive identification of El Marcado. Trails between here and Vegas. Do you copy, Mount Charleston?"

"Shit," hissed Houston. "That was fast. Hurry, Angel. If we don't respond soon, they'll know something's up."

"And…we're in." Lightfoote smiled at the screen. "Got the search grid. You were right. This is a node. They were going to coordinate from here. Reinforcements called in, expected tomorrow morning."

"You find us a way out?" asked Houston.

"Yeah. They're spread very thin right now. Lots of holes. We're going to have to trust my memory of the map. There are several minor roads they can't cover. We can thread around their checkpoints. If we move *now*."

"Not in this!" said Houston. The truck might as well be firing off flares. The darkness outside pressed in on her, the dragnet all but visible to her eyes and tightening around them. They needed to move!

"No. We steal some wheels. Get to the next town outside the search web. Ditch the wheels. Get new wheels. Three cycles and we're ghosts."

Houston grunted. "Okay. Plenty of cars around here. We hotwire one of the older ones. Let's go!"

"Wait! Hold on a sec as this finishes," she said. "There. I downloaded some malware modules. If they're stupid enough to use this truck again, their data feed gets routed to some servers I control. And the GPS data, if I can just…"

"We don't have time for more!"

Lopez put his hand on her arm. She stared at him and glanced to the skies. Angel worked in mysterious ways.

"I found the chip signals," said Lightfoote.

"The ones in the detainees?" Houston's skin tingled. "How?"

Lightfoote's typing filled the space inside.

"Part of the command and control data. Easily accessed."

Houston still couldn't wrap her mind around things. "These soldiers are tracking detainees through the chips? *Why?*"

"Maybe thought we brought some chipped folks with us," suggested Lopez. "Could track us that way."

"Okay, and so?"

Lightfoote stopped typing. "This map shows all the chip locations. Have a quick look."

A monitor glowed in multiple colors. There were six circles of light and a host of small dots for miles around them. One of the circles dwarfed the others. "What the hell is that?"

"Five blobs. The camps, I'd wager. The sixth one's different, several times the intensity of the others. It looks like tens, hundreds of thousands of chip signals."

Houston's mouth hung open. The numbers were impossible, the concentration of people difficult for her to grasp. The blob of color on the monitor throbbed like a million hearts pressed together. "Where is it?" she whispered.

"Yucca Mountain," said Lightfoote, her eyes a green fire. "The nuclear waste facility."

Lopez called from outside. "Lights are coming on around us. We need to move now, or we'll never be able to act on any of this!"

The pair continued to stare at the screen. Lightfoote touched her hand. Houston gripped it back. Warmth flowed between them, a balm in the face of something cold and inhuman. She glanced toward the Fuchs doors.

The pair leapt out, Lopez indicating a line of parked cars. "Old '80s Toyota someone's kept up. Angel and Sara get it started. I'll ditch the plates."

The trio sped toward the vehicles.

36

VAXAGEN

"**G**race Gone!"

Gone opened her eyes to the voice. She was greeted by a green forest outside a giant window in the new biotech's building. The trip to the vaccine biotech had already exhausted her. Sacker and the doctors were, of course, right. Her body needed much more rest, certainly more than it would get pounding the beat of this case. A sea of pines disappeared as Sacker spun the wheelchair. He stopped on a dime when she faced their tour guide.

He's getting adept at this.

A woman in a white lab coat beamed at her in the doorway. She wore an ID clipped to a top pocket that held markers and a folded pair of glasses. *Triller, Nina. PhD.* A pair of purple nitrile gloves poked up from a set of pockets at her hips. She sported jeans and sneakers, an attractive face, and a severe blond ponytail. It gave her the appearance of a whiz kid from a science romcom.

She gasped, out of breath from the dash to meet her guest. "You have no idea how excited I am to meet you. Speaking as a biologist, your work on the Eunuch Maker case was amazing. Riveting!" She frowned, catching her enthusiasm. "This assassination attempt—horrible. You're an inspiration. Welcome to Vaxagen!"

Well. That's nice.

She smiled and held out her hand from the chair. Triller leapt toward her and shook, sending flashes of pain through her injured shoulder.

"Please forgive me for the short notice," Gone opened, her voice strained. "And the time constraints. I'm really not supposed to be here. My physicians would have a fit."

Triller nodded. "As a basic researcher, I understand your devotion. Not always great for health or quality of life."

"I'm also sorry about the armed guards." Gone indicated the two men in black suits outside the building. "Mr. Sacker here is a bit over-protective. We try to scramble my schedule, only tell a few people my plans."

"Completely understandable after what happened."

"Would you like to begin the tour now, then?"

"Yes, please. Thank you."

The scientist gestured to Sacker. "Follow me, please."

She led them out of the office and down a glass-walled corridor.

"I'm sure you've noticed all the glass," she gestured, swiping a keycard over a scanner. There was a click and two glass doors separated in the middle. She led them through.

"Yeah," said Sacker. "I'm starting to feel a bit like a wheelchair in a China shop."

"It's to foster a collaborative atmosphere. Transparency between the groups."

"Very interesting," said Gone.

"So must be this case you're working on," lilted Triller, giving Gone a glance from the side.

"One I can't talk about. But your company's work could help me understand one aspect of it."

She stopped in front of a large, automated platform. Robots moved samples from cold storage to warm cultures. Plates and vials danced through a series of space-age equipment. "I'll show you our basic setup. Some things are proprietary, so that could only come with some serious NDAs. Anything non-confidential I'm happy to share and explain."

Gone ogled the rows of machines and computers, sighing.

Tens of millions here. What I could do with a tenth of this.

She refocused. "From what I could gather online, you produce antibodies and vaccines for addictive drugs?"

"Yes!" Triller's eyes lit up. "As a postdoc, I helped develop a new immunological platform. Everything in front of you is the end result of those early years. But instead of me working sixteen hour days to do it by hand, now we have some automation and AI."

"How does it work?"

"It's based on a naturally occurring surface coat of a virus, a dense carpet of protein. We can tag this coat, cover it with anything we want. That includes small chemicals like nicotine or heroin. We inactivate the pathogen, inject the dead coats into animals or people. That creates a powerful immune response to the attached chemical."

She motioned to several rows of robotic arms hovering over rows of plastic plates. Each plate contained hundreds of tiny circular wells inside.

"These machines are part of that process. Here we're taking immune cells from the blood of vaccinated subjects. We clone antibody genes from single cells."

Gone's eyes narrowed. "So the animal or person develops antibodies that bind the drug, remove it from circulation."

"Exactly. The goal is for addictive diseases to have immunological treatments. Just like any infectious disease or cancer."

Sacker leaned in. "What about alcohol?"

She frowned. "Well, I can't go into details, but it's tricky. For drugs that reach high levels in the body, our approach hasn't been so effective. There are only so many antibodies a body can make. The immune response can't clear enough of the substance for significant efficacy."

Gone leaned forward in the chair. "Which brings me to some very specific questions which I hope that you can answer. From what you've said, I would expect this approach to work best for the most potent, most toxic of substances. Those that are deadly at very low concentrations."

She beamed. "Yes! You've likely read about our work with fentanyl. It's been in the papers. Fentanyl is very potent at much lower concentrations than heroin. That's why so many people overdose on it. But we've shown in mice that our fentanyl vaccine sops up enough to render the drug impotent. Early human trials are very promising."

"You can prevent overdose?" gaped Sacker, his eyes widening.

"In animals, yes. Obviously, the ethics of inducing overdose in humans precludes direct testing in a controlled scientific environment, but we believe it will in the field."

"And if it works with fentanyl, which is a hundred times more powerful than morphine," said Gone, "then it would work even better with carfentanyl, which is ten thousand times more powerful."

Triller's face tightened. "Ah, yes. That would be a logical deduction."

"A deduction? You haven't pursued this line of research?"

"Carfentanyl isn't widely available on the street. It's not a problem in addictive diseases."

"But of course, regarding carfentanyl, there are other areas of interest." She locked eyes with Triller.

Triller drew a long breath. "Possibly."

Gone held her functional arm out to the side of the wheelchair. Sacker placed a manila folder in her palm. She brought it to her chest and removed a piece of paper. "These government documents indicate that Vaxagen recently signed several contracts with Homeland Security. Including for the production of carfentanyl antibodies and vaccine doses. Not R&D. But actual product production contracts."

The woman's mouth hung open as she stared at the printout. "How did you get these?"

"Isn't the Department of Defense very interested in such products? If I remember correctly, carfentanyl has been weaponized by Russia. They even used it on terrorists in that Moscow theatre. Killed *everyone* along with the terrorists, sadly, including some British nationals that MI6 did autopsies on."

Her face was slack, eyes wide. "We...I...can't comment on any of that." She looked back to the paper in Gone's hand. "Please. Can you tell me how you got that?"

The woman would say no more, but it was enough. Tumblers clicked in Gone's mind. Homeland contracting for countermeasures to an opioid chemical warfare agent sent shivers through her. She suppressed the reaction. She needed to focus. She was going to get her hands on those countermeasures. *The antibodies.* This called for a trick play.

Gone's eyes fluttered to the side. "Wow! Those are some big minus-eighty freezers! What do you store in there?"

Triller blinked several times. She followed Gone's gaze. "Our freezer farm? You'd like to see that?"

She grinned and nodded.

Triller glanced at the folder in Gone's lap. Hesitating, she led them toward several towering box-shaped machines humming by the glass wall between rooms. "These hold our antibody clones in cryo-preservation."

"And what, you just keep the DNA of the clones in some big freezer or something? Why?"

She ignored Sacker's glance.

Play along, Tyrell. Let me lead.

Triller's shock faded as her enthusiasm returned. "DNA can be a very stable molecule in the right conditions. We have DNA stored in refrigerators and freezers, as well as in certain microbial cells that act as carriers."

"You really have DNA of clones stored here? Inside? This feels like a movie."

"Sure!" She smiled. "I'll show you."

Triller reached for a pair of clean gloves on a bench. She yanked on a huge lever, popping open the freezer door. Fogged air and shards of ice spilled out as she scanned inside and pulled out a plastic box. In the box were rows of small plastic tubes the size of disposable eyedroppers. "These are actually pretty fresh. Optimized antibodies for…well, for certain compounds after multiple rounds of enhancement. These will be shipped to GMP facilities soon to produce the antibodies that the clones code for."

Triller displayed the box in front of Gone. Before the scientist could stop her, Gone grabbed the tray of tubes with one hand. The rack jerked, and the tubes spilled over her.

"Oh God!" Gone shouted, trying to grab the tubes, dragging them over the piece of paper in her lap.

Just a little DNA. Only a little from the lip of the tube.

Triller swooped in and scooped the tubes up, replacing them in the box. "Don't touch, please!" she cried. "I'm sorry. We don't touch anything without gloves!"

Sacker glared at her. "Is it dangerous?"

"Not to us," she said, replacing the box in the freezer and pushing the level up to seal it. "But we can introduce contaminants. It's easy to pick up DNA from the environment. Bacterial, viruses, that kind of thing. Some of these things could impact our cellular expression systems down the pipeline. Sorry to snatch it. I should have given you the rules. My fault for getting so excited."

"I'm *so* sorry," said Gone, plastering as silly a grin on her face as she could muster. "I was *dying* to look. It was just so interesting!"

"Yes, well. Okay, then." She inhaled. "What else did you want to see?"

Gone grimaced and moaned, touching her shoulder with her good arm. "I think my doctors know a little more than me about healing. I'm sorry, Dr. Triller. You've been so kind. But the pain is returning." She turned to Sacker, who stared with a perplexed look. "Tyrell can take me to the van. I think I need to get back and rest."

Triller's face fell. "Oh, of course. I'll show you out. But if you ever want to visit again, ah, maybe talk more about your case…"

"Oh yes. I'll call you. I hope to come back soon."

The woman frowned but led them to the exit.

37

ANTIBODIES

S acker held his finger to the button on the van's chair lift until the lift reached position. He moved behind the chair, pulling it inside. He secured the runners to the floor, attached the tie-down to the hooks, and positioned the vehicle belts, careful to avoid her injured shoulder.

"You're getting very good at this," said Gone, focused on him.

Sacker couldn't endure her glance for very long. There was too much emotion. Too much power there.

From me, or from her?

A question with an answer he didn't want to face. He walked around the outside, secured the doors, and ducked into the driver's seat.

Work. Focus on work.

He checked in with their newly hired security team. Their head-lights flicked on and off behind him. Ready to roll. "So, that exit we just made. What the hell was all that about?"

"Interview was over. I got what I wanted, and she wasn't going to spill the beans. They've got them all gagged there about the contracts."

"What about the bit at the end? You were grilling her like a prose-cuting attorney and then, *bang!* Suddenly you're a clueless high school science wannabe. And a clumsy one. I don't know *what* you were doing, but I know you were doing *something*."

He started the engine, released the brake, and pulled out from the parking space. A few short turns, and there was a ramp directly to the highway.

"Decades ago," said Gone, "a big-name lab claimed to have made a pivotal discovery." Her voice hiccupped as the van bounced along the asphalt. "Turned out they'd co-discovered a new and medically relevant gene. Problem was that it exactly matched the gene a competing lab had recently published." She laughed. "And it just so happened that the competing group had sent them some other samples and paperwork in response to a request for materials, common in science."

Sacker swerved onto the highway, his brow furrowed.

Where's she going with this?

"Long story short, because the competing lab had made so much of the gene in question, the DNA was everywhere. Like dust all around the lab. In other samples, on the paper and fabrics in the rooms involved. This unscrupulous group was able to clone it from pieces of paper. They homogenized the paper, processed it with the appropriate chemicals and protocols, amplified tiny quantities of contaminating DNA. They then tried to pass it off as their own discovery."

He peeked in the rearview window at her. "How were they caught?"

"Never proven. Just a rumor." She padded the manila folder in her lap. "But the principle is valid."

Sacker's eyes widened as his gaze returned to the road. "Wait a minute. Are you saying that your crazy clumsy act…did you just try to steal their clones?"

"I'm banking that I got a little plasmid DNA from the tubes on the papers in here. These were fresh carfentanyl antibody clones prepared for expression at GMP facilities. High concentration and purity, Likely in standard expression vectors for this sort of thing."

"Did she say they were carfentanyl? She confirmed it? I thought she was dodging you there."

"She was dodging. She stopped herself. Nearly said it. I was paying attention. Anything else, she would have just named the target of the antibodies, But she bit her tongue because this production contract is top secret."

"Why? What is going on?"

There was a pause. Sacker knew those few seconds were like three days of processing time for mere mortals like himself.

"I don't know," she said. "It *could* just be protected for military use. But that feels weak. Those were large orders. There hasn't been any rash of chemical warfare attacks with carfentanyl, that one Russian test case notwithstanding. The army can't be screaming for such countermeasures. It's for something else. Something that someone thinks they need right now."

"But what?"

"Good question. Why would you want truckloads of a cutting edge prophylactic countermeasures against a deadly and weaponized version of an opioid drug? A drug that isn't any sort of real threat to the US military at the moment? Why would you contract that out in a clandestine, likely illegal, multi-departmental government program named after these drugs?"

"China Girl," whispered Sacker. A chill ran up his spine. Putting together a dark government program with paranoia about a chemical attack was getting too close to James Bond doomsday scenarios. "They're seriously interested in protecting themselves from it, spending all that money. Why? And what's the bigger picture?" He shook his head. "Something's going on."

"Which is what I've been saying." She thumped the folder again. "So, the genetics and function of antibodies is well mapped. I'll be able to use that knowledge to clone the genes."

"To study them?"

"That would be interesting, but no. It's not hobby time. This is survival. Someone wants a lot of people protected from aerosolized carfentanyl. These same someones want us *dead*. I figured, maybe it would be good to have some countermeasures ourselves. Because I'm afraid we might need them."

"Wait. Make it? How? Don't tell me you have GMP-or-whatever facilities in that basement!"

"No," said Gone. "That's way beyond even our enhanced yet still humble budgets. But we know someone who can. Someone with the secrecy and resources to do this. Someone we've worked with before to do scientific forensics. Someone who'll have *a lot* of interest in Mirnateghi trying to kill me to cover up a US governmental scandal."

Sacker sucked air. "Intel 1, huh, sister."

"I think it's time."

He put his arm on the seat and swung his head around to look her in the eye. "You think things are really that big?"

"Turn around and look at the road."

He smiled and did so. She continued.

"Yes. I think it's that big. And that bad. I don't have all the pieces of the puzzle, but I really don't like the outlines we've assembled."

They drove on into New York City traffic in silence.

38

AHAB

S avas waded through a sea of blue and red light. Flashes from police cars and medical ambulances turned the neglected block in Queens into a rave. Coded squad-car radios crackled in the soup of conversation buzzing around him.

Local and national media gathered behind blue NYPD barricades, their vans, trucks, and reporters pressed like some swelling tide. They strained and jostled for a glimpse of the scene. A crowd of onlookers amassed and threatened to overwhelm the police presence.

It's not every day that a part of New York turns into a war zone.

Squinting, Savas stepped over the police tape. He sidestepped bodies and debris. Two Intel 1 agents led him under rickety scaffolding that groaned in the breeze. The entrance to the warehouse led down a short hallway. Small fires smoldered on his left and right. More bodies slumped along the path, both terrorists and law enforcement officers. He left the dead to the medical personnel, marching with a blind zeal into a larger room.

The extended firefight had centered here. The musty interior smelled less of the rust and mold coating the walls and more of gunpowder and blood. Bodies were moved to the sides to create space for a large set of tables in the middle. The wounded groaned from cots, the Mjolnir survivers restrained despite their injuries. Emergency responders tended them in the presence of police and FBI.

Savas moved straight to his second team. Intel 1 technicians had opened up boxes of portable electronic gear. Keyboards, cables, and monitors sprawled across the floor, chairs, and tables. Phones, thumb drives, and laptops were plugged into several of them. Blood smeared across many of the tethered devices, the carnage around them impossible to avoid.

Let's hope this works.

The information age had transformed law enforcement. Digital seizures procured key evidence that was often more important to an investigation than unreliable, fleshly criminals. Intel 1 possessed a rapid response team dedicated to locking down the brittle digital data present at a bust.

Angel's doing.

Before the odd genius disappeared at the mere mention of the Eunuch Maker. Before she teamed with Lopez and Houston after the election.

Doing I don't know what. Doing what I don't want to know.

He zeroed on the team leader, Karen Young, a former gymnast with back-length, braided hair. At the rapid clop of his shoes, she turned around.

"Anything?" he asked.

Her smile sent a fresh injection of adrenaline flowing through him. "We're running Agent Lightfoote's old code," she said. "You know, the one that stopped the Fawke's Worm."

Savas smiled. "I'm very familiar with it. That was the above-ground version of Intel 1, and Angel basically stopped a world-wide digital meltdown with it."

"Well, I hadn't seen it before. I guess it makes sense you kept it under lock and key. It's something. Successfully hacks into several devices, especially the Android mobiles. The procedures from Apple are generally working, but the encryption is taking longer to break, even with the modules they provided. On the devices we got into, we defeated one autowipe. A laptop."

He inhaled, steadying himself on the table, lightheaded. "And?"

"It's going to take time. But we did find something of interest."

Of interest. With Young, that meant it was big. She tended toward over cautious.

Bending down, she pointed toward two computers and operators in front of them. "The key was cross-referencing phone call GPS locations with laptop IPs. They've used proxies, VPN, Tor, you name it. But not consistently or with the best procedures. NSA monitoring of ISPs and a lot of their spyware helped. We can compare the locations and some clean IP geolocations." She straightened and locked eyes with Savas. "Bottom line: there's a nexus."

"Meaning?"

"Different people, on different occasions, through different devices and means, accessed a similar set of IP addresses. Likely a single location."

He slowed his breathing. This was too easy. He needed to devil's advocate this. "But it could be anything though, right? A terrorist server farm, or middling personnel only critical for this cell?"

"Maybe, but even that would be a huge catch. Could lead us up the food chain." She paused. "But we think it's more."

Young indicated a bloodied man on a gurney. He was unconscious, wounds apparent on his legs and chest. Bags of blood and clear liquid hung over him as the EMTs wheeled him toward the exit.

"Mr. Shot-Up-To-Hell there was likely the leader. Our frontline team—well, what's left of it—reported him giving orders. He was carrying critical plans for the Jamaican Mosque sight in this thumb drive." She tapped a drive plugged into a black box. "We broke the encryption."

Savas glanced back at the exiting gurney. "I look forward to talking with him later. We're going to need to break all this down. Get a mission report, reconstruction." He turned back to Young, her expression still intense. "What else?"

"The best part. The new deals with the social media companies are paying off, lets us sample his supposedly-encrypted text app. He's gotten recent messages on his phone from a 'PR.' Just the initials."

"Patrick Rout."

"And PR is contacting him from the nexus site."

My God.

The implication stunned him. Rout was holed up at the nexus point, or very near it. The monster didn't know it, but they had his damn coordinates. "That's incredible work, Karen. Lightning fast for a raid like this. You might have just blown this wide open. Get everything back to the bat cave."

Young held her head high like an Olympian who'd just nailed the landing. "Thanks, boss," she smiled, turning toward her team.

Savas scanned the room. His wounded and dead agents lay around the room. He didn't give them so much as a glance. He was utterly, maniacally focused on the results. That he was out of balance, that his perspective was deeply warped wasn't in question. But it didn't matter. The target of the hunt was all he could see.

I've got you now, you son of a bitch.

PART III

ENDGAME

The people can always be brought to the bidding of the leaders. That is easy. All you have to do is tell them they are being attacked and denounce the pacifists for lack of patriotism and exposing the country to danger. It works the same way in any country.

— Hermann Göring

SUITE PROTECTS AMERICANS, DECLARES MARTIAL LAW

by Sean Ingraham, *Canid News*

The spate of high-casualty terrorist attacks on innocent Americans along the east coast and in the southwest have prompted Daniel Suite's administration to take actions to protect law-abiding citizens from the growing menace.

Issuing an executive order today from the Rose Garden, the president declared the attacks "acts of war" led by those that "violate American customs and laws, inciting outbreaks of lawlessness and mob action."

The Protect Americans Order immediately goes into effect for a set of twenty US cities, including New York, Philadelphia, Washington, Atlanta, Birmingham, St. Louis, Houston, Dallas, San Francisco, Los Angeles, Las Vegas, Seattle, Miami, Detroit, and Chicago, among others.

"Today, I'm ordering the activation of the National Guard to secure these vulnerable cities from the invasion of terrorists killing Americans," said President Suite. "These killers are pouring into our country from our southern border, but more importantly, are already here after years of treasonous inaction by leftist administrations. These sleeper cells are activating, killing us, so that no one is safe. But we're going to make you safe. The army is coming in. In Chicago. New York. Las Vegas. The bad hombres are going to have to deal with our finest soldiers."

The president went on the stump for his massive deportation program, a plan stymied by federal lawsuits and Mexico's unwillingness to take ten million purportedly Mexican citizens into the country without vetting. Tensions between the two nations have grown since Mexican president

Miguel Ángel Garcia Gonzalez demanded a negotiated treaty to consider such a massive population move.

The new presidential action sets curfews and martial law in "problematic areas," a term many leftists have claimed to be a code word for minority communities.

"This is the first step toward the formation of state-sanctioned ghettos," argued Senator Anastasia Ortega-Cruz. "Vulnerable populations of minorities and the poor will be surrounded by armed troops under the excuse of protecting Americans from terrorist threats. Even though, as FBI statistics show, the greatest threat to America is statistically from right-wing terrorism."

Celebrity activist Gerald Tanaka, whose family was held in Japanese internment camps during World War II, saw something more ominous in the move:

"This sort of thing isn't new. They locked up a hundred thousand innocent citizens, families, in the 1940s. In Hawaii after Pearl Harbor, martial law was also declared, but the Army took it very far. There was a military government where the Constitution did not apply. A military dictatorship, in all practical terms. Now it's military control of inner cities. What are we seeing now? How far will this go? What's next? Fencing? Barbed wire? Who are we keeping under guard, terrorists? Or innocent citizens that this administration doesn't like?"

Director of Homeland Security Kiltss Neerijnen defended the new action, reminding America that the first job of the president is to safeguard the well-being of the people.

"It is completely within the powers of the president to declare martial law. When the nation has been invaded and attacked in the past, the government reluctantly did what it had to do to protect the country. Today is no different. Today radical killers are trying to destroy this nation from within. You've seen the attacks. Entire buildings destroyed. Roads, bridges, gang members and other illegals freed from captivity and set loose on the public. Some loss of freedom is a small price to pay for your life and the lives of your children."

39

RECYCLED

L ightfoote yawned and stared at the enormous piece of machinery in a daze. Since the skirmish at Mount Charleston, there had been little sleep. Their escape plan worked almost perfectly, the one wrench in the gears being the new martial law decree by the Suite administration. Law enforcement presence had increased everywhere, even National Guard, even in areas not directly affected by the districting and troop mobilizations. Now, any neighborhood could be a minefield. But they'd threaded the needle. They'd stolen and ditched cars, identified and bypassed roadblocks, and outright avoided violence.

They'd called in help from their resistance forces and now found themselves back in Vegas. Their return was ominous. Things were changing in the nation, faster and darker than they had even anticipated. They no longer had only ICE and local law enforcement to contend with. Suite had gone from blurring the lines of domestic military intervention to outright erasing them. Special forces troops now operated within US borders. Top of the line US military equipment was employed against US citizens. The National Guard poured into new militarized zones in big cities.

It's a matter of time until they stop us. Unless something breaks this regime apart.

A twenty-five-foot crane hoisted the remains of a blue 1993 Honda Civic hatchback into the air. The claw dropped the rectangular remains on a conveyer belt in a line of compressed vehicles where the hammer mill tore into the metal and plastics, ripping the remains like they were made of thick cloth. Parts rained down on separation belts. Fragments jostled and jumped to massive magnets on rollers. Light-foote shuddered at the detached, inhuman, and inevitable process.

She turned away and watched a van approach. The cursive logo of the Sandoval Casino decorated the sides. The Latino community in Vegas had provided an unexpected operations base for their resistance. They'd recruited second and third generation immigrants, drafted floods of the documented and undocumented from south of the border. All of them were flamed with emotional investments toward their communities. All of them looked on in horror as their communities were demonized and torn apart by Daniel Suite. More and more decided to act every day.

In no small part because of Francisco.

Lopez nucleated the resistance, having left Intel 1 for this quest. And like a missionary, he'd devoted himself to the task.

You can take the priesthood away from a man, but you can't take the priest out of him.

Lopez spoke with two men who exited the van. They motioned for her and Houston to enter. Lightfoote shuddered, glancing back at the shredder once more. The Civic was gone, all evidence of its existence wiped from the planet. That was good for them. The car was stolen and now there would be nothing to trace them back to Vegas. But she couldn't shake the chill running through her limbs.

"Angel?" Houston called, hanging half outside the van.

Lightfoote jogged over and leapt in. She cast herself against the opposite door and secured the belt. Lopez sat in the front, speaking with the driver in Spanish.

"Raphael Sandoval, right?" she asked as the door was shut from the outside. Lopez and the driver climbed into the front seats.

"His brother, Mario," said Houston. "They co-own the casinos, but it's Raphael who is the force of nature behind everything. Including the help to our little insurgency."

"We've never met him."

Houston continued as they pulled out from the scrapyard and onto Interstate 15. "And we likely won't. That his brother's running this pickup himself shows how sensitive things are. We barely made it. People are shook. Shook that they almost lost the leaders of the resistance. Shook at what Francisco is telling them."

Lightfoote smiled. In the middle of all this madness, seeing Houston brought calm. How could vision so completely reprogram a mind? Cascades of emotions, hormones, neurotransmitters. *A mystery.* But she was staring at yet another face of a chameleon.

Houston's look changed faster than the seasons. Recently, she had let her hair return to its natural blond-brown. Lightfoote ogled old photos of her whenever she got the chance. A master painter had once mixed the rich honeyed hue, but the natural look was rare. Houston colored since she and Lopez became America's Most Wanted. The hikers they spared could identify them, so her appearance morphed again. Today it was raven black, shorn much shorter. She'd ditched the hat in the mountains and transformed the rest of her appearance with makeup.

But it's the force of nature inside that's most beautiful.

Years before, she'd met Sara Houston in a crucible. The digital world had collapsed, and a coup nearly destroyed the country. Now they fought and fled together as the nation slid toward fascism.

In all that chaos, Lightfoote wasn't exactly sure when she'd fallen in love with her. A terrible complication in a terrible environment.

Another mystery.

She tugged at her white hair. After years shaving her scalp, the mass growing above was alien to her. Unlike Houston, she didn't alter her appearance. The hikers didn't know her real hair color as the filth in the desert darkened and matted her fine strands beyond recognition.

Lopez pared his epic beard to a broad mustache, completing the trio's appearance changes. The single change restructured his face. He also had reapplied a latex false skin to the scar on his forehead.

The shredded hatchback returned to her mind. She couldn't block out the image. It set her stomach to a vicious churn as the van bounded along the asphalt. "We have to get to those mines," she said, trying to distract herself. "To Yucca Mountain and see what the hell's going on."

Houston wrapped her arms around her chest, squinting. "I don't want to think of the conditions they're keeping those people in. And why? They already dumped so much money into the tent cities. As bad as they are, why move millions *away* from the border? Are they looking for another way into Mexico since the border's closed? By sea, maybe?"

"Through Nevada?" Nothing made sense. "Yucca Mountain. The answers will be there, maybe enough to blow this whole thing open. Maybe the country might finally care enough to stop it."

Houston sighed. "If ripping families apart on live TV doesn't do it, if kids dying in camps doesn't, what's going to make a difference? Entire communities destroyed by raids. Local economies tanked. It's like the nation is drugged. Numb."

"That's what I mean. Maybe the answers will be a shock. A real shock."

Houston locked eyes with her. "Well, if conditions there are *that* much worse than what we've seen, I'm terrified to go."

Lightfoote stared out the window to the growing midday traffic. A dream sense flooded her. A monster approached from behind, large, powerful, and famished. Its shadow fell over the three of them.

"I think we're in over our heads, Sara. We were good at weak point strikes. Disruption. At breaking things in a fragile system. But this is different. Suite's brought the military home. We saw that with the special forces and army equipment, all on US soil. He's militarizing law enforcement. Now military barriers and martial law in cities? *Districts?* It's bigger than what we can handle. It has the full power of the US government and military behind it."

Houston frowned, her shoulders slumped. "So, what do we do?"

"We can't go it alone at Yucca Mountain. We barely made it out this time. There won't be a next." Her glance fell back on Houston. "We need some serious extra firepower. And I only know one place we can get that."

40

INTERROGATION

"**J**ohn, we've worked together several times. Your reputation is unmatched. You're a damn legend."

Assistant Director in Charge Tim Cox stood outside a doorway in a dim hallway. Following up on the case, he'd flown in from DC to assist in the interrogation of the prisoner. After the raid in Queens and the capture of higher-level Mjolnir operatives, after possibly zeroing the location of Patrick Rout and the core of the terrorist operations, decisions had to be made. Verifying the location of the killers, that the intel was real, was critical. And this prisoner was the key. Cox was there as a courtesy from the DC FBI. He was also there because Savas needed a gut check on what was about to happen.

Cox faced Savas and several men in white coats. One pushed a cart with medical tools and electronic devices. Cox's eyes danced between Savas and the tools.

"I know you want to nail these guys," he continued. "But don't do this."

Savas grimaced, the words stinging. *You don't understand, Tim.* He spoke flatly. "It's cleared all the way to the top."

"Goddamnit! I don't care if Jesus himself said you're good to go.

Don't do this! I know you're better than that. Hell, that those extremists at 1600 approved it is all you need to know to step back. Rethink."

"Tim, respectfully, this is war. Mjolnir declares war. They prosecute that war. Last time we barely stopped them from killing tens of millions with a nuclear device. I'm not going to let them succeed this time. This is a small line to cross to prevent that."

Cox shook his head. "That's what every terrorist group says to justify what *they* do. That's what pre-emptive war is about. And the track record of success isn't good. You want the ends to justify the means. Well, in my book, usually the ends are products of the means."

Savas stared at the ground. Cox was right. This was crossing a line, stepping through a barrier that would transform him. Change the man he was into something else.

But the alternative is worse.

He signaled the men beside him to move into the room. They avoided eye contact with Cox and walked inside.

"I've got to make a choice between violating decency and allowing indecency to commit horrors." He held up his hands as Cox protested. "I know it's not a sure analysis, but I'm certain enough. That's the choice before me. And if there's a price to pay, then I'll goddam pay it."

Cox's face slackened, his eyes doleful. "Then may God have mercy on your soul."

The Assistant Director turned and marched down the hall.

Savas entered the room. The medical technicians were busy around the unconscious Mjolnir soldier. His wounds had been stabilized after the Queen's firefight. All evidence pointed to the likelihood that he was a senior ranking member of the cell, likely the leader.

This is our ticket to confirming Rout's location.

"How long does it take?" asked Savas. The sooner this was over, the better.

The lead interrogator glanced up from the work. "The prep? Less than half an hour. We have a lot of experience with covert intel missions. It will take some time longer for him to awaken from sedation and recover sufficient awareness to be effectively questioned."

Savas swallowed. The techs shaved the man's scalp.

"Is there much pain?" Every moment the procedure progressed was a step into darkness.

"None at all. Not physical, anyway. We anesthetize the scalp. There are no pain receptors in the brain, ironically. We can place the electrodes in the proper locations to achieve the effect we need without discomfort." He reached over and adjusted a scan on a laptop placed on the cart. "Psychologically, however, there's usually tremendous distress."

"Will it affect his answers?" *Dammit, John! As if that's all that matters?*

"Not their truthfulness. We will access the brain regions associated with conscious will, trust, and threat evaluation. We're quite experienced at manipulating the signaling in these regions. The electrodes induce weak currents that shut down pathways of skepticism and distrust. Other probes stimulate acceptance, desire to share socially, and so forth. His higher cortical functions remain intact. It's like the mythical truth serum, just messier."

"The distress?" asked Savas, his mouth burning with a bitter taste. His hands already felt soiled.

"That comes after. While stimulated, the subject acts as he has been induced to feel. When the electrodes are removed, he'll return to his normal cognitive states. Then, he will feel violated not only by us, but by his own flesh. Since we equate our flesh with our souls, many feel a permanent sense of personal sin, if you will. Counseling is recommended."

Maybe I'll earn my trip to hell today.

The doctor glanced at the techs as they marked locations on the soldier's bare scalp with black markers. He double-checked the scans on the computer and removed a large metallic cage from a box.

"We've learned to sedate the subjects during prep," he added. "As you can imagine the preparation is stressful. Most tend to respond very primitively when we restrain the head. We do try to make this as humane as possible. We will wake him slowly and allow some time for his consciousness to sharpen."

Savas squeezed his temples. He gave a quick nod to the interrogation team. "I'll be out in the hallway. Come get me when things are ready."

This I will never tell Rebecca.

He stepped outside, a long breath escaping his lips. Today, he lost his soul. He crossed a line, and there was no coming back. He couldn't bear the idea that Cohen would forever see him as tainted, but he also knew that knowledge would hurt her every day for the rest of her life. She didn't need to know. Not today. *Not ever.* At the least he could spare her that suffering.

He closed his eyes. No matter what he did, Mjolnir extracted its price. That's what monsters always did, even—or especially—in defeat. But he was going to save thousands of souls for it and end this malignancy once and for all.

Maybe it's a bargain.

41

ACE IN THE HOLE

He's wrecked.

Cohen sat at Savas's desk and stared at the computer screen. Savas had called to update her on his progress. The case was moving at light speed, important breaks in the case leading to central figures in the organization.

That's how mistakes get made.

First, they captured the lone, wounded soldier after the hit on the Washington mosque. That led to the seizure of critical digital files that left a trail back to the hive, possibly to Rout himself. Today, Savas expected to question one of the men captured in that raid.

So why does he look like the case has collapsed?

She expected to see the burning zeal of the hunt in his eyes. Instead, there were only the downcast eyes of a troubled man.

What isn't he telling me?

"So, everything is okay?" she asked.

"Yes. Yes." Again, his eyes wouldn't meet the camera. "We'll see what he says, but I'm sure we'll get what we need. Even without confirmation, we're going to move on the site. Quickly. But the more we know, the better."

"You sure you can trust his information?"

He swallowed, clenching his jaw. "You never know. But I'm hopeful."

Cohen sighed, unable to shake the feeling that something was off. "Then we shouldn't delay. It's clear to them now that the attack failed. The press coverage of the raid has tipped them off. If they're smart, they'll relocate their center of operations in case we made progress."

"Agreed," said Savas, the intensity back in his face. "We're already planning the strike." The image froze, his voice sounding like distorted robots. "And how's it on your end?"

"You're breaking up. Things are good. I'm moving the suspected Suite moles into a group of teams who will get lesser cases, be more distanced from critical Intel 1 operations. But I can't shut them out completely without tipping my hand."

The image remained frozen, their connection breaking. Text scrolled in a messaging app at the bottom of her screen.

"Underground. Poor signal. I'll text later," Savas wrote.

She pushed her chair back, her palms pressed together with the tips of her fingers touching her lips. The agony in his eyes was seared in her mind. She'd seen him hurt before, all those early years at Intel 1 when "Mad John Savas" had lit up the FBI and nearly gotten himself killed more times than she could count, and the pain of 9/11 lurked behind his passionate intensity. But something was different now. Something darker behind the flame. Some torment in his soul.

What's wrong with John?

She shook her head to break the spell of gloom hanging over her. Savas was stressed, no doubt. Things were moving insanely fast. And she had a job to do.

Mirnateghi.

She pushed the chair toward the desk and opened computer windows. Through one shone the polished teeth of Reza Kazemi, the new ambassador to Iran.

Suite had managed a domestic political success in reestablishing diplomatic relations with Iran, a needed win following a year of disastrous summits and tumultuous international conflict. *Canid News* heralded it as another Nobel Prize-worthy presidential achievement. Other reports were mixed. But Iran promising to end its nuclear weapons program? Several oil deals in the mix? The president received a lift in his low approval ratings.

But why wasn't Saudi Arabia throwing the proverbial excrement fit? Those two powers had battled in the region for centuries. The last decade was an ugly set of power plays for dominance. One either allied with Iran, like Russia, or the Kingdom of Saud, like the USA. But suddenly, Russia, Iran, Saudi Arabia, and the USA were a big, happy family.

Times like this, I wish we still had the Bilderberg analysts.

In freeing the world from Bilderberg, Intel 1 had set loose an ancient tribalism. They'd also lost an important analysis tool to understand human nation-states. The socioeconomic predictive algorithms of that star chamber were destroyed. The ability to model populations, manipulate them to specified ends, were lost.

Like Angel said, we weren't ready.

Lightfoote destroyed that knowledge by unleashing the Anonymous worm on the Bilderberg computers. Ready for that power or not, it was gone.

Back to old-fashioned methods.

Now, Cohen struggled to decode the movements of powerful people and nations. She focused on Kazemi. Coming out of nowhere, this bright Harvard Business School graduate was everywhere at once, and always in the company of VIPs.

Reports placed him at critical meetings during the presidential campaign. She scanned photos she'd collated from the internet. There he was at the Seychelles archipelago for a gathering of heavyweights from Russia, the UAE, Iran, and Saudi Arabia with former mobster and New York developer Phillip Schaiter. Smiling with them was Derek Nobleman, former head of Dark Rivers, the American mercenary company. The meeting was Exhibit A in online sleuths' cases against Daniel Suite. A Great Conspiracy with several foreign nations. A *quid pro quo* for election interference, money laundering, and political favors.

Kazemi had no previous background or contacts that would garner him a ticket to such an event, yet Suite put this moneyman on his foreign policy advisory panel during the campaign. It only increased her suspicions that something nefarious was going on.

And now he's Ambassador to Iran. He was in the Oval Office when Suite dragged John and me up to DC. Why?

She was going to find out.

Cohen pressed a button on her desk phone, opening a connection to her assistant. "Melinda? I want you to clear my calendar for tomorrow. Call a meeting of the Cyrus team. I don't care what they're doing or where they are. They need to be here tomorrow in my office."

"Yes, Agent Cohen," came the girl's lilting drawl. "Ma'am, there's also a call for you on one of the protected numbers."

Cohen sat upright. "Which one? Who is it?"

"A Ms. Grace Gone, ma'am."

42

FOOT IN THE DOOR

Gone held on the line, the absence of hold music unnerving. The call was on speaker, a soft hiss leaking from the device like steam from a broken pipe.

Sacker stared at her across the desk in the small office. *Former family kitchen*, she reminded herself. He'd pulled it out from the wall to accommodate the wheelchair. He'd also arranged a mounting platform for her laptop. She sure as hell was going to continue working, blasted shoulder or not.

"Ms. Gone?" came the nasal voice of the receptionist.

"Still here," she said, biting her tongue.

"Agent Cohen will speak with you now. Please hold while I transfer you."

Cohen? Where was Savas?

"Grace," came an analytic flatness. "Of course I know what happened. Hard not to since you're basically a celebrity now. I would have contacted you once I knew you were healing, but…it's good to hear from you again. Surprising, even."

Okay, she knows something's up.

She put on her cheeriest voice. It was time for a favor.

"Great to hear from you, too, Rebecca! I'm doing much better. A little high-caliber military round's not going to stop Gone Investigating." She winced and repositioned her shoulder, trying not to gasp out loud. "So, where's John? You taking over Intel 1?"

Cohen laughed, her voice rising in pitch from its mellow alto. "Don't put ideas into my head. But no. I'm sitting in the big chair temporarily. John's very busy with a case."

"Mjolnir. I'm not surprised. I'm sure this is important for him."

"Indeed." It almost sounded like a sigh. Cohen recovered quickly. "To what do I owe the pleasure of this phone call?"

Shock and awe. With a smile.

"Rebecca, I need access to pharmaceutical grade monoclonal antibody production facilities."

Cohen paused. "I'm sorry?"

"I have several clones of an anti-carfentanyl immune-therapeutic. I need GMP mammalian tissue culture expression systems to crank out gram quantities for injection into humans."

"Wait. Slow down, Grace. What are you talking about? What injections? What is this?"

"After what happened four years ago, I hope you have some respect for my work. My judgment."

"That's putting it mildly."

"I'd like to arrange a meeting. Tyrell and I will stop by your Lex Luther hideout underground. I've got a list of companies I'll send you if you agree. You use that Intel 1 magic to strongly encourage them to send representatives. I'll give a little presentation, explain in detail what I need. You and they decide if it's feasible and if you want to do it. It will cost a few million."

A short silence followed. Gone knew she'd hit hard, but she feared there was little time. She had to trust Cohen to make the right call even with the pressure.

"I'm willing to help you, generally speaking, of course. But this means pulling some big strings. Can you give me a little more to go on here? What's carfentanyl? Why injectable antibodies? Why Intel 1?"

"It's related to a case we're pursuing. We have come across some documents that reveal a massive governmental cover-up. Financial malfeasance for sure, but it's weirder and scarier than that. There's Department of Transportation. Prison construction companies. And in the middle of it, a vaccine biotech startup paid millions by the government. All to produce antibodies against the opioid drug, carfentanyl."

"Carfentanyl?"

"It's related to fentanyl and heroin."

"The government is paying for *antibodies* to this drug?"

"Yes. For a lot of it. And it's all part of a single giant project called China Girl. The huge and illegal money transfers. Contracts off the normal books."

"China Girl? That's not…."

"Not me. Although, with the recent assassination attempt, it might as well be now."

Keyboard clacking sounded over the speaker. Cohen was digging. "What's China Girl, then?"

"Street name for these drugs."

Gone held her breath. Cohen was bright. One of the smarter ones at Intel 1. *Her and that wild card, Angel.* She was going to make the connection. Gone wouldn't make it for her.

"Wait a minute. I saw the flowers in the paper. *The hyacinths.* Is this connected?"

Bingo!

"No. No coincidence. The flowers were a small *digitus impudicus* for my assassin. She got cocky and sent hyacinths to Tyrell. We were tracking down critical players in this case when they tried to take me out."

"*Mirnateghi.* Everywhere I turn, this woman is haunting my life." There was a long silence. "No way it's coincidence. John and I speculated that our Iranian princess might be involved. The hit seemed too professional. So from what you say, it could be because you're poking around in something she has a stake in. Two birds with one stone."

"Exactly," said Gone.

"Which means, it's a direct route to Suite. Iranian money. Influence in the election. But this places her in something big and secret his administration is undertaking. What are these documents you have? How'd you get them?"

"I can talk about those if you'll work with me on the antibodies."

Cohen continued typing. "Tough negotiator. So you think there's some kind of danger? I'm finding a lot of military interest. The drug was weaponized. Some kind of gas or aerosol. Maybe it's a military contract?"

"We've considered it, but there are problems with that hypothesis. Outside of the one use in Moscow, there's no information suggesting it's an active threat to US soldiers. Something for research, perhaps, but not for industrial-scale production of the countermeasure."

"And the other is China Girl."

"Precisely." *So nice to have someone that always keeps up!* "It's embedded in something dirty. One of the biggest governmental efforts in decades, buried. Tens of billions of dollars going missing."

"I need to know your sources."

"You want to verify? You can't. I don't know the identity, but the records are legit."

"Verification would be good, but having such internal sources— and this one has to be internal—would be really useful to us right now."

Sacker spoke up for the first time. "Suite messing with you?"

"Hello, Tyrell," said Cohen. "Thought you might be there. Yes, he is. And it's all hands on deck here."

Gone continued. "If we're going to keep investigating, this level of concern over the drug is a red flag. Someone is frightened enough to buy enough antidote to the poison for a small army. We felt it might be useful to have ourselves inoculated. Get the countermeasures inside us."

Cohen's tone was cold. "And have some in stock in case this stuff finds its way to more widespread use."

Yes! She gets it. Gone locked eyes with Sacker. "So you'll help us?"

"You got your foot in the door, as always. I'll arrange this. I want to hear it in more detail. I want to see the reactions of some professionals. And we'll do it tomorrow. This sounds serious."

Sacker mouthed "tomorrow," his eyes wide. Gone kept her voice neutral.

"We believe it is. The sooner the better." Gone smiled. "And can we skip the blindfolds this time?"

"Policy dictates that we do it, but it's likely pointless. I assume you've already figured out where it is?"

Gone's grin covered her entire face. "I plead the fifth."

43

POWERPOINT

Sacker rubbed his eyes as the lights came back up. *Holy God damn, that was long.* He was ready for a break. A week-long nap. Maybe even a therapist after all that bio-babble.

A bottle of peated iron dram and a pack of smokes.

He flushed the urge out of his mind and glanced back at Gone. She looked as tired as he felt. Her dog-and-pony show before Cohen and the biotech reps had drained her. Her eyes were sunken, black rivers of hair rebelling against her tie. She slumped, fatigued from navigating the wheelchair, pointer, screen, and audience.

She should be resting. Recouping. This is crazy.

She was still low on blood. Anemic. And here he was dreaming of getting liquored up, focused on his vices when she'd sacrificed so much. The trip back down into the bowels of Intel 1, now complicated by her condition and movement needs, sapped her energy before the meeting even started. Even he had been bewildered by the blindfolded journey through the maze of underground tunnels and internal passages. The long delays topside from Suite's National Guard deployments had stretched the day out further. For someone who had nearly lost her life not too long ago, it must have been far worse.

If they could harness her willpower, they could light the world.

"The constructs are industry standard," pronounced Bearded Pony-tail Dude. Sacker was long past giving a damn about their names. "Have you done any pilot experiments on expression? What are the yields? Any concerns we need to know about before we get into it?"

Gone shook her head. "You'll be going in blind beyond the sequencing information and plasmid maps I sent you."

Bollywood Babe piped in, her thick hair like a shroud around her fashionable glasses. Her tight shirt strained against the pressure of her ample chest. "The time frame to produce certified human monoclonals is extremely tight. I don't know anyone in the industry who can meet that schedule."

Ponytail Dude wagged his head in agreement.

Gone frowned, exhaling slowly. "I don't want certified anything. This is not for general distribution. It's for a covert governmental operation you've sworn secrecy to. And this is not rocket science. These are, as Fredricks noted, standard expression vectors. I'm sure there are variations from antibody to antibody, even in the same system. Deal with it."

Well, that's that.

Cohen stood, moving beside Gone's wheelchair. "I think that's enough questions for our speaker. The real question is for you." She glanced back and forth between the two reps. "Your companies topped my list for a number of reasons. Discretion. Reputation. Previous contracts with the US government. Now the question is just how much do you want some easy tax-payer money? I'll escort you out and you can confer with your superiors. If we don't have offers today, or if we don't like the offers, we'll reach out to others. Again, this is a matter of national security and highest secrecy. And highest priority. *Someone's* going to make these for us."

On cue, her assistant Melinda Banks entered the room, opening the door wide. She smiled at Ponytail and Bollywood Babe. The pair rose, Ponytail frowning, Babe smiling off center, wagging her head side to side. They followed Banks out of the room and down the hallway.

Cohen closed the door and sat down beside Sacker. Gone pressed buttons on the wheelchair and it came to a rest beside the table.

"How'd those two take the blindfold tunnel trip?" laughed Sacker.

"Like grade schoolers," she smirked. "I think I'm getting old." She turned to Gone. "How did you get these clones?"

Gone assumed an expression of angelic innocence. "Funniest thing. I visited Vaxagen. When I got home, my stuff was just *filthy* with DNA. *Disgusting.* But before throwing it in the laundry, I did some plasmid isolation and transformations in the basement. In some of my colonies, out popped these antibody expression vectors!"

"You stole it," shot Cohen, her eyes boring into Gone.

Gone didn't flinch. "I isolated an environmental contaminant."

The corner of Cohen's mouth tightened, but she let it go. "I've looked over your documents. Thanks for sharing. Would you mind if we worked with these? This is something Intel 1 will be interested in."

"John, too?"

"I'm sure of it, but I have to make the call myself. He's assigned me to the big chair." She shook her head and smiled. "First thing I do without consulting him is spend millions of dollars. Next, I plan to open a case of fraud against the US government, possibly involving a target we've been obsessively hunting for years. The irony is that when I tell him today, I'm not sure it will even register."

Sacker frowned. "Not register?"

"Overstated. He'll care, but his mind's locked on the Mjolnir case."

"And how's that going?"

"It's all confidential." Cohen rolled her eyes. "But what— I'm keeping secrets from you? You might as well be honorary members of Intel 1. I think half our celebrity collars over the last few years trace back to you."

"Sometimes in our cases, we have to outsource to law enforcement," he said, glancing at Gone. She didn't return his gaze but focused intently on the Intel 1 agent.

"But it's going very well, actually," said Cohen. "We caught one of the participants in the mosque attack. Wounded. He didn't know much but was trained to be part of the next mission. John set a trap."

"Queens," he said. "Read about that. I know the neighborhood."

"They hit the jackpot. We used several devices to uncover a center of operations. Maybe *the* center of operations. Confirmed through intel from a soldier captured at the raid as well. John's planning to hit that soon."

Gone's lower lip protruded. She tapped it with the index finger of her good arm. "That was awfully fast," she said.

Cohen glanced at her sideways. "Yes. I suppose so. We were lucky."

"Or they were very sloppy."

"Yes." Cohen stared into the distance. "Not what they used to be, perhaps."

What is it with these two?

Sacker huffed. "They seem pretty awful to me. A bombing and then a mass shooting of mosques within a few weeks? If they've lost a step, thanks be to God."

The two women held each other's gaze, the room deathly quiet. Cohen broke the silence.

"I'm going to need to see the files you got from your source. All of them. Or nothing goes a step further."

44

SEED MONEY

The desk lamp provided the sole light in the underground office of John Savas. Cohen worked late in the converted fallout shelter seven stories below New York City. Without others needing to see someone in the "big chair," she'd taken her usual position across the desk, but it had become too awkward to rotate the screen and stretch the keyboard wires to work. At last, she'd let go of her reluctance and sat in his chair.

She rubbed her eyes. Replacing her glasses, she stared at the rows of data. Organizations, people, and contracts arrayed in the spreadsheet. Gone's files were stunning. Extraordinary sums of money appropriated funneled toward this massive China Girl project without Congressional approval, coordinated efforts across several massive departments to circumvent oversight and regulation. The grafts and levels of malfeasance were so large, no one would think to look for it. It was an audacious betrayal of the country and the norms needed for it to function.

A Suite-sized scandal. So, what am I missing?

Her intuition prodded, taunting her to forgo sleep. She juggled a collection of unsavory actions, associates, and governmental leaders. She had no doubt many in the Suite administration had committed prosecutable crimes. Crimes she would refer to the DoJ in due time, damn the new rules protecting them. But there was something else.

What? Dammit, Rebecca, think!

Her mind flashed to the brilliant PI Grace Gone, now wheelchair bound by the minions of Mirnateghi. She remembered Gone's slides, the presentation of biotechnological systems to produce antibodies, the production systems "creatively acquired"—*stolen*—from Vaxagen. Perhaps she should share all Intel 1's files with Gone. She would likely cut through the webs of deceit to the truth.

"Wait a second. Vaxagen?"

She sat up in her chair. The name was familiar to her and not only from Gone's records. She had come across the name. Her mind swam through rows of text and names, pages flitting through her memory. But the ghost refused to be caged.

"Brute force."

She opened the full spreadsheet file and prayed the automated scripts grabbed the relevant information in this complex mire. She hated relying on the AI, but there wasn't time to manually search through thousands of pages. She typed the name of the company.

One hit.

Her finger traced the horizontal cell back to the column for names. One name cross-correlated the Vaxagen records from Gone and those of Intel 1.

Reza Kazemi.

She scanned for the description box, reading out loud to convince herself of the reality.

"'Founding investor in Vaxagen, providing seed funding for the startup company.'"

The entry ended. Inconsequential. A random angel investor in a biotech company. There were thousands of such. Except of course Kazemi was anything except a random investor. His ties to Mirnateghi, his positioning within the Suite administration as the future ambassador to Iran, brought together two seemingly independent threads of corruption with the Vaxagen connection.

No wonder Gone missed it.

Suite hadn't yet officially announced Kazemi as his choice for

Iranian Ambassador. The president was too busy basking in the press coverage of his Iranian negotiations.

Which could end again as soon as some Ayatollah insults him.

Reza Kazemi and Vaxagen. Gone had a cache of TNT with her documents, but the PI didn't realize how explosive it was. Cohen combed the internet for keyword phrases combining the names. There wasn't much, but money trails were hard to hide. Investors were a unique set of private investigators looking into companies and people. They sifted through the wheat and chaff for moneymaking opportunities.

And they'd documented this one.

"'Hedge fund manager Reza Kazemi lent his weight to a young biotech startup today,'" she read from a Yahoo Business report. "'In doing so, he becomes one of five VCs to invest seed funds to launch the company. Vaxagen seeks to leverage a proprietary technology to develop novel monoclonal antibody therapies.'"

She checked the date. It was only a year before the election. Leaked emails proved that Suite had put a run for presidency in motion many years before the primary, which meant that whatever China Girl was about, it was long planned.

Lining up all his ducks in a row.

Whatever Suite was using the biotech for, Kazemi made the Iranian connection. A link to Mirnateghi went through the soon-to-be Ambassador to Iran. Cohen had her key lead.

She opened her email app and entered "Cyrus." The software filled in a group of email addresses. She copied her assistant in as well. Moving back to the spreadsheet window, she highlighted the row of interest. She saved the file and returned to the email.

Cyrus Group,

Clear your schedules. Everything else can wait.

See the attached spreadsheet. There is a link between Kazemi and the biotech company Vaxagen.

You are to follow up on this connection. We'll discuss this first thing in the morning, but you'll be going over every detail of every file on Mirnateghi and of the documents provided by Gone. Examine all our records. If we find anything suspicious, we'll target a friendly judge, garner warrants, and raid it.

This is a breakthrough. I know we're all a bit stunned from the content of Gone's files, but now we've potentially linked this corruption to Mirnateghi.

That means two things. First, it gives us another route to finding out more about her. Second, more critically, it means that whatever is going on, given her past record, it's likely very bad, very dangerous, and likely destabilizing to the country and the world.

I need every one of you bringing your best to this. With Mirnateghi involved, with the highest levels of our nation's government involved, I can't emphasize how serious this work is.

Rebecca

Cohen pushed her chair back from the desk. *John's chair,* she tried to remind herself. She gazed to the ceiling, the tiles dim, the halo of light from the desk lamp a star in the midst of darkness. She closed her eyes.

The waters are getting deep, now.

'ISLAM BAN' PASSES SENATE, HEADED TO PRESIDENT

by Edward Gelles, *The Boston Globe*

Bill H.R. 1123, officially titled the American Laws Protection Act but called the "Islam Ban" by Democratic leaders and activists, narrowly passed the Senate today on a vote sharply divided along partisan lines.

Among some of the proposed law's most controversial points are the categorization of Islam as a political ideology based on Sharia Law and the criminalization of Sharia Law at the federal level. The bill classifies observance of Islamic law as sedition, proposing sentencing guidelines in the felony range punishable by up to twenty years in prison.

Conservative advocates have long pushed for a criminalization of Sharia Law, but rights groups have argued that the informal system of codes and ethics Muslims have turned to around the world is not a threat to US laws, and that the banning of it, particularly while declaring Islam a political ideology, is designed to strip Muslims of their First Amendment Rights.

"This is a naked attempt to dehumanize and criminalize Muslims simply for practicing their religion," said Democratic Congresswoman Maryam Mazandarani, who is Muslim. "Once Islam is declared a political ideology and not a religion, it can be criminalized. Mosques can be closed. Muslims can be targeted and rounded up simply for praying. Because now our prayer is outlawed political activity."

To bolster her argument, Mazandarani referred to comments made by President Suite during his campaign and since he was sworn in as president. Far from softening his tone, Suite took to the bully pulpit and spoke strongly in favor of some of the new bill's more extreme interpretations:

"Islam hates America. Christian and Jewish America. Our laws. Our way of life. There's a huge amount of angry hatred. America needs to get to the bottom of it. We aren't loved by Muslims. Look, I saw in New York thousands of Muslims celebrating when the towers fell. Can you believe that? Thousands cheering. How are we supposed to deal with that kind of hate? Across generations? Non-assimilation? Kids of Muslim immigrants are killing us. We can't just take out the terrorists. With them, we have to take out the families, too."

Many of the president's assertions have been repeatedly challenged as inaccurate, such as the claim that Muslims celebrated the destruction of 9/11. When pressed on the denial of First Amendment rights, Suite did not address the point directly but instead returned to his campaign promises about closing mosques.

"I'm definitely going to have a serious look. It would be sad. I'd hate to, but the truth is we're going to have to strongly consider doing it because of all the absolute hatred coming from these places. So much hate. Coming from Mosques. Why is that? You have all these people leaving mosques with death and hatred in their hearts and minds. Well, we can't just sit around doing nothing. The mosques have to be dealt with, whether some people like that or not. If we don't, Americans won't be safe."

When reporters continued to press the president to answer the question, he appeared to become irritated, ordering several to sit down. "This country has a serious problem. All of us can be stupid, politically correct, act like there isn't a problem. Are we that dumb? But we have a big, big problem. It's not just terrorism. A huge, huge problem with Islam. It's a war. That's the real news. Not the fake news. Maybe you should be reporting on that, the real news for a change."

Later in the day, the topic again returned during the president's meeting with strongman Duterte of the Philippines. Reporters ignored his controversial guest and continued to press for clarification of religious rights for Muslims under the new law he was to sign later that day.

"Everyone's upset because I labeled it with the word Muslim. 'Oh, you can't say that, can't say it's the Muslims.' But it is the Muslims. Not all of them. Some very bad ones. But the others don't do anything, so it's all of them. Think about it. Our Constitution is great. The greatest document. And I know documents. I sign a lot of them. I've probably signed more documents than anyone. But I don't remember it giving us the right to commit suicide, you understand? Sure, there are the rights—you know, everybody wants rights. Protection. Who doesn't? And that's super. That's one of the wonderful things about our wonderful Constitution. All the rights. But I gotta say, I see this differently. Why are we committing suicide, America? Why would we do that?"

In comments to *Canid News* and the *New York Times*, Suite declared himself open to the idea of creating a database of all Muslims living in the United States. "America needs to know where these people are. Where they live and what they're doing. Or no one is safe." Later, when questioned, his aides refused to deny that law enforcement was already monitoring Muslim citizens as the ACLU has challenged in recent lawsuits.

Osama S. Addin, a religious liberty scholar and attorney, condemned the president's words and the new law:

"If Congress and this administration strip American Muslims of their constitutional rights to practice their faith, a freedom Christians cherish and fight for, it's American Christians — not the Muslims they are so terrified of — who will be the ones setting the Constitution on fire and destroying religious freedom."

The president's staff and Republican members of Congress have flooded the news cycle with spirited defenses of the new law. Suite's National Security advisor Gabriel Fenn minced no words. "Islam is a political ideology," he told an audience at an ACT for America conference in Dallas. "It disguises itself as a religion to hide its purpose: world domination."

"Islam is not really a religion, but a political system that uses a false god to advance an agenda of global conquest," said newly elected GOP congressman Ralph Bennett on *Meet the Press*. He continued by comparing the religion to "a malignancy" and tweeted that a fear of Muslims is "the mark of wisdom."

Former Suite campaign manager Stan Brennem, who worked for years in several nationalist media outlets, labeled Islam "the most diabolical political system in the world," warning that Muslims in the United States constituted "a fifth column" in the war on terrorism.

Even American evangelicals, long proponents of new laws to protect religious expression and freedom, appeared to view the legislation in a favorable light.

"Religious liberty has to be protected for all belief systems, of course," said Toohell Falbad, president of Freedom University in Lynchburg, Virginia. "But the country needs clarity. Is Islam truly a religion? We've come to believe it is not. It's a political system disguised with spirituality. Our report details this analysis."

Falbad referred to Freedom University's recently published book called *The Gospel and Islam*, in which considerable space is devoted to the topic of the political nature of Muslim religious beliefs. "There are spiritual elements," the report noted, "but the misapprehension is that Sharia Law is a code of religion in the Western sense." It concluded by noting that the Travel Ban was in keeping with other national security efforts to protect the United States: "Immigration of those following Sharia Law, which is basically all Muslims, should be prevented. This is no different than previous denial of admission to the nation with followers of other seditious ideologies such as communism."

The report harkened back to president Suite's words when he announced his Travel Ban in his first term: "I am demanding a complete and immediate stop to Muslims coming into the United States until we can determine what is going on."

Gabriel Chiggar, a long-term critic of Islam and friend of the White House, went so far as to label every Muslim a traitor to the nation, stating, "A faithful Muslim, who accepts the Qur'an as scripture, can't be loyal to the United States of America and should not be a true citizen."

Activists and Democratic lawmakers have expressed rising concern that this sort of rhetoric incites violence and is antithetical to the spirit of the Constitution. Other religious leaders have responded similarly, some with a call to arms to defend Muslim religious rights.

"Threatening the religious freedom of anyone threatens it for everyone," said Rabbi Noam Gordon. "Every belief system is under attack by this new law. We see the favoring of particular religions like Christianity, where Congress and the president labor for laws to ensure bigoted practices against gays and transgendered people, while they dismantle protections to different religions. Of course, who is favored and who is persecuted often changes with the wind."

The president plans to sign the bill into law at a large ceremony in the Oval Office today.

45

CONNECTIONS

"I'll get it."

Sacker jumped from the chair toward the ringing desk phone, knocking his hat to the floor. Gone stewed in place. Three days after she had turned the whistle-blower's files over to Intel 1, Rebecca Cohen was scheduled to call, but Gone couldn't manipulate the wheelchair to reach the receiver.

"Thanks, Tyrell."

Her own voice sounded odd to her. Raspy, a frog's gargling, the fatigue of the last week setting her recovery back some days. The shoulder pain had flared. The swelling increased. Worst of all, her mind was a blur. Without the meds, the pain distracted her. With the painkillers, everything was a fog.

My mind is everything. I'm running at fifty percent right before the finish line.

"Gone Investigating," answered Sacker.

Gone managed a weak smile at his formality. Nothing touched her more than seeing him take pride in her business. His respect meant everything.

"Rebecca," he said, white teeth flashing. "Good to hear from you again. Let me put you on speaker so Grace can hear."

He pressed a button. Cohen's voice burst into the room.

"I'll have to brief you quickly. A lot has happened since we got hold of your files. You can imagine they were shocking. And as you likely guessed, the probable crimes involved are not something Intel 1 can ignore. I have a team on that, but there are a few more pressing things."

Sacker sat down across from Gone, his eyebrows up. Gone continued to fight the wheelchair, trying to line it toward the phone. "Let's begin with the files," said Cohen. "We used them to connect Suite and Mirnateghi."

Gone's lip jutted out, her forehead creased.

How did I miss this? Damn meds!

"What connection?"

"The bridge is a man named Reza Kazemi."

Gone's mind raced through the files. She possessed the rare gift of a photographic memory. The name came to her, but it offered no explanation. She pouted all the more. "Some investor in Vaxagen. Managed the Wiley Fund. How is he connected?"

"Suite's about to name him the ambassador to Iran. When we got dragged up to the White House, he was in the Oval Office with Suite as he assigned Intel 1 to the Mjolnir attacks."

Gone tilted her head back and closed her eyes.

This is insane.

Sacker tapped the table with his index finger. "Wait, you mean the antibodies, the company and all the other contracts, this Kazemi is involved?"

"Yes, or it's one hell of a coincidence. He became an early investor in Vaxagen a year or so before the election campaign began. He's now part of the new opening of diplomatic relations with Iran. *And* he was called in for the meeting with us and Suite. What does the new Ambassador to Iran have to do with the Mjolnir case?"

"The Mirnateghi connection is probable, then, but not proved," said Gone, rubbing her eyes. She leaned forward. "But this is big."

"We've got teams pulling all-nighters," replied Cohen. "And now, finally, the last bit of news for you and then I have to go."

"Shoot," said Sacker.

"Through an NYPD-to-FBI handoff, we were brought in to examine a body. Gunshot wound. Fatal it turned out. Victim had taken a taxi from Manhattan to a Bronx trauma center."

Gone's face tightened. She locked eyes with Sacker. He cocked his head in confusion.

Cohen continued. "He died in the ER. No identification. Nothing in the police databanks. Likely would've been filed a Joe Doe and forgotten, but the detective had some FBI contacts. Good ones, it turned out."

Gone interrupted. "And you're going to tell me there's video footage of him on the Upper East Side. That he's a foreign national with ties to Iran?"

There was a pause. "I'd swear you have a mole in my office if I didn't know you. Yes. Remember when Suite relaxed the visa requirements for Iranians last fall? There was a flood of applicants. The FBI ran this guy's prints through the database. He's a recent visa recipient from Tehran. Lighting fast approval from State. Technical engineer of some kind. But the paper trail vanishes when you try to chase it down."

"Ballistics?" asked Gone.

"Exactly. Tyrell, what kind of firearm is your go-to?"

"I shot the bastard with my Glock 19 Luger. Nine millimeter. My first NYPD issued firearm."

"Two hits," noted Cohen. "Pretty damn good shooting with Grace bleeding out at your feet."

Sacker's glance flicked to Gone. A warmth spread through her seeing his eyes, the concern on his face.

Cohen completed the data dump. "And those were the two rounds still in the vic. We aren't going to find more on the Iranian side. Everything we have about him is likely a lie, except for his country of origin. But this guy miraculously achieved a speedy visa right after Suite makes it possible. His reason for coming is clearly a fraud. And he ends up with a rifle nearly killing Grace in New York."

"The flowers were enough of a confirmation," said Gone. "But this makes it airtight."

"I'll let you know if we come across anything else," said Cohen.

"I'm late for another important meeting with some of my teams. Thank you for the files. And stay safe."

The line went dead.

"They went through a lot of trouble to get to you, Gracie. Suite helped moved some major obstacles. He's got to be knee deep in this shit river. And so is the deadly *Sonbol*."

Gone glared at her aching shoulder. She could feel Sonbol's toxins as if she were still poisoned. But the word for a flower wasn't enough to capture the woman's vindictiveness.

"I'll stick with the other nickname for Mirnateghi. *Nemesis*. Fits the hole in my shoulder better." Gone angled the chair from the speaker toward Sacker. "We need to get out more."

Sacker leaned back and raised his eyebrows. "If you're thinking…."

"We need to take Dr. Triller up on her offer and visit Vaxagen again. She's dying for me to return, remember? Let's go find out what they know about their not-so-angelic investor."

46

REGROUP

"How long, Lord? Will you forget me forever?
How long will you hide your face from me?
How long must I wrestle with my thoughts
and day after day have sorrow in my heart?
How long will my enemy triumph over me?"

L opez examined the fake IDs as he whispered the words of the psalm. It was top-notch work visually. But the real skill hid behind the plastic. Function demanded useful social security numbers, addresses, and state driver's licenses. The kind of data that survived a run through a police scanner or credit card reader. The kind that linked to innocuous bank accounts from which they could operate.

The special forces' attack on the camp had taken some of their best. Had nearly taken their own lives. But their numbers only grew, two replacing every one lost. They had spent years cultivating an underground network that filtered and funneled talented and sympathetic rebels to combat the policies of hate spreading across the nation. These tributaries fed their movement, at first in trickles, increasingly in small streams. But those small streams now raged as churning rapids.

Fighters flooded into their ranks. Some fled the new districting orders, leaving homes and jobs in urban areas slated to be walled off into open-air prisons. Others came from untouched regions, radicalized from the oppressive steps the Suite government had begun to take. People of color demonized in propaganda-filled media tirades. Religious groups. Muslims found their way to the resistance as their faith was redefined as politics and their mosques closed or subject to terrorist attacks. They were all dedicated to the cause of stopping Daniel Suite and his minions in power. Lopez counted on them now.

He whispered the prayer of the Virgin Mary:

> *"He has brought down rulers from their thrones*
> *but has lifted up the humble.*
> *He has filled the hungry with good things*
> *but has sent the rich away empty."*

He turned from the table and smiled to see a short woman in a hijab. Her eyes sparkled at him, and she answered back.

"By the power of your hand, O Lord, destroy those who look to this world for their reward. But satisfy the hunger of your treasured ones. May their children have plenty, leaving an inheritance for their descendants."

"I didn't know Muslims took an interest in the Psalms," he said.

She beamed. "The Surah An-Nisa of the Qur'an states, 'and to David We gave the Psalms.' Christians usually forget that Islam holds all the scriptures sacred."

"Great work, Amna." He gestured to the items on the table. "I assume the plastic will support my luxurious lifestyle."

She put a hand on his arm, tears in her eyes. "We're all glad that you're alive. Everything that's happening, this darkness coming after us. Our faith. Our mosques and homes. Our families. We don't go out at night anymore because of the patriot gangs, and those black shirts are more and more violent. Hitting our stores. Killed and raped the daughter of a friend. Only you are fighting it. *Really* fighting it." She looked at the ground. "I don't know what we'd do without you."

Lopez's shoulders rose and fell as he exhaled. "I'm just the face,

Amna, not the body. We have a small army. Our methods are treasonous resistance. But there are many who work within the system for what is right." His eyes scanned the basement room and found those of Houston. "I know them. Don't doubt that they fight. They just fight within a corrupted system and have chosen different weapons. I'm not sure who has the tougher battle."

Amna nodded, gathering the items she'd help produce. Heavy boots approached. She retreated from the table, making room for Lightfoote.

"Where's Sara?" she asked.

He indicated the far end of the crowded basement with his eyes. On other tables were weapons and gear. Houston lounged on a chair in front of a cache of firearms like a bored cat. She ignored those splayed out around her. Instead, she held the large Browning over her knees. The two women connected across the space, their glances fleeting, yet charged.

He frowned and turned to Lightfoot. "Progress?"

"I've got a com network activated," she answered, eyes returning. "Secure tunneling. We can burrow through the dark web and pop up in Rebecca's messaging."

"*You* can burrow. The rest of us will watch." He called across the room. "Sara!"

Houston stood and slunk over to the pair, holstering her sidearm. "Is it time?"

Lightfoote gave a thumbs-up.

Houston crossed her arms over her chest. "You sure about this? They have to suspect what we've been up to. Maybe they *know*. We don't know who's after us and what evidence they have. This could be leading the law to us."

"Intel 1 hasn't been after us. I still monitor the place. They haven't chased my code out yet. All the communications I've spied on are either about Mirnateghi or more standard cases. Well, and now Mjolnir."

Lopez turned to Lightfoote, his expression hard. "Let's go find out," he said. "You were right. We need help right now. The Man is coming down on us hard, and it's likely that whatever hellhole they've set up at Yucca Mountain, it's going to be a fortress. We can't do it alone."

Houston shook her head. "Still. Why would they help us? Even if they don't think we're the rebellion in the southwest, why believe all this? *I'm* having trouble believing it."

Lightfoote snapped back to attention. "Rebecca will trust me. She'll think we got something wrong. That we have bad data, wrong conclusions. But she'll take me seriously."

Lopez grunted. "I hope so. But some persuasion will be in order. You're going to give her everything? Like we agreed?"

"Yes. I know my security systems there. I've already dropped folders of information from the hacked military and ICE files. Give her a little time. She'll come around."

"Time is something we don't have much of," said Lopez, glancing around the room. "I have to keep up a positive face. These people are desperate. Entire Latino communities are disappearing, Muslim businesses and mosques closed under this new Sharia Law Bill. I can't tell them the truth."

Houston held his gaze, pain in her eyes. "What truth?"

His mouth twisted, anger flaring. "That we're losing. That the noose is near." He turned to Lightfoote. "It's time to reach out to Savas."

"He won't be there," said Lightfoote, her face furrowed. "Rebecca. She'll be making the decisions now."

Lopez squinted but said nothing. Houston shrugged as Lightfoote continued to stand in a trance.

Angel "angeling" again.

"Let's go to the second floor," she continued. "The setup's ready."

They followed Lightfoote's sprite-like bounding up a short stairway into a crowded storage room. The three huddled around a mess of computer equipment from a dystopian film. Laptops and wires. Odd blinking boxes whose purposes remained enigmatic except to the former FBI woman.

Lightfoote sat before a monitor. She *onioned* and *VPNed*. She used proxies and backdoors and secure exit nodes, a dash of encrypted routers and endless technobabble. Lopez fidgeted. He just needed to see if Intel 1 would put its mighty resources into the fight.

"She's in John's office," said Lightfoote, grinning and hopping in her seat like a teenager. "See, I'm monitoring his keyboard. She's typing. Definitely Rebecca's prose, not John's. I'm logging it too, so we could find out what's she's doing."

"You're spying on Intel 1?" asked Lopez, an eyebrow lifting.

"Not usually. But I can. I'm not taking any chances."

"Then John's IT people suck," scoffed Houston. "Gone downhill since you left."

"It's worse than that," said Lightfoote. "They have some sloppy breach attempts. From *inside*. Likely some new hires trying to compromise security. I'm always intervening."

"So she's there," said Lopez. "What now?"

"We ring." She popped a huge wad of gum in her mouth and chewed. The smell of fruit exploded around them.

"Ring? His phone?"

"Yup. Got it wired with encrypted voiceover internet protocols." Her words were slightly garbled by the gum. "He never uses it that way. But we will. Right now."

She tapped on the keyboard. Numbers raced across a field in an open app. There was an old-fashioned bell ringtone.

"Hello? Who is this?" A clipped tone to the voice indicated surprise and anxiety. It was Cohen.

47

OLD FRIENDS

"Greetings, Kemo Sabe," bubbled a woman's voice over the line.

Cohen caught her breath, her eyes darting around Savas's office. As she waded through the sewage of an accelerating case of international intrigue and scandal, as the nation seemed to burn down around them, the last people she had expected to hear from were some of the arsonists themselves.

"Angel?" Cohen's voice rose. "How the hell did you get this number?"

"Hacker girl, Rebecca. Remember?" The sound of gum smacking was unmistakable.

"Wow." Cohen tried to shift gears, dig herself out of the labyrinth of money transfers and shell companies. She tried to accept the fact that some of the dearest people in her life were calling. People who were in danger, risking their lives. People she should, by all rights, be arresting. "This is the week of phone calls."

Rough shuffling sounds erupted on the speaker as the voice changed. "Rebecca? Where's John?" Houston's. Lopez was likely near.

"Not here. Hold on. Let me verify with someone I trust that this is secure, that no one's listening in."

"The only people listening in are us." Lightfoote again. "I've checked."

"As my former IT genius, I guess I'll take your word for it. But things are a little different around here these days."

A male voice boomed. "What's going on at Intel 1?"

Cut through the bullshit. Let's get to it.

"Let's leave that aside a minute. What's going on with you three? We haven't heard a thing in years and…." she paused. "We have our suspicions."

Houston cut in. "Look. We have something very big. Something very bad. Hundreds of thousands of lives could be at stake."

Her disorientation deepened. Could these three just stop being a hurricane for some part of their lives? "Hundreds of thousands of lives? Sara, what are you talking about?"

"Please listen! Angel will give you the details. You can make up your mind."

"Make up my mind about what?"

Lopez replied. "About whether Intel 1 is going to help us. Whether you're going to go rogue and work against your own government. Because the government has gone rogue."

Help them? Help America's most infamous terrorists. Go rogue. They were calling on Intel 1's secure lines to ask them to join in their seditious acts. She fought to slow her breathing.

"Listen to me. John doesn't want to know about what you're doing. And we've been specifically ordered by the powers that be to leave the terrorist El Marcado alone. Other divisions of law enforcement are on it. But *I* know. I know what you're doing. I can't condone it. I should be turning you in!"

Lightfoote's voice crackled over the speakers. "We're not going to discuss those issues. Another time. There's something more important."

"More important than you turning into domestic terrorists? You've killed federal agents, for God's sake! People like me trying to do their jobs, trying to help the country."

"Not with what they're doing," Houston shouted. "You have to listen!"

"No! I won't listen. I'm making myself complicit in terrorism even to have this conversation. This is the last communication we can have. We end this now."

"Wait!" cried Lightfoote. "Several *hundred thousand* undocumented detainees are missing from official governmental records. They've been bused, trucked, and secretly sent by train to Nevada. They're taking them from across the country, siphoning them from the border tent cities. They're *all* going there, to a growing set of off-the-record camps, unknown to the public or even official government records. Who knows how many others have been rounded up accidentally, caught in a coarse dragnet?"

"What?" *Complete madness.* She placed her hand to her temples, squeezing.

Lightfoote only deepened the headache. "Listen! Whoever is behind this is systematically moving them to a single location. Hundreds of thousands."

She shook her head, gesturing with her hands to an empty room. "How do you know this? How can this be true? People would know. You can't hide something like that."

Houston spoke. "We hit one of these new camps. Angel hacked into their systems. We have the data. We've uncovered other things. Worse things."

"They're chipping people," said Lightfoote. "All these secret detainees. Injecting them with microelectronics. We know where they are because of the chip GPS."

"Injectable microchip GPS? These don't even exist yet!"

"They do! It's been under development for years. A company called PowerID has some new line of them. Government has them, is *using* them. It's buried in innocuous-sounding contracts, but what they're really doing is GPS chipping the masses of illegals they're rounding up."

"Why, for God's sake?"

"That's what we need help with. The chip signals are massing at the Yucca Mountain site."

The insanity approached some crescendo. She felt multiple threats converging from different angles, the mists still too dark to align her defenses. "The nuclear waste mines?"

Lightfoote continued. "I've sent you a digital care package. It's on your desktop. Name's *Messenger*. Double click on it, type the password: name of our favorite evil hacker. It has all the governmental data."

She checked the screen. *Damn.* The hacker girl was playing around with everything. She double-clicked on the file and typed "Fawkes" into the prompt. It opened.

"Found it," came her distracted voice, distant to her own ears. "You hacked into John's computer."

"But be *careful,*" Lightfoote warned. "If you try to verify what's in there, some parties will find out. And they are not the good-government types. Talk only to people you trust completely if you need to double-check. Don't share the file over any internal or external channels."

"Get John," added Lopez. "He needs to see this. You have to move quickly."

When it rains, it damn tsunamis.

Cohen felt overwhelmed as she scanned the documents. The content set off bombs in her mind. The weight of the scandals she pursued crushed her from the sides. She couldn't speak for several moments. "Jesus. These numbers. How can this be real?"

"It is, Rebecca," said Houston. "We've seen it."

"What timing. Everything is going to hell at once. God is punishing me for my pride and ambition."

"Sorry?"

"John's not here. He's not going to be here for some time. He's moving on Mjolnir. He has some incredible leads. He's gone dark until it's done. Meanwhile, yours truly is in the big chair."

Lightfoote's voice was flat. "This could be the most important thing Intel 1 has ever done. This could determine the future of the country."

Cohen glanced at the ceiling. They were asking her to work with traitors and terrorists. Betray her oath. Believe treasonous rebels. To make the call herself.

She leaned forward.

"You have to give me time." Her voice was firm. "I trust you. All three of you. We've seen too much together. But I have to be convinced of this."

"We understand."

"I'm not going to destroy everything we've built, bring down Intel 1, unless I'm sure. And if we're wrong, this *will* be the end of Intel 1. I need more time."

"Look into it," said Lightfoote. "But don't take too long. Hundreds of thousands are waiting."

48

NORTH BROTHER ISLAND

S avas paused, staring at the image from the projector. He was rushing things, he knew that. But there was no choice. They had a possible fix on Mjolnir's location, but that could change at any moment. For all he knew, it could already be too late after the failure of the group's last mission. Rout could have decided to move their center of operations to avoid the risk of discovery. There was no time to waste.

He let the reality of the situation sink in. His audience consisted of some of the best field agents of Intel 1. They would form the initial strike team that would assault the Mjolnir headquarters. He'd just revealed the location to them.

Rebecca should be here.

He missed her professional input. He missed the long-developed rhythm of their work. But most of all, he missed her. It was a hell of a time for them to work a major mission separated.

One of the young members of Savas's strike team shook his head and stared at the projected image in the dark room. "I've lived in New York City all my life. How do I not know about this place?"

Savas held a laser pointer in his hand. Its red circle of light centered on a green oval in the middle of a small bay. Packed grids of buildings and roadways lined the surrounding lands of the Bronx. Interstate 278 snaked its traffic-packed course along the northwest side of the bay. The tip of Queens and Riker's Island were south and southeast of the small land mass.

"You've all heard of Typhoid Mary?" Heads nodded, accompanied by a low murmur. "Well, this is where they isolated her. Up until about fifty years ago, North Brother housed a series of hospitals and retirement homes for the military. During the TB epidemics, sanitariums sprung up. When that faded, some hospital duties remained, addiction clinics. They even built residential housing for vets."

"How'd they get there?" asked a woman from the back, her features in shadow, obscured by the projector light.

"Ferry from 138th street. And that's what killed it. Without a bridge or tunnel, it's too damn inconvenient to get there. By the 1960s, everyone had left and the city let the entire place die." Savas laughed. "Except the opposite happened. Nature moved in. It's now twenty-two acres of dystopian film backdrops and a bird sanctuary."

He flipped through several slides showcasing the abandoned buildings and structures. The windows of brick mansions were shattered from the wild growth of vines. Entire shacks were overrun. Moss and mold covered crumbled masonry, collapsed walls, and vanishing roads. A mangled mass of rusted and collapsed iron marked the location of the ferry dock. It was framed by a towering rectangular derrick isolated in the water. The dock had long collapsed into the water.

Savas paused on a slide showing a split screen. On the left was a bright daytime image of a ruined hospital building overrun by vegetation. On the right was a satellite infrared image revealing many heat signatures. "And recently, something else moved in as well. These lands are off limits. Travel to North Brother is forbidden by New York City ordinance. And from the photos, you can see that for most of the last half century, that law's been obeyed."

The slide changed. A schematic of the hospital building rendered in three dimensions occupied the screen.

"You've seen the intel. The digital trail led to an office in the Bronx right across the water from the island. But that location is only their telecommunications nexus. As the satellite images show, and as our captured Mjolnir soldier has confirmed, the personnel are there. Right here in this former heroin rehab center. We estimate on the order of forty people have taken up residence."

"How are they living there? There's no power, right?"

"No power. No sewage, waste removal, running water. Nothing," said Savas. "But these guys used to hunt terrorists in the Afghan mountains. They're ex-special forces. They're a boat-ride away from supplies. This isn't hard for them. They've found the perfect hideaway to launch their new terror war from right under our noses."

He pressed a button and a map of the bay returned. A red box covered the land due north of the island.

"We don't know how they're getting on and off the rock, but it has to be by boat. Likely small ones put out at night." The red laser stopped on the red box. "But we'll be pushing off from Barretto Point Park in the South Bronx. Let's go over the strike plan outline first, before we get into details."

A new slide appeared. Bullet points and arrows traced across the screen to a smaller map image.

"Our NSA contacts have hacked into the server they're using in the Bronx. We assume a lot of their communications run through that. We're going to shut it down during the raid. Cellular signals will be jammed across the island minutes before we land."

A black man to his right spoke. "Won't this tip our hand?"

"Yes," said Savas. "But by then it'll be too late, not to mention likely pointless. These are ex-military extremists. They plan missions like special forces. They probably rely on tailored comms gear like those they used on the battlefield. There isn't much we have at our disposal to counter that. So, we'll do what we can."

"Won't they have some kind of security system? Motion detectors? Lookouts? They'll be looking for trouble coming in from the north."

"Indeed. But we're not going to be that obvious. While we depart from Barretto Point Park, we're fanning out. We'll have a contingent of six boats with six personnel on each."

Several red dots appeared along the shore. Now came the core of the plan, a military-style assault on military-trained targets. It was as dangerous as anything Savas had ever done.

"We'll land at these locations, coordinate our approach through our own radio frequency communications equipment. It will be important that you memorize these maps. And remember that a lot of it is getting close to thick forest density." He turned from the screen to his team. "As for their defenses, anything goes. We don't know what they've had time for. But I recommend extreme caution. These are battle-tested soldiers. They have no qualms about killing. They don't fight fair."

The slide altered, with blue dots appearing around the shore.

"Once we're in position, our backup will arrive. The NYPD police boats will have been taking up positions around the island. Before we strike, they'll pull to the shore. Officers will converge on our position at the hospital site. They are there to help us, but I will be honest with you—we're the troops on the front lines."

He looked across the room, the whites of eyes still visible in the darkness.

"It's quite possible some of us won't be returning from this raid. You need to come to terms with this danger, so I'm here to say now. If anyone, for any reason, feels they're not up to this, you aren't. I need a dedicated team that sees this as a war assignment. Because that's what it is."

Savas paused, gazing again across the faces. He gave them the time they needed. No one spoke.

"Okay then. Let's focus. We'll go into the details of the approach and raid. Pay attention. And remember, everything I tell you tonight will need to be adjusted on the ground as this plays out. Probably with guns pointed your way."

49

BACKUP

"Look, Gracie, you're just going to have to let this go. And can you slow the hell down?"

She hadn't lasted two days. After the conversation with Cohen, Gone's idea to revisit Vaxagen had become an obsession. She'd arranged another visit. And then, just like that, they'd called her back and canceled. She hadn't taken it well.

Sacker slept through the evenings on the couches in the lobby of Gone Investigating. He'd heard her tossing fitfully in her mechanized hospital bed. In the morning, the first words from her mouth were to head to the biotech. He'd argued, tried to reason, but the combination of her normal drive to penetrate mysteries and the personal nature of this case could not be stopped.

Sacker chased the wheelchair as it sped out of the office. Gone drove the mechanism with irate abandon. She bumped a magazine stand, sending pages flying across the empty waiting room. As she backed it up, trying to navigate around the strewn journals, he moved in front, raising his hands.

"Tyrell!" she hissed between gritted teeth.

"Vaxagen's closed the doors to you."

"If you don't get out of my way—"

He pled with his eyes. "If it's all connected to Mirnateghi, it makes sense. They were bound to find out you paid them a visit. They shut that down."

"I had an appointment *today* with Triller," she fumed. "We were hours away from getting a shot at information on Kazemi!" She placed a hand to her temples. "I need more data. There's something we're missing. I can't hang all the pieces on any model. Huge money transfers. All these disparate groups from industry to government. What's the purpose? What is driving this? We're missing something huge!"

"Well, we'll have to find another way to put the pieces together. Maybe we should reach back out to Intel 1, trade some information. Cohen likely has a lot we don't. Maybe you can make some connections." He met her burning gaze as best he could. "But I can promise you, they aren't going to reschedule this meeting. There's not going to be a rain check."

"We go anyway. *Today.* Show up for our meeting time and pretend we never got that message. We bang on their door. I'll drive through the damn glass walls in this damn cripple car!"

Ah, hell.

He winced, her bitterness burning. The words struck him like an arrow in the chest. He understood. He wanted to help her overcome all this. But the risk was just too great. He was torn in half from concern for her physical well-being and sympathy for her emotional anguish.

"It's already too late in the day," he said. "Nearly noon."

"I'm slow to get moving now. I'm sorry."

"No, that's not what I mean. The Guard's set up roadblocks and shut down streets in Harlem, the Bronx, I don't know where else. Could be Queens next, and we'll have trucks and fences going up around us. Goddamned *districts* for this martial law bullshit. Damn Patriot Corps parading about in the middle of it all. Traffic's like nothing before in the city. Let's regroup, work this out, and go another day."

"I'll drop some threatening accusations. Someone will talk to me. I'll shake out some answers."

Sacker wrung his hands, his eyes lingering on her form. Her body slumped in the chair, eyes defiant. If lasers burst out of her eyes and burned a hole in the wall, he wouldn't be surprised. But Gone shaking down someone? He didn't dare laugh or she might prove him wrong. Personally. "Can we just—"

"We have the van until tomorrow," she said, her voice softening. "*Please*, Tyrell. Don't make me try to drive the thing myself."

Damn this stubborn woman!

"All right," he said, lifting his chin and giving her the side eye. "Wrestling a freight train is easier than talking sense into you. But, okay, dammit. Let's hope we don't end up with the Guard on our asses and in some cage." His brows narrowed. "We're both the wrong color."

She disregarded his warnings and beamed. Her expression bathed him in warmth, a spell he didn't want to dissipate. He could drown in that radiance in the midst of so much trauma.

He smiled back. "Let me get you around this mess you made."

He steered the chair toward the door.

I'll clean it up when we get back.

Once again, he struggled with wheelchair and narrow doorframe. The paint was wearing off from the repeated scrapes.

I'll get to that later, too.

The early morning cool vanished, leaving the promise of another sweltering day. Sacker inhaled, pushing the chair toward the van. *What further mischief is this little woman brewing?* As always, the trouble would be interesting.

He steered to the side as a wino staggered toward them, bottle dangling to one side. The body odor overpowered even the moist wafts of uncollected garbage nearby. The wino paused and raised the bottle toward them.

Except it was a gun. He aimed at Gone.

"Grace!"

Ambush. Sand blew across the streets of Queens. *Where were the damn scouts?* You didn't send in a team without clearing the sector, dammit! The thoughts flowed with the images of Iraqi buildings as he pivoted, drawing his weapon.

Shots exploded. He watched as the head and torso of the assassin ruptured, blood blasting from flesh in different directions. The body dropped to the pavement with a sickening slap.

Crossfire. New York. Fallujah. Not a squad. Not Iraq. Queens. *Gone.*

"Tyrell!" she cried, her head arched backward.

His own gun drawn, finger on the trigger, Sacker gawked as several Asian men sprinted toward them and converged on Gone. They took positions around her, scanning the streets.

"Hold fire, Sacker. Assess the scene." His commander's voice. He blinked the ghost away. Were they hostiles? His finger ticked on the trigger. *No.* He removed it, ran the digit along the side of the gun. He stood down.

One of the men spoke in Mandarin, handing Gone a mobile phone. She spoke several short phrases into it and handed the phone back. She shook her head, closing her eyes.

One of the Asians grabbed it and touched the glass screen. He stepped toward Sacker and offered the device. "Mr. Gon will talk to you now."

Sacker stared at the scowling face in front of him and took the phone, placing it to his ear. "Hello?"

"Some bodyguard you have made."

He adjusted the gadget, trying to process the near assassination, the appearance of hidden backup, and the voice of Gone's father. "These were your men? What were they doing here?"

"What were they doing?" The man on the other end exhaled. "What *you* should have been doing! Protecting my daughter!"

"You've had us followed?"

"Of course I have. Do you think after the last attempt on her life, I would leave her vulnerable? If you had kept her indoors, hidden as I would have, it would have been so much easier. Instead, you let that headstrong child order you about. I'm lucky your escapades did not get her killed. It was impossible to predict where you would go or clear every site. I've had my best people involved."

A spectrum of emotions churned through him. Anger, embarrassment, surprise, fear. *Love?*

Not that. Not now. Once that door opened, he knew it couldn't be closed. He shook his head, hoping to avoid a brain meltdown.

"Thank you," he said at last, meaning it.

"You are welcome. Now take my daughter back inside this instant. I would like to speak with her under different conditions. It is not safe outside."

50

CRYSTALLIZATION

"I'm grateful to your help, but that doesn't mean I owe you anything." Gone set her jaw, a field of distain emanating toward the speakerphone. "I'm not going to let you try to assert control over my life again. That time is over."

She couldn't look at Sacker, who listened raptly. The entire dynamic between father and daughter left him with a mystified expression. She caught glimpses of disparate emotions running over his face. No doubt he longed to know the full story.

And he deserves it. But it was so hard.

"Controlling you was never in question," came the exasperated tones over the speaker. "But a little rationality. Some small grain of prudence. Some respect for your father would be nice to see."

"Respect can be won and lost," said Gone. The muscles in her face hurt, her teeth grinding as she balled her fists. "You have a lifetime to atone for."

"And you now have a lifetime to reconsider your behavior because of me."

The line went dead.

"Family." Sacker smiled. "Can't live with them, and you can't live with them."

"He's a drug kingpin," said Gone.

His eyebrows launched upward. "Holy meth balls."

She eyed him closely for the first time. He fought an urge to straighten. He forced his mouth closed and brought his eyebrows down. He was trying to act cool.

And she knew why. The insight tugged at her heart. He knew she needed an ear and not a reaction. He was putting what he thought she needed over his own emotions.

That's why the world hurts you, Tyrell. You've got too much heart.

"The thug brought my whole family from Shanghai to Mexico when I was a kid." She turned her face from him, the shame too much. "I didn't understand for a few years. But even at eight or nine years old, everything fell into place. The constant bodyguards and tutors. Fake friends brought in to play with us while my siblings and I remained under house arrest."

She could imagine his thoughts. Siblings. Crime boss father. Gone's family.

I'm sorry, Tyrell. Now you know.

"I remembered everything the adults said. And heard a lot. By the time I was a teen I knew my father sold narcotics. Knew he ruled with an iron fist. Knew he had blood on his hands." She bared her teeth, eyes still away from him. "We fought. Constantly. He was grooming my brothers to take over the family business, idiots though they were. My sisters were like my mother. Huge hearts, no spirit. They did what they were told."

"And then there was you."

She flashed him a fiery glance. "Then there was me. I despised him. What he was. The false life we had. The cage I was in."

"So you ran away."

Her eyes rolled away from him. "I figured you had some idea. Poking around into my past when you were at NYPD."

"Well, due diligence was required. I wasn't gonna let some random gumshoe nobody into the biggest case in the city in half a century. So, yeah, I knew something was off. But this? No. I can't say I'd guessed all this."

She chewed her lower lip. *Please don't look at me differently, Tyrell.*

"I used his own money, his contacts and systems. Judo flipped the entire infrastructure against him. I disappeared for as long as I could. He was bound to find me with all the success."

She sighed, closing her eyes. Freedom, even illusory or temporary, had been such a gift. Freedom from the tyranny of a monstrous parent. Now it was gone. The monster, her father that she loved and hated, was back.

"You're alive today because of him." Sacker swallowed and reached toward her, placing his hand on hers. "I'll take it."

She opened her eyes, their glances locking. She felt the pull between them as their heads tilted toward each other. This time, after everything, escape from it was impossible. And unwanted. He reached toward her cheek.

The phone rang.

Both jumped. Her eyes flicked to the device, growing wide. "Cohen."

He pulled away, short of breath, and pressed a button on the phone. The Intel 1 agent's voice broke into the room.

"Grace. This is Rebecca. Are you okay?"

Sacker shook his head as Gone replied. "Seems everyone in the region is keeping tabs on me," she said.

"I'm not apologizing for it."

"Neither was my dad."

"Were those his men that intervened? We had a team monitoring you. They saw the threat too late. Our assets laid low when it was clear you had back up."

She straightened in the chair and focused on the phone. "I appreciate the concern, but I'm okay. You sound shaky. What else is on your mind?"

There was a short silence. "I need your thoughts on data that we have. I'd like to share with you what we know. I've just sent you an encrypted file. You can unlock it with the name of the researcher who produced the androcidal virus."

This is it. What we wanted. And it sounds big.

Her eyes darted to Sacker. His eyes widened. She ignored his stare, focusing on the words crackling from the speaker.

"Let me give you a summarized data dump. You can go through the details after. I've been in contact with former agent Angel Lightfoote and her two…associates."

"Gabriel and Mary," said Gone. "You realize I know to whom these aliases refer?"

"God, I'm glad you're on our side."

"Then you also realize that I have some idea what they're doing. So, why is Intel 1 in contact with terrorists?"

Sacker blinked. He mouthed "*We need to talk.*"

"There's no time for that," said Cohen. "Your scandal. The documents on China Girl. Well, these three are knee-deep in it."

Her left arm trembled, even in the sling. The right remained firm as her gaze bored holes in the phone.

Cohen continued. "As part of their recent…activities…they've stumbled on a clandestine set of detainee camps in the Southwest. These aren't known to the public or in governmental records, at least any we can access. And at Intel 1, our reach is broad."

"The prison companies," whispered Gone.

"*Visiting* one of these camps, they discovered something extraordinary. The odd contracts, D.O.T. monetary expenditures—it's part of a massive detainee relocation program."

"Ethnic cleansing."

"I take your point." Cohen exhaled. "Their numbers are drawn from existing camps and fresh round-roundups from ICE raids. We're talking hundreds of thousands."

Sacker gaped. "Are you serious?""

"It gets worse. They're systematically microchipping them. State of the art, biometric, GPS microchips. Angel got her hands on the data. Tracking the signals, she discovered that all these new camps are just feeder sites. The mass of detainees are all being gathered at one place: the former Yucca Mountain Nuclear Waste Repository."

Sacker slapped a hand on the table. "Holy Jesus Jeans! What in the ever-loving fuck?"

"Go on," said Gone. The web of connections were linking, gelling.

"That's what we have. The details are in the files. They're begging me to intervene, ship our agents to Yucca Mountain and investigate.

Beyond that, they're demanding a strike force to *seize* the place. I hardly have the numbers with what is going on with Mjolnir. But beyond that, it would be treason."

"That's for sure," said Sacker. "This is crazy!"

"I trust them," said Cohen. "They believe this. Angel especially is completely spooked, convinced we have to act. Even they admit they don't know *what's* happening, but they're very frightened. If they're wrong, it's the end. For Intel 1. For our careers, our efforts to stop Mirnateghi. They're calling our hand, demanding we go all in."

Cohen's voice faded. A fog settled over the room, Sacker misty behind a screen of Gone's thoughts. An absolute stillness possessed her form.

"Here she goes," whispered Sacker.

His words floated past her, ignored, irrelevant to the information processing.

When the puzzle pieces clarified, the trance emerged. It was impenetrable. Stone tumblers glowed from within a magical artifact. They rolled through a sequence of obscure runes and numbers. One by one, they clicked into place, broken spells, spilled magic, until the artifact opened. Opened to death in the desert.

"Listen to Angel," said Gone.

Her words were calm but firm. The mist over her eyes dissipated. Bright light flared.

"Rebecca, I can't say this strongly enough. Do whatever you have to. Sacrifice everything. Your career. Your organization. Lives, if need be."

Sacker froze. Tension locked his body in place.

Cohen's voice dragged. "What are you…"

"Send everything there. As soon as you can arrange it. Be smart about it, but make sure you can get the job done."

"Tell me why," demanded Cohen, her tone sharpening. "Please."

Gone breathed through pursed lips. She leaned over the desk and grasped Sacker's hand. "The key clues to the mystery are here. One, the concentration of people into the camps, the prison construction, the D.O.T. transfers. Two, the unexplained presence of a company with undersea habitant construction experience. Three, the carfentanyl antibodies. And four, the choice of the name for the project, China Girl."

The room fell silent. Sacker scrunched his brows, parsing the information. Cohen was silent as Gone continued.

"Underwater habitats are pressurized environments. They control the passage of atmosphere. They divide an exterior from an interior with many safety features. Carfentanyl's been aerosolized. Weaponized. It's deadly in gaseous form. And antibodies to it would protect those exposed." She let out a long breath. "Protection for workers at death camps."

Cohen gasped on the other end. "Dear God. This *can't* be."

Gone didn't bat an eye. "Tell me your contacts in biotech are churning out liters of antibodies."

"They are." Cohen's voice rasped. "They're not happy. Had me sign a lot of forms saying I know this material isn't vetted for use in humans. That it needs proper clinical trials, and so on. Liability is all on us. That legal release and the money helped push them. Your clones were the real thing. It's working."

"Have them prepare injections. Expedite distribution to your people and our friends in the southwest. Anyone going to the site needs to have an antibody infusion."

"Heaven help us. Okay. We'll rush the drugs."

"Now get people there. As soon as you can. The population of entire cities hangs in the balance! Every minute matters."

The weight of a star fell on her shoulders. She felt crushed to the ground. Not even the wheelchair seemed sufficient to hold her up. Sometimes, being the first to understand was a terrible burden when the insight was terrible. And what had crystallized in her mind from the data was more horrible than anything she had ever encountered.

And will Intel 1 even be enough?

National Security Advisor George Darton stood beside the slumped yet tense form of President Suite. The pair were alone in the Oval

Office. A voice crackled on a speaker from a large conference phone in front of them.

"The situation is critical," came the distorted voice of Reza Kazemi. "The moles you have within Intel 1 can't get the details, but it is clear that her Cyprus group has had a flurry of activity following the communications with Gone. In addition, our communications hacks were able to intercept penetrations from outside, directly to the Intel 1 command center, perhaps even to Savas's office."

"How is that possible?" asked Suite.

"We don't know, but all of this converged immediately before Intel 1 began a scramble. Our plants are still trying to get their hands on what is happening, but it is likely the former agent, Lightfoote, has also been communicating with Cohen."

"She's with El Marcado!" shouted Suite.

"Very likely," Kazemi sighed. His voice rasped with fatigue. "We have to conclude that the PI has deduced the essence of your Nevada location. The cat, as they say, is likely very much out of the bag. My employer can have no more to do with you or this operation. I suggest you move aggressively to shut things down. Good luck, Mr. President."

The line went dead.

"That son of a bitch!" Suite slapped the phone across the desk. It pitched over the edge and fell, crashing to the ground in the dim light. "I'll expose them all!"

Darton leaned in. "They have much more on us than we have on them. I half believe they're relishing the chaos of this disaster. They never were our allies, only a party with temporary mutual interests."

"He's saying Intel 1 is going to get involved. We have to stop that. They could interfere, expose us."

Darton nodded. "Authorize a strike force. I'll accompany them to the Intel 1 headquarters. We'll arrest Cohen on whatever charges the Attorney General and the DoJ can manufacture." He stared at Suite. "Assuming they will comply?"

"Of course they will! He's my appointment. He shut down the Special Counsel. He'll do what I say. Anyone who doesn't is just next on the chopping block and they all know it!"

"Good. It will just be Cohen and a thin team. Savas is already committed to the strike on Mjolnir with a good part of their forces. That Iranian witch saw to that. He won't be there to help her. We'll march in with warrants for their arrest and a lot of guns. The little girl will fold, and we will shut down that entire underground police force." He smiled at the scowling president. "Intel 1 is over. They won't be doing anything to stop us."

51

ASSAULT PLAN

Lopez gazed over the interior of the large warehouse from the top of a mobile elevated work platform. He took in the thousand-strong standing before him. A rebel army, assembled from across the country in clandestine fashion, brought together at great risk, hidden by the millions in cash from Latino businessmen from Vegas and the spirit of communities pushed to the brink. Enabled by the skills of former CIA, FBI, military, and technological experts who turned against the regime in power.

It was insanity. It was unstable, certain to be discovered and crushed by the might of the most powerful military the world had ever known. And so tonight, he would likely send them to their deaths. He would likely seal his own fate, Houston's, Lightfoote's. The great hope was in their sacrifice to free entire cities worth of people from bondage.

Lord in Heaven, let my people go.

His voice rang through the space.

"And that is why a fight tonight. That is why we gather in such numbers, break our secrecy, put aside our guerrilla war. Because our people need us. And they need us with a desperation we've never known before."

Houston and Lightfoote stood on each side of him along with a cohort of his most able and trusted fighters. Before him the crowd focused on his every word.

"You know the facts. You know that the monsters in DC have taken hundreds of thousands captive. Our families. Our friends. The old and the young. Imprisoned them together at that mountain waste site for God knows what purposes and under what suffering. We are here tonight for our people."

Murmurs and cheers rose from the crowd. He raised his voice.

"And who are our people?" He held his breath a moment. "I see a sea of color and form. I see men and women, black, white, brown, yellow, red. I see Sikh and Buddhist, Muslim and Jew, Christina and atheist. I see laborers and managers. Why are you all here? Who are our people?"

He glared at the forms below, the tense silence a string taut and ready to be plucked.

"The disciples of Jesus asked him something similar once. The Lord told them to love their neighbor as themselves, a phrase no one examines because it is so old and familiar. But it is radical. *Impossible.* Transformative. And what did these would-be holy men say in return? *'Who is our neighbor?'*"

He paused, letting the question sink in.

"Immediately, they looked for a way out. Even they sought to divide, to lessen the demand of divine love, to place limits on decency and humanity. So Jesus hit them hard. He picked a despised ethnic and religious minority, a Samaritan, to make a point with a parable. Many of you know the story. A man was beaten by thieves, left naked on the road to die. The best and brightest of the nation of Israel walked past this victim. Left him to die in pain and shame. Who would save him? Who would be the neighbor to love the man and care for him? Jesus picked the lowest. An alien. A foreigner. A stranger in custom, appearance, and belief. That despised Samaritan was his example of divine love. *'Go and do likewise'* he told his wayward students."

Lopez slammed his fist against the podium. The echo reverberated through the warehouse.

"Who is my neighbor?"

Boom. He pounded his fist again.

"My neighbors are the migrant families building the homes and roads in America, harvesting and feeding the nation, caring for the children of the country. Who is my neighbor?"

Boom. He struck the lectern again.

"My neighbors are the desperate families fleeing strife and poverty who seek refuge and the chance to build a human life in a nation that once so promised."

Boom. As his fist hit the wood, a collection of feet stomped in unison, some hands clapped, and others beat a fist on their chest.

"Who is my neighbor? Every child in a camp."

Boom. The drum beat spread, swelling the space.

"Every family suffering." Boom. "Every child of God!"

Boom. Boom. Boom. The rhythm shook the walls, the fighters discarding caution, the fire hot within them.

"We are our neighbors! Every one of us! Of every creed, color, and custom!"

Boom. Boom. Boom.

"And we will go tonight to a holy conflict. We will step up as true neighbors, but not only for one by the road. Not for a single camp or caravan. For hundreds of thousands caged by devils and men sick with hate and power. And we will liberate our people!"

Boom. Boom. Boom. Boom. Boom.

The beats faded as Lopez paused. He closed his eyes, nearly chanting.

> *"Then the King will say to those on his right, 'Come, you who are blessed by my Father; take your inheritance, the kingdom prepared for you since the creation of the world. For I was hungry and you gave me something to eat. I was thirsty and you gave me something to drink. I was a stranger and you invited me in. I needed clothes and you clothed me. I was sick and you looked after me. I was in prison and you came to visit me.'"*

Silence accompanied his words. He continued.

> *"And the righteous will answer him, 'Lord, when did we*
> *see you hungry and feed you, or thirsty and give you*
> *something to drink? When did we see you a stranger*
> *and invite you in, or needing clothes and clothe you?*
> *When did we see you sick or in prison and go to visit*
> *you?'"*

Lopez smiled, a feeling of warmth spreading through his body. The power of the love of God became more real to him in this moment than at any other time in his life.

> *"The King will reply, 'Truly I tell you, whatever you did*
> *for one of the least of these brothers and sisters of mine,*
> *you did for me.'"*

Lopez hoisted a duffle bag of weapons on the truck bed with a grunt. Dust rose in the artificial light, the dawn still hours away. He turned to Houston. "Should we be glad Cohen is responding like this? Or terrified?"

"Both," she replied, tossing up another canvas bag bulging with ammunition.

He sized up the small convoy. Ten trucks carried all the fighters they could conjure. The chaos after the camp military strike left many still scattered around the region, and a large number were now in captivity.

The poor bastards. *Enhanced interrogation.* The brand on his forehead tingled. Visions of captives flooded his mind, the broken men and women who vomited any reality to stop the pain. Truth. Lies. It didn't matter. Half the intel would be garbage. The other half would expose them all. The only question was how long it took the inquisitors to sift through the chaff.

We'd have had to bug out anyway.

But not like this. Not under these circumstances. They weren't running away *from* the enemy. They were launching a full assault *at* the enemy. They had a mission.

He'd given his speech. He'd revealed the horrific facts. The impact was raw and devastating. The resistance was motivated. *Committed.* He ground his teeth. His forces lined the abandoned lot, each prepared to meet their maker.

They'd have marched to their doom even without the outside help.

But now Cohen augmented their corps. Intel 1 had committed treason, mixing legitimate law enforcement with outlaws. Heroes with terrorists. He hadn't believed it possible. "So why'd she help us?"

His lover paused, dropping a bag of supplies. She crossed her arms over her chest. "Honestly, I have no fucking clue. Ask Angel. Maybe she understands. All I know is what we both heard. The PI convinced her. Grace Gone."

Lopez stared into the desert sands. "Intel 1 is coming, calling in favors from law enforcement across the region. The needle's in the red."

"It's all moving very quickly. I hope we can coordinate this."

"We'll have a head start, but we need to navigate in stealth mode until the site. Split the group, different routes, avoid the feds, regroup. She'll call in one thousand national security and emergency codes to speed her mobilization. Given that, we should be arriving at Yucca Mountain at about the same time."

"We won't have any reconnaissance. No mission prep. We're flying in blind."

"We need an assault plan."

"Yup," she said, slapping a magazine into her Browning. "That, an army, and to win the lottery. We'd better not miss."

Lightfoote jogged toward them, a laptop in her hands. She placed it on a crate of explosives, waving them over. "You prayed for an assault plan. Angel provideth."

Houston and Lopez approached. He touched a bandage on Lightfoote's bare arm. "You get your infusion?"

"One of the last. Few more in line."

"Like things weren't crazy enough. Then Intel 1 sprints boxes of some miracle injection vials to us from a Cali biotech. Chemical warfare threat! At an illegal detainee camp. Next to a burial pit for the nation's radioactive waste." He shook his head.

"There isn't time to parse it," she shrugged. "We have to trust them, or why the hell did we call them in?"

She drew their attention to the screen. A diagram glowed in the night, schematics and images of the Yucca Mountain repository. A long tunnel snaked in a U-shape north to south on the map, framed by a vasculature of roadways.

"Keep in mind this is old intel. Publicly available. I don't have the gear or time to hack into real-time satellite imagery. There's likely a lot of changes to accommodate the hundreds of thousands of *guests* that have arrived. New camps, bigger than most we've seen."

"And they'll need the troops to serve and guard it," he said.

"Right. There are two construction zones, each around one of the entrances to the waste site." Her finger tapped on the screen. "The north entrance is larger, more developed, likely has water and a line to the grid. My guess is that anything they've added to the place was done for the camps."

"And this will likely be the most fortified area," injected Houston. "Roads, buildings, whatever tent cities they have."

"That's why we should come in from the south. Likely less surveillance and personnel."

"If they're in the north zone," said Lopez, "we'll have to hit it anyway. But maybe you're right. We'll have a little more surprise coming in from the south. I assume the approach is a hundred times harder?"

"Yes, we'll have to cover some tough terrain without good roads. But we'll also move more like the eagle flies, cut out a lot of road looping. And the bulk of the mountain is north and west. We can valley-hug for a good part of it." She tapped several keys and moved the pointer. A more detailed map revealed the structure of the underground waste repository. "But I've got a cooler idea."

He smiled. "Of course, you do, Angel. I would've been disappointed if you didn't."

"We split our forces. Send half our people from the south across the plain to the north. Well, that's assuming that's where they've settled. Otherwise, we adapt."

"And the other half?" asked Houston, her brows knitted.

"We go underground. Through the tunnels."

Lopez blinked. "*Through* the tunnels?"

"Wait," paused Houston, pulling her head back. "Did they ever put any nuclear waste in there?"

"No," said Lightfoote. "And no one uses it now." She traced the tunnel through the path into the mountain. "They bored out giant twenty-five-foot diameter tubes in the rock. It makes a horseshoe from south to north, going down into the earth. This is the main tunnel. The nuclear waste was to be stored in emplacement tunnels shooting off the main one. We can enter from the south portal, move unseen under Yucca Mountain, and pop out at the other entrance."

"How far?"

"Above ground is three miles, but the tunnel's five," she said.

He circled the south entrance with his finger. "Security?"

She clicked on a window. A photograph appeared, shot from inside the tunnel. It framed a round opening to a blue sky. A silhouette with a hardhat stood in the foreground. "*USA Today* article from a few years ago. I don't see any large mechanical devices like a door. There's some fencing in the background. My guess, not much in the way of security. Who's going to trek through the Mojave Desert to an abandoned nuclear waste facility?" She grinned. "And if there's a sealed entrance, we always have Bomb Girl." She winked at Houston.

"But things might've changed," he said. "We need to arrive in waves. If they have developed security, countermeasures, then we won't be taken out at once. But I like the idea. If we can get access to the tunnels, we'll come up on them from inside completely unexpected. Time it right with Cohen, we make a hell of a surprise strike."

Lightfoote pulled up a map of Nevada. "To make any time, we have to take I-95. We could send some trucks in parallel on 160, but it's another half hour, so we need to account for that. But even with secret detainment camps, they're not going to block off the highways. It's when we get close that all bets are off."

Lopez turned to face the congregating platoon of fighters he'd recruited. Young and old, trained fighters and street scrappers. He was about to march them all into war. That they were idealists bent on a righteous cause only made it that much harder.

"All bets were off once we decided to invade a clandestine detainment site." He exhaled. "The game is on."

52

WAPO

"You can hold my hand, Tyrell."

He peered under the brim of his Ice Topper. Her wheelchair added an incongruous quirk to the lobby of the *Washington Post*. They'd taken another trip to DC, this time to the new home of the *Post* at the One Franklin Square high-rise. The entire train ride had been exhausting. Not for the struggles of managing a wheelchair-bound traveler. He'd learned to deal with the handicap-unfriendly infrastructure of the nation. It was Gone's increasingly anxious state that drained him. That, and the need to move her with the caution of someone wheeling a president.

Two assassination attempts already. Sacker was not going to let there be a third. He'd swallowed his pride and contacted her father. The drug lord had helped create a security convoy. With some paranoia in the route, false departures, and dummy cars, they had made the trip without incident.

Now he focused on her mental state. He'd never seen her like this. Her analytic focus was shattered. The warmth of her gaze had dimmed. Shadows hung under her eyes and she fidgeted without stop.

He grasped her small hand in his great paw, squeezing gently. "With your rep, Gracie, he'll listen. They'll do the right thing."

She tried to steady her hands. She'd seen a lot in her life. A biological hazard zone in the basement of a madman. Half-dead zombies strapped to tables, their insides oozing from a man-made hemorrhagic fever. A helpless Tyrell Sacker in that hellhole, his eyes desperate after an injection of a live virus. And she'd had the guts to pull off her biohazard mask. Share the risk with him, quarantine and all.

But this was different. This was the bloodied claws of hell breaking through cracks in the earth and dragging people into the fires.

She trembled, her breathing rapid and shallow. "Thank you for this. I couldn't just sit back and wait for Cohen and Intel 1 to report back. Or for them to do the right thing. We have documents. We have the story of monstrosity." She wiped tears from her eyes. "And this country needs to know. The world needs to know."

A bald man in a tight suit shuffled through a set of glass doors opposite them. He was trim, in his mid-fifties, a razor-thin paint of gray beard over his chin and lip.

Sacker sat up on the couch. They locked eyes. "That's him."

The man marched toward them, shaking Sacker's hand. His eyes were wide and never left the wheelchair. "Tyrell Sacker," he said. "A long time. And this is surely the lovely Grace Gone?"

She extended her right arm, the left side still in a sling. "Maron Bartin," she replied as he stooped to grasp her hand. "I would stand, but circumstances have intervened. Will we be headed to your office?"

Bartin tipped his head forward. "Of course. I received your email. *And* the documents. I'm still recovering a bit from that. A hell of an attachment to read on the ride to work. Follow me, please."

Bartin sped through an array of reporters' cubicles. Devoid of office walls, the packed density made the space open and claustrophobic. At the end of the floor, he stopped at a side door and unlocked it. It led to his office. Sacker angled Gone's chair through the door and to the side of Bartin's desk.

He sat as Sacker pulled up a chair. "Let's get right to the point. I already have this out to my best teams. They're chasing down everything they can. And well, it's a lot to chase down."

"We don't have time for that," said Gone. "This is happening now.

The raid I told you about. *Today.* You need to run with this story now."

Bartin shook his head. "Even with such a source as yourself, Ms. Gone, there has to be a modicum of quality control. With a story this explosive, more so. But thank you for going on the record."

"I'll go to Bezos if I have to," she said. "He likes to get things done."

Bartin's mouth twitched to a smile. "You're a hard-ass, I see. Never judge a PI by her cover. The God-Emperor is in the loop. Don't waste your time. And if anything, he's pushing us. We're going to hit this story from every angle. We have an exclusive. But you will like to hear that we are sharing this with our newspaper competitors."

Sacker leaned forward. "You are?"

Saves us the trouble of several repeats.

Bartin nodded. "Jeff's idea. Some things are bigger than any one business. The *New York Times*, several other papers of consequence, major TV news organizations—he's personally reached out to all of them. Even Canid. From what I understand, news crews will be converging on the Nevada desert."

Sacker's face brightened. He touched Gone's arm. His smile faded at the harsh lines between her eyebrows.

"What they find there will change America," she said. "It's going to explode our politics, our sense of what and who we are. And our research shows that the current administration is responsible. This can't just be about ratings. If you really believe this is bigger than the *Post*, you know what you have to do. You and every editor in the country have come out strong. You have to call for the removal of those in power."

The editor's face remained locked, expressionless. Only his drumming fingers betrayed any emotion.

"I'm late for a meeting on this right now to coordinate not only our content in this news cycle, but also with the other presses." He locked eyes with her. "We understand the gravity."

Her face did not soften. "Suite might use the new law to shut you down."

"He probably will, but only after we've released it. And after that clumsy first attempt, our legal team is vaccinated. You can bet we'll launch a carpet bombing of the courts when they try." A corner of his mouth ticked up. "Besides, once it's out, you can't cage information on the internet. What they do to the press after is part of this historic story. We will see."

"We're here to do whatever we can," assured Sacker.

"I see that. Your willingness to go on the record, do this video today, is critical. We could never have run this without a strong public statement from our source, even from someone of your reputation, Ms. Gone. But I would like to address one missing element."

"Our sources from within the government," said Gone, anticipating him.

"You've said the document leak is anonymous. I believe you. But the other information, I'm sure you have a source in the DoJ somewhere. But you won't share that."

"No. I won't. It may come out in what's happening. It might not. But that's not my call. There's a reason that's staying secret."

He sighed. "You're cracking the dam. Releasing a flood. It's going to cause pandemonium. Cameras and protestors are going to descend on that salt mine like a locust swarm. DC is going to have a nuclear meltdown."

She leaned back in her wheelchair. Sacker saw the first hints of a smile creep over her lips as she spoke.

"That's exactly what we're hoping for."

53

GHOSTS

C ohen stared at the benzodiazepines, little pink pills arrayed in neat, foil-coated rows. Ready for use. A little thumb pressure to pop them out, and she swallowed one with a glass of water. Then, she shoved the leaf of drugs back into her purse.

I need to be sharp. Damn the turbulence.

Too much was happening all at once. Too little solid information. John in New York. Mjolnir. Grace Gone dropping documents signaling the largest scandal in American history. Intel 1's research suggesting possibilities she struggled to face. Now she was thousands of feet in the air blasting through the atmosphere in a tin can, heading for a humanitarian disaster in the making. Once she landed, then came the fun of an additional helicopter ride.

So what about those pills, girlie?

No. She had to process the recent data from her Cyrus team. Her brain could not be dulled.

She adjusted the computer on the desk of the jet. The message had come from New York. Her quivering finger mashed a button, opening a file.

Her lips tightened. The connection her team made linked to events a decade ago. Events she knew only too well. Back to William Gunn and the years when Mjolnir first surfaced. The link was through one of the companies in Grace Gone's files, Forster LLC. They acquired a subsidiary of Gunn International, formerly Operon Shipping, now Danville Shipping.

Operon.

Waves of nausea swept through her. Gunn had smuggled arms for his terrorist war against Muslims through Operon. Operon conjured ghosts better left forgotten.

While she was in transit, her team had followed her instructions. They had moved aggressively, raiding the offices of Forster. Their ships had come up empty with the information search, but not with the chemistry.

Cohen tightened, her stomach nauseous as much from the data as the flight. They had swabbed the cargo holds. They had run it for the explosive S-47. The result of that analysis was in the file.

Please no. Please don't tell me this.

She opened the lab report. Strong S-47 signal. Every muscle spasmed. It was positive.

As her adrenaline spiked, her mind functioned analytically in parallel. Mjolnir was running weapons and explosives through Danville, their old shipping system. Which of course meant that there existed a direct link between Mjolnir and Forster.

"Gone's files," she whispered.

The chords on her neck bulged. The damn files. Forster was one of several corporations that possessed a money trail leading back to Iran. Those sources funneled funds into the China Girl project as well as several of Suite's election and inauguration budgets.

Operon to Danville. Danville to Forster. Forster to Suite and his co-conspirator in Iran.

She couldn't bury the fear inside. Evidence incarnated her nightmare: Mirnateghi was behind the resurgent Mjolnir. The puzzle pieces slammed together.

"John. Oh, my God."

"Rebecca, you're breaking up."

Gone tried again, fiddling with the speakerphone remote control. It was past midnight. Part of her just wanted Sacker to end the phone call, pick her up, and drop her in bed.

And join me there.

Gone groaned, redialing the number. The static on the line returned, but Cohen's voice was clearer.

"Grace? Can you hear me now?"

"Better. This connection's terrible."

"I'm mid-flight. We're bouncing this across who knows what set of sats and lines. Did you get what I said?"

She shook her head. "No. You mentioned something about a company linked to William Gunn."

"There's no time to flesh this out. Please listen. We found S-47 residue on the boats of a shipping company that links to Iranian funds. To Mirnateghi."

Gone's haggard eyes widened. "Then that means Mjolnir is Iranian funded!"

"At least in part, yes."

Sacker gestured to the phone, leaning toward it. "Then what the hell is John walking into?"

Cohen's voice rose. The static worsened. "That's my fear. Mjolnir is terrifying enough. Knowing it's backed by Mirnateghi—I don't know what to expect. I can't reach John, now. He's gone dark for the mission on North Brother Island."

"North what? Where?" he asked.

"An abandoned island near the Bronx," she said. "It used to house sanatoriums for TB patients and the like."

"Never heard of it. What's going on there?"

"Mjolnir's secret headquarters. Right in front of us. He's planned a covert strike tomorrow. He hopes to deal a death blow to them, capture their leader."

"A leader with Mirnateghi's backing." He looked at Gone. "With that monster, I'd be worried, too."

The speaker erupted as Cohen exhaled. "They don't need help to be monstrous. But yes. Everything is going mad at once. That's why I'm going to ask a hard favor from you, Tyrell."

Gone grimaced. The endpoint was obvious. Sacker's response assured. A strong urge to lock him in a closet flowed through her.

But I can't. I'm trapped in this chair. Rebecca, do you know what you're asking?

"Favor? What could I possibly do?"

"Call in your NYPD connections. Warn them. Get more support than the small force he's arranged. If he knew Mirnateghi was involved, he'd have planned more carefully, used overwhelming firepower."

He squeezed his temples. "I'm sorry. You know what happened to me, how I left the NYPD. They'll never forgive me for bringing Grace in on the Eunuch Maker, showing them up. I'm a pariah. No one will pick up the phone, let alone lift a finger for anything I ask."

"*Please*. Can you at least try?"

The plaintive tone stabbed her. She glanced at Sacker, images of him in Dyer's home laboratory flooding her. He'd dashed off, fueled on raw emotion, to that near death as well.

"Of course," he said, his eyes shifty and glancing to the floor. "I'll try. With everything going on, maybe I can convince them to commit more people."

"*Thank you*, Tyrell. I mean that. Please update me if you make any progress. I don't know if I'll be able to respond. I'm about to land in a tempest. And that's not about the weather."

"We understand," said Gone, her chest constricted as she stared at Sacker. "Good luck."

The line went dead. The room froze, silent and still. When she yanked her wheelchair toward Sacker, the wheels screeched, raking her ears.

"I'm coming with you," she said.

He startled. "What? How did you—"

"I'm coming with you. And there'll be no debate. If you try to leave me here, I'll hire a boat and land this damn wheelchair on the island."

"Gracie, what makes you think—"

"Don't *Gracie* me right now. Don't try to outthink me. I'm sorry if that's rude, but I'm angry. I know you lied to her. We *both* know NYPD is dead to you. But you feel you owe Savas. And maybe you do. Without Intel 1, you'd be dead." She coughed, trying to hide her emotion. "So I guess I owe them, too."

He stiffened, his eyes wide.

"I *know* you're going there yourself. Like an idiot. Like the idiot who tried to take on the Eunuch Maker all by himself. You'll do it no matter what I say because that's the kind of impulsive loyalty you have." A tear dropped down the side of her cheek. "But I'm not going to boil in my own juices waiting to hear if you took a bullet for John Savas."

He gaped, shaking his head. "I…I don't know what to say."

"You'll leave me outside. I don't hold any delusions that I can do anything else. But I've got to be there with you."

54

TREASON

"Seven western state FBI field offices are on board."

A young agent panted in the doorframe of Savas's office. Cohen nodded and returned to her phone call. The agent turned and rushed back down the hallway.

"I don't care if you have to break every union rule, pay ten times the overtime, hire a damn drug cartel shipping group, but get all the antibodies out! It doesn't do one damn bit of good to have made them if they sit in your warehouse. I have a local team coming in to advise. Do what they say and get the rest of that stuff shipped!"

She slammed the receiver down and mashed her temples between her fingers.

John! You picked a hell of a time to go independent.

Her assistant popped her head into the doorway. "Your plane is ready."

Cohen exhaled. "Thanks, Melinda."

This was going to work. She would make it work. They would twist enough arms, call in enough favors, put the entire power of a black ops governmental agency with a substantial dark budget into motion.

And for what?

She hoped to God this mad risk was worth it. But they had to move. Everything was converging in the Southwest.

An Indian woman appeared behind her assistant. Her face was slack, eyes large.

"Yes, Seema? I don't like that look."

"Emergency. They're at the gates. With *troops*."

Cohen blinked. "Who's at the gates? What troops? What are you talking about?"

"There was no announcement. No warning. FBI. National guard! We're trying to ID all the forces, but Darton's there. He's demanding entrance."

"What? This is insane."

"He says he has warrants for your arrest."

Cohen set her jaw, glaring at the Intel 1 agent. She stood up and straightened her pantsuit jacket, the blue fabric stained from several nights sleeping in the office. Pushing the chair back, she marched toward the two women. "What's the threat level? If we engage?"

"Engage? You don't mean—"

"What's the damn threat level? Or did we hire you for nothing?"

The woman stepped backward and focused, the muscles in her cheeks tight. "High. It will be a blood bath. But they don't have the numbers, even with half our forces gone. They don't know the site here." She nodded, as much to herself as to Cohen. "We'll win. But it will cost us."

Cohen smiled, placing a hand on the woman's shoulder. "Good. Assemble a force. Not just of our fighters. Put a gun in the hand of every clerk and secretary who can fake it. The bigger mass we show, the more we intimidate. This is all going to come down to guts and psychology. Meanwhile, stall. Don't let those bastards through security until I okay it. Then we'll meet them with a welcoming party. They'll get to decide whether obeying Daniel Suite is worth losing their lives."

The woman stood motionless.

"Seema, go! Get the remaining squad leaders in the loop and they'll take over."

The agent turned and sped down the hallway.

Cohen's assistant glanced at her with wide eyes. "I've never shot a gun."

Cohen squeezed her hand. "And hopefully you'll never have to. We don't want a fight. We can't afford a fight. We need all our strength in Nevada. Get to the operations room, find someone to give you an unloaded weapon. At the first sign of trouble, run. But until then, look the part. Can you, Melinda? So much depends on this."

Banks locked eyes with Cohen. "Maybe I'll ask for bullets. Real's got to be real."

She dashed from the office. Cohen returned inside and opened a large drawer in the desk. She removed a shoulder harness, the holster bulging with the weight of her firearm. She strapped the harness over her suit, making the presence of the weapon overt. After closing the drawer, she stepped across the room and into the hallway.

Dashing down the hallway, bringing along increasing numbers, she soon stood in the cavernous entrance to the underground lair of Intel 1. They had dramatically modified the old cold war bunker. Here, the roadway from the tunnel under the Hudson River ended before the underground caverns. A secure doorway, massive like that sealing NORAD, provided enough thickness to survive a nuclear blast. Darton's short-notice team wasn't going to enter without their permission. Unfortunately, the doorway was also the only practical way out.

"Open the gate."

Agents manning the doorway turned from her to the control panels. Seconds later, the massive structure groaned as it swung open, a troop of armed men entering as it did. They jogged in quickly, tactical armor and helmets glinting in the artificial light. Their body language was aggressive as they cleared the door, but they slowed with a growing uncertainty as the crowd of armed men and women inside came into focus.

Intel 1 positioned people in a broad semi-circle flanking the invading troops at every angle. Directly in front was Cohen and the largest mass of people. Spread to the corners parallel with the gate were armed members, some on elevated man-made or natural structures in the cavern.

Through the ranks marched the mustachioed Darton. His eyes opened to large circles, his mouth twisted in a snarl.

"What is the meaning of this?" He glared at Cohen, but stopped beside the front of his forces, not daring to approach her and the heavily armed agents aiming guns in his direction. "I have a warrant for your arrest, Agent Cohen, and am here on the authority of the Attorney General himself—"

"Since when does the DoJ send presidential cabinet members to a raid? You folks have done wonders for the executive's operations."

"Agent Cohen, by the order of President Suite, I—"

"We don't have time for this dance," snapped Cohen. "*I* don't have time. You've got one minute to decide if you want to try and shut us down. Fair warning: if you do, most of us won't be walking out of here."

He took a step backward, his face a bright shade of red offsetting the white of his mustache. "This is treason."

"I might have to agree with you. But, if we're going to do treason, we're going to do treason in a blaze of glory. Is that how you want to go out?"

Her voice echoed off the stone of the high ceiling. The colossal door pinged as the weight of the open gate strained the metal. Darton licked his lips, glancing across her forces. His shoulders slumped, his arm dropping to his side with the warrant crumbled in his hand.

"No? Then I'll give you an out. Order your forces to stand down. Turn the hell around and march out of Intel 1. Go back to Suite and tell him whatever you have to. The pain of that is infinitely less than getting your chest ripped open in gunfire."

Sweat trickled down his cheek. He scanned his forces, men with fingers on triggers, some appearing eager for a firefight.

A cornered and cowardly rodent. Take the exit, Darton.

"Thirty seconds, sir."

"God damn you!" He turned from her to his forces. "Stand down. Now!" he yelled, the men lowing their weapons. "We're leaving."

He stormed out through his murmuring ranks, the National Guard and FBI troops more cautiously backing away from the armed

Intel 1 contingent. As the last of them passed through the doorway, Cohen gave a sign and the operators shut the gate.

Melinda Banks exhaled next to Cohen, her eyes fierce. Her voice trembled in the stillness. "And don't let the door hit you in the ass on the way out."

55

ASSAULT

Savas hugged the rigid side of the inflatable boat. His was one of six deployed to North Brother Island. Each made a simultaneous incursion along the shore surrounding an old sanitarium. He'd brought the core of his tactically-trained operatives from Intel 1. Six to a boat, two as crew to launch and pilot the craft from the Bronx. The other four members of the team carried automatic weapons. He'd stuck with his old NYPD-issued Glock firearm. He wouldn't lead the charge, anyway.

Too damn old.

There was no moon, but the background glow of New York compensated for it. The shape of the island appeared as a shadow in its radiance. As they neared, the engine cut, and the darkness dissolved into vegetation and rocks. The hull scraped against the pebbled shore. Several shapes leapt out of the boat and into the shallow water, beaching the craft. He swung over the side and landed on the ground.

He tested his earpiece and microphone. "Archangel planted. Status."

One by one, the team leaders of the other boats reported in. They'd completed the first stage without incident, placing their teams on enemy territory.

"Blue Boys, you're next. Seas are clear."

The sea captains of the NYPD signaled back. They launched their police boats toward the island.

Backup.

They'd likely need some.

A former Navy Seal rushed from the jungle of vegetation in front of them and straight toward him. "Benson and I scouted ahead. Maps were right. There's some remains of a roadway ahead. Overgrown, but the vegetation is lighter there. He's with Thomas, checking for sentries and unpleasantries."

"Unpleasantries?" he asked.

"Mantraps. IEDs. I figured we treat this like combat."

"Right. You read the briefings."

A voice cut in on their radios, crackling in his ear. "Archangel. Coast is clear. Join us up the road."

They sprinted. A swift jog to the younger men, but for Savas, it was an all-out haul. Wild undergrowth complicated the dash. Untended by human hands since the middle of the last century, it took some navigation. He arrived last, gasping as he approached the others.

Benson sported a pair of night vision goggles and pointed toward the looming hospital structure. Even in the weak lighting, Savas could see its decayed form. Ivy coated it like paint, stones and mortar broken and falling from the sides. A part of the roof had collapsed.

"Sentries at each corner," said the soldier. "Two at the back entrance, likely more in front."

Savas relaxed. The attack plan was solid. Two other teams confirmed positions at the rear. The remaining two planned a delayed rush. They would storm the front once the guards there had moved into the building. That was assuming the rear assault would draw them out of position.

The best-laid schemes o' mice an' men....

He wasn't going to finish the poem.

His receiver crackled. "Archangel. Do we have the word?"

Savas exhaled, the breath long. He locked eyes with Benson, speaking into the receiver.

"Go. Repeat, all teams, go, go, go!"

Chaos erupted. Mjolnir scouts picked up their forces seconds after they pushed through the vegetation. As the strike teams zeroed on the building, gunfire blasted toward them. He heard the whiz of bullets, the screams of men, the retort of high-powered rifles and automatic weapons. The flash of gunpower became a firefly show in the night.

The sounds brought him back to the madness in the plains of the Midwest, when a military coup d'état had split America in two and brought battle to the shores of a land peaceful since the Civil War. This skirmish paled in comparison. Smaller. No heavy artillery or air deployment. And yet, just as in the bloody snow in Ohio and Kansas, the bodies fell. Men cried out in pain. Blood flowed.

Like the manager he now was, he ran from the rear toward the battle lines, but the firefight slowed before he was truly engaged. He stepped over corpses and writhing injured bodies, leaving the tending to the medical teams. The leader of his squad was still alive, identifying Savas and signaling silently that they were going to move into the structure. He nodded and gave his leader a thumbs-up, and the group of men converged with the other teams as they approached the aged stone walls of the sanitarium.

Less men.

The Mjolnir defenses had performed well, cutting his forces down by at least a third, but now they had access to the building. Now the rats were cornered with nowhere to go.

His com crackled, the radio signal weak and jammed. He could barely make out the words.

"Honey pot....one eighty...."

They had no code with that name. This was breaking protocol. This was an emergency. Honey pot? That was a term for false treasure, cyber or sexual. It was used to lure hackers or spies. Did it mean...

"Heat signatures...forest...."

His team leader spun to look behind them. Savas felt his stomach tighten. The garbled communications continued to sound.

"Sudden...shielded. Repeat, rear ambush!"

Gunfire exploded from behind. Men dropped around him like dominoes. Savas and the rest reacted with instinct, dashing into the building, fleeing the assault of bullets ripping through them from the forest.

Inside, they were met with a second barrage of weapons discharge. Mjolnir had positioned forces on both sides, the vice of projectiles squeezing with death's grip. Now they were trapped between a hammer and an anvil.

A trap long planned. Savas grimaced, the reek of gunpowder thick in the air. *They were waiting.*

He crouched behind an overturned table in the large room. It was an old lecture hall, complete with stadium seating. The rotted wood of the benches and chairs reeked, the fibers molded and broken by time. Now they were shattered in places by weapons fire. Mildewed books coated the floor like some art project. Blood splattered the pages from several downed soldiers. He was alone.

"Archangel here," he said into his comm. "Status! All teams report!"

Static crackled.

The assault was in disarray. By driving the Mjolnir forces inside, they'd won entrance to the sanitarium, only to find it a feint. Terrorist reinforcements flooded from the forest and trapped his teams inside. Machine guns ripped through the tactical armor his people wore. For every downed Mjolnir soldier, he'd lost five.

A massacre.

Savas's forces were gone. He feared the worst for the NYPD patrols around the island. Men had died and the hydra was still alive, still able to strike the defenseless. He had failed. And his gut told him that he would not walk off this island.

I'm sorry, Rebecca.

"Special agent John Savas," came a booming voice.

He turned his head to the side. The tones were familiar. The bass and rasp unmistakable.

Patrick Rout.

Savas popped the magazine out of his pistol. The gray polymer mag was dark in the low light, but enough for Savas to count the four rounds remaining. He didn't doubt that Rout had marksmen set to shoot the second he showed his face. The question was how fast his aging muscles could move, aim, and pull the trigger.

Rout was close. By sound alone, Savas could pinpoint the voice to the middle of the rising seating. If he could roll to the side of the table, set his aim, there was a chance.

I won't make it back, Rebecca. But I can take that monster down with me.

Shards exploded from the wooden table. Holes ruptured at either end, moving inward, squeezing. Dust and mold choked his lungs. The killers of Mjolnir left him with only one option.

He slapped the magazine into the gun, leapt up, and aimed.

Several shots ripped through his body armor. His gun arm exploded, the joint vaporized at the elbow, his weapon falling to the ground before he'd fired a single shot.

Fire raged in his belly and the right side of his chest. He let out a furious growl and slumped to the hard table edge, rolling to the floor. A warm river flowed over his torso.

Heavy footsteps echoed off the stone walls, the impact muffled by decaying books. Savas glanced up, the room spinning. Above him loomed the chiseled bulk of an older man, his head shaven, a weapon in his right hand. A diabolical grin wrapped around his face like a tumor as he spoke.

"I've waited a long time for this."

56

YUCCA MOUNTAIN

The band of the Milky Way spilled in majesty over the sky. Lopez turned away, focusing on the Earth. He peered through binoculars across a shrubbed plain near the Yucca Mountain ridge. Weapons discharge echoed in the distance. Flashes of light accompanied the retorts from the North Portal.

The enemy was near. American or foreigner, patriotic flag wavers or bloodthirsty Islamic radicals, it didn't matter. Those that would harm his people were the foe. Again, the psalms of King David came to his mind.

> *Deliver me from mine enemies, O my God:*
> *defend me from them that rise up against me.*
> *Deliver me from the workers of iniquity,*
> *and save me from bloody men.*
> *For, lo, they lie in wait for my soul:*
> *the mighty are gathered against me;*
> *Consume them in wrath,*
> *consume them, that they may not be:*
> *and let them know that God ruleth*
> *in Jacob unto the ends of the earth.*

But unto thee, O my strength, will I sing:
for God is my defense, the God of my mercy.

He lowered the binoculars. He reoriented his gaze to the South Portal through the powerful scope of his rifle. Five ICE agents guarded a chain link fence blocking access to the tunnel entrance. A small generator powered a set of lights by a makeshift guard station.

He spoke into the microphone on his headset. "They're getting spooked, but holding in place. We can't wait much longer." He mouthed a prayer, his words lost to the desert wind. "Take them out."

A series of sharp pops played around him. Through the scope, he saw the guards drop one by one to the ground. He focused on each for several seconds. None moved.

He gave the all-clear, and a set of snipers rose from the desert around him. Engines roared to life in the distance. Headlights sliced the dust as trucks shifted into gear and approached. They stopped before the advanced party, kicking sand into the air and fogging the light. Drivers from each jumped down and jogged to Lopez, forming a circle. Lightfoote and Houston arrived from different directions.

"We stick to the plan," he said. "Angel, Sara, and I will lead two teams into the mountain. We'll take the main tunnel around to the North Portal. We exit there and bring an element of surprise to the mix. The rest of you, haul your asses over the roads—secrecy be damned. Cohen's forces are fighting already, and we need to get in the churn now. You'll take some flak but also split their focus and aim. Divide and conquer. Questions?"

"Anyone *not* get the magic serum?" called Lightfoote, glancing around the assembled fighters. "Countermeasures for a possible chemical attack. If you didn't get it, don't be stupid. Sit this out."

No one responded.

"Then let's move!" he shouted.

The forces heading to the North Portal scrambled back to their vehicles. The trucks coughed, roaring past the remaining group. After they passed, he jogged toward the fencing in front of the South Portal, the others falling in step behind him.

A minute later, they came to a stop before the barrier. Five bodies lay at their feet, the victims of their snipers from moments ago.

Lightfoote examined the links, signaling with her hands. "Bolt cutters!"

Several figures rushed forward brandishing tools, tearing into the metal. Lopez watched her smirk at Houston. "No bombs tonight, Honey," she said

"The night is young," Houston replied.

He tore his gaze from the pair and focused on the incisions into the metal. Seconds later, there was a vehicle-sized hole in the fence. The troop rushed through, passing gigantic tunnel-boring equipment. The machinery was long abandoned and left to decay along the roadway to the tunnel. The entrance was unbarred, the interior lit dimly by LED lights along the ceiling.

Rail tracks extended from outside and down into the heart of the mountain. Ahead of them, a set of cargo wagons sat perched on the tracks.

"Hitch a ride?" said Lightfoote, examining the front car.

"No way the cars still work on this," said Houston. "We'll have to leg it."

Lightfoote held her hand up. "There's a manual set of brakes. If we can heave the thing forward, gravity will do the rest."

"At least halfway. Assuming we don't lose control and crash to an early demise."

"We can fit all of us in the first two cars. They're joined by manual couplers. Let's unhook the rest and start pushing."

His people moved toward the tracks. They struggled with the attachments. He removed a set of large flashlights and handed them to Lightfoote. "I don't know how long these lights last. I'm amazed they're still on."

She squinted down into the tunnel. "There's been activity here, that's for sure. But what the hell are they doing?"

"We're going to find out." Metallic clanks signaled the decoupling of the first two cars from the rest. He moved to the front. "Let's try to get this moving by hand. Angel's the lightest, so she'll drive and work the breaks. Once we get some speed, leap in or find yourself chasing us down the hill."

The team lined up on each side of the small train and behind. Lightfoote slammed metal and shouted. "Loose!"

They pushed. The rusted rails screeched under the friction of the metal wheels, the troop wincing as one. But the wagons moved. The grade increased, the tunnel sloping downward, and their walk transitioned to a slow jog.

"Everyone up!" he cried.

Even as he spoke, they gained speed, the sound earsplitting. Members of their team struggled to keep hold and hoist themselves over the edges and into the holds.

Lightfoote duct-taped a pair of flashlights to the front edge. She leaned in and out on the break, slowing the cars, then allowing them to accelerate.

"You think you've got this?" Lopez yelled over the sound of wailing metal.

Her bleached hair puffed backward as they hurtled downward. A grin spread over her face. "Oh, yeah. I got this."

The LEDs ended. The tunnel strobed to the pair of lights at the head of a screaming snake.

They plunged into blackness.

57

MISSING PERSONS

The pilot set the helicopter down roughly. Two Intel 1 agents opened the door. Dust from the whirling blades overhead mimicked a storm in the Sahara. Red lights flashed from the aircraft. Cohen covered her mouth with a scarf and stepped on the sands at the North Portal entrance.

Fires raged around her. Bodies littered the ground. ICE agents. Uniformed soldiers. Police and FBI that she had brought, some with grisly wounds. Entire groups, fallen without a scratch on them. Smoke mixed with dust and rose into the night sky, obscuring the stars.

"My God."

Cohen winced as her stomach lurched, bile heaving toward her throat. The information linking Mjolnir and Mirnateghi that she received en route had shattered her concentration. Savas was in terrible danger, but she had to focus. Even greater events unfolded in front of her.

Hold it together, Rebecca.

A man jogged up to her, his face sooty and smeared with sweat. Several others accompanied him in uniforms too filthy to discern. "Agent Cohen?" he shouted over the helicopter engine.

She squinted at him. "Agent Rodríguez? I hardly recognize you."

"It's been a real shit storm, ma'am, if you'll excuse me."

"Tell me."

He glanced behind him. "Come with me. I'll take you to the main site. We've established a makeshift command center."

The group of soldiers escorted her into the heart of the chaos. The odd retort of gunfire sounded sporadically with, floating like whispers on the wind, the high-pitched tones of...

Children's voices?

"As you can see, the fighting's done," coughed Rodríguez, wiping grit from his eyes. "We've got things under control. But I'm glad I insisted you stay out."

"Because I wasn't treated with the antibodies? There wasn't time!"

"Yes, I understand. But there was a chemical attack at the beginning."

She swallowed. "Did the countermeasures work?"

"Saved our asses. Got nothing but thanks to you for that. But, well, we had help from some local law enforcement, FBI. They didn't get the infusions. They're all dead."

She placed her hand to her throat.

Gone was right.

"But most of us and the forces from the south were protected. They can fight, let me tell you. The resistance here collapsed, and we took the site."

"That was faster than I had hoped."

His face tightened. "Their numbers weren't what you'd guess. We had a three-to-one advantage."

She cocked her head, staring around the site. Medics tended to the wounded. Prisoners were marched past her. "The entire thing doesn't look like I'd thought," she mused. "There's not much here. How do you house hundreds of thousands of people without a lot of infrastructure?"

"That's the thing, ma'am. You don't." He continued as her eyes bored into him. "There's not a hundred thousand here. Not even ten thousand. Just a couple thousand in just one new tent, right over there."

He pointed, indicating a towering structure behind them. Cohen watched as agents led a bewildered and terrified crowd from the canvas shelter. Men, women, and children shuffled past with darting eyes.

"This can't be right," she said. "We tracked them. They're chipped."

"I don't know about that, ma'am. Never heard of that tech. But I do know there's only a few thousand people here, not your four hundred thousand. There's no infrastructure for that many—ten thousand at most. Only a few tents. Well, and these weird buildings."

She followed his gaze. The fog around them obscured all except a faint shadow in the distance. An encroaching doom rolled through her psyche like a storm front.

"Show me," she whispered.

He walked her past the center of operations toward a three-story building. It was the strangest construction Cohen had ever seen. Long and rectangular, it spanned the width and length of a football field. The design defied any normal sense of architecture. A small doorway at one end and a broad, loading dock platform at the other. The dock faced toward a lone road running straight toward Yucca Mountain. There were no windows.

"That's the entrance to the tunnels?" she asked.

"Yes. Can't make heads or tails of this thing. I've got some men inside trying to now. Some kind of negative pressure environment, one said."

"Negative pressure." The chill inside her deepened.

"Yeah, what's inside isn't let out. It's all sealed and pressurized."

"Like an underwater habitat? Or submarine?"

"Ah, sure. I guess. But no water, of course. Just, well, air outside."

He pointed to a set of expansive ventilation shafts. The tubes were the width of buses and running to a smaller structure housing machinery. A set of larger electrical generators hummed nearby.

"There's some kind of pump system there that feeds air into the main building. The Nevada grid here's active, but likely a bit flaky from not being used for so long. They got a bunch of backup generators running. They power the pumps."

Cohen froze in the cool desert air. The industrial structures before her phased in and out of her awareness. Unreal. She imagined her body melting and dissolving into the dry sands. Her mind flashed to memories of documentaries, films, and history books.

Smokestacks and raining ash.

"It's almost like a giant air conditioner system," he concluded.

Her eyes tore from the hideous architecture and to the road leading into the tunnel system. A man was sprinting out, waving toward them.

"Jesus Marshall," said Rodríguez. "What's got into you?"

He closed the distance, bending in half to catch his breath a few feet in front of them. He panted as he spoke, his sentences staccato. "Agent…Cohen. Ma'am. Agent Rodríguez."

God, he's pale. The man's hands trembled.

"We've found…something. You need to come…see."

Rodríguez put a hand on this shoulder. "What's going on Marshall?"

"We've…found…the detainees." He gasped, inhaling and trying to compose himself. "All of them."

Rodríguez took a step backward, cocking his head. "Where?"

Marshall's eyes flicked up as he rested his hands on his knees. The whites glowed in the darkness.

"Inside…the tunnels."

58

AIR DROP

The helicopter approached the exposed beach on the eastern side of North Brother Island in the darkness. NYPD patrol boats drifted offshore with an ominous stillness.

Sacker checked on Gone. A large headset and seat swallowed her small form. Her body had become more diminutive since the assassination attempt.

She curls up more. Like a pangolin.

She smiled at him, haggard eyes betraying her anxiety. All the remaining assets of Intel 1 buzzed around them. That included local FBI and the NYPD Emergency Service Unit, the SWAT team of the city. He assumed Cohen had spent her last favors.

And not for no reason. Already it was clear a slaughter had occurred. The NYPD police boat units were floating tombs. Savas's teams were nonresponsive.

He was privileged to be included in the mission details of Intel 1. But there was a price. An expectation. He and a special team risen from the bowels of the earth under Manhattan would enter the fray.

To save Savas and bring down a terrorist group.

He shouldn't be here by almost any rational metric. But he owed them his life. And Cohen had called in that debt.

The bird shuddered as they hit the sands. Doors flung open and the team spilled out, waving him on.

He turned to Gone. "This is crazy. I just can't leave you here. It's not safe."

"Just go, Tyrell. No one cares about a hobbled Asian chick in an attack helicopter."

The blades beat over their heads, the shouts of men around them echoes in a wind tunnel. The deep brown of her eyes glinted in the strobe lights.

"I'm sorry. This isn't the time or place. Or maybe if this isn't…I mean, dammit, I can't lose you! Not again. I need you." He nodded, finally agreeing with himself. Accepting his fate. "I need you, Gracie."

Words came from deep inside, spilled from emotions that the moment unleashed beyond his ability to suppress them. What he was saying was the truth.

She grabbed him with her healthy arm, pulling his face to hers. Her breath was warm. Her smell, dizzying. "I need you, too! Haven't you deduced that, *detective*? Come back to me. *Don't* leave me alone. Promise me!"

He swallowed, the revelations stunning. Barriers, real or imagined, tottered and fell. *She needs me?* Doors opened to the future, exhilaration flowing through him. "Well, okay, then."

"You were a soldier. Be a soldier again. Whatever it takes. This is war. And you have to come back to me."

Despite the madness around them, he smiled, patting his old hat in her lap. "Don't lose it. From the Harlem Renaissance. I plan on wearing it a long time."

"Let's go!" cried a man outside.

With a last glance at Gone, he leapt out and followed them into the underbrush.

The thwacking beat of the craft's blades faded as they plunged into a thick forest. The sanitarium was near, as everything was on this tiny island. Within minutes, they came to a busted roadway.

Bodies lined the path. They multiplied as the team jogged forward. Scouts ahead beckoned them after securing each advance, the numbers of dead adding up. *Which side were they on?* The combat gear was similar, dark and camouflaged, the fighters easily swappable. In the end, the dead had no affiliation.

Which is going to make any live engagement tricky as hell.

His firearm was in his hands, an automatic rifle similar to the one he'd carried in Iraq. Old intuitions returned. His senses heightened, balancing on the edge of paranoia and superpower.

They reached the shell of the old building. There was a back entrance. The Intel 1 team would enter there.

Intuition.

He grabbed the team leader and pointed to an access ladder leading to the upper floors. "I'll take that, give you some eyes above."

The man squinted, unsure what to make of the improvisation. He nodded and left, joining the others moving in.

Sacker sprinted to the ladder. It was rusty, the links to the stone loose, and rose thirty or forty feet to multiple sets of windows.

A deathtrap.

But it was an unexpected entrance. He holstered his weapon and climbed. The ladder swung back and forth, threatening to dislodge at any moment. Halfway to the second floor, he'd decided this was an extremely stupid idea.

Get off here, Tyrell. Don't push your luck.

He reached a broad window. The glass was long shattered, vines exploding through the frame.

Perfect grip.

He grasped two thick canes from the main trunk and pulled himself off the fragile ladder. Several yanks and a roll later, he spun onto a creaky wooden floor. The pre-dawn glowed behind him, outlining the shape of the room. *A study.* A giant book was presented on a stand in the middle of the room. Thick pages the size of a dinner tray erupted from its spine. They were stained, torn, and molded, several pointing skyward in rebellion to gravity.

Voices.

He couldn't make them out, but someone was speaking inside. He thought he heard the groans of the injured.

He rushed out of the room, rifle in hand. The hallway outside opened to a vast inner chamber. A lecture hall of some kind was below him. He crouched beside a broken railing, peering down toward the sounds.

Savas.

The former FBI agent lay on the ground, severely wounded, covered in blood, and defenseless. Outside the building, weapons fire sounded along with the shouts of men. A broad man with a military assault weapon stood over him, gloating. His voice rose over the cacophony of battle.

"And now, the end of Intel 1 begins."

59

TUNNELS

Houston's breath came in rattled gasps. She considered herself in good shape. The requirements of survival in her profession demanded she stay sharp. But everyone had limits, and they were pushing themselves to the brink.

The crazed rollercoaster ride into Yucca Mountain saved time and energy. Lightfoote steered them on the edge of safety into the heart of the earth at high speed. Any obstacle meant potential disaster. Visibility was minimal, the brakes were slow to respond, but they'd escaped without incident.

The cars petered out in the darkness of the tunnel's minima. The resistance fighters took to their feet. A herd of tramping boots resonated off the surrounding rock walls. Blackness shrouded the sides of the tunnel. Only the strobing flashlight bounces lit the way forward as they jogged.

She repositioned her backpack as she ran. Feeling for the holster, her hand touched the cold metal of the Browning 1911. The lethal chill soothed her, returned her focus. She centered her mind on the coming chaos.

It won't be long now.

Time was as much their enemy as the diabolical forces of Daniel

Suite. The battle at the Yucca Mountain detainee camp raged, its outcome a complete mystery. Their other contingent had certainly arrived and engaged. Cohen's Intel 1 forces were likely present as well. They'd entered the fray with little preparation. There'd been no time to scout the camp design, its defenses, or the number of troops guarding it.

And if it's ten squads of Navy Seals, we're in trouble.

Lightfoote's idea was to come up from behind, through the tunnels, in a sudden and devastating element of surprise. Many humorous analogies ran through her mind. She shoved them aside, pacing her breathing as they raced up the incline toward the North Portal.

And what if this entrance is blocked?

The weight of the C4 in her pack reminded her of the options. Nothing was going to slow them down for long. And if there was one thing she was good at, it was blowing things to hell and back.

Lopez spoke through heavy gasps. "Light…ahead."

He was right. First, only a glow was distinguishable from the darkness, but it strengthened and soon became unmistakable. Like the South Portal, a strip of LEDs ran along the ceiling as they neared the exit. Only, something was different with this end of the tunnel.

An odd odor, earthy yet mixed with antiseptics, assaulted her nose. She squinted, the dim illumination confusing her. The large metal pipe paralleling the LEDs was familiar, but it was pressed on each side by something unusual. The gray rock walls morphed into a material both dark and shiny. Even the sounds changed. The familiar echoes became muffled and deadened.

Is the tunnel narrowing?

"Slow down," said Lopez, holding up his hand.

The pack stumbled to a stop, chests heaving. The dark fog around them dissolved ahead in the face of the lighting. She followed the circumference of the tunnel.

It's definitely tighter.

There were additions to the sides of the concrete walls. Black plastic glinted like oil, puffed bags of insulation, a thin layer of paint that grew much thicker in the direction of the entrance. The smell grew. Ahead, the tunnel constricted to a thin cylinder. The diameter was hardly wide enough to allow passage of freight along the tracks. The black bags choked the passage like plaque in an artery.

"New construction?" she asked.

Lopez shook his head. "I don't think so. It looks like…"

Lightfoote whipped around, her eyes haunted, shaking her head. She marched toward Lopez. "Francisco, stop. This—"

He shoved her to the side. His eyes widened but remained focused. Planting one foot in front of the other, he lumbered forward like a sleepwalker.

Houston squinted.

What the hell's going on?

She stepped toward Lightfoote, glancing between her and Lopez. "Angel?"

The former FBI star turned around. Tears were in her eyes as she shook them loose. She embraced Houston and buried her head in the crook of her neck. The pressure of her ribs was rhythmic as she wept.

The contingent behind them murmured and whispered. She heard Spanish and English. Curses and prayers. Lopez stepped toward a nearby train car in the middle of the tracks. It was filled with the black insulation, the bags stacked to the top of the car. The plastic was zippered from top to bottom, the mirrored steel of the teeth flashing under the lights.

He grasped the metal slider, pulling it forward. The sound ripped through the still space, the teeth popping obscenely.

Hair.

Long black hair spilled out of the bag like blood from a wound. He stepped back, his head jerking in short bursts, trying to shake "no" as his body failed him.

The murmuring behind crescendoed. There were cries and wails. Killers wept. Lightfoote held tighter, never lifting her head.

She followed the curve of the tunnel walls, reappraising. The twenty-five-foot diameter narrowed for a great distance. Stacks and stacks of black bags piled as far as her eyes could see. An ocean of them congealing like a blood clot.

Not insulation.

Dear God.

Bodies. Thousands and thousands of bodies.

Lopez fell to his knees, gazing up at the horror encircling them. A primeval howl ripped from his lips and echoed through the hellish space.

60

DEBTS PAID

Savas moaned, straining, writhing to one side.

Patrick Rout.

The devil was revealed in all his diabolical splendor. Bulging muscles even in his fifties. Combat scars along his neck and jaw. A sharp crew cut with blond hairs like sharpened spikes. Rout smiled at the futile lunges of a dying man. The terrorist sited his prey down the barrel of a gun.

"We don't have much time together, I'm afraid to say," said Rout. "I'm due on a boat out before too many of your sweet wife's reinforcements arrive."

"You leave her out of this!" Savas choked on ragged coughs.

I'm dying.

"That's exactly what I will not be doing. My benefactor—a woman of a most singular focus, as I'm sure you're aware—has contracted me for several kills. Yours, the first and most satisfying. But Intel 1 must die, and along with it, your lovely Agent Cohen."

No! A trap, but not only for him. A long-set ambush for everything he and Rebecca had worked for. A pit to bury both of them as well.

Savas arched his back, frantically searching the space around them for an escape. *Anything.* All he could see were two guards. One posted near Rout, another high in some balcony and concealed in shadows, aiming a rifle toward him.

"After I've killed her, Nemesis has her own plans, even as she funds us to complete ours. She's a master chess player. As was my friend, Liam. But he died that day you and Intel 1 destroyed our movement. When you shot both of us down that day at Tampico. Nemesis helped lay this long trap. Every step, designed. Each person you captured, a strategic sacrifice. We plotted for a long time to lure you here. Fortunately, our new president has been most accommodating, following our suggestions to help steer you to this moment and the end of everything you have tried to accomplish."

Rout raised his weapon, aiming squarely at Savas.

"This is for William Gunn and Mjolnir."

Defeat and blood loss drained his will. Inevitability froze his limbs. This was how his life ended, before the hands of this monster, knowing the beast would turn next on all her cared for. And he could do nothing. Savas shut his eyes. *Goodbye, Rebecca.*

A shot rang. Even in his near delirium, he knew something was off.

Too far.

A heavy thud sounded next to him and the wood platform shuddered. He opened his eyes, ignoring the outline of the body beside him and focusing on the origin of the shot.

The shadow in the balcony whipped a weapon twenty degrees and locked on the guard nearby. The Mjolnir soldier zeroed the assassin, raising a gun.

A round burst through the guard's neck. The soldier staggered backward and clutched his throat. He dropped off the stage to the floor below.

Savas relaxed, exhausted even in the effort to gaze around him. He lowered his head, angling it to his right. Alongside him lay the twitching form of Patrick Rout, the right side of his skull missing. Screams continued outside, but few shots were fired. One way or the other, the battle was ending.

Out of the corner of his eye, he sensed a shadow above as it rose. The marksman rushed toward a collapsed portion of the balcony near

Savas's head. Across the lecture hall, the floor had given way, large planks running down like a gangway.

Throwing caution aside, the man sprinted to it and slid down. The wood cracked and he tumbled, catching himself in a roll. His shoulder slammed into the wall.

Moving toward Savas, he raised his weapon and scanned the room. The killer's face clarified.

"Tyrell…." His voice cracked, his eyes rolling up as he struggled to maintain consciousness. "Rebecca…."

Scrambling forward, Sacker leapt over debris, sliding to a stop beside him. "Dammit, John. You're a clusterfuck."

Of course he was. Multiple gunshot wounds. Massive rounds blown past his body armor and through his lung and mid-torso. His right arm nearly severed at the elbow. *Blood loss.* None of that mattered.

He croaked, his eyes unfocused and wild. "You need to protect… Rebecca. *Nemesis.* She'll kill her."

"Rebecca's fine, John." Sacker's eyes were sad. He knew the truth. "*Jesus.* After this, it's Mirnateghi who'll need protection."

"Tell father Timothy…pray for me. For what I've done."

"Shut up, John." Sacker ripped off his tactical gear and removed his shirt. Sweat dropped over the stained wood of the lecture stage. He pressed the shirt over Savas's chest wound.

"Tempted. They planned it all. A fool. I failed."

"Rout's dead! You didn't fail. Now, hang on. We have help on the way." The shirt was already saturated, Sacker's hands dyed crimson.

"Tyrell…don't. Mortal wounds. Only minutes."

"Damn, man, I can't just—"

"Got to accept it. *She's* got to accept it. Let me go. Tell her to…let me go. Hold what we had. The good we did. Then…*let go.*" Savas coughed, the smell of copper misting the air. A crimson line ran from his left nostril. His words bubbled through blood. "Her story's not over yet."

Footsteps stampeded into the room. Sacker kept the pressure on the chest "Someone get help here now! He's dying!"

"Ah. Funny." Savas stared toward the ceiling, the world drawing away from him like a child's toy.

"NYPD! Hands up, now!"

Large shapes gathered around them. Light blasted through the side of the building, forcing the ex-detective to squint. The men were a dark silhouette, their faces hidden in shadow.

Savas whispered. "Can't see. Can't…"

The barrels of their guns glinted and then faded to a deep darkness.

PART IV

EPILOGUE

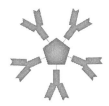

O heart! heart! heart!
O the bleeding drops of red,
Where on the deck my Captain lies,
Fallen cold and dead.

— "O Captain! My Captain!", Walt Whitman

AMERICA'S AUSCHWITZ

How a Tenacious PI, a Modern Deep Throat, and the Deep State Unseated a Genocidal Administration

by Ronen Landler, David Goldman, and Tomoko Tabuchi, the *Washington Post*

America continues to reel from the devastating revelations of a covert program of ethnic cleansing undertaken by the Suite administration. In this plan, millions of undocumented immigrants were targeted for arrest and detention, relocated from the "tent cities" along the Mexican border and secretly transported to the Yucca Mountain Nuclear Waste Repository in Nevada.

There, it is alleged that an industrialized execution system surpassing that of Nazi Germany was employed to kill hundreds of thousands of people. Only the combined heroic efforts of fortunately-placed individuals and agencies brought this heinous slaughter to an end before it could achieve its purpose.

Shocking photographs and videos of underground tunnels filled with the dead have stunned the world. Evidence linking the program to members of the Suite administration include devastating revelations of a modern opioid-based Zyklon B, whole-scale commandeering of law enforcement and transportation departments, and an influx of mysterious foreign money, leaving Washington and the nation stunned.

A constitutional crisis was immediately precipitated as Special Counsel Ronald Tiller claimed authority to lead the DoJ in issuing an unprecedented indictment and arrest of a sitting president, his immediate staff, multiple heads of departments, and members of Congress. Court challenges slowed the American judiciary to a crawl. Simultaneously, riots consumed larger cities from New York to LA to Houston as

Americans took to the streets, demanding the impeachment and arrest of the president. Conflicts with counterdemonstrations degenerated into violence as left-wing and right-wing extremist groups faced off.

The vice president resigned as the remaining cabinet sought to remove Suite through the 25th Amendment, stating that "the president is unable to discharge the powers and duties of his office" due to the influence and compromise of foreign powers.

Events reached a fevered pitch this week when Air Force One was surrounded by federal officers from an undisclosed division of the DoJ. In a plot out of a political thriller, President Suite himself was led off the plane by armed troops and has not been seen since Wednesday. The apparent arrest and detention of the nation's leader set a fresh wave of protests as thousands of Suite supporters poured into the streets. Armed gangs like the Proud Boys and Patriot Corps assaulted counter-protesters and reporters, and set fire to the New York Times building.

Based on correspondence revealed in a document dump from a still-anonymous inside source in the US government, it appears that President Suite's failure to secure the deportation of over ten million illegal immigrants led to increasing desperation and frustration. The plan to kill detainees seems to have been developed by some of the more extreme white nationalist elements of the president's staff but was tabled in the earlier months of the young administration. How it was greenlit and developed is still under investigation.

Stuck in the middle of this flurry of revelations is celebrity PI Grace Gone of New York. The young investigator skyrocketed to fame four years ago when she solved the Eunuch Maker case, stopping a serial killer and terrorist bent on killing men. Ms. Gone obtained a treasure trove of classified government documents from a shadowy figure many on the internet have taken to calling Deep State Throat. Using this inside information, she was able to unravel the covert program of genocide. She went public with multiple newspapers just as federal authorities were raiding the Yucca Mountain death camp.

"They tried to stop me, silence me," said Gone in reference to the two assassination attempts on her life that occurred while she investigated the case. "And those forces aren't gone, whatever mess we clean up here in America."

A killer's bullet left her hospitalized for weeks, her recovery still ongoing as she spoke to the *Post* from her wheelchair. Despite the near-death experience, Gone continued to pursue the case until she had the evidence required.

"I didn't want to believe it myself. It sounded ludicrous. Impossible. Something hysterical that couldn't possibly be true. But facts are stubborn things. Thank God. Because the heart of darkness had been opened in the middle of the nation."

Another familiar face from the Eunuch Maker case also found his time in the spotlight. Former NYPD detective Tyrell Sacker, an associate of Ms. Gone at her investigative firm, participated in a raid by New York and federal law enforcement on North Brother Island near the Bronx. In what has been described as a scene from a war zone, they engaged the terrorist group Mjolnir, who were using the island as a secluded base of operations to launch their attacks against Muslims. The FBI reports that their leader was killed by Sacker in the melee, and the terrorist group routed.

"We did what we had to do," said Sacker, dodging questions of how he became involved in the Mjolnir raid. "And it came at great cost."

It is unclear what he referred to, but a number of NYPD and federal agents died in the strike on the hardened terrorist compound. In what many have called a tragic loss for the nation, FBI agent John Savas, who stopped an earlier incarnation of the deadly group, lost his life on the island. Savas was a decorated veteran of many law enforcement agencies.

As Congress prepares to vote on articles of impeachment,

as challenges to the arrest of Suite and others in the Executive Branch wind their way to the Supreme Court, as a nation holds its collective breath about what will happen next, more and more people are asking the question "How?"

How did something so heinous, so contrary to the foundational principles of the nation happen? How could ethnic cleansing and genocide occur under the noses of the population in the United States of America?

At present, the country can only struggle with these and other difficult questions, unsure of what the future brings in the face of such monumental betrayal and crimes against humanity.

61

FUNERALS

Blessed are You, O Lord, teach me Your statutes. Alleluia.
My soul has slumbered from sorrow; strengthen me with
Your words. Alleluia.
Despair took hold on me because of sinners that forsake
Your Law. Alleluia.

Houston tugged at the formal attire as the cantors chanted in the Greek church in Astoria.

Don't they believe in air-conditioning?

Inside the packed church, old ladies in black jostled and pressed against her. Clouds of fragrant incense caused her eyes to water. A service mostly in Greek left her bored and distracted. She was reconsidering the decision to attend the ceremony.

Catholics on steroids.

She glanced at the broad form of Lopez beside her. Once a Catholic priest, then defrocked, he still worshipped his God. He said last rites over men he killed. Even buried them when there was time.

But something's wrong.

After Yucca Mountain, the man she knew had transformed. Receded. Disappeared into himself. His broad frame sagged. His step, slowed and unsure. His words, distant and flat. She shuddered in the oppressive heat of standing next to him.

I don't know who this is beside me.

> *For You are the Resurrection, the Life, and the Repose of*
> *Your servant John Savas, O Christ our God;*
> *and to You do we send up glory, with Your Eternal Father,*
> *and Your All-Holy, Good and Life-creating Spirit,*
> *both now and ever, and to the ages of ages.*

Still, she'd come because the man before would have wanted her to. She glanced up at the front row of the church. Cohen, the Jew, sat unmoving, her face still as stone. Next to her was the Greek family of John Savas. Sisters and brothers. An ex-wife at the end of the pew.

She came also for Rebecca Cohen. Along with Savas, she'd saved her and Francisco from imprisonment and death many years ago.

> *You Who of old did fashion me out of nothingness,*
> *and with Your Image divine did honor me;*
> *but because of transgression of Your commandments*
> *did return me again to the earth where I was taken;*
> *lead me back to be refashioned into that ancient beauty of*
> *Your Likeness.*

She tried to focus on the old priest. His long white beard was trimmed precisely. He limped across the altar, his back bent with age. She tried to recall his name.

It looked like his sunken eyes held back tears.

> *Where is the pleasure in life which is unmixed with*
> *sorrow?*
> *Where the glory which on earth has stood firm and*
> *unchanged?*
> *All things are weaker than shadow, all more elusive than*
> *dreams.*

In the end, she came for Savas. When she'd stumbled, dying near the burning home of the former vice president, he'd come for her. When she was under arrest and the subject of hatred and scorn for a crime she didn't commit, John Savas was there. He'd dared believe in their innocence, put his career and reputation on the line, Broke the law to free them, handed them a hidden life protected from the pursuit of the law. He'd brought them on as clandestine agents for the resurrected Intel 1 at the bottom of New York City. The life she had, the chance to make a difference in the world, the life of her lover, she owed it all to him.

> *Terror truly past compare is by the mystery of death*
> *inspired;*
> *now the soul and the body part, disjoined by resistless*
> *might, and their concord is broken;*
> *and the bond of nature which made them live and grow*
> *as one, now by the edict of God is rest in twain.*

The priest approached the casket and prayed over it. Several assistant priests joined him and chanted the same prayer.

> *O God of all spirits and flesh,*
> *Who has trodden down death,*
> *destroying the power of the devil,*
> *bestowing life on Your world,*
> *to the soul of Your servant, John Savas,*
> *departed this life, do You Yourself, O Lord,*
> *give rest in a place of light,*
> *in a place of green pasture,*
> *in a place of refreshment,*
> *from where pain and sorrow and mourning are fled away.*
> *Every sin by him committed in thought, word, or deed,*
> *do You as our good and loving God forgive,*
> *seeing that there is no man that shall live and sin not,*
> *for You alone are without sin:*
> *Your righteousness and Your law is truth.*

She left Cohen with the Savas family. She returned to the table in the cafeteria next to the church and spooned odd wheat balls into a small plastic glass. Her nose wrinkled. The smell of sugar and cinnamon wafted upward.

At least this place is cooled.

She thanked whatever God there was for AC. After frying in the Mojave, heat was poison. She squinted at the strange concoction in the glass.

"It's called Koliva," said Lightfoote behind her.

Houston's heart skipped, and a flash of warmth ran through her. She turned, nearly drowning in a sea of white hair. It shrouded Lightfoote's face, which she was stuffing with food, her blazing emerald eyes staring back.

"According to Wikipedia," she mumbled through a full mouth, "'in the Eastern Orthodox Church, koliva is blessed during funerals, as well as during the memorial service that's performed at various intervals after a person's death and on special occasions, such as the Saturday of Souls.'"

"Okay, thanks." She fought to slow her breath. The threat of imminent death no longer existed as an excuse to postpone hard realities. She dreaded the necessary resolution, the calm after the storm, more than the storm.

Gazing at the beautiful, dangerous, and elfin woman before her, Houston's only desire was to step forward. Bridge the distance. Reach out and touch her. But touches set off other kinds of bombs. "How's it taste?"

"Awesome." Lightfoote grinned, sugar coating her lips. The smile faded, and she wiped her mouth with a napkin, furrowing her brows. "We have to figure things out, Sara."

The weight of the world dropped on her. Houston shook her head, eyes large and watery. She turned, leaving Lightfoot behind and marching outside.

The heat of the day struck a body blow. The sounds of the city rushed around her. Rhythmic slams of the Queens subway line exploded above their heads on an elevated track. Cars sped through the busy intersection below, rivers of pedestrians a constant murmur. She steadied herself on a balcony railing, focusing on the stairway running to the street.

Please don't follow me, Angel. Please just stay inside.

The door behind her opened. Lightfoote stepped up beside her, exhaling. Her breath smelled of cinnamon. "Life's short. Like we need reminding. John's body is in there. But he's not. He's gone. He'll never know another day. We'll never talk to him again. Rebecca will never see him again. She'll never hold him again."

Houston's throat closed up. She struggled to breathe.

Lightfoote leaned into her, and warmth and electricity flowing through her body. "What about us? What about life?"

"What about choices, Angel? Repercussions?" Her face flushed as she pushed backward. "You could study up on consent, you know? You kissed me out of the blue, without ever giving me the chance to walk through that door myself. Make the choice. You jump-started a thousand feelings, and I had to deal with them. My body, my heart, whatever the hell it's all about! You walked in, flipped switches without asking, firing things up, but I didn't want that! I was where I wanted and needed to be. Francisco and I were happy!" She glared. "Why did you do it?"

Lightfoote's lip trembled. She looked to the ground and shook her head back and forth. "Dark time. Angel saw the cages again. Angel was a small girl again. She *needed*. Angel…needed you." Her eyes flicked up to meet Houston's.

"I know," she said, swallowing. A tear ran down one cheek. "But it's a *mess*. My choices are fucked now. I'm torn between something I want and something else I love. The love is deep and real. I've got to make a hard choice. I just can't do it."

A deep voice rolled behind them. "Let me make it easy for you."

Both turned to see Lopez framed by the closing doorway.

Shit.

Houston stared at the sky, her eyes rolling back to earth as she blinked water away. She hoped to avoid this, tell Lightfoote she was too much in love, survived too much with Francisco. Then they could just walk away, leave the feelings untouched.

The last thing she wanted was him involved.

But in the midst of this triangle train wreck, her thoughts centered on his face. *His change.* His eyes were empty. The passion of resisting Daniel Suite's monstrous policies, gone. His devotion and spirituality, absent. The moral and ethical burdens that often weighed on him, vanished. Instead, she could see nothing. Only an emptiness.

He took a step forward and grasped each of their hands. He placed Lightfoote's left in her right, pressing the palms together. He held his own hand there as he spoke.

"When the church betrayed me, some part of me died. But you made a difference, Sara. And my trust and love in God. My belief in a force of goodness and justice and decency in the universe. These kept me from falling into the pit."

His grip remained firm as Lightfoote cocked her head and stared into his eyes. Houston's shoulders shook.

"Everything we went through. All we've seen. Maybe my view of creation hardened." A rueful smile crept over his face and then faded. "You once told me that I would need 'retraining,' that I didn't understand the world around me. I finally see now that you were right. I don't understand it. And until I do, I can't be here anymore."

Houston startled, but Lopez wouldn't let her pull her hand back. "What are you saying?"

"I can't see a God of justice and love. Not anymore. Not in a world with tunnels inside of Yucca Mountain."

His gaze peered through the city and into the depths of time. *He's falling and I can't catch him.* This wasn't like a mission. There was nothing she could do. No rope to throw down, no assailant to counter. Only some battle inside him that she was cut off from. She'd never felt so alone beside him.

"I stood there, dropped into the bowels of hell, filled with vileness and corruption." He turned to Houston, his face terrifying in its emptiness. "And I died. Whatever I was, it stopped. Duty. Faith. And love."

He turned away again. A long silence eating into her bones like corrosive acid.

"I have to find myself, or it's over. I'll go into the wilderness like some lost repentant, searching for God. For myself. Until then, there's nothing I can give. To others. Or to you."

"Francisco, *please*." Tears dropped from her eyes. "Don't go. We can work through this. We can find you a way back. *Together.* The world shut us out. We're exiles. Don't leave me alone out there."

"There isn't a human way back for me. I need something greater than genocide. Something greater than a tunnel of death that eats at my dreams. Something that can transform the darkness. And I don't have it inside me. Service and work don't have it." He stared into her eyes. "And not even you, beautiful Sara. It's bigger than you or me. I'm hurt too deep inside. I'm sorry."

She fought to keep her shoulders from shaking. She battled the sobs that clawed their way to the surface. He turned to Lightfoote and kissed her cheek.

"Take care of her, crazy FBI girl."

His firm grip disappeared from her hand, leaving it numb and clasped to Lightfoote's. He turned and sped down the steps. She moved to follow him, but Lightfoote placed her other hand in the middle of Houston's chest.

"Don't," she said. "Don't make it harder."

Torn, hesitating, she spun at the sound of the doors opening, glancing inside.

Cohen stepped out, confusion on her face at the sight of the pair holding hands and weeping. "Everyone okay?"

Houston returned her gaze below, seeking out Lopez. But he was gone.

62

OPTIONS

T he bathroom in Gone's apartment dripped with water. Steam filled the space, and Sacker stepped carefully over the slick tiles. He needed to run an obstacle course to carry the clean towels into the room while avoiding any stares at the naked woman in the tub.

After the attack, she required a full-time nurse. But she's proud and stubborn as hell. Instead, she'd nominated him for the position. Most of the time, it was innocuous work. Pushing her around, helping with meds or PT, going on supply runs.

But hygiene, that was another story. *Bath time.* Panic.

Her eyes were closed, her wounded arm draped over the glistening ceramic, her skin shining. The curve of her arm moved to her chest, and he fought his own eyes to look away. But he lost the battle as her eyes opened.

Damn.

"It's okay, Tyrell," she said. "I like it when you look at me." She grinned, her canines pressing into her lower lip. "I could use a second sponge bath."

He paced his breathing. The only thing worse than wanting to stare at her was being encouraged to do so. "We don't want to irritate the skin. You just got that sling off. The skin's raw there."

The corner of her mouth twitched. "Well, you could arc around those areas. You have very good hands."

He turned away and placed the towels on a shelf. He adjusted his pants. Things had gotten crowded inside.

"I want you to come to the doctor with me next week, Tyrell."

He nodded, keeping his gaze away. "Of course I will. But I think you're healing so well, we might not need to see the surgeon much more."

"Not the surgeon," she said, water sloshing. His mind painted the picture of her sitting up in the tub. Every square inch of her as she moved. "Dr. Lauren Fischer."

He paused. "Fischer? Who's that?"

"My neurologist."

He turned to face her. The throbbing below faded. "You have a neurologist? For the shoulder motion?"

"No. Not for that. I've had her for several years now. Before the shooting."

He didn't move. A thousand small factoids and thoughts danced in his subconscious, little voices that had cried to be heard resurfaced from the soundproof box he'd stuffed them in. Except now, the voices came from in front of him. From Grace. *Doom's footsteps.*

"The wound in my shoulder is healing. That's good. But it was an acute threat in the slow tsunami of greater concern."

"I don't understand."

"The stress of the injury. Inactivity. I'm not sure what, exactly, or the combination, but I've deteriorated much more rapidly."

"Deteriorated."

A sad smile touched her lips.

"Tyrell, I think you know. But don't want to know. My left side, the leg can't support me anymore. The cane isn't going to be enough. The truth is, I might never leave the wheelchair again." Her face scrunched in pain. "I want you to understand why."

She's finally saying it. Finally making me see it.

She had tried to keep it hidden. Of course. Not a hard mystery to crack, really. Certainly not for a former NYPD detective. But like she said, he hadn't really wanted to know. By the time it was obvious to him, he'd already plunged headfirst for the brilliant woman. A pair of facts he tried to suppress.

He was shaken. She was revealing this to him, letting him see without masks just how hard it was for her. *She'll be a prisoner in her own body one day.*

That was why it hurt her so much that her father had discovered the truth, vulnerable before a man she had hoped to never see again. *Now she's letting me in.* The implications of such trust overwhelmed him.

"But later," she said. "I want you to come here."

He approached, a terrible weight settling on his shoulders.

"I want you to look at me."

His awareness drowned in her eyes, the irises like shimmering pools of brandy.

"I love it when you gaze into my eyes," she smiled. "But right now, I want you to look down. I want you to take in all of me. I know you want to."

There could be no resistance. His gaze left her eyes. He drank in her skin, traced the contours of her naked form.

"I can see it in your eyes. Your muscles. Your breathing. How your skin changes."

"See what?" he managed, his throat dry.

"Arousal. Affection. Need and love."

All cards on the table. All masks and shields lowered. She'd confessed her illness, risked lowering her defenses to him for a purpose. Because the bridge she wanted him to cross wasn't only emotional. It was physical. His head spun. "Gracie…"

She reached with one wet hand and touched his shirt. She unbuttoned this collar and moved downward.

"I…"

"Shhhhh."

Her nimble fingers danced. With each opening of his shirt, the blood in him beat harder. Soon, his shirt slid off, the light fabric falling down the sides of his arms and to the wet floor.

"I can't do more," she said, laying back in the water. The effort had tired her. "Take off your pants. Get in here with me."

"Grace, you know...*a lot*. But, not...everything. Things are *complicated*. It's not going to be exactly what you expect."

"Really?" She gestured to her shoulder and her leg. "My leg hardly works. My shoulder's half gone, People want to kill me. Is this what you expected? I certainly didn't. I want a refund."

"You're so much more than I've ever expected in this life."

"We just came from a funeral. Across the country and in Mexico, there are hundreds of thousands more." She closed her eyes and shook her head, her entire body in motion. He followed every movement. "Death. Death and more death. Pain. Can we do one thing that isn't about pain, but about joy and pleasure? In this godawful sea of all the suffering, can we just make love?"

He removed his clothes. The pants caught on his erection, his hands trembling. He wasn't a virgin, far from it, but he picked partners on a practical combination of desire and tolerance. Rejections in the bedroom were frequent. By now, he was stoic and jaded.

But this was different. This was Gracie. This time, it mattered how a partner reacted. Rejection today would devastate him like nothing else.

Gone placed her fingertips to his lips. She dragged her nails down his neck, between his large pecs, along this stomach. Grasping his erection, she drew an involuntary gasp. Her hand stroked. She held his eyes to hers. Pleasure rippled through him as he entered the tub.

"Now, let's see what we have here."

He froze, knowing well what she meant. Her fingers moved down beneath his small scrotum, the crease of skin below opening to her swirling digits.

He couldn't think. The limbic stimulation shut down his mind. He was drugged, his mouth open, his hips thrusting.

"Well," she smiled. "Don't let anyone say you don't give a girl options."

She pulled him down on top of her.

63

HUNT

Cohen stepped into the room, freezing a moment. Two shapes waited inside. Lightfoote had returned to her GI Jane look, the bursting shock of dyed white hair gone, the scalp bald. The piercings along the right side of her face were more visible with the hair removed. Houston curled on a couch in feline brooding, her eyes downcast. Lightfoote tracked Cohen's entrance into the room. Houston continued to stare at the floor.

This was John's office.

Simply walking inside was a gut punch. She wrestled with her body, strangling the urge to cry. A thousand memories rushed through her from a thousand days working and living beside him. His smell lingered in the room, the furniture and decorations a tangible reflection of his personality. Photographs were portals to joy and pain. It was as if some essence of him floated in the atmosphere, unerased even by death. *Maybe that's what ghosts are.* She would never be free of his presence, a psyche always over her shoulder in this room and with every step she took.

Good. Her muscles tensed. *Let me remember every day. Let me do something about it.*

"How'd the Speaker do?" asked Lightfoote, her black combat boots clashing with the pink gum she chewed.

She snapped out of her trance and stepped behind the desk.

"Acting president Bryant's still in shock," she said, sitting down. "These politicians are such snowflakes. Enabling Suite was a wonderful power trip. Nothing he said or did was too monstrous to remove support. Until it was. Until they woke up to something they couldn't wrap their minds around. Then their partisan club fight turned into something monstrous."

Lightfoote popped a bubble. "So he's a changed man."

"I wouldn't go that far. But for the time being, I think he sees the bigger picture. The nation's balanced on a knife's edge. I think he'll try to steer it out of this until the election next year."

"And that should be a shakeup," Lightfoote smirked, glancing at Houston. Her smile faded. Houston didn't respond.

"And for now, at least, he's going to leave Intel 1 alone. I think our role in all this has many spooked. Those that know of our existence are scared to mess with the dark ops former president York setup. We're the people who revealed this horror. They're going to maintain our funding, give us free rein to direct our investigations. At least until the next administration arrives."

She sighed, staring at the desk surface.

"We need to rebuild. The nation needs to rebuild, of course, but that's out of our hands. Beyond our pay grade. Maybe the politicians might start to put the country before their ambition for a change."

She held up a silver-framed photo. Bright blue water surrounded the caldera from the island of Santorini. Savas stood next to her on a small fishing boat. The left side of her mouth twitched upward. She returned the photo to the desk.

"We need to rebuild Intel 1. Suite tore us down piece by piece, case by case. He ripped good agents and assets from us. Filled us with moles and sycophants." She turned to Lightfoote. "Angel, you're going to purge this place digitally. Do whatever you have to. Fortify us for the coming war."

"Coming war, huh?" The wad of pink gum protruded from between her clenched teeth. She resumed chewing. "I guess I knew it was coming." She glanced at Cohen. "We have to finish the job. But Mirnateghi's going to be harder to reach than ever."

"Perhaps," she said, her eyes two glowing coals. "But I have some ideas. A long-term strategy. But first, we need to right this ship. Get our house in order." She turned to Houston. "Sara, you and I are going to work on the personnel side. We need to start a pink slip avalanche. We need to hire agents worthy of what we're doing, recall many that we lost."

Houston said nothing. Cohen focused on the former CIA agent, silent for some time. She stood and stepped around the desk, moving beside the couch along the left wall. She sat next to her. "I'm sorry Francisco's gone."

Houston inhaled and pivoted away.

"I'm sorry for Intel 1, because he brought more than just a rare talent we could use. We're going to need talent like that more than ever, but he brought us something harder to replace. A conscience." She tilted her head to the ceiling. "Secrecy, power—we're the poster child for executive overreach. Maybe it made sense when York did it. But the longer it goes on…. He questioned our actions, our choices, our motives. He helped keep us from turning into some version of the things we were trying to stop. We need him. I know *I* need him now, because what I plan is on the edge of decency."

Houston's breath quickened, but she said nothing.

"But I need you to come back. I know it's hard. But right now, I'd give both my arms to know that John was still alive. Hiding in Canada. Up in some monastery in Tibet. Meditating in some cave in the desert trying to figure things out. *Anything.*"

Houston turned toward her, eyes red and swollen.

"And since that's not going to happen, not ever, there's something else I want."

Cohen stood, marching back to the desk and standing over it. She looked back and forth between the two women in the room.

"Something I need your help with. Both of you, one hundred percent engaged and willing to risk everything."

Lightfoote turned to Houston. "Sara?"

Houston peeked up toward Cohen, her face slack. "I'm here, but I can't promise how much of me. You'll have to give me some time. You'll have to decide what I'm worth now."

"Some time, we have. We have a long and careful trap to set. But I know your worth. And I know you will want to help me win this fight."

Houston shrugged. "What fight? What do you want to do?"

She glared across the room. Her gaze burned through the bedrock of Manhattan and across the ocean to the sands of the Middle East. "I'm going to hunt down the creature that took John from me."

Her lip curled, her left eye squinting.

"And I'm going to kill her."

The United States is extremely lucky that no honest, charismatic figure has arisen. Every charismatic figure is such an obvious crook that he destroys himself, like McCarthy or Nixon or the evangelist preachers. If somebody comes along who is charismatic and honest this country is in real trouble because of the frustration, disillusionment, the justified anger and the absence of any coherent response. What are people supposed to think if someone says, 'I have got an answer, we have an enemy'? There it was the Jews. Here it will be the illegal immigrants and the blacks. We will be told that white males are a persecuted minority. We will be told we have to defend ourselves and the honor of the nation. Military force will be exalted. People will be beaten up. And if it happens it will be more dangerous than Germany. The United States is the world power. Germany was powerful but had more powerful antagonists. I don't think all this is very far away.

— NOAM CHOMSKY, *POWER AND TERROR: CONFLICT, HEGEMONY, AND THE RULE OF FORCE,* 2011

AFTERWORD

My thrillers are based on contemporary events, conflicts, and particularly the moral and ethical quagmires arising in the modern geopolitical landscape. In previous books, I've tackled issues of how civil societies respond to terrorism, the fragility of the digital infrastructure undergirding modern societies, the threats of biological weapons, and the struggle of developed nations to live up to their purported creeds and commitments to equality, fairness, and decency. I'm inspired to ground the action and my characters in these critical conflicts.

There is no hiding what this thriller is actually about. I don't shy away from that in the imaginary world that reflects an extreme version and direction of our own. *China Girl* sets the scene with a particular conceit drawn from certain interpretations of contemporary events: what would happen if a true autocrat came to power, one that possessed the charisma and competency to wrest control of the government, unhinged the checks and balances of the US Constitution, and moved to implement the age-old strategy of demagogues seeking power, namely Orwellian propaganda, societal division into desired and undesirable groups, with the demonization of the latter central to accruing power through fear of "the other," thereby convincing enough in the nation to jettison decency and previous norms. How would our heroes in Intel 1 respond? When the government goes rogue and commits atrocities, who is the terrorist and who the hero?

This scenario, while extreme, is hardly a stretch for America. The nation was built upon the genocide of an entire continent. Even as the hallowed Founders were writing the near-worshipped documents enshrining freedom and governance, they were enabling the enslavement of tens of millions of human beings, etching that dehumanization into the Constitution itself, many profiting from that most complete abuse of power and insult to the idea of freedom. From a century of KKK terrorism, apartheid laws, the disenfranchisement of fifty percent of the population until women won the vote one hundred years ago, discrimination by race, nationality, gender, sexual preference, and religion, the nation has both acted upon the most monstrous of human instincts and slowly, painfully, struggled to raise itself to match the profound statements of rights in the governing documents.

Therefore, as a nation, we've been there. Done that. And we could do it again all too easily. History smirks at any doubters.

In the face of many abuses of power and the assault on the rights of minorities, as politicians brazenly spew vile, racist slander and enact discriminatory laws, the reactions of the people show just how vulnerable America is to a totalitarian seizure of power. "How did the Germans allow it to happen?" How did the Rwandans? Or the Turks? Or the colonists that systemically erased the indigenous populations in the Americas? When we see seemingly decent and normal people excuse, justify, defend, or otherwise turn their eyes from violations of human rights and decency, when a nation slowly allows itself to be transformed into a caricature of what it espouses, their mental gymnastics aided by vast propaganda outlets, and the ever siren call of fear and the arrogance of racial superiority, it is only too clear just how much on the knife's edge we stand.

China Girl is my personal response to our current crisis. While I can vote, debate, even march or protest, my unique contribution has been and is in what I can produce with my own hands. In my daily work as a scientist, I try to find ways to make the world better by adding knowledge and working toward therapies. As a writer, I am inspired to address what appear to me to be the great moral quandaries of this age.

Unfortunately, everything is polarized, so calls to decency and warnings of societal madness are viewed through political lenses. And so America limps along, blinded and increasingly numb, dangerously close to toppling over the cliff into utter ruin. With the power of nuclear weapons, the planet's largest economy and military, and the ability to stop any effort to reverse the coming climate catastrophe, America's fall would be the world's as well.

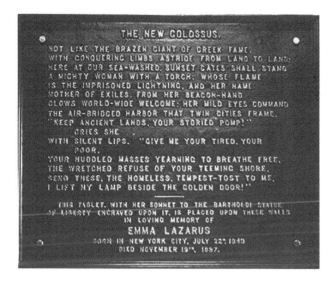

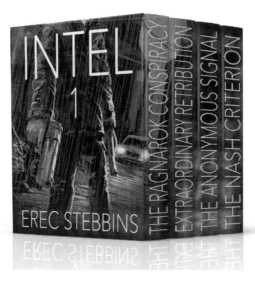

ANDROCIDE
The 5th Book in the INTEL 1 Series

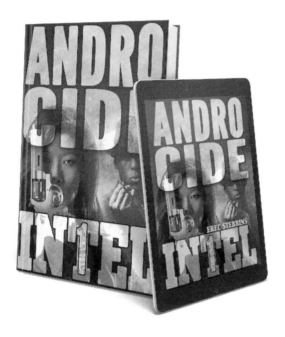

"Integrating police procedural, holmesian puzzle-solving, bio-thriller, and political commentary, Androcide's style and substance will prove irresistible for readers." —The Booklife Prize

HARD TIME ADVENTURE NOVELLAS
WHERE SURVIVAL IS THE MEANING OF LIFE

HARD TIME SCIFI Series

Where survival is the meaning of life. A speculative fiction serial of adventure novellas set in a strange and punishing world. In Book 1, **METAL** a woman finds herself in two different worlds, as two different people. In one she is a criminal, sentenced to a new and terrible punishment. In the other, she is a stranger and then a prophet, granted the visions of God.

48217007R00237

Printed in Poland
by Amazon Fulfillment
Poland Sp. z o.o., Wrocław